MW00580532

What the Ravens Sing

The London Charismatics Series

Explore the dark, mystical streets of Edwardian England with The London Charismatics, a supernatural historical fantasy series full of deadly mystery and arcane powers.

~

Book One
The Fire in the Glass
Lily's visions could stop a killer if she'll trust a reclusive aristocrat with her darkest secret.

Book Two
The Shadow of Water
A dangerous prophecy threatens London. To stop it, Lily must uncover the truth behind her mother's murder.

A London Charismatics Novella
A Wrath of Sparrows
When an old enemy resurfaces, Lily is forced to choose between friendship and fate.

Book Three
Bridge of Ash
When Strangford is accused of murder, Lily is plunged into a game of secrets that could shape the future of the war.

Book Four
What the Ravens Sing
In the maelstrom of the Great War, only Lily can stop an ancient and terrible charismatic ability from tearing the world apart.

What the Ravens Sing

THE LONDON CHARISMATICS

BOOK FOUR

Jacquelyn Benson

VAUGHAN WOODS
PUBLISHING

Copyright @ 2022 by Jacquelyn Benson
Cover design by Sara Argue of Sara Argue Design
Cover copyright © 2022 by Vaughan Woods Publishing
Proofread by Casey Fenich of Thoth Editing
Typeset in Minion Pro and ALS Script based on design by Cathie Plante

First edition: April 2023
Library of Congress Catalog Number: 2023900733
ISBN: 978-1-959050-06-3

Published by Vaughan Woods Publishing
PO Box 882
Exeter, NH 03833 U.S.A.

Stay up-to-date on new book releases by subscribing to Jacquelyn's newsletter at jacquelynbenson.com.

Content warning for What the Ravens Sing:
Contains warfare, catatonia, post-traumatic stress disorder, animal death, plane crash, murder, medical experimentation, captivity, violent fights involving death and serious physical injury, blood. Descriptions of pregnancy loss. References to prostitution and human trafficking. References to sex.

"Sed fortuna, quae plurimum potest cum in reliquis rebus tum praecipue in bello, parvis momentis magnas rerum commutationes efficit; ut tum accidit."

(Fortune, which has great influence in affairs generally and especially in war, produces by slight disturbance of balance important changes in human affairs.)

- GAIUS JULIUS CAESAR, *THE CIVIL WAR, BOOK III:68*
(TRANSLATION BY A.G. PESKETT)

~

"If a man were to know the end of this day's business ere it come;
But it suffice us that the day will end, and then the end be known.
If we meet again, well then we'll smile, and if not then this parting was well made."

- WILLIAM SHAKESPEARE, *JULIUS CAESAR, V.I*

ONE

Monday, April 8, 1918
Eight-thirty in the evening
Kentish Coast, outside Whitstable

 LILY RIVERS, LADY STRANGFORD, roared across the cliffs on the back of her motorcycle, pushing for speed as though it were possible to shorten the distance to London by sheer force of will.

The headlamp of her Triumph spilled across the pale, winding path of the road, the sky deepening from purple to cobalt over the fields to the east. To the west lay the sea, a darkly moving mass she could hear rushing against the coast over the engine's roar.

The motorbike had been improved since Lily first rode it four years earlier. After the pistons wore out on her original configuration, His Majesty's government had arranged for a retrofit, installing the new 550cc three-speed block onto her old frame. Lily could feel the difference in the way the motorbike sped out of the turn, the force pushing her against the narrow seat.

She had been granted the upgrade for the same reason she now rode through the dark on the remote Kentish coast. Lily wore the uniform of the Wrens—the Women's Royal Naval Service. For the last three years, she had served as a courier shuttling messages from the naval listening stations that peppered the coast. The intercepted, encrypted German wireless transmissions picked up by the stations were too sensitive to be trusted to the telegram lines.

1

Lily dropped gears and rolled the Triumph to a halt at the top of a slight rise. She took a long draught from her canteen, washing the dust from her throat. The road was dry today, the sky clear and cloudless. Stars glittered overhead against the dark blanket of the night, emerging with a splendor that was rare to see in perpetually fog-bound England.

The sight of those distant points of light gave her a distinct twinge of unease.

The hour was later than she would have liked. The Triumph's chain had loosened as she arrived at the Herne listening station, and it had taken nearly two hours for her to fix it. In a way, the accident was a boon, as the delay meant one last additional intercept found its way to her before she departed, a communication that would otherwise have waited at the station until the next courier arrived in the morning. Lily had shoved the slim yellow paper into her pocket just before firing up her engine. She could feel it there now, the envelope slightly stiff against the wool.

Wind rippled the long, coarse grass beside her, soft with the scent of the sea and touched with spring warmth. The waves sounded a gentle susurration against the shore at the base of the cliffs below.

She slugged once more from the canteen and twisted on the cap. Pulling down her goggles, she tugged her linen scarf up to block the worst of the dust from her nose. She would not stop again before reaching London.

Spinning the pedals, Lily sparked the Triumph back to life and roared down the road.

~

She tore into the city two hours later, covered in a film of dry earth. London was dark as she rode towards Whitehall, the gas lamps that lined the streets either unlit or painted to direct their dim light down at the ground. The windows of the houses she passed were blackened with shades or cardboard, and the shops and taverns were already closed for the night. Few automobiles or carriages ventured out on the roads at this hour, and those that did navigated by shaded head-lamps that gave out only a vague illumination. No one wanted to make the city an easier target for a German air raid.

A policeman turned at the sight of Lily's own headlamp, necessarily undimmed to allow her to safely speed across the rural roads of Kent. He blew his whistle, motioning for her to halt, but waved her on as he noted her uniform and courier's satchel.

The Admiralty Building, headquarters of the Royal Navy, could barely be made out against the neighboring government offices lining Whitehall. It was nothing but a crenelated silhouette against the softer darkness of the clear night sky. No one inside would risk revealing a glimmer of light through a poorly-shaded window. The Germans would happily have bombed the place to dust if they could find it.

Lily sped past the shadowed facade, leaning into a quick turn around the statue of Charles I that marked the entrance to Trafalgar Square. She whipped into a narrow alley closed in by monumental buildings. The shadows were darker here, the light of her headlamp more starkly painting the paving stones.

She stopped the motorbike near an unobtrusive door nestled into a corner, killing the light and dismounting. Grabbing her satchel, she stalked up to the uniformed sentry who stood by the step.

"Good evening, Mr. Greene," she said as she approached.

"Lady S," he acknowledged with a tired nod, opening the door.

The hallway beyond was cramped, the floor a patchwork of chipped tiles. It was lined with offices, most of the doors shut at this hour. The few that were open revealed men in shirtsleeves leaning over desks covered in papers. Farther along, a room full of lady typists clattered with the noise of their keys. A fellow Wren in the conventional skirted uniform pushed along a trolley with urns of hot coffee and tea. She eyed Lily's trousers with a note of envy as she passed by.

Lily neatly navigated the labyrinth until she reached the central hall, a wide space framed by open-air staircases that rose in elegant angles to the floors above. During the daytime, it roared with hurried conversations and rapid footsteps. It was quieter at this late hour, the noise dimmed instead to a low hum of activity.

The weighty oak desk at the center was manned by a single duty clerk, a grim young lieutenant with a stiff back who wearily set aside a stack of papers as Lily approached. She pulled three thick envelopes of intercepts from her satchel and handed them to him.

"Manston, Westgate, and Herne," Lily announced.

She abruptly recalled the final Herne intercept, pulling it from her pocket.

"Oh—and this," she added, slapping it onto the pile.

"Acknowledged," the clerk replied stiffly.

He set the envelopes on top of a teetering stack of similar manila packages on his desk and turned away.

"Aren't you going to put them in the tubes?" Lily pressed.

The pneumatic tubes ran like arteries throughout the massive complex of the Admiralty. Lily could see the mouth of one behind the clerk's desk. Papers were inserted into cylinders that fit neatly into the tube and were then sucked into a distribution center on the ground floor. They were sorted there and shot on to their destinations. It was a far faster and more efficient method of moving documents through the building than relying on couriers running up and down the massive staircases.

"The tubes are down," the lieutenant clipped out in reply without looking at her. "Someone will be along shortly."

It was a perfectly reasonable answer. Lily's only charge was to see that the intercepts were delivered to the Admiralty. She had completed that task, and the hour was already late. The notion of crawling into her bed was deeply appealing, but as she stepped aside to let a postman drop his enormous bag of mail onto the desk, that late yellow message from Herne glared at her from the top of the pile.

A resonance rose in her bones, one that Lily both recognized and did not welcome. It was the distinct buzz of her onmyōdō.

Lily had been plagued with a straightforward form of foresight for as long as she could remember. It was a power that subjected her to both humdrum and terrible visions of what was to come. Something critical had changed four years ago on the night that she plunged into Regent's Canal. In a strange moment between life and death, a transformation had taken place, one that left her coughing up muddy water onto a slab of concrete carrying something far different back with her.

Lily's power to glimpse the future had been joined by an ability to feel out the places in the present upon which different outcomes rested. She thought of them like switches on railroad tracks, little changes that sent the course of things to come rattling down an altogether different path.

Onmyōdō was the name James Cairncross had given her complicated new gift. As The Refuge's former librarian, Cairncross knew perhaps more than any other living soul about the arcane gifts their mentor, Robert Ash, had called khárisma.

Lily's onmyōdō glared at her unexpectedly from objects, moments, or people, filling her with an often irresistible urge to make some seemingly innocuous change to the present. One of the earliest impulses of the power had led her to a fight that broke her relationship with her closest friend. Then three and a half years ago, Lily had succumbed to the onmyōdō-fueled compulsion to shift the position of a single decorative porcelain vase and, in doing so, turned her fiancé into a suspected murderer and fugitive.

A wise and difficult man had once told her that her visions of the future weren't random. They had a cause, one that lay with the powers that moved the universe—fate, perhaps, or what Ash had poetically referred to as the Parliament of Stars.

Lily acknowledged that the actions driven by her onmyōdō had ultimately prevented greater evils from coming to pass, but the power had never shown a great deal of concern for her personal stake in the whole business. If it really was some impulse of the divine, then the divine seemed indifferent to Lily's own well-being or that of the people she cared about.

It left her instinctively wary of the unmistakable pull of the onmyōdō—a pull she felt now from that ordinary slip of yellow paper.

She could ignore it, walking away from the desk and leaving the intercept where it lay. The future would play out as it was currently meant to, the alternative promised by the yellow paper remaining forever unrealized. No one around her would ever know the difference.

But Lily would know. She knew it now, looking at the page and feeling something very like a scream ring through the back of her mind, desperate and unrelenting.

It was not a choice she necessarily had to make blindly. If posed the question of why the late intercept from Herne mattered, her onmyōdō would respond. Sometimes the answer was simple—an heirloom mirror that would no longer be broken or an automobile accident avoided. Other times, the push to know more unlocked a barrage of foresight, throwing open doors to complex and confusing outcomes spilling far into the future. It was an experience over-whelming enough to bring her to her knees.

Falling to the ground in the throes of a prophetic maelstrom in the hall of the Admiralty was not an ideal proposition.

A pair of admirals strolled past, ambling like men on their way to the club. Another courier pushed his way through the door behind her. Lily's skin burned with the feeling that she was running out of time—that in a few more minutes, the window to choose between two possible futures would close.

Now, the onmyōdō hummed inside of her. *Nownownownow …*

The courier's briefcase spilled open. Papers slid across the tiled floor. The duty clerk's head snapped to the right, and Lily's hand flashed out as though making the decision for her. Her fingers closed around the slip of yellow paper, and then she was gone, turning for the stairs with the intercept shoved into her pocket.

She climbed quickly, moving as though she knew exactly where she was going. To do anything less in this place would invite ques-tions about her purpose Lily couldn't possibly answer.

The onmyōdō pulled at her, drawing her like the needle of a compass. It tugged upward.

It wasn't until Lily was halfway to the top of the building that the rest of her brain caught up, and she realized where she must be going.

Her destination was one of the Navy's most carefully guarded secrets. Lily certainly wasn't supposed to know its location—or even that it existed—despite the fact that her husband often collaborated with the people who worked there.

Strangford had been serving in the Naval Intelligence Division for nearly four years now, ever since the memorable day when he was recruited by none other than Winston Churchill, then Lord Admiral of the Royal Navy.

Churchill had since moved on to serve as Minister of Munitions, and Strangford had evolved from an analyst and translator to more active forms of duty. He had been to both Ireland and Norway, help-ing to foil attempted uprisings and an effort by the Germans to infect Scandinavian livestock with anthrax.

It was forbidden for officers of the NID to discuss their work with their spouses, but Strangford had good reason to trust Lily's ability to keep a confidence. The balance of secrets in their relationship was also terribly skewed for reasons that could not possibly be avoided. Hiding the true nature of his employment from her had felt wrong.

Lily knew that what she was contemplating could earn Strangford a reprimand or worse. Before she chanced it, she ought to know exactly what was at stake.

Reaching the third-floor landing, she left the main staircase and strode down the hall. She blended in well enough in her uniform. Even at this late hour, there was still a scattering of other Wrens about, shuttling orders from the kitchens below or serving as typists and telephone operators.

Lily caught only a few uninterested looks as she moved purpose-fully past the offices until she reached a narrower, enclosed service stairwell at the back of the building. She pushed inside and stopped, listening.

The noises of the Admiralty hummed around her—the faraway ring of a telephone bell, the murmur of quiet voices. None of them came from within the echoing enclosure of the stairwell. She was alone here . . . for the moment.

It would have to do.

The onmyōdō still pulsed through her blood. Steeling herself, she took a breath, pushed gently at that uncanny hum—and fell.

Lily lands on a railway platform.

It is a location she knows well, one she has passed through dozens of times—London's Waterloo Station, situated on the south bank of the Thames.

The glass ceiling overhead is painted black, blocking the glare of the electric lights from escaping into the night. The lights themselves are dimmed, leaving long shadows where, before the war, everything blazed with illumination. It is late, the sprawling space around her sparsely populated.

A train emits a soft hiss of steam. A conductor cries out a

departure.

From somewhere above those familiar sounds, Lily hears the low, dull buzz of an enormous bee.

It fills her with a mix of confusion and dread—and then the urgency washes over her like a wave.

Remember, she thinks, clinging to the habit of her years-ago training. Her gaze snaps to the clock that hangs over the platform, all four faces of it precisely calibrated to show the correct time.

It reads five minutes to eleven.

The world around her shifts, tearing at the seams with a sound like the roar of a winter storm. Painted glass overhead shatters, raining needle shards down on the few people inside, who share a scream of panic. The concrete under Lily's boots splits, iron girders screeching against some enormous unseen pressure.

Plumes of dust burst from the shops lining the east side of the terminal.

The cataclysm is abrupt, stopping as soon as it has started. Following a terrible instinct, Lily flies across the platform to the doors.

She spills out into something that is not the midnight-dark streets of South London.

Where blocks of flats and shops should be is only a wasteland—a dry, dead sprawl of twisted wire and blackened trees. The air smells of burnt meat and smoke.

No, Lily desperately thinks. *Not that. Not there …*

She blinks, and the landscape shifts, turning to something else— something she has seen before.

A crater lined with earth and brick, jagged with broken pipes spewing water and flaming gas. The far side of an apocalypse marked with the icon of a bloody red hand.

Her throat closes, the old horror choking her. She shoves back the terrible association—a dark memory she knows has been dredged up by her mind as it struggles to translate the raw information thrust at her by the onmyōdō. The scene before her clears into a sprawl of crumbled stone and shattered glass. She hears people crying for help, running both toward and away from the remains of a bakery, from the isolated sign for a boy's school standing before a blackened heap.

Lights flash overhead, great white beams brushing across the sky. They dance across the form of a great gray insect, a monstrous wing-span with a terrible sting.

And then she returned.

Lily held herself upright with a hand braced against the wall, quietly gasping. She pulled in a breath, forced it back out, and fought to steady the erratic, racing beat of her pulse. The yellow intercept was crushed in her hand, her fingers clenched into an involuntary fist.

She forced them open. Carefully, she smoothed the page against the leg of her trousers, her hands still unsteady. It was clear now what the cryptic string of numbers and letters typed on the page meant— how desperately important it was.

A German bomber was coming for London tonight.

TWO

*I*T HAD BEEN TWO MONTHS since the last raid when a single one-ton shell from a monstrous German bomber had landed on a quiet street in Maida Vale, destroying three homes and killing over a dozen people.

The area around Waterloo was even more densely populated. Lily recalled with a lurch in her gut that a boarding school stood directly across the street from the main entrance to the station. How many children would be sleeping in their beds when the bomb hit?

Even if one of the naval listening stations on the coast picked up the plane's engine as it approached England, they wouldn't know where it was headed. If they did, the Admiralty could alert the Royal Air Force to scramble planes to intercept. The air raid alarm could be raised in the targeted areas, and there would be hope of minimizing the damage.

The irony of it tasted bitter. Lily could tell them exactly where the German bomber was headed . . . but they would never believe her.

The information had to come through a channel the Admiralty leadership recognized, and there was only one place where the message she held in her hand could be transformed from a string of gibberish into a warning.

Lily raised her head, pulling herself away from the wall, and looked up the dim length of the staircase. She could climb to the top and try to infiltrate one of the most secret and carefully-guarded locations in England, or she could let the future she had just foreseen come to pass.

Time inched towards inevitability.

Lily mounted the stairs, taking them two at a time. She reached an innocuous gray door at the top marked only by an indication of the floor. It would be locked.

Raising her fist, she pounded on the barrier.

The lock snapped, and the door swung open. A solidly-built sentry in Navy blues stood across the opening, a sidearm holstered at his shoulder. The bulk of his body blocked almost the entirety of her view of what lay on the other side. He glared down at her.

"Wrong door," he barked.

Electricity danced across her skin, raising the hairs on her arms as the knowledge of what would come next rose up inside of her.

A telephone bell was about to sound in the hallway behind his shoulders. Someone would drop a stack of files. He would swing the door shut, closing her out.

She could stop him. It tugged at her, a dark and whispering promise. If she did not resist it, Lily knew what it would mean. Violence would spill through her veins, marrying her skill as a fighter with the awareness of the next move her enemy would make. It was like battling someone grappled, their inability to move through time granting her a deadly advantage.

The power brought with it a fierce and thirsty pleasure, one that had previously drawn her to the brink of murder. They were moments that continued to haunt her even as unrealized possibilities. In the quietest hours of the night, Lily could not avoid the truth that part of her had wanted it. The death. The victory.

She fought the impulse now, teeth gritted against it. Mauling a naval guard at the door to a top-secret program would benefit neither her career nor that of her husband Instead, she swung her courier's bag off of her shoulder and jammed the leather into the door's hinge.

The obstruction jerked the door to a stop, bouncing it back against the sentry's hand. The big man glared down at her. Lily had perhaps three seconds before he either shoved her out onto the landing or tossed her over his shoulder to carry off to more dire consequences.

Behind him, a telephone bell blared. A clerk startled at the sound, dropping a stack of files onto the floor. Someone bent down to help him, putting his face into the narrow field of her vision.

It was a face she recognized.

"Mr. Adcock!" Lily called.

The face swiveled toward her, blinking with surprise behind a pair of round spectacles. His gaze moved from Lily to the sentry at the door. A rapid calculation took place behind those glasses.

"Lady Strangford," he said, straightening. "My apologies. I did not expect you quite this early. I see you found your own way up."

Lily breathed a silent sound of relief. The sentry frowned, but he was no longer pushing at the door.

"There weren't any visitors logged for tonight," he noted, his disapproval clear.

"Weren't there? An unconscionable oversight," Mr. Adcock replied, stepping up to the door.

Frank Adcock, Cambridge lecturer in Ancient History, was a man of inconspicuous build, balding at the crown of his head. Unlike the sentry, he was not in naval uniform. Instead, he wore a rumpled brown suit. Lily wondered if perhaps he had fallen asleep in it earlier that afternoon.

Lily had been introduced to him at a charity tea a few months before and had noted the careful way he and Strangford had greeted each other.

The guarded suite of offices Adcock had just bluffed her way into was known as Room 40, though it now took up far more than a single room. It was not a typical naval department. Its staff included a bevy of civilians, many of them scholars of history and linguistics. Few knew that these men had taken a leave of absence from lecturing and reviewing papers to crack German codes.

"Come along, my lady." Adcock said, gesturing her in with an easy assumption of authority.

For a moment, it looked like the sentry might resist, but at last he stepped back. Lily flashed him a thin smile as she hurried past, following the unassuming university fellow into the hall.

It was far more cluttered and busy than the floors she had passed through below. Wires hung in thick bundles along the ceiling, branching out into the various offices that lined the way. Even the broom closet appeared to have been converted into a sorting station.

13

The program was rapidly outgrowing even this expanded space, but its officers and civilian volunteers could not simply spill over into less secure areas of the Admiralty.

The hall was jammed with filing cabinets, trolleys, and stacks of equipment. The entire place hummed with activity. No offices were closed up for the night here. She might have been passing through in the middle of the afternoon.

Lily was far from the only woman present. Others typed furiously at rows of tightly packed desks or strode past with files under their arms.

Adcock opened one of the doors and motioned her inside. Lily found herself in a small room with a shaded window. It was dominated by a desk heaped with papers, the space made more narrow by the bookshelves that lined the walls. They were packed with volumes in an array of languages that even Cairncross would have found impressive.

The small man in the rumpled brown suit pushed the door shut behind him and turned on her, back stiff.

"I hope you realize how irregular this is."

"I know. I'm sorry." Lily replied.

"If you're looking for his lordship, he isn't here. He's at a debrief in Greenwich. I expect he will return directly to your home once he is done."

"I'm not here for Strangford." She held out the yellow paper, still wrinkled from being crunched in her fist. "I have an intercept from Herne."

Adcock's expression shifted to one of exhaustion. Lily noticed that the cuffs of his shirt were stained here and there with spots of ink.

"Yes. Right. I shall add it to the incoming pile. I assure you we will examine it as soon as possible."

She heard what he was careful not to say—anything that indicated what, exactly, that "examination" might entail. That she was here at all indicated she already knew more than she should about Room 40. Adcock did not intend to reveal more than was strictly necessary to her.

She took a breath. Figuring out how to navigate this was like walking through the dark.

"This one is important," she urged.

"They are all important, my lady." he returned, taking the paper gently from her hand. "Now, we had best get you out of here before you raise a stir."

She could feel the uncomfortable pressure of her onmyōdō. It told her that death still hung in the air over her head.

As she followed Adcock back out into the hall, Lily tried to tell herself that she had done all she could. It was a singularly unsatisfying argument.

They were halfway back to the door when a young clerk in rolled-up shirtsleeves poked his head out of an office.

"Spotters confirm single R.VI off Margate!" he called out.

There was a shift in the atmosphere around her as the people crowding the suite of offices paused in their work to take in the announcement. The activity picked up again with a new and more determined energy. She caught words buzzing through the air around her: *flight paths, observation, targeting.* Her own thoughts were locked onto the terrible significance of those three letters: *R.VI.*

Lily knew what an R.VI was—a Zeppelin-Staaken bomber, an enormous German aircraft that crossed the sky like a beast from a nightmare. It was a single bomb from a Zeppelin-Staaken R.VI that had leveled an entire neighborhood in Maida Vale back in March.

Adcock stopped, his hand tightening on the paper he had taken from Lily. He looked down at it, then whirled back to her, holding up the page.

"Herne, you said?"

"Yes," Lily confirmed.

"What time?" he demanded.

"Seventeen minutes past eight."

At the charity tea, Adcock had been pulled into a comfortable and meandering debate about Latin declensions. He was far more tightly focused here, that innocuous frame coiled with sharp and ready intelligence. At her response, he neatly pivoted on his heel and stalked back down the hall.

Lily followed him.

"Dilly." he barked, forgetting her presence as he yanked open another door.

15

Over his shoulder, Lily was mildly horrified to find herself looking into a bathroom.

It was also clearly an office. A desk sat parallel to the tub, holding precarious and yet obviously organized stacks of books and papers. More items were tacked onto the walls, overlapping each other as thick as a tapestry.

The tub itself was full, the water no longer steaming. It held a tall, thin man with a high forehead and thick, small glasses. He reclined in the bath, a pipe hanging out of the corner of his mouth as he made a mark on a clipboard.

Lily blanched a bit to realize that she recognized this gentleman as well. He was Alfred Dillwyn Knox, another Cambridge scholar who had been at the tea, renowned for his work on translating Egyptian papyri.

His bare knees poked up from the water like the limbs of some awkward bird. A metal tray of papers suspended over the tub thankfully blocked the most compromising portions of the papyrologist from her view.

"I am thinking, Frank," Knox replied patiently without looking up.

Adcock seemed not the least bit surprised to find his colleague in such an unorthodox position. Rather, he gave a short huff of irritation and hurried into the room, holding out the yellow paper.

"You heard the Margate warning?"

"Mr. Morgan has quite capable lungs," Knox returned, finally lifting his gaze from the clipboard. "Good evening, Lady Strangford."

"Mr. Knox," Lily returned politely as Adcock whirled back to her, raised his eyes to the ceiling in a very brief and silent prayer, and then snapped the page at the man in the tub.

"Herne Bay. Two hours ago."

Knox paused, his pencil hovering over his paper. His eyes shifted to the intercept, narrowing with quiet and intense interest.

"Right, then. Just a tick," he responded.

With a swish of tepid water, he launched himself out of the tub. Lily was treated to an alarming display of pale, scholarly flesh before she swiveled to put her back to Knox and took a step into the hall.

Adcock joined her there.

16

"That was . . . ahem." He struggled to find the words. "Mr. Knox is a very effective—ah, translator. The water helps him think."

"Yes. Of course," Lily murmured, unsure of what else to say. At least in his embarrassment, Adcock seemed to have momentarily forgotten that she wasn't supposed to be there.

The door behind them flew open a moment later, revealing Knox with a towel wrapped around his waist. He pushed the intercept back at them along with a quickly scribbled scrap of paper.

"Waterloo. They're targeting Waterloo."

There was no surprise in the information for Lily, and yet she felt the impact of it all the same. Her thoughts shot back to the hiss of the broken gas lines, the shattered field of brick and earth.

Adcock reacted more quickly. He snatched both papers from Knox's outstretched hand.

"Where is Blinker!" he shouted down the hall.

A reply echoed back.

"Canteen!"

Adcock bolted forward, Lily on his heels. She was vaguely aware of Knox striding behind them, still in his towel. The sight of the half-nude scholar seemed to make clear the urgency of their errand, and others dodged back out of the narrow hallway as they approached.

At the far end of the suite, Adcock pivoted through another doorway. They raced through a room full of lady typists who glanced up as they passed and then immediately returned to their work.

The canteen lay on the far side. A samovar bubbled on the counter next to a plate of buns. A diminutive officer with a captain's bars and a bevy of ribbons on his jacket stood by the platter, a slice of pound cake moving toward his mouth. He sported a pair of bushy white eyebrows, a hawk-beak nose, and bright, very intelligent eyes.

One of those eyes twitched reflexively as he looked sharply to Adcock, Lily, and Knox.

"Report," he barked.

"Margate has called a raid warning, and we've this message from Herne," Adcock replied.

The captain—Blinker—snatched the papers from his hand, scanned the contents in a breath, and then shouted.

"Don't just stand there! Open a priority line to RAF Uxbridge and ring Scotland Yard to get out the warning!"

Adcock raced off. Knox lingered by the pastries, selecting an iced Belgian bun with a glazed cherry on top of it.

"Who's the Jenny." Blinker demanded, gaze shifting to Lily with another twitch.

"Courier," Knox replied smoothly through a mouthful of bun. "Duty clerk sent her up as the tubes are out. Apparently thought it might be important."

Blinker frowned.

"Remind me to have a word with him," he noted narrowly.

"My motorbike is downstairs. I'll help get out the warning," Lily offered before the sharp-eyed officer in front of her could draw further conclusions about her presence.

Blinker studied her with an uncomfortable intensity. Then his hand shot into his pocket, emerged, and tossed something at her through the air.

Lily caught it with reflexes honed by both her kali and a touch of foresight. She opened her hand to see a shining silver whistle.

She straightened, knocking out a sharp salute.

"Sir."

She turned and hurried out, resisting the urge to run. She had just exited the typing pool when she realized that Knox was strolling beside her, his long legs making it easy to keep up.

"It will pass over Sheppey and the Hoo," he noted casually, flicking a crumb off his pectoral. "Then overland from Gravesend through Oxley."

Lily took mental note of the directions. The air raid warning would need to be called out as far along the likely route of the plane as possible. Once the bomber became harried by the Royal Air Force defense fighters, it might drop its bomb at any point rather than returning to Germany without scoring a strike at all.

Her mind skipped forward, drawing a mental line between Oxley and Waterloo. What she saw there made her heart skip.

"They'll cross Greenwich," she blurted.

Knox looked back at her with quiet understanding.

"His lordship is at the college. King Charles Quarter, Room 105."

"Thank you," she said, meaning every syllable.

The towel-clad cryptologist popped the rest of the bun into his mouth and made her an elegant bow in reply.

~

The warning was already sounding along the streets approaching Waterloo Station when Lily crossed the bridge on her Triumph, the whistle clamped between her lips. The police telephone lines had moved faster than her motorcycle. Constables bicycled down the deserted roads, shouting with practiced volume as families began to gather their essentials and scurry for shelter. One man carried a still-sleeping toddler in his arms as Lily approached the station. At the boy's school, a queue of children, still in pajamas and clutching stuffed bears, hurried across the street to the entrance to The Underground.

The sight washed her with relief, signaling as it did that with the aid of Adcock and Knox, she had at least managed to change something of that terrible future she had foreseen.

The work of spreading the warning along the rest of the bomber's potential route still needed to be done. Lily swung the Triumph around to head east along the river, the shrill note of Blinker's whistle piercing through the stillness of the night.

Searchlights blazed to life, swinging across the sky on both sides of the black current of the Thames. Fueled by acetylene, they burned a ferocious white. Gunners would be hurrying to the antiaircraft nests concealed on top of buildings scattered across the city. The lights would also help the Royal Air Force planes that must already be scrambling from their base in nearby Uxbridge.

She found herself painfully conscious of the time. In the future she had shifted, the bomber would have hit Waterloo in twenty-five minutes. That meant it must already be leaving the fields of Kent for the suburbs of southeast London—including Greenwich, where Strangford would be just finishing his debriefing.

Following the curve of the river, Lily passed the distinctive silhouette of Tower Bridge and the narrow glimmer of St. Saviour's Dock. She gave the empty place where Joseph Hartwell's warehouse once stood only a brief glance as she flew by, shivering a bit at the memory of the flames.

19

A constable was hurrying out of Southwark Park as she passed, pulling on his uniform jacket with his whistle clamped between his lips. It felt as though she were racing the hands of the switchboard operators as voices on the telephone lines worked the warning out to the other neighborhoods in the R.VI's flight path.

As yet, there was no sign of the RAF defenders overhead.

Lily swung from Jamaica Road to weave through the warren of denser streets by the river. Windows popped open as she passed, neighbors pounding on doors, the call of "air raid" echoing through the night air.

It was ten minutes to eleven when she crossed the bridge over Deptford Creek, entering Greenwich to find the police were already hurrying people to basements and shelters.

The switchboard operators had won. Lily celebrated her defeat by pausing for a moment under the searchlight-crossed sky to breathe a sigh of relief. The sense that she alone carried the responsibility for what must come next finally lifted.

She spun the Triumph back into ignition and buzzed down another lane, emerging at the sprawling campus of the Royal Naval College.

During the day, it was one of the most splendid pieces of geography in the city. The long, white-columned buildings faced broad green lawns that opened onto the muddy waters of the Thames, looking like soot-stained Grecian temples to the gods of military supremacy.

At nearly eleven in the evening, it was swathed in shadows. Like the rest of London, the windows of the college were blacked out with shades, the lawns deserted. The only illumination came from a searchlight set in a park to the west, which blazed across the sky overhead, painting a line to the river and then further east.

Lily neatly glided her motorbike around a gate blocking vehicle access to the campus at night, following a footpath up to the shadowy and timeless facade of the King Charles Building. She halted before it, killing the engine.

The two men standing by the door looked over at her.

Strangford was in uniform, the distinctive shape of it apparent even in the gloom. He extended his hand in a farewell shake as the fellow beside him gaped at the motorcycle-riding apparition on the lawn. Remembering himself, Strangford's companion took his leave, hurrying away as Strangford approached her.

Her husband's Navy blues were well-fitted. He had been able to give the patterns to his usual tailor, and thankfully the required fabric was simple wool.

Strangford could tolerate wearing wool.

The patch over his missing eye stood out starkly against his pale skin under his close-cropped hair. Serving in the Navy required him to cut it more often than he liked. The shorter trim revealed the fine glimmers of gray starting to show at his temples.

He stopped just shy of where she straddled the motorbike, close enough that she had to look up at him.

"To what do I owe the pleasure?" he asked, his voice a warm rumble that set off an answering hum inside of her.

"Air raid," she replied. "Targeting Waterloo."

He arched his eyebrow.

"I believe we are in the flight path to Waterloo."

"We are," Lily confirmed, swinging her leg off the Triumph and standing.

Strangford paused a moment, his ear tuned to the night where the police whistles could be heard, their sound softened by distance.

"It would seem the warning is out," he noted.

There was something in the possessive and admiring gaze he turned on her that made her bones heat.

"I have the oddest suspicion that those currently finding shelter might owe that to you."

Strangford moved in close enough that she could feel the brush of his uniform against her leg. He slipped his gloved hand around her lower back, pulling her nearer.

"It was Knox who deciphered the intercept," Lily protested as the hand on her back moved a little lower, setting her nerves tingling and her thoughts into a crawl. "Bloke named Blinker."

Her husband straightened, looking at her with dark amusement.

"You were in Room 40."

"I . . . er, yes," she admitted with a flush of embarrassment. "I'm sorry. It was terribly important. Will I have gotten you into trouble?"

21

"Most likely. Though I expect the fact you helped raise an air raid warning may soften the blow." His fingers paused in their delicious track up the length of her spine as he considered. "Perhaps I'll tell them you used your feminine wiles on me."

"Don't you dare. They'll suspect I must be a German agent."

He pulled her closer, his mouth exploring the sensitive skin beneath her ear.

"Your wiles are very effective," he noted.

"Anthony." she protested weakly as his hands explored further. "We are on the lawn."

"Not yet," Strangford returned. "But we could be."

The blackout had never seemed quite so much like an invitation, but her attention abruptly shifted as a low hum caught her ear. Lily gripped Strangford's arm, looking up.

"Do you—"

"Yes," he confirmed, looking up as well.

"There!" Lily pointed.

It slipped through the beam of a searchlight farther down the river—something like an enormous gray dragonfly. Two tiers of wings were marked with the black imperial German cross, four engines framing an enclosed cockpit. In the bay of that body would be a bomb capable of flattening a city block.

The R.VI was a marvel of engineering, moving over the blacked-out city like a creature from a myth. It was just as threatening as any dragon.

The night crackled with the sound of machine gun fire.

Smaller airplanes zipped into view like sparrows harrying an albatross. The RAF fighters had found their target. Though diminutive in size compared to the hulking German bomber, they moved quickly and carried a sharp sting, strafing the R.VI with bullets.

Strangford pulled Lily up into the shelter of the doorway to the looming Baroque building. The angle still provided her a view of the firefight taking place in the sky over the river as the R.VI shot back at the smaller, more nimble RAF aircraft.

His arm tightened around her waist. With his chest at her back, Lily could feel him deliberately deepening his breathing. Strangford was more sensitive than others to blaring sounds and flashing lights.

It was a reactiveness rooted in the same place as his discomfort in crowds—namely the exquisite vulnerability of his own khárisma. The breathing exercises were a part of his tàijíquán practice meant to help moderate those naturally heightened responses.

The threat was real. At any moment, the crew of the R.VI could decide to cut their losses and drop their payload regardless of the intended target, deeming a cluster of suburban homes better than nothing. Still, the dance taking place in the sky was oddly beautiful as the aircraft swooped and dove amid the racket of deadly gunfire.

The enormous frame of the R.VI shifted, pulling into a turn that would take it back out over the Thames, signaling its intention to retreat. As it moved, a strafe from one of the fighters found a lucky mark, and the side of the bomber burst apart in a ball of flame.

The great structure of it dipped, twisting in the sky as it fell. It hit the surface of the river and pinwheeled, pieces of the wings snapping off as it spun until it finally splashed to a stop, resting half-submerged beside a rowing club on the far bank. In the light of the flames from the wreckage that floated, scattered, on the water, she could see the small figures of the German crew scrambling out of the broken windows of the floating shell of the cockpit. A cry sounded from nearby, a lifeboat crew assembling by the college docks.

She leaned against Strangford, shoulders sagging with relief. It was over. Those who only an hour before had been meant to die would wake in the morning ignorant of how close they had come to a different fate.

And for once, following the demands of her onmyōdō had not cost her something more.

THREE

Tuesday, April 9
Half past seven in the morning
Lancaster Gate, Bayswater

LILY WOKE TO SOFT sunlight streaming through the bedroom windows and the sound of something thumping against the bedroom door. The sound was regular and slightly muffled. It was followed a moment later by a whispered reprimand as her housekeeper, Mrs. Jutson, shooed Cat down the hall.

The animal had adopted Lily at her old flat on March Place and followed her to Bayswater upon her marriage. It was not allowed in the bedroom as its hair on the sheets caused Strangford to either sneeze or snore.

Cat was not overly fond of this restriction, demonstrating a maniacal determination to violate it.

Strangford was snoring gently now as he sprawled across the bed beside her. He wore only the bottom half of his pajamas. Their maid, Theresa, had left them two years earlier for a better paying job in a munitions factory, which meant no one would be coming in to relight the fire. Strangford had decided to take advantage of the lack of morning interruptions by wearing fewer clothes. The sheets were a good Northumberland flannel, comfortable against his skin, and forgoing nightwear saved him from hunting for more garments he could wear without flinching.

Strangford's tendency to absorb the history of whatever he touched had improved since he and Lily had married. Impressions no longer forced themselves upon him from every surface he contacted unless they were of a particularly potent variety. He was able instead to exercise his power with a bit more discretion. Lily suspected it was because he more routinely opened himself up to contact with the world around him. Things like his books, their garden, and the objects in the house were reliably safe for him. And Lily, of course— Strangford made a habit of touching her quite regularly.

The same could be said of her foresight. Those more conventional glimpses of the future that once forced themselves upon her, almost exclusively in the form of unavoidable disasters, had become a rarity once she opened herself up to simpler and more regular moments of precognition. It was as though her power was a system under pressure that must burst out now and again if not offered more controlled forms of release.

It had made for a quieter life despite the rigors of the war, and Lily could feel it as the morning sun streaked through the window, spilling across Strangford's chest as it evenly rose and fell with his breath.

His snores hitched, breaking their rhythm, and he let out a long exhale.

"I was doing it again. Wasn't I?" Strangford demanded, his remaining eye still closed.

"Whatever could you mean?"

The eye opened, shifting over to her with a look of warm skepticism before closing again.

"I'm still asleep," he declared.

Lily contemplated her possible responses, at least one of which set a wicked flush through her. In the end, a rumble from her stomach settled the matter.

"I'll leave you to it, then," she said, slipping from the bed.

She plucked her dressing gown from the hook, shrugging it over her shoulders as she slipped from the room.

Cat immediately inserted himself between her ankles, a maneuver that could easily topple the unprepared. Thankfully Lily had been expecting it. She pulled the door shut before the animal could slip past her, neatly stepped over his bulk, and quietly made her way down the stairs.

As Lily reached the hall, a savory and mouthwatering smell rose to meet her. Voice rose from the further steps down to the kitchen.

The household at Lancaster Gate had grown even smaller since the start of the war. In addition to Theresa leaving for the factories, Strangford's awkward, countryish footman, Roderick, had been drafted in 1917. It was still hard for Lily to imagine the young, easily startled Roddie living through the violence and terror of the Western Front, but he wrote letters every week to Mrs. Jutson. Lily knew that as of last report, he was not only alive but intact and not generally minding the food.

Only Mrs. Jutson remained, and it was not Mrs. Jutson that Lily heard talking from the far end of the hall.

"And this notion that Maud Allan is having an affair with our former Prime Minister's wife is simply ludicrous. I can't imagine Margot Asquith throwing up her skirts for a bit of fun if I try. And besides, everyone knows Maud is quite devoted to Verna, her secretary."

Lily descended into the kitchen, a cozy space nestled into the ground floor of the house. Narrow windows near the ceiling looked out into the back garden.

"Good morning, Estelle," she said from the doorway.

Estelle, resplendent in caftan and turban despite the early hour, rose from the scarred kitchen chair like a goddess and glided over to Lily, greeting her with a kiss on each cheek.

"Darling! How refreshing to catch you en déshabillé. You are too often in uniform these days. It's noble and depressing. Come join us. One of my clients graced me with a pound of ham after I connected him with his departed mother, and I was just regaling Mrs. Jutson with the sordid tale of the Cult of the Clitoris while she fried it up."

Mrs. Jutson stood by the stove, neatly flipping slices of ham with her tongs. The offering was indeed a treat, something that had been next to impossible to come by since the outbreak of the war.

The housekeeper was in her early fifties, her hair coiled into a slightly off-balance bun. The kitchen was her realm, which was why the walls were mounted with plates paying tribute to various jubilees and anniversaries. Mrs. Jutson was a devoted royalist.

"It's right alarming," the housekeeper said. "Women with women and such, and the Germans turning them all into spies. Begging your pardon, my lady."

Mrs. Jutson's manner was somewhat less than precisely proper, but then she had not been trained by one of the agencies that nobles usually hired from. Instead, Strangford had found her through one of his tenants who lived on the family estate in Northumberland. What she lacked in tact, she made up for in hard work. More importantly, she was a woman uniquely devoid of jealousy and spite. Though not exactly grandmotherly in her manner, she was motivated by compassion, loyalty, and affection—feelings that Strangford did not mind sharing when he touched the objects Mrs. Jutson had come into contact with.

"I have not received a single note from a German blackmailer yet," Estelle complained in response, flashing Lily a wink. "I am feeling quite left out."

"Tea's ready." Mrs. Jutson said, plucking the kettle from the stove.

"It's warming up a bit outside. Why don't we take it in the garden?" Estelle suggested.

Returning upstairs to change had felt like too much effort for wartime, and so instead, Lily plucked a light coat from the stand by the door and shrugged it over her dressing gown. She was glad for it once they got outside. The sky had clouded over, and there was a breath of chill to the air.

Once in the garden, Estelle draped herself across one of the white wrought iron chairs.

"Aren't you cold?" Lily demanded as she took the other chair.

"Not anymore. As you will understand in another twenty years or so, I should expect."

Lily allowed Estelle to cool off as she soaked up the quiet beauty of the garden. Even with the cloud-covered sky and the chill, she was happy Estelle had prompted them to come out here.

The walled space behind the house was not as ornamental as it had once been. Strangford had pulled up the overgrown shrubs and perennials to make room for vegetable beds, building more boxes over the lawn and patio. They were already bursting with crisp heads of spring lettuce and curling tendrils of peas. Fresh vegetables were nearly as hard to come by as ham, so growing their own was the only way to ensure the house had a regular supply. Lily knew it was not particularly fashionable among the upper classes, but she found the sight of all those useful growing things very pleasant.

"Where is Gwen this morning?" she asked. "Raising donations for veterans with her suffrage group again?"

To the outside world, Gwendolyn Bard was Estelle's roommate. The two women made no secret of the true nature of their relationship to those they called friends.

"No," Estelle replied. "I finally convinced her to take a holiday, which she was rather desperately in need of. I had been thinking perhaps of the seashore or the Lakes District, but she's hared off to some tiny village in Kent for a festival where they bake loaves of bread in the shape of a pair of conjoined twins who died eight hundred years ago. Because that, of course, is Gwen's idea of fun."

Miss Bard was a rather well-respected folklorist. Because she published under her initials, there were very few who realized that the learned G.W. Bard was not a gray-bearded old scholar but a plump and pretty middle-aged suffragette.

"What about you?" Lily pressed. "Are you taking a holiday, or are you still working all hours of the day and night?"

Estelle made her living as a medium. Her business had initially combined her very real talents for speaking with the dead with a fair amount of show and spectacle. The war had changed that. An exponential increase in demand for her services had allowed her to do away with the tricks that brought in the punters and focus instead on communicating the genuine messages of the departed.

Lily knew that Estelle had been struggling to balance the needs of the dead and the grieving with her own well-being.

"It is not as though I am capable of sleeping anymore," Estelle complained. "I might as well be doing a bit of good. It's that or sit around overheating. Gwen says I am coming into my power as a crone and, apparently, that is why I am constantly melting. Because I am so splendidly powerful."

She emphasized the point with a graceful sweep of her hand and then slumped back in her chair.

"Ahh, the tea. Bless you, Mrs. Jutson," she added.

Mrs. Jutson set the tray down on the table, along with a small stack of letters and the morning newspaper. Lily's stomach grumbled in response to the smell of the ham. There was also a porridge but no toast. The porridge was of indeterminate origin, made up of whatever grains Mrs. Jutson could get hold of, but she always had a bit of bramble jam for it sent to her by a sister back in Northumberland.

"I'm afraid it's that Chinese stuff again," Mrs. Jutson warned. "Ration day isn't till tomorrow."

"Tea is Chinese, Mrs. Jutson," Lily gently corrected her, pouring out a cup.

"Is this Mr. Wu's gòngjú?" Estelle asked, perking up as Lily handed her the cup. "I quite enjoy it. It reminds me a bit of my favorite vermouth."

The gòngjú was made with dried chrysanthemums by Lily's old friend Mr. Wu, who cultivated the flowers in his garden outside the city. He spiked the blend with a hint of the herb known in the Americas as sassafras, which gave it an earthy and spicy flavor Lily found quite pleasant, even if it lacked the invigorating qualities of the usual stuff.

She was grateful to Mr. Wu for providing them with it. Many other families simply went without as they waited for their next ration pickup, or they steeped their leaves over again until the liquid they brewed had roughly the consistency and flavor of bathwater.

Thinking of his father always brought Sam to Lily's mind. She had not seen him since the start of the war, though at least now the pair of them regularly exchanged mail. Lily filled pages with inane details about her work and life in London, and Sam would send back a postcard with nothing on the back of it or an envelope with a few news clippings or other things he picked up like a magpie. It was enough to know he was alive but so much less than what they had once shared. Of course, Lily knew she had very possibly shattered that closeness forever with her actions the last time they had been together—on the night Jack Cannon died.

She missed the closeness—missed Sam. She wondered what might be left between the two of them when he finally did return home from the war . . . if he came home at all.

For a moment, the thought left her gazing blankly down at her tea.

When she caught herself and raised her eyes again, Estelle was looking at her with quiet, knowing sympathy.

Lily turned from it, stabbing a piece of ham with her fork. She took a bite and frowned. After months of deprivation, it should have tasted like heaven, but for some reason, the flavor was unpleasantly metallic. Perhaps it had simply been too long since she'd had any.

She forced herself to swallow and turned her attention to vaguely shuffling through the mail.

"Anything good?" Estelle prompted, cutting her own slice of ham in half and plopping one of the sections onto Lily's plate. Estelle always ate like a bird.

"Looks like another update from Dr. Yates," Lily replied.

The doctor was a female physician Lily had met through Gwendolyn Bard's suffrage club. She ran a charity health clinic exclusively for women and children. Many of her patients were prostitutes with limited options for health care. Lily knew all too well how easily such women could be taken advantage of. A few years ago, she had made a significant donation—the entirety of the accumulated money her father had sent her over the years before she married Strangford. The checks had been deposited into a bank account in Lily's name, one that she had refused to touch even when it left her impoverished to the point where she had to work the most menial jobs to survive.

Once she had emptied the account, Lily had asked her father to close it and cease his deposits. He had agreed, which was a relief to her, but he still found ways to inflict his wealth upon them. They were simply more subtle now and, therefore, more difficult to refuse. She would come home to find that someone had paid for a cracked windowpane to be replaced or a new chair would be delivered when an older one lost a spring.

The gifts were occasionally exasperating, but Lily knew they were different than those earlier payments had been. This wasn't some substitute for genuine love and support, but rather her father's awkward way of showing that he cared about her.

Her relationship with Torrington had never evolved into something conventional. There was too much history between them, and too much was complicated by the antagonism of his heir, Viscount

Deveral, and the ever-present fear and hurt on the part of his count-ess. Still, the pair of them managed to meet at least once every couple of months, and those engagements had come to feel increasingly comfortable.

There were still things that hurt. She had never been back to Brede Abbey, her father's rambling country estate in the Sussex Weald. The one time she had seen it, the manor had made her ache with thoughts of what her life might have been like had her father succeeded in convincing his family to adopt her after her mother's death.

"I see you have another from Miss Eversleigh," Estelle noted, reaching across the little table to flip up an envelope more volumi-nously stamped than the others.

"Portia?" Lily said, reaching for the missive. It had indeed come all the way from Cairo, Egypt. Lily's quiet, bookish niece had joined Queen Alexandra's Imperial Military Nursing Service the day she finished school. After her training, she had requested a transfer to the army hospital in Cairo, of all places. She was lodging with friends of the Eversleigh family, Neil and Constance Fairfax, nursing soldiers wounded on the African front.

"How is she enjoying Egypt?" Estelle asked.

"It is hard to be certain, as her letters are generally stuffed with information about the pharaohs of the 18th Dynasty or the relative merits of tourniquet materials, but if I had to guess, I should say she is rather taken with it."

Lily still wondered how much of Portia's decision to join the nurs-ing service was driven by the events of that night in December 1914 when the girl had calmly helped to hold back the blood gushing from the gunshot wound in her father's chest.

Her deeply observant niece had never mentioned anything about Dr. Harold Gardner's ability to diagnose the nature of her father's injury with a touch that night, or how Strangford had drawn the intentions of his assailant from cold steel with his hands, but Lily felt certain the girl missed nothing from behind those owl-like spectacles.

Portia was quite capable of recognizing a secret when she saw one.

Her eldest niece was not the only Eversleigh who knew of Strangford's powers. Her mother, his sister Virginia, was aware of them as well. She occasionally brought up the fact that Strangford had hidden them from her for thirty years when she wanted to best him in some verbal battle.

Lily would read Portia's letter later when she had time to delve into its dense descriptions of Arabic grammar. As she set it aside, her eyes fell on the newspaper—locking onto the date printed boldly under the header.

April 9

She slowly set down her fork.

"So that's why you came," she said numbly as the significance of that little line of type shattered through her.

It had been exactly one year.

On April 8th, 1917, Lily's mother-in-law, the dowager Lady Strangford, had finally slipped away after a three-year battle with cancer of the ovaries. The following day, shortly after the telegram arrived at the house, Lily lost a pregnancy she had only just discovered—a pregnancy that she and Strangford had almost given up hoping for.

Lily told herself it had barely been real yet. There was hardly anything to lose. She might not even have known had she not been so carefully counting the weeks even as she pretended not to mind anymore.

She hadn't told anyone about it, still so hesitant to believe it could really be happening. Only Strangford had known, and Strangford had been sent off to analyze some debris salvaged from a sunken German destroyer off the Yorkshire coast. Lily knew he must go directly from there to Allerhope, the family estate in Northumberland, to help Virginia make the funeral arrangements.

If she wired to tell him what had happened, he would be torn between those two responsibilities, and so Lily had hovered in the bedchamber, paralyzed by the simple and terrible decisions she must make. The monster of her own looming grief had risen up inside of her even as she chided herself for being so horribly weak, knowing she must simply get on with things—clean up, pack her bags.

Get up off of the floor.

Then Estelle had come.

She still wasn't sure how Estelle had gotten past Mrs. Jutson when Lily had not yet come downstairs for the day, but then Estelle had always known what to say—it was rather her gift. One minute she was more alone than she had ever been in her life, and the next, Estelle was opening the door and kneeling down beside her, pulling her very gently, very carefully into her arms.

"I know," she had whispered as Lily started to shake, the careful dam she had built against her pain beginning to shatter as Estelle's long fingers swept through her hair. "I'm here."

Lily had not shared the news of her pregnancy with her friend, but Estelle had means of collecting information that went beyond the cries of the newspaper boy. Lily had never asked her which spirit had raised the alarm about her distress—in the end, it didn't really matter. It was Estelle who had helped her wash up and change. Who had packed her things and joined her on the ride to the north, and then taken Strangford carefully aside when he met them at the tiny station two miles from Allerhope. She had slipped her fingers into his hand and allowed him to learn the news in a way that did not also burden him with the terrible weight of Lily's sadness and that awful sensation that she was somehow at fault, even though she knew rationally that could not possibly be the case.

Back in the soft gray quiet of the garden, a year later, Estelle poured a splash more gòngjú into her cup.

"Are you doing anything to mark the occasion?" she gently asked.

"I have to work," Lily returned shortly.

She forced herself to eat another bite of the ham, even though the flavor of it was wrong. She did not want Estelle to know she had lost her appetite.

"Rituals help, Lily." Estelle pushed back softly. "Grief heals better when you honor it."

"I honor my grief perfectly well, thank you," Lily snapped back.

Estelle made no comment, not even the typical arch of one of her fine eyebrows. Somehow that said more than any words would. Lily felt her defenses crumble a bit.

"It just seems like it should hardly matter anymore. It isn't as though I lost someone I knew."

"That's not how love works," Estelle replied, pushing aside her porridge and sipping her gòngjú.

"No," Lily acknowledged. "I suppose it isn't."

Estelle's hand slipped across the table to cover Lily's. It stayed there, holding her gently, and something in her uncoiled just a little. She wondered whether perhaps this was her ritual—this quiet tea in the garden with a friend who knew exactly how hard this day would be for her.

The door at the top of the steps cracked open. A bolt of orange fur streaked out, hurrying down to entwine itself around Lily's ankles. Cat then moved to Estelle, who firmly nudged the animal back with her foot.

"Not on the caftan, thank you very much," she asserted.

Strangford sneezed from the doorway.

"Good morning, ladies," he said.

Unlike Lily, he had taken the time to get dressed. His hair was still damp from a quick wash in the basin, and he wore one of his old black suits. There was something comforting in the sight of it since so much of the rest of the time he was in uniform.

"Hello, Anthony." Estelle greeted him in return.

Something in the unusual solemnity of her tone alerted him. His expression shifted, the casual cheer fading from it.

"Oh," he remarked quietly. "Yes, of course."

He descended, crossing to the table. He stood by Lily's chair, his bare hand falling to where the dressing gown covered her shoulder.

She was torn between two opposing instincts. One urged her to pull away, to protect him from the emotions that roiled inside of her. It was an urge she would almost certainly have given in to four years earlier.

Lily lifted her hand, entwining his fingers with her own.

Though she knew Strangford's power only worked one way, she could almost swear she felt something pressing towards her through the warmth of his touch—a pulse of comfort. The overpowering sense that she was not alone.

He bent down, his lips brushing against her hair.

"Here," Lily said, pushing the word past the lump in her throat as she straightened. "Come join us. There's ham."

Strangford released her. He touched the back of the seat as he sat, a habit he developed after he lost his eye to make certain he didn't misjudge the distance. It was the odd chair at the table, added a couple of years ago after they kept finding themselves with company. It didn't match the others, but Lily found she preferred it that way.

"We must have pleased the rationing gods," he noted as Lily pushed the better part of her ham onto the plate in front of him.

He took a bite. The pleasure that flashed across his face was genuine.

"Estelle brought it," Lily said.

Estelle waved a dismissive hand.

"No tribute is required. Pass it on to your wife."

Strangford's eye brightened a little mischievously.

"This is quite excellent ham. Whatever could I offer that would be sufficiently pleasing?"

Estelle snorted out a laugh. Lily felt her cheeks warm, and just like that, the morning reclaimed itself. The grief was still there, but so was the tea, the growing things, and the laughter of the people she loved.

With that soft and sure glow inside of her, she enjoyed another sip of her tea. She reached for the last letter. As her fingers brushed the envelope, her power abruptly sparked to life.

Her breath fogs before her in a room of ice.

Black feathers rustle against a familiar voice in her ear.

You don't know what I've done.

Glass shatters in the heat of an inferno.

Monsters scream across the dark.

Strangford gazes at her through a snow that falls warm against her skin, scented like a funeral.

… the only choice …

Lily slammed back into the garden, the fear threatening to choke her as she clenched the envelope in her hand.

"What is it?" Strangford demanded, breakfast forgotten as he studied her face.

Lily forced her hand to open, looking down at the ordinary shape of the letter. It was postmarked from London, made of plain white paper and addressed in a quick, neat hand, one that spoke of control and efficiency. It might have held a bill or a request for a charity donation.

"It's for you," she managed to say, acknowledging the name neatly printed on the surface and holding it out to him.

Strangford's bare fingers rested against the wrought iron table. Everything about him went very still, his eye on the envelope as though it were a wild animal that had wandered into the garden.

Lily continued to hold it out even as part of her wanted to tear it into pieces—but that could not be her choice. It was Strangford's letter. It was for him to decide what to do with it.

"Is it bad?" he asked her, still not lifting his hands.

"It's ... important," she stammered out, shaking her head. "I can't be sure of anything else but that."

He absorbed her words in thoughtful silence, then pulled his gloves from his pocket and tugged them on. Finally, he accepted the letter, tearing it open with an unused butter knife from the tea tray.

"Well?" Estelle prompted impatiently.

"It's from Inspector Tariq Kazi," Strangford replied.

The name was as shocking as a rhinoceros wandering into the garden. Lily had not seen or heard from Inspector Kazi since they last spoke on the cliffs at Taddiford the morning after Strangford was cleared of suspicion of murder.

Tall and elegantly put together with his watchful golden-brown eyes and fine mustache, the inspector missed nothing. He had pursued Strangford in a manner that was both relentless and woven through with a deep vein of integrity that might ultimately have saved both of their lives.

Kazi was no longer their enemy, but Lily was far from comfortable with the prospect of his reappearance in their lives.

"What does he want?" she demanded.

"He asks if I would consent to being transferred to MI1c for the next month for a special project. The Foreign Section of the Secret Service Bureau," he clarified, looking up to meet her eyes.

Faced with war, England had leveraged the collective powers of three distinct intelligence agencies. There was the Naval Intelligence Division, which Strangford worked for and which included the code-breakers like Knox and Adcock in Room 40. A parallel organization ran within the British Army, designated as Military Intelligence 1B.

Finally, there was the Secret Service Bureau, a joint operation of both military officers and civilians that was run directly out of the War Office, the branch of the British Cabinet that oversaw all war operations.

Kazi had been working for the SSB when they first encountered him back in 1914. He and several other officers from the Special Branch of the Metropolitan Police had been detached to the intelligence bureau at the outbreak of the war to aid with their counterespionage efforts.

Apparently, he must still be involved.

"What kind of project?" she demanded.

"He doesn't specify."

He handed Lily the letter. She read through the text, which took only a moment. It said little more than what Strangford had already told her.

"Is that all we can know?" she asked carefully.

Strangford did not object. He took off his gloves and accepted the page back from her. He lowered his head, a posture that made it easier to conceal what he was doing—at least if none of the emotions burned into what he held were too powerful.

"Noise. It's . . . children arguing." He frowned at the page, pushing himself deeper. "A woman . . . Tidying up. Everyone is always leaving things lying about."

A touch of that other soul's exasperation found its way into his voice, and then he set the letter back down on the table, straightening and coming back into himself.

"There was also a girl at the factory who was upset about a tiff with the vicar," he added. "Nothing more. Nothing of the inspector."

"How very odd," Lily commented uneasily.

"Did someone else write it for him, then?" Estelle asked.

"I'm not sensing anyone putting a pen to this page. It's as though it should still be blank."

Estelle tapped at the paper with an elegantly shaped fingernail.

"And this is definitely your inspector's hand?"

"I never saw it," Lily admitted.

"Nor did I," Strangford agreed. "But it would make little sense for someone else to impersonate the man. No one who knew the history

WHAT THE RAVENS SING

of our relationship would think our connection such that it could be imposed upon."

"He did accuse you of murder," Estelle cheerfully agreed.

"Suspected," Strangford corrected.

"He got you indicted," Lily pointed out tersely. "I should say that counts as an accusation."

"He was doing his duty." he gently countered.

Lily bit back her instinctual retort to that. It was true that there had been nothing dishonorable in Kazi's actions four years ago, and he had come through for them in the end.

None of that meant she had to be pleased about the prospect of the man turning back up in her life.

"Well, I hope you aren't going to agree to what he's asking without more information," Estelle commented, giving voice to what Lily had been quietly thinking.

"No," Strangford confirmed.

He picked up the envelope, turning it over.

"There's a return address. St. Mary's Garden's, Lambeth."

"But that's nowhere near Whitehall," Lily protested, pulling up her mental map of the city. "It's all residential. There certainly aren't any offices there, intelligence bureau or otherwise."

"Then it would appear the two of you shall be paying a call this evening," Estelle noted blithely, taking another sip of her tea.

FOUR

Five-thirty that afternoon
Lambeth, South London

$\mathcal{I}$T WAS APPROACHING SUPPER time as their tram rattled across
the Thames.

Lily was fairly certain she was the only baroness in London who
took a tram. It was not a status she particularly minded. After four
years, she had become more accustomed to the fact that she, who had
once swept stages and worked as a chorus girl, was now a member of
the nobility. She still had little desire to take on the usual accouter-
ments of her rank, even if Strangford had been able to afford them.
Those few times they had ventured into higher society together, she
had been conscious of a deep and strange disconnect between herself
and the bejeweled aristocrats who talked about their art purchases
and New York fashions as though there wasn't a war on.

They did, in fact, own a carriage, but the conveyance had been
kept in Northumberland for the use of Strangford's mother. At the
time of her passing, the family chauffeur had reached the venerable
age of sixty-nine, and Strangford had offered to pension him off. At
any rate, it would have been a bother to acquire the animals to pull
it, even for a family of horse breeders like Strangford's. Any stock
they raised was subject to an ongoing contract with the Army, which
snatched up the beasts as soon as they had reached maturity.

Some of the shops were already locking up for the night as they

41

disembarked in Lambeth, though the streets were still busy with pedestrians heading home from work for the evening. The scent of boiling potatoes and fried fish floated out from the open windows of the flats above the storefronts. The sky had cleared a bit since the morning, the air warming into a pleasant April afternoon.

Lily wore a gray tailored suit and blouse. She carried her walking stick with her, a solid and sturdy length of yew topped with tapered brass. To those they passed on the street, it looked like a mildly eccentric fashion accessory. In reality, it was a weapon.

Strangford had raised an eyebrow when she came down with it as they were leaving, once more clad in his Navy uniform.

"I doubt you'll need that," he commented, setting his officer's cap on his head.

"One can never be too prepared," Lily had countered.

She did not know this area of the city particularly well. Only the main roads were familiar to her, and so she was a bit surprised when they turned the corner onto St. Mary's Gardens. The neighborhood was a quiet delight.

North and west of London's heart, the presence of a green square inevitably meant a doubling of real estate prices. The lawn would be lined by fine homes and enclosed with a locked gate to which only residents had a key.

Here, the square was open, a triangle of green dotted with bright tulips and softly flowering trees. The houses were not looming mansions but rather quaint two-story row homes of the sort that working families could easily afford. They were universally well-kept, with swept steps and tidy front gardens, many of which had been converted into vegetable beds. Part of the square had been turned over to farming as well, maintained by volunteers from the neighborhood.

Children chased each other among the sprouting beans and carrots. One kicked a football as an older gentleman planting potatoes waved the lot of them off toward the remaining lawn. The horde of small bodies wheeled towards the grass, colorful and loud.

The address on the envelope took them to a house at the end of the row marked by well-tended flower boxes hanging from the windows and pots of herbs lining the steps. The trim was freshly painted, and

Lily could smell something cooking inside as she mounted the steps. The spices made her mouth water.

Strangford raised his hand to knock.

Lily's arm instinctively shot out, stopping him as her brain was crowded with a familiar buzz. The sense of imminent significance rang through her skull like a tolling bell in the distinctive tones of her onmyōdō.

"Should we turn around?" Strangford quietly asked.

"I ... I don't know," she stammered. "I just ..."

He waited for her with quiet patience. She took a breath, the sensation already receding, leaving behind a thin and frustratingly vague awareness.

"It ... feels like we're supposed to be here," she admitted.

"That's good?" Strangford offered tentatively.

She flashed him an uncomfortable look.

"Just get on with it," she ordered in lieu of an answer.

He rapped out three neat blows.

The door opened to reveal a sturdy, chubby boy of perhaps five. He looked up at Lily and Strangford with wide, deep brown eyes.

"Have you lost an eyeball?" he demanded.

"I have," Strangford graciously replied.

The boy's gaze widened with happy fascination.

"What'd you lose it on?"

"Part of a train," Strangford returned.

"Which part?" the child pressed as a tall, slender boy of around twelve ducked quickly into the hall.

Strangford frowned.

"I'm not precisely certain."

"Chotu!" the older boy scolded. "You're not supposed to answer the door."

"Well, he knocked on it," the five-year-old countered crossly, pointing at Strangford.

The older boy neatly shoved the child's finger back into place, then straightened, quickly smoothing himself into a proper comportment.

"May I help you?" he asked with cool politeness.

The effect was somewhat marred by the buckling of his left knee as Chotu elbowed it from behind.

A certain familiar symmetry of features suggested a connection Lily felt was confirmed by the thick brown hair and copper-hued skin on both of the children. That Strangford had obviously leapt to the same conclusion was revealed in what he said next.

"Lord and Lady Strangford calling for Inspector Kazi."

"I shall see if he is receiving—" the boy began before being promptly cut off by his younger brother.

"Bābā!" the smaller boy bellowed, his big eyes locked with interest and suspicion on Strangford. "There's a one-eyed lord outside!"

The announcement was greeted by sounds of interest from elsewhere in the house. Footsteps pounded elephant-like down the stairs as a girl of eight barreled into the hall, staring unabashedly at the visitors.

"He isn't a lord. He's a Navy officer." the girl declared, hands on her hips, clearly disappointed.

"I am both, as it happens," Strangford replied as he removed his hat, tucking it under his arm.

A petite and lovely woman marched into the hall from a door at the back, an apron tied around her waist. Her shining dark brown hair was pinned up elegantly. By the fine lines of her face, she appeared to be perhaps a couple of years older than Lily. Though slight in size, she wielded a wooden spoon like a field marshal's baton as she barked out orders, her voice warmly accented.

"Rani! Chotu! Into the kitchen!"

"Why not outside?" the girl complained.

"I want to see the lord," the youngest added, drawing out every syllable painfully.

The woman sighed, raising her eyes to the ceiling. "Motka, fetch your father from the garden."

"He is already here," a voice smoothly cut in as Kazi entered through the back door, pulling off a pair of gardening gloves.

The inspector was dressed in his shirt and trousers, sleeves neatly rolled up. A canvas apron was tied at his waist, though not a speck of dirt was visible on it or any of his clothing, despite the fact he had clearly been working. He still wore a tie, which was neatly tucked into his shirt.

"Good day, my lord. Lady Strangford," he said calmly in greeting.

The woman looked from her husband to the children, waved her arm, and hissed another order.

"Go! All of you!"

The children scurried out, but not through the back door to which she pointed. Instead, they stampeded past Lily and Strangford toward the square where the other children could be seen playing.

Their mother closed her eyes, let out a controlled and eloquent huff of frustration, and then regained control of herself.

"May I present Mrs. Kazi?" the inspector offered.

"A pleasure to make your acquaintance," Mrs. Kazi replied.

She admirably mustered a gracious curtsy, but there was an audible edge to her voice as she addressed her spouse.

"Dearest husband, where would you like to receive your guests?"

"The parlor will do," Kazi replied as he took off his boots and put on a pair of house shoes, hanging the apron on a hook by the door. "We will require a bit of privacy."

"Tea?" Mrs. Kazi asked with forced brightness, directing the question to Lily and Strangford.

"I'm not sure that will be—" Kazi began.

Lily cut him off, her eyes on his wife, intuiting what the proper response should be.

"That would be lovely." she replied determinedly. "Thank you."

Mrs. Kazi nodded, satisfied. Shooting a brief but potent glare at her husband, she slipped back into the kitchen.

The inspector rolled down and buttoned his sleeves, straightening his tie and slipping into the coat he had left hanging on a hook by the back door. The transformation took only a moment, and he was once again as impeccably put together as he had been four years ago. His dark hair was untouched by gray, and Lily was fairly certain he had not gained a single wrinkle.

It was a little irritating.

He gestured to the door to their left.

"If you would."

They stepped through into the parlor. It was modest in size, the furnishings carefully chosen and well-arranged with a distinct lack of clutter. Hints of the family's origins punctuated the decor, from a colorful woven throw blanket to the photographs on the wall of distant family members in kurta tunics and saris. An elegant arrangement of Arabic script was framed on the wall, hanging above the place where a violin leaned on top of a pile of sheet music. Lily found herself easily able to picture the oldest of Kazi's children being compelled into lessons.

She was still surprised to find herself inside the inspector's home. In fact, it had come as something of a shock to discover that he had a family at all. Some part of her had assumed he must simply materialize each morning in his office and then blink out of existence again when he was no longer needed.

"You are a bit later than I expected," Kazi said, taking a seat in an armchair that seemed perfectly designed to fit his frame.

"Than you expected?" Lily echoed, lowering herself to a spot on the very comfortable settee across from him. "If you had wanted to speak with us, you might have extended an actual invitation."

"Invitations can be refused," Kazi replied. "I suspected a mystery would be a more reliable means of enticing you here."

That he was correct only deepened her ire with the man.

"Lady Strangford had a shift with the Wrens," Strangford offered easily.

He looked quite at home on Kazi's couch as though this were a casual chat between old acquaintances. Lily was prepared to be annoyed with him as well until she noted the watchful focus of his eye. He might be playing a friendly role, but he was just as wary as she was of the purpose behind this encounter.

"You might have left her at home," Kazi pointed out.

Lily's temper flared.

"It would hardly have been wise for me to venture into a meeting with you without reinforcements. Would it?" Strangford returned.

The door opened as Mrs. Kazi strode into the room. Her apron was gone, revealing a very fine day gown, her already tidy hair further neatened. Strangford stood as she entered, offering her a bow.

"Ma'am," he said in greeting.

Mrs. Kazi flashed him a look of approval as she set an elegant tea service down on the table.

"Can I offer any further refreshment?" she asked, dark eyes darting a challenge at her husband.

"Thank you, Mrs. Kazi. I'm sure that will do," Kazi said, the words obviously a careful dismissal.

His wife smiled, flashing white teeth. Lily was briefly reminded of a tiger.

"If you're quite certain, Bhuto," she replied.

At the sound of that word—*Bhuto*—Kazi's jaw twitched with suppressed irritation.

"Lord Strangford. Lady Strangford," Mrs. Kazi said gracefully, offering an elegant curtsy and then departing.

Lily was not one to leave a gift on the table.

"Bhuto?" she casually asked as she reached out to pour the tea.

Kazi's fingers drummed against the arm of the chair.

"I believe you would refer to it as a nickname."

"Does it have a meaning?" Lily pressed sweetly.

"Ghost," he replied, his voice edged with annoyance. "I was very quiet as a boy."

Lily found she could easily picture it—a thin, silent child hovering in the background of some busy family life, too serious and far too observant. It was strange to comprehend how he fit into this busy and obviously affectionate household with a strong-willed wife and the three energetic children she could even now hear joyfully calling out in the square. She wondered whether he was always so serious with them, sticking out like a sore, stuffy thumb. Or did his family draw something more pliable out from under that dour exterior?

"I have given you no reason to think I am a threat to you," Kazi continued, neatly picking up the earlier thread of their conversation now that his wife was out of the room.

"You came rather close to slipping a noose around my neck," Strangford countered cheerfully, pouring a cup of tea.

Lily could tell by the scent that it was actual tea, but it came already blended with milk and fragrant with other spices. Strangford offered the first cup to Kazi, who accepted, and then made one for himself.

"I was following a compelling chain of evidence to its logical conclusion," Kazi returned just as comfortably. "You can hardly blame me for failing to reason that one of my suspects might be capable of appearing in two locations at the same time."

Lily's hand froze on the teapot. It was that or risk fumbling and dropping it on the fine carpet.

It could not be a surprise, she fiercely reminded herself. Kazi had long ago proved to have an impeccably logical brain. Certain facts revealed during that final confrontation at Taddiford would have been sufficient for him to unravel what had really happened the night Felix Brockmeyer died—never minding what he must have witnessed directly in the intermittent glow of the lighthouse beam.

It was still unsettling to hear that truth spoken aloud. It made Lily feel all too keenly aware of the other secrets she and Strangford had carried into the room.

"This is delightful!" Strangford exclaimed from beside her, taking another sip of his tea.

"It is Mrs. Kazi's recipe," Kazi replied politely.

"Do you think she would share it?" Strangford asked hopefully.

"What do you want?" Lily cut in, her eyes on the inspector.

That careful, penetrating gaze shifted to her.

"As I said in my letter, I would like to request Lord Strangford's assistance with a mission."

"What sort of mission?"

"The debriefing of a British Army liaison officer currently convalescing in Paris."

"Army Intelligence has its own debriefers," Strangford relished another sip of the tea. "Does she actually steep the leaves in milk?"

"Yes," Kazi replied shortly. "And I'm afraid the Army debriefers are of rather little use with this particular case."

"Ginger." Strangford sniffed the cup. "Perhaps a little nutmeg?"

"Why." Lily demanded.

Kazi did not insult her by pretending she was asking about the tea.

"The officer in question is catatonic."

Outside the parlor, time continued to move, measured in the happy cries of the children playing on the green. Inside, under the watchful gaze of the gray relatives on the wall, everything had gone still. Strangford's teacup paused halfway to his lips, then lowered slowly back to his knee.

"Ah," he said quietly, a world of expression in that single terrible syllable.

The sense of threat roared up, rushing in her ears like the crashing of waves. Lily found herself clutching her teacup with both hands. Had she been holding her staff instead, it was entirely possible she might have risen from her chair and done her best to kill him.

No, she thought quietly, desperately, as the tea slowly scalded her fingers through the thin porcelain.

She was not sure if she was resisting the terrible truth of what Kazi had just revealed or the unwelcome urge to violence that ran so quick and hot in her blood.

The latter had lain mostly dormant for the last four years, and those few flashes of it she had experienced, she had managed to resist.

That did not mean she had forgotten it or the awful things it could do.

Strangford reached carefully across the settee to rest his gloved fingers on her knee. To anyone watching, it must look like a gesture of comfort. Lily wondered if he was actually holding her in place.

As quickly as it has risen, the violence ebbed, settling into a low and simmering hum in the background of her mind. It left her feeling weak and shaken.

"Are you capable of lending assistance with such a case, Lord Strangford?" Kazi softly demanded.

Though Strangford didn't move, something in him felt coiled and ready to spring.

"Why don't you tell me what you believe I am capable of."

Lily wondered if the inspector could hear the thread of danger in his voice.

"There were certain aspects of the Brockmeyer case—and of the train accident at Ludgate the previous summer, which Lady Strangford was so kind as to bring to my attention—that remained unsettled after Mr. Anstruther-Fields's death," Kazi said. "I am not a man much tolerant of loose ends, and so before very long, I found myself at a discrete and well-appointed rest home in Berkshire speaking with the late Lord Bexley."

Lord Bexley.

The name sent a chill across her skin despite the warm comfort of the room. It pulled up memories of a terrible prophecy and a desperate encounter in a brothel on Primrose Hill. She could still recall the look of outrage on the face of one of the leading peers of the realm as Strangford used his hands to pull the knowledge they needed to save the city out of Lord Bexley's skin.

How the bloody hell do you know that?

The sun had risen the next morning with Lord Bexley fallen into disgrace, and word had reached her not long afterward that he had quietly retired to a secluded location in the country. Dr. Gardner had informed them that this "rest home" was in fact a posh but secure lunatic asylum and that Bexley was likely suffering from a genuine nervous disorder.

If any of his ravings were based in truth, no one there would know how to tell the difference.

In 1916, after the death of his eldest son at the Somme, Bexley managed to hang himself with a strip torn off of his bedsheets. Lily thought that chapter of their lives might finally have closed . . . until now.

"The story his lordship told was fantastical by any measure, but it undeniably meshed with certain other unanswered questions I had about the Brockmeyer investigation," Kazi continued. "Why you went to his home in Scarborough. How you knew that Anstruther-Fields would be on the beach that final night or that he had gone to Taddiford at all."

Lily's heart pounded as her tea began to chill. Outside, Kazi's children argued, their voices drifting past the window. She could hear the youngest, Chotu, complaining about losing the ball.

They had always been so careful, taking every precaution to hide the truth of what they were from the world, knowing that nothing good could come of being exposed. It was a secret far too dangerous to share, one that would leave them open to persecution and exploitation. What might Strangford have been ordered to do if his superiors at Naval Intelligence understood the true nature of the power he held in his hands?

The might of the British Empire had churned through the bodies of countless men in the name of this war. Lily found it hard to believe they would extend Strangford any special consideration, no matter the cost to his sanity or his soul.

"You wore gloves when you wrote the letter," Strangford said quietly, breaking the silence that followed the inspector's words.

"I did," Kazi acknowledged, sipping his tea.

Lily flinched as though his words were a blow.

That was why Strangford hadn't been able to feel anything about the composition of the letter that brought them here. Kazi had used Strangford's own trick to block any impression he might have left on the page . . . because he had known exactly what Strangford could do when his own gloves were off.

"Who else knows?" she demanded.

"No one," Kazi replied.

"Not Churchill? Not the NID?" she pressed.

"I recommended your husband to the Lord Admiral based on his lordship's other merits, which were more than sufficient. As far as I am aware, no one in Naval Intelligence is privy to the matter we are discussing unless you have informed them of it yourself."

"I have not," Strangford flatly returned.

"You realize your talents could likely be put to better use were your colleagues and commanding officers aware of them," Kazi pointed out.

Strangford did not answer right away.

"There are limits," he finally replied, looking down at his hands. "It does not come without a cost."

"Ah. I understand."

"How could you possibly." Lily challenged, the words firing out of her like weapons.

The inspector set down his teacup, taking a moment to reply.

"I have known Lord Strangford's secret for nearly three years. I did not inform NID. I did not request his transfer to my own division, though his abilities could certainly have made a great deal of difference over the last four years. I have kept the matter entirely to myself because I understand you to be a man who does not shrink from his responsibilities."

"Are we supposed to be grateful for that?" Lily seethed.

"My point," Kazi continued, forcibly calm. "Is that I would not be approaching you now were the matter not of the utmost delicacy and importance."

Lily bit back her retort, as much as she burned to continue her attack. This was Strangford's secret, and it must ultimately be Strangford's decision what to do about it.

An automobile rattled past in the lane outside the window. Out in the square, the voices of the children rose and fell like the soft rush of waves.

"What makes the matter so important?" her husband finally asked.

"I am afraid I cannot answer that," Kazi replied.

"I see," Strangford frowned, fingers tapping against the arm of the chair.

Lily knew the anger that flared up in her at his response was the child of a primitive and instinctual panic. She fought to moderate it, resisting the urge to throw her cup at the wall.

"Why ask?" she demanded instead. "Why bother when you might simply order him to be transferred to your unit?"

"I would prefer that Lord Strangford's participation was voluntary."

"Prefer?" Lily echoed carefully.

"I am trying, Miss Albright," Kazi snapped, then caught himself, pressing his fingers to the bridge of his nose as he strove for patience. "Lady Strangford. I cannot pretend that we are friends. Our history is an unpleasant one. I can only ask—hope—that you might allow logic to speak for me. I have kept this secret. I am keeping it even now. I am asking for help because I need it."

He paused, taking a breath, and met her eyes.

"Because we all need it."

There was something unexpected in that look—something she would never have thought to see in the urbane and collected man before her. It was a deep and serious unease.

"To Paris and back," he continued, collecting himself once more. "One afternoon in the American Hospital there and nothing more. No one outside this room will know the true nature of your involvement."

Paris.

The word hung suspended in the air like a curse. Rather than elegant boulevards, it conjured the acrid stench of burnt cordite and

52

set the ground trembling under her feet.

She could hear Strangford's voice screaming in her ear, telling her to run as the world blew apart around him.

The vision sparked by the blue bottle she had stolen four years ago from Robert Ash's apothecary cabinet had never left her. That unwelcome chain of foresight had already come to pass in so many ways, including the closing of The Refuge, now serving as a school for boys, and Sam's heartbreaking decision to enlist on the day of Ash's funeral.

The injuries Strangford sustained during the train wreck in Ludgate had offered her a reprieve, disqualifying him from regular military service. And though his duties at the NID had evolved from translation and analysis to occasional work in the field, it had not yet taken him to the European mainland—to the place where the war waited to devour him.

Paris was not the front, she forcibly reminded herself. It was not and could not be the place where he was meant to die. Lily knew, logically, that going there could not pose any more risk than walking down the streets in London, where a rogue German air raid could just as easily blow him from the earth . . . but it didn't feel that way.

She was conscious of Strangford's heavy silence beside her and knew he was struggling with the weight of both Kazi's revelation and the decision he was being forced to make. Kazi had been right when he described Strangford's character a moment before—he was not a man who shrank from duty. It was no small part of what had made her fall in love with him in the first place. She could not wish him any different, not even when it left her tangled up in knots.

Her husband raised his scarred face. Lily felt the imminence of his answer and tensed herself for whatever it might mean.

"I would like to discuss the matter with my wife."

She reached out to slip her fingers over his gloved hand, overcome by gratitude . . . but his gesture was ultimately futile.

There was nothing to discuss.

"If the stakes are as high as you say they are, you cannot allow Strangford to refuse you," Lily stated. "If he does, you must resort to coercion. He will go because agreeing to do so now at least keeps you from sharing your knowledge with his superiors or your own."

Lily stood, releasing Strangford's hand and looking down at the inspector, feeling the force of her intention like a fire in her blood.

"But you will only receive his full cooperation if I go with you."

Kazi's face went blank with surprise.

Behind her, Strangford settled back against the settee and drained the last of his tea.

"Cardamom," he declared triumphantly.

"You will not find me a burden. I am quite capable of taking care of myself." she asserted.

"I am well aware," the inspector dryly returned.

Lily abruptly recalled that one of her last meetings with this man had taken place as she battled an enemy in the dark with an antique Roman spear while dodging machine gun fire. She awkwardly brushed a bit of dust off of her skirt.

"I suppose I may assume you are in alignment with this?" Kazi pressed, looking to Strangford.

"You may indeed," Strangford returned, setting down his now empty cup.

The children burst into the hall, announcing themselves in a boisterous clatter beyond the parlor door. Something that sounded distinctly like a football bounced off the walls, followed rapidly by Mrs. Kazi speaking in a loud and clearly disciplinary Bangla.

The inspector stood, Strangford following suit.

"We will leave on the Vigilant out of Dover at one o'clock Thursday afternoon. Pack your uniforms but do not wear them. I shall take care of all the necessary paperwork. Have you any questions?"

"None that I imagine you would answer," Lily retorted.

"Excellent," Kazi concluded blithely. "Then you will want to be getting on with your own arrangements."

It was an infuriating dismissal, but Kazi had already won what he wanted. Strangford was going to Paris. If he had to bring along a bit of unexpected baggage, he did not seem particularly perturbed by it.

Strangford put his officer's cap back on his head and extended his hand.

"Shall we shake on it?"

Kazi hesitated. It was brief, just a flicker of sharpened attention as his eyes shifted to the black leather covering Strangford's fingers, then rose again to meet her husband's gaze. A quick tension rose between the two men, one potent enough that Lily could feel it thicken the atmosphere in the room.

Her husband was not offering a handshake. It was a subtle and effective threat, one that promised Kazi could not keep his own secrets for very long.

Not if Strangford was determined to acquire them.

At last, Kazi accepted the hand, his bare skin looking particularly vulnerable in Strangford's grasp.

"Inspector," Strangford said.

"My lord," Kazi returned with a careful nod of respect.

Strangford's hand came to the small of Lily's back, steering her into the hall as the children pounded on the ceiling overhead, and then they were back out into the soft light of the square.

"Not here," he said under his breath.

He offered her his arm, and they strolled together down the street.

~

Lily tossed her gloves down on the table in the study, finally released from the careful silence they had maintained through the tram ride back to Bayswater.

"Tell me what you're feeling," she demanded. "Please."

It was getting late. Her stomach reminded her that the hour for dinner had already passed, though she found it difficult to conceive of how she could manage to sit down and eat it.

"I am alright," Strangford replied, setting his hat on the table and coming over to slip his hands around her waist. "I'm more concerned about you."

The room was their sanctuary. It had changed only a little since Lily had first encountered it. A few more paintings had been added to Strangford's uniquely personal selection of artworks that covered the wall. His desk was still tidy, though the translations sitting on it hadn't been touched in months as his work at NID consumed his time. A settee had joined the two green armchairs by the fire. Beside it stood a magazine rack—Lily's guilty pleasure.

"Me?" Lily protested, pulling the pins out of her gray felt hat and tossing it on one of the chairs. "I'm not the one who's being blackmailed."

"It isn't precisely blackmail."

Something in his tone raised a flag in her mind. She gaped at him in shock.

"You're making excuses for that man."

"He is not without honor, Lily." Strangford pushed back.

"How can you possibly know that?" she demanded.

He responded with a knowing quirk of his eyebrow, and she let out a huff of frustration. Of course, he would have taken the opportunity four years ago to read anything Kazi had come into contact with in order to get a sense of what he was up against.

"Honor isn't monolithic, Anthony. It is all tied up with loyalty, and we have no idea what Kazi is loyal to."

"Duty is important to him," Strangford replied. "Upholding the law. Protecting the vulnerable."

"You are aware, aren't you, of what is conspicuously missing from that list? You," she snapped, jabbing a finger at his chest. "Inspector Tariq Kazi owes no loyalty to you."

"Perhaps not," Strangford quietly replied. "But those things are important to me as well, Lily."

She bit back her retort, conscious of the naked honesty in his voice. She turned away instead, stalking across the room to sit down on the desk.

"You might at least have taken your gloves off." she pointed out. "We could have learned a great deal more from the house."

Strangford crossed to her, using his gloved fingers to brush the loose hairs back from her temple.

"That would have been terribly rude of me," he murmured.

The meaning of his words sunk in. She caught his hand, halting its explorations.

"Because you had already guessed that he knew?" she asked dangerously.

"The absence of impressions in the letter made me suspicious," Strangford admitted.

"And you went anyway."

Lily was aware that she had descended into more or less shouting.

"It hardly would've changed the situation if I had stayed home."

She pulled away from him, withdrawing to the window as she struggled to get hold of the whirlwind of emotion that spun through her.

Strangford slipped his arms around her waist.

"Tell me what you're feeling," he asked, gently echoing her words from a moment before. "Please."

"I'm not sure I know," she admitted.

There was a surprising unevenness to her voice.

Strangford started to pull back.

"If you need more time—"

The kindness of it undid her. She knew he would grant it to her if she asked him, but this wasn't about her. It was Strangford's threat—Strangford's danger.

She turned, taking hold of him before he could move away. She pressed herself to him, tucking her face into his shoulder as her hand slid up into his hair. Her skin tingled with that familiar electricity as her power resonated with the contact of his own.

His arms tightened around her back as he pulled her closer.

"Oh, Lily." he said, and upon hearing the deep sympathy in his voice, she was finally able to put a name to the tumult of emotion that raced through her.

It was terror.

"It's just Paris," he whispered.

"You can't know that's where it will end," she protested.

His gloved fingers came to her chin, gently lifting her head so that he could meet her eyes.

"But I have you to protect me," he replied, that familiar smile tugging at the corner of his lip.

She blurted out the rest—the thing that frightened her more than anything else—knowing there was no point in hiding it from the power of his touch.

"What if I can't?"

He didn't give her an answer. She hadn't expected one. She knew well enough what the truth was.

FIVE

Friday, April 12
Eleven o'clock in the morning
Approaching Paris

THE TRAIN TO PARIS was crowded with young men. It was the most of them Lily had seen together in quite a long time outside the rows of uniforms drilling in the park. Many of them were British soldiers on leave from their posts at the front, heading to Paris for a few days of fun. They were a loud and boisterous crowd at the front of the carriage, watched with indulgence by the old men smoking pipes and the grandmothers tending infants.

A woman passing down the aisle dropped a hatbox as she moved past their row. Strangford jumped up to fetch it for her, murmuring in flawless French to catch her attention as she blinked at the sight of his scars and eyepatch.

Across from where Lily sat, Tariq Kazi turned the pages of a newspaper. The inspector was elegantly turned out as usual in a dark tweed suit and long gray overcoat. He had taken off his fedora and set it on the seat, but his dark hair was still perfectly swept back, his mustache elegantly trimmed.

The woman with the hatbox cast him an appreciative look before continuing on her way.

Lily felt less appreciative of the inspector's presence. She was still resentful of this entire excursion, though it had admittedly gone off smoothly so far. Their boat had left Dover precisely on time, Kazi meeting them at the docks with all the necessary passports and paperwork—none of which could have been easy to come by with the government strictly regulating who came in and out of the country.

"I am glad to see you packed lightly." he had commented.

"To Paris and back," Lily had returned coolly. "What else could we possibly need?"

The trip across the channel had been uneventful. Their smaller passenger ship had joined a convoy of troop and supply transports guarded by a flotilla of naval vessels. The convoy was necessary to prevent ships being picked off by the German U-boats that managed to slip past the minefields into the channel.

Lily was in no hurry for another close encounter with a U-boat. She had been on shore during her last and only meeting with one and that had still been quite enough for her.

The only complication had been how ill she had felt the entire time she was on the boat. The gray, gloomy docks of Calais had been a welcome sight, even though the city's charms were buried under the sprawling military encampment that had more or less swallowed it. The docks were a labyrinth of men and materials, loud and stinking of diesel. Rows of wounded from the front waited there for transport to the rehabilitation hospitals in England.

Lily compared her memory of those soldiers with the young men passing a flask around the front of the train car. Some of the casualties had also been laughing as they traded stories, but they had cracked their jokes with bandages, crutches, and empty sleeves while other men on bath chairs or stretchers remained silent.

The evening train to Paris had already been booked, so they had stayed the night in an overcrowded inn by the docks before setting out in the morning. In all that time, Lily had not heard so much as a rumble from the front. The war itself was at a distance here, even though the clusters of troops and clattering military lorries were more or less ubiquitous.

Outside the window of the train, a formation of airplanes looped overhead, flying in a tidy formation like a flock of oversized swallows.

It was nothing like the nightmare landscape of mud, noise, and wire from her vision, but Lily still held herself on the bench of the train carriage as though, at any moment, the whole thing might disintegrate and drop them into Hell.

The whistle pierced the air as they approached a crossing, a farmer waiting with his sheep blurring past the window. Kazi briefly raised his eyes from the newspaper as Strangford took his seat again, making a quick scan of the people in the car. The movement had the feeling of a habit, a trained watchfulness that reminded her how very little she knew about their traveling companion.

His gaze crossed to Lily as he completed his survey. It halted there as he realized she was glaring back at him. He absorbed it, revealing nothing of his own feelings in return, and went back to his reading.

Lily turned her glare out the window.

~

They disembarked at the Gare du Nord. The interior of the train station felt like that of a Gothic cathedral with its tall, narrow windows and long shadows. It was marked by subtle signs of damage and disrepair, from a cracked pane of glass that had not been replaced to a pile of rubble swept into a corner.

Their luggage retrieved and sent on to their lodgings, Kazi led them out into the late Paris morning.

The city was both beautiful and battered. The elegant buildings that lined the streets seemed immune to the coating of soot that covered everything in London. The sky had cleared now that they were away from the north coast, the sun burning bright and high. The air was rich with the perfume of flowering cherry trees. A cluster of mourning doves fluttered by, cooing with gentle irritation at a passing omnibus.

As soon as they turned the corner, she noticed a cordoned-off pile of rubble in the middle of one of the rows of houses. The missing building stood out like a gapped tooth, a glaring reminder that the war was still felt here as well.

Kazi flipped open his pocket watch with a sharp click.

"It is half past eleven," he noted, adjusting the angle of his hat. "I should like to proceed directly to the hospital unless anyone has any objections."

Lily knew she should be glad the inspector was eager for them to get on with it but found herself blurting out a protest.

"Actually, might we grab a bite to eat first?"

Her hand dropped to her stomach, which answered her with an audible rumble.

Kazi studied her for a thoughtful moment, then snapped shut the watch.

"Certainly." he said.

~

Lily looked down at her empty bowl. A few moments before, it had been filled with a simple and hearty fish stew, drizzled with cream. She had sopped up the last remnants of it with a slice of bread—real bread, albeit brown.

Technically, of course, it was Strangford's bowl. The chicken Lily had ordered tasted off to her as though the dressing used to season it had gone a bit sour.

Strangford had tried it, insisted it was fine, and cheerfully swapped lunches.

"How do they have so much real bread?" she asked, appreciatively eyeing the last bite.

The cafe spilled out onto the pavement, close little tables packed under an awning that blocked the worst of the midday sun. It was jammed, noisy, and cheerful. Women sat at tables with little dogs tucked under their feet, many of them already sipping a cocktail or glass of wine. Lily could almost trick herself into thinking that she was here on holiday—as though there was no war and this was simply a romantic jaunt to Paris with her dashing husband.

Except, of course, that she wasn't just here with her husband.

"The French government has been aggressive about rationing and securing supply lines," Kazi replied, falling into the obviously comfortable mode of a lecture. "And their climate is more suited to domestic production of wheat."

The inspector took another crunchy bite of his toast with sardines, and Lily allowed herself the brief luxury of quietly resenting his presence.

"The Germans have taken Armentières," Strangford announced.

Kazi paused with the toast halfway to his mouth, then slowly lowered it.

"When did you hear that?" he asked.

Strangford nodded towards the next table, where a silver-haired gentleman held up his newspaper over an empty glass of cassis.

"It's in the French papers," he replied.

"I have been out of contact with my HQ since we left Dover. The line has held?" Kazi asked grimly.

"It would appear so," Strangford said.

Lily absorbed the news with a chill that defied the warm spring air. The pundits had been predicting a major German attack for months. Since Russia had left the war following its revolution, the Eastern Front had become irrelevant. Germany had been free to withdraw those troops and apply them to the task of breaking the French and English defenses in the west. It was an effort they had kicked off a week or so before, harrying the British line around Oise and Amiens.

More troops would still be en route across Germany to join the attackers, while the remaining Allied nations, already desperately overextended, could only pray that their new American allies would train up and ship out reinforcements in time.

She hoped the news of the loss of Armentières was not a harbinger of far worse things to come.

~

Through the opened windows of their hired carriage, Lily caught further glimpses of the city's astonishing loveliness. Many of the people strolling the pavement projected an elegance rarely seen in London, though she knew that fabrics and tailors were in just as short supply here as they were elsewhere. The French demonstrated a remarkable prowess for making the best of their circumstances. Even the white bands of protective tape that crisscrossed many of the shop windows had been put up in elaborate decorative patterns, turning a defense against shell damage into a work of art.

Paris had been plagued lately by more than just air raids. Since the month before, the city had also been subject to attacks by a massive German gun capable of striking from behind the front line over fifty miles away. The papers had been touting the French air raids targeting the gun's supposed location, but as of yet, they had been unsuccessful. The city continued to be subject to random shelling, an effort aimed as much at destroying morale as at shattering buildings.

At one point, they skirted the edge of the massive roundabout that surrounded the Arc de Triomphe, the iron peak of the Eiffel Tower just visible in the distance.

Ten minutes later, the carriage jolted to a stop. Kazi tossed open the door.

"We're here," he said, striding out.

The American Hospital sprawled across the better part of a city block, its two enormous wings towering over a pretty tree-lined suburb northwest of the city center.

"It looks like a palace," Lily exclaimed.

"It was a school," Kazi informed her shortly. "The hospital expanded into it at the outbreak of the war when it began offering its services to Allied soldiers rather than just American expatriates."

He turned to the driver, settling their tab with his awkward French. His grasp of the language was fairly rudimentary compared to Strangford's fluency or Lily's schoolgirl competence.

A handful of orderlies lingered outside one of the doors, smoking cigarettes and laughing, their flat American accents ringing strangely. They flicked the butts aside as a line of ambulances arrived, walking over to help them unload.

The reception hall inside was crowded enough that Strangford had to turn his head to ensure he didn't collide with someone stepping into his blind side.

Kazi led them to a busy desk staffed by a trio of women.

"Lieutenant Neville Casey." he announced to the first who was available, a graying blonde with a robust figure. "British 68th."

The receptionist pivoted to what looked like a library card catalog and popped open a drawer, fingers flicking through the entries with obvious practice. She stopped, giving a card a quick scan, and then snapped the drawer closed again.

"All visits to Lt. Casey must be cleared by Captain Hume," she replied in a Yankee drawl.

"Hume," Kazi echoed thoughtfully. "Yes, of course. Can you let him know we are here?"

The receptionist blinked at him with just a touch of hostility, her eyes flicking to the line of people waiting behind them.

"Agnes!" she barked.

A young girl hovering behind the desk rushed over, standing ready behind the older woman's shoulder. The receptionist plucked up a little square of white paper, her pen poised.

"Name?" she demanded.

"Inspector Tariq Kazi," he replied, leaning over the desk to watch her write. "That's not a 'C,' it's . . . Never mind."

He straightened as the woman shot him a dangerous glare. The blonde flicked the note up in her hand like a knife she was about to toss at the inspector but held the pose. The young girl behind her darted forward, snatching the paper from her fingers before hurrying away.

"You may wait there," the receptionist ordered, pointing like a sergeant to the left of the desk.

Kazi, clearly annoyed, turned on his heel and stalked off.

"Madame," Strangford said, his bow somewhat more curt than usual.

After a quick once-over, the receptionist honored him with a brief nod of acknowledgment before barking to the next person in the line. Lily stepped closer to the two men to allow a pair of the smoking orderlies from outside to pass, carrying a stretcher between them.

"It would be best if you kept your contributions to the conversation minimal," Kazi said quietly.

"Why." Lily demanded. "Who is Hume?"

"Second-in-command of the Folkestone Office, British Army Intelligence," Strangford replied with a sideways glance at Kazi. "If I am not mistaken."

"He runs France for MI1b," the inspector begrudgingly confirmed.

"Runs France?" Lily echoed.

"He's the lead on all Army intelligence operations here," Strangford explained.

The man who cut through the crowded lobby toward them was shorter than Strangford and moved with force. His figure was lean and weathered, skin permanently tanned in the manner of someone who had spent much of his life in far warmer climes than England. It made it difficult to guess his age, as the sun had also carved fine lines around his eyes and mouth, but Lily put him at somewhere around forty. There was just a hint of silver in his sandy blond hair, and his blue eyes looked startlingly bright in his tanned face.

"Inspector," he said as he arrived, extending his hand.

"Captain Hume," Kazi returned. "Allow me to present Lord and Lady Strangford."

Lily found herself watching Hume's reaction very carefully, even though Kazi had promised them he had shared his knowledge of Strangford's power with no one. The captain eyed the pair of them now with a mix of curiosity and mild disapproval. She found herself glad she had opted for a conservative tailored skirt and jacket that day rather than the trousers she had packed in her valise. Strangford, of course, was in one of his habitual black suits, though this one at least appeared to be somewhat less frayed at the cuffs.

"Charmed," he replied curtly, shaking Strangford's gloved hand with a quick and thoughtful look at his missing eye and scars.

He returned his attention to Kazi.

"Cameron mentioned you were coming, but I rather thought you would be alone."

"Lord Strangford has a childhood connection to the fellow," Kazi replied. "I promised to help him pay his respects."

Lily searched his response for some tell that he was lying. There was none. Had she not known better, she would have believed the inspector herself.

"We met on a family trip to the Cotswolds. Corresponded on and off after that," Strangford offered. "I can't say we were close, but when I heard he'd been injured, I thought at the very least I might stop in while I was here and bring word back to his mother."

Strangford's accent had gone a bit plummy, and the response was far too detailed and ready-to-hand to have been invented on the spot. He and Kazi must have worked it out ahead of time, perhaps on the boat during one of the intervals where Lily was emptying her guts into the waves.

"And what brought you to Paris in the first place, my lord?" Hume asked.

"I'm on assignment with the War Office Lands Branch, looking for yet another building to let," Strangford replied.

"His lordship is with the RNVS," Kazi offered, using the acronym for the Royal Navy Volunteer Service, to which Strangford was formally attached.

It was something that would check out neatly enough were Hume of a mind to look into it.

"The Navy is looking for a building in Paris?" Hume inquired carefully.

Lily felt a prickling of the nerves along the back of her neck. Paris, of course, was nowhere near the sea.

"To facilitate prioritizing transmission of materials between the Mediterranean and the Channel," Strangford returned. "And, I suspect, to give some of the top brass an excuse to take in the cabaret."

"Yes. I see," Hume concluded tiredly.

"Shall we, then?" Kazi prompted.

With a glance at his fellow spy, the captain gestured them forward.

"We'll have to go around the flu wards. They're under quarantine. This way."

They navigated a maze of stairways and halls. The hospital felt much like any other Lily had been inside of, busy and smelling of carbolic, save that the patients were almost uniformly soldiers. Those who were ambulatory stepped aside as Hume approached, flashing off a salute even if they wore the sky blue of the French ranks.

The place reminded her of Gardner. She had last seen the doctor a year ago, just before he had been transferred from the military hospital in Portsmouth to a unit in Northern France.

Hume finally stopped at the door to a ward that looked like any of the dozens of others they had passed so far. The beds were lined up in neat rows, all of them occupied by men with wounds of varying levels of awfulness. It was quiet save for the soft clatter of the tea trolley being rolled in, the intravenous bag stands like sentinels keeping watch over the fallen.

Hume nodded to one of the nurses.

"Matron Kaminski."

With her soft brown hair and pretty, unlined face, she looked far too young to be a matron, but she answered him with a calm authority.

"Captain," she replied in a clipped American accent.

"Any change since this morning?"

"If there had been, I would have sent for you as instructed," Kaminski replied shortly, scribbling something on a clipboard and then handing it to the nurse waiting patiently in front of her. "And make sure the pharmacist gives you the right dosage. Last time the pills had to be cut in half. Anything else?"

Her last words were directed to Hume.

"No. Thank you, matron," he replied respectfully.

She did not deign to offer him any further remark, turning to one of the beds and instructing the nurse there about the proper positioning of an IV needle.

"Efficient woman," Kazi noted from beside the captain.

"Quite," Hume agreed.

He led them to a bed at the back of the ward. The man who lay there could not have been older than his mid-twenties. A few lacerations were visible on his face, along with some old bruising. His hip was strapped to a brace. He looked wasted, the knobs of his bones poking through the skin. Lily wondered with alarm just how long he had been in this coma. It was not a state a man could survive in for long as the means of providing him with any sort of nutrition beyond the IV drip were highly limited.

Kazi's urgency began to make a bit more sense.

She glanced over at Strangford. His power was not one of observation but of immersion, plunging him into the most intimate memories and experiences of another person as though they were his own. It was something he generally avoided inflicting upon another person, particularly in the absence of explicit consent. At the moment, Lily found herself more concerned with what was going to happen when Strangford put his hands on the young lieutenant here in the quiet hum of the hospital ward with a British Army spy chief watching everything they were doing.

This was a terrible idea.

"Why don't we give them a moment?" Kazi suggested, gently steering Hume towards the window. He dropped his voice to a confidential murmur and pulled the captain into another conversation.

Strangford sat down in the chair next to the bed, tugging off his gloves. He looked down at the young man wasting away under the sheet, taking a breath to steady himself.

"You don't even know what you're looking for," Lily whispered sharply.

"Kazi said to focus on the night he was attacked."

"Attacked?" Lily echoed, the word sounding oddly specific. "You mean whatever battle he was in?"

"I am not at all certain how long the inspector will be able to distract the captain with a discussion of Dutch beef imports. Perhaps I'd best get to it?"

Lily bit back the rest of her questions, knowing he was right.

He husband reached out and took the dying man's hand. His eye lost focus as he slipped into the current of his power.

Lily hovered beside him, nerves anxiously edged. The regular hum of activity from the room around her remained unchanged. Water bottles clinked. Bed linens rustled. Her gaze flicked over to Kazi and Hume. The two men remained at the window, seemingly engrossed in their conversation. To them, it would look as though Strangford were bowing over the comatose man's hand, perhaps offering a prayer for his recovery.

Certainly not scouring through his memories.

The muscles behind Strangford's eyepatch twitched, his mouth twisting as he fought his way through the overwhelming morass of history a single human held within his skin.

There would be the gentle or agonizing hands of doctors and nurses. The fellow soldiers who carried him from wherever he had fallen. A lover back home, perhaps. Children and parents, childhood humiliations. The shock and grief of some unexpected loss.

"Lavender," Strangford said, pushing the word out under his breath, the feeling connected to the memory strong enough that he was compelled to speak it aloud. "She smelled of lavender."

He shook his head, trying to move past it. His mouth twisted into a grimace of pain.

"The shells... The stink of it." His voice wavered, the emotion in it intensifying. "Gregory... he's all over me ..."

His volume threatened to rise, his grief and horror visceral.

Lily set a hand on his shoulder, careful not to brush his skin and interrupt the reading.

69

"Shhh," she urged softly as Hume glanced back at them.

Kazi recaptured the captain's attention, his eyes flashing her a warning.

Lily urgently studied the prone figure of the man on the bed. They could not take much longer, or Strangford would risk his secret being known by more than just Kazi. Nor did she think the inspector would accept Strangford's failure with equanimity—not when he clearly believed something terrible was at stake. She needed to find a way for Strangford to home in on what mattered.

The night he was attacked.

The thought burned with frustration. Kazi had given them almost nothing to work with. Lieutenant Neville Casey was a soldier. People would have been shooting at him more or less since he joined up.

Her eyes stopped on the cut across his forehead, framed by the blue and purple discoloration of an old bruise.

She tightened her grip on Strangford's shoulder.

"The blow to the head," she whispered fiercely at his ear, bending down as though comforting him. "Find it and go back."

He nodded, the gesture almost imperceptible. She felt him take a breath before his muscles abruptly stiffened under her hand. His next inhalation sounded more like a gasp, edged with an animal terror.

"Blood," he croaked softly. "Blood on the snow."

The quiet routine of the hospital continued around them, underlain by the regular rumble of traffic from out in the street. It was entirely ordinary, unimpeachably present, and Lily knew in her bones that Strangford was not there anymore.

The chill crept up from where her fingers rested against the rigid tension of his shoulder. He had gone was somewhere else—somewhere she could not possibly imagine.

"They're screaming," he breathed, the word thin with another man's terror.

"Who?" Lily pressed.

"The monsters in the dark."

The air around her split with a crack like thunder.

Kazi and Hume both flinched from the window, moving by quick instinct. The captain twisted behind the wall, shifting into a crouch. Kazi made an elegant pivot to do the same on the opposing side, and

Lily was surprised to see a pistol had materialized in his hand.

Matron Kaminski's voice pierced the shocked quiet of the ward.

"The Cannon is live!" she called out, her words ringing with authority. She repeated the warning in clear French, and a cascade of orders followed, resounding through the room in a mix of the two languages as she variously directed them at the American staff and the French soldiers capable of moving under their own volition. Crutches and bath chairs were fetched, the whole operation moving like a well-oiled machine.

Strangford yanked his hand back from where Lt. Casey lay. His breath was still rapid, his body tense under Lily's hand.

The matron stalked over as her staff whirled into action.

"I am moving him to the cellar," she said, her tone leaving no space for debate. "We don't have room for non-patients. You'll have to find another shelter."

She grasped the cord of her watch, sliding the neat little silver orb into her hand with practiced efficiency, flicking the dial into her line of sight.

"You have thirteen minutes."

Lily realized she was expecting Strangford to make his usual gentlemanly response. His silence indicated he wasn't yet capable of it. She quickly stepped into the void.

"Thank you, Matron. We'll get out of your way." she promised— and became painfully aware that she hadn't the foggiest idea how to do so.

She needed to get Strangford out of the hospital, which meant she needed to know where to go—and there was only one person who could help her with that.

"Inspector!" she called through gritted teeth.

Kazi snapped to attention by the window. He neatly slipped his sidearm back into a shoulder holster concealed under his tweed coat and strode over to them.

Lily bent down, putting her lips to Strangford's ear.

"Can you move?" she demanded lowly.

"Yes."

The word was more or less a groan.

He put his hand on her sleeve, using her arm for support as he

71

rose from the chair. Lily took a closer look at him as he stood. His skin had gone over with a cold sweat, pinpricks of it visible at the roots of his hair. She could feel the tremor in his hand.

Kazi reached them, radiating a tightly coiled impatience.

"A moment," Lily ordered, knowing another measure was required before they could leave the ward.

She slipped her hand over the back of Strangford's glove, clasping her fingers around the bare skin of his wrist, and projected as much strength and steadiness as she could muster.

His breath caught, then slowed. Muscle untangled beneath her touch, a palpable release. He inhaled again, this time more deeply, and lifted his eye to hers, giving her a nod.

"Bit of shell shock?" Hume guessed, not unkindly, as he joined them. "The nearest public shelter is the Porte Maillot Metro station, about a mile down Victor Hugo. Should only have to weather one more hit before you reach it if you walk a quick pace. Inspector, debrief in the morning if you don't mind? Eight o'clock at Rue St. Foch."

"Certainly." Kazi agreed, his voice a bit thin.

"Till then. Lady Strangford." Hume offered her a polite bow, cast another sympathetic look at Strangford, and then strode from the room.

"Is he unwell?" Kazi demanded once the captain had gone.

"Not anymore," Strangford replied, gradually straightening up.

Kazi cast another potent glance at the catatonic lieutenant, but a pair of nurses were already hurrying over with a gurney. There was no time for anything more, even if Strangford were capable of it.

Lily saw the inspector draw the same conclusion, marked by a flash of frustration.

"Come along," he ordered, leading them out.

~

Outside the hospital, families hurried past with bags of supplies, heading for the shelter of a neighbor's basement or an underground room at one of the nearby universities. Others strolled down the pavement, walking their dogs or chatting as though nothing untoward was going on. Woven through it all was a worn-out air of acceptance.

"How long will the bombardment continue?" Lily asked, quickening her pace to keep up with Kazi's long stride.

"It has generally held up for around twenty rounds or so, each landing at roughly fifteen minute intervals," he replied, leading them across a lovely boulevard lined with flowering trees.

Lily made a rapid calculation.

"That's five hours."

"If the Germans do not pause to make repairs or recalibrate," the inspector confirmed.

The tired air of inevitability made more sense to her. Who could afford to spend five hours of every day huddling in a basement? London's air raids had been far more intermittent, a terrifying midnight interruption followed by weeks or months of quiet. She did not presume to guess how she would react if faced with the same unrelenting and random threat.

"Didn't the captain say the shelter was the other way." Lily pointed out as she recovered her bearings.

"We're not going to the shelter," Kazi corrected her, setting his fedora back into place. "We need to talk."

He took them around another corner, emerging at the banks of the Seine. The river in front of her was divided around a long, looming island covered in fine and obviously expensive houses. On the bank below, a tidy and colorful line of boats sheltered in the narrower waters.

Behind where they stood, an old man slept on a bench, his head fallen back as a dog waited obediently at the end of a leash still wrapped loosely around his wrist. A courting couple meandered past, clearly having decided to ignore the warning hit of the first shell.

Kazi eyed their surroundings, then jogged down a narrow stair leading to the water where the dozen or so weathered péniches were tied along the slender beam of the dock. A slight, wrinkled fellow sat in a camp chair beside the barges, ostensibly there to guard the as-yet-unloaded cargo. He sipped a glass of wine, turning the pages of a novel.

"Anthony, what is this about?" Lily demanded under her breath as she and Strangford lingered above, watching the inspector make some negotiation with the watchman in stilted French.

Strangford tugged back on his gloves, his hat still tucked under his arm. The tremor had not yet gone out of his hands.

"I'm not entirely sure I know," he replied. "But it isn't good."

A few coins exchanged hands on the dock, and Kazi looked up to where they watched from the embankment, motioning to them with a jerk of his head.

"Come on," Strangford said, leading her to the stairs.

The inspector had hired a rowboat. The diminutive vessel was tied to the end of the dock. Kazi held it in place as they descended, Strangford pausing to offer a smooth French greeting to the man in the chair, who nodded acknowledgment before returning to his book.

Strangford boarded nimbly, extending a hand to help Lily inside. Kazi waved her to the bench in the back, leaving Strangford the prow. He pulled off his naval officer's cap as he sat, tossing it down by his feet.

Kazi loosed the rope and hopped into the middle with an easy confidence that surprised her. Stripping off his coat, he folded it neatly across his lap, turned up the cuffs of his shirt, and picked up the oars. His torso moved with practiced grace under his waistcoat as he propelled them out into the river with strong, even strokes.

"UCL Boat Club," Kazi said shortly, noting her surprised attention.

The inspector's solution was an elegant one. There was no debris out on the water, no collapsing ceilings or shattering glass. Only a direct hit from above could cause them any damage, and the chances of that were as thin as a lightning strike. Though Lily knew another shell must be coming shortly, she found she was not cowering at the prospect.

Her breath was tight in her chest for other reasons.

Kazi rowed them past the island out into the broader waters of the Seine. The buildings to either side were fine and large, set back against spacious lawns. They had more privacy here than they would have even in a hotel room.

A boom resounded softly through the spring air, punctuated by the twittering of the birds that darted across the water. Lily did not need to check her watch to know another shell had struck, this one in a more distant part of the city.

Kazi stopped, resting the oars in their locks and allowing the boat to drift gently with the current.

"What can you tell me?" he demanded.

It took Lily a moment to realize that Kazi was addressing the question to Strangford, not to her. As rower, he faced the back of the boat, and Strangford was behind him. She was in the odd position of being able to see both men while they could not see each other, at least unless the inspector uncomfortably turned about. It made her feel like a strange and awkward bridge between the pair of them.

Strangford took a moment before he answered, looking down at the soft shimmer of the water over the side of the boat.

"I would like you to tell me what you know," he finally replied.

Lily recognized his tone. It was the one her husband used when no amount of reasoning was going to dissuade him.

Kazi frowned, struggling with how to respond.

"I have been expressly ordered not to share that information with anyone."

"I have a high level of security clearance, as you are well aware," Strangford returned.

"Not this high," Kazi retorted tiredly.

Behind him, Strangford looked down at his gloved hands.

"What I know," he began slowly. "Is that you have far greater need of me in this affair than you could possibly have guessed."

He raised his head, his gaze finding Lily's from behind the inspector's shoulder, each of his words ringing with an import that sparked a rising sense of dread.

"Of both of us."

Kazi stilled, then finally turned in his seat, giving up control of the boat in favor of a better look at Strangford. What he saw there made him pale, his careful facade of professionalism momentarily dropping for something less certain and far more human.

The inspector closed his eyes.

"On March 15, there was a raid on the Stelvio Pass outside Bormio in the Italian Alps," he said.

Lily summoned up what she knew about the Italian front, where on the rough slopes of the highest peaks in Europe, Italy's elite mountain troops, the Alpini, faced off against a similarly hardened

Austrian army. It was remote, icy, and wind-rattled, especially during the frigid month of March.

The current had carried them back to the island. Kazi grasped the oars again and shot them powerfully forward. The boat cut across the water like a blade, leaving disturbed ripples behind it.

"Two platoons of the 137th Italian Alpini were stationed at the pass with the rest of the company on relief in the village," he continued, barely short of breath. "A telephone wire had been laid to connect the pass to headquarters. The evening check-in was completed with all reported quiet. The next scheduled call at two o'clock in the morning was not answered."

A chill danced across the skin of Lily's arms, raising the small hairs there. She was reminded, uncomfortably, of something Robert Ash had once told her.

The flesh is quicker to recognize truth than the mind.

"A cut wire leads to silence. This one rang," Kazi went on. "The company headquarters tried again for the better part of an hour before dispatching a scout team to investigate. The road was still snowbound. The team was forced to navigate the last half-mile on foot and did not arrive until dawn, at which point they found the entire complement at the pass were dead."

Behind the inspector, Strangford's face was grim.

"The entire complement?" Lily pressed tentatively.

"Seventy-five of them, to a man, with the sole exception of the liaison officer we just left in that hospital, without the use of artillery or a single enemy casualty on the ground."

The shock of it silenced her.

The battles of this war had been terrible, the loss of life entailed in them profound. Entire regiments had been devastated in a single charge, reduced to only a handful of men, but there were always some who had managed to scrape their way through alive. The enemy had paid its due price in blood as well.

"Were they sleeping?" she finally pressed. "Or drugged, perhaps, leaving them vulnerable to a raid?"

Strangford, slouched in the prow, offered nothing.

"It's possible," Kazi acknowledged hesitantly. "If the Austrians managed to slip a man undetected past the sentries and the machine gun posts into the heart of the encampment and a kitchen where staff hover around the fire for warmth. Or maybe a man was turned. But we cannot rule out the alternative explanation that the Central Powers have acquired or developed some new technology that grants them an unthinkable advantage, even in the most hostile terrain of the war."

The rest of the words spilled out of him, driven by something she now recognized as a very deep and genuine concern.

"Our forces are depleted, spread abominably thin. With the collapse of the East, the Germans have just regained hundreds of thousands of men, and we are already losing ground to them. Our only hope for victory in this war lies in our ability to hold the line until American reinforcements can arrive in force, which will take another eight weeks at the least. That Germany itself is half starved by our blockade is the only thing that should allow any of us to sleep at night. If it turns out they have developed some means of slaughtering two platoons of elite soldiers in a well-fortified location without losing a single man ..."

He broke off the thought, but it required no further explanation. The Germans had already pushed the French and English back across miles of land won two years before with the deaths of a million men. If a mass of German troops was able to break through the line and storm Paris, or cut off the British forces and roll them back against the sea...

England was safe from a German invasion only so long as France continued to fight. If she fell or surrendered, there would be nothing to stop the Germans from throwing the full force of their military might against her home.

There were no more men to send as reinforcements. Parliament had even taken the extraordinary measure of pushing eighteen-year-olds into active service immediately upon completing their training instead of waiting for them to reach nineteen. All their hopes were pinned on the Americans, who had entered the war the previous winter with only a small standing army. The United States was rapidly training up millions of men who would be ready to ship come summer, but in the interim, the Allies were desperately vulnerable.

It was suddenly clear to her why this mission had felt important enough to Kazi that he was compelled to violate the sanctity of a secret he had otherwise kept for four years.

In the prow of the boat, Strangford tugged off one of his gloves. He dipped his bare fingers into the water.

"MI1c," he said.

Kazi's arms stilled at Strangford's reference to Military Intelligence 1c, the designation given to the Foreign Section of the Secret Service Bureau, his oars halting mid-stroke in the water. The boat began to turn against the force of that unintentional rudder until he snapped them up, resting them against the rails.

"What about it?" he demanded flatly.

"A handful of Special Branch police officers were seconded to the Domestic Section of the SSB at the outbreak of the war, charged with locating and apprehending those identified as potential spies," Strangford began.

It was a fact Lily herself was already familiar with. She had learned it after the death of the man who had called himself Felix Brockmeyer. It was the reason a London Metropolitan Police inspector had turned up at a murder scene in a remote Hampshire country house.

He had been hunting for spies.

"So, how did you end up with the Foreign Section?" Strangford quietly demanded.

Of course, she realized with a blink of surprise. There was no established progression from policeman and domestic enforcer to foreign service agent. Something had happened during the four years since she had previously encountered this man, something that had sent him on an unexpected course.

"I know that you do not yet particularly trust me," Kazi slowly replied. "But I assure you that the answer to your question bears no relevance to the issue we are investigating."

He wasn't just hiding it. Lily was abruptly certain that Kazi genuinely didn't want to talk about the matter.

From across the city came the distant crash of another German shell.

The water lapped softly at the hull of the boat. The Paris sun warmed her skin where it was left unshadowed by the brim of her hat. A fish broke the surface a few feet away, chasing the delicate shadow of an insect.

"If it becomes relevant, can you promise you won't keep it from us?" Lily pressed.

"I can," Kazi snapped back neatly, pivoting to face the man in the front of the boat. "Now it's your turn."

A pair of sparrows danced along the water, dipping and swirling before they slipped from view.

"I cannot tell you what attacked those men," Strangford replied.

Kazi's jaw tightened, his hands squeezing the handles of the oars. Lily could not entirely blame him. He had revealed far more than he had intended, violating his precious rules to do so. To be thanked for that with nothing had to gall him.

Except that it wasn't nothing. Lily could read that in every line of Strangford's body, in each of his careful silences. She held her tongue and waited.

"No one was drugged," he finally continued. "It wasn't some new gas. The man in that hospital bed—the lieutenant—woke to the sound of gunshots, confused in the dark . . . intermittent, defensive. There was a . . . sound . . . outside the tent. Something dull. Wet."

The chill returned to her skin again. Despite the spring sunshine and the fine houses lining the water, Lily felt as though they were approaching someplace darker.

"Wet?" she echoed carefully.

The look Strangford gave her in response was bleak.

"When he scrambled out of his barracks, he tripped over a man whose torso had been mostly separated from the rest of his body."

Kazi frowned.

"The reports indicated there was no shelling."

"That is correct," Strangford replied.

The chill crept deeper, closer. It occurred to her that she was afraid of what was coming next—of something that happened in the night on a mountain five hundred miles away and a month into the past.

"What else besides a shell could do that sort of damage?" Kazi demanded.

Strangford didn't answer.

"He found three other men of the company trying to repair a

79

damaged machine gun," he continued instead. "Shortly after he joined them, they were attacked."

He halted there, brought up short in a way that seemed to choke him.

This wasn't something he had read in a briefing, nor had Strangford been a mere observer of the horrors he was describing. He had lived it. The memories belonged to him now as much as they had the dying man in the hospital, the lieutenant's terror still sharp and clear enough to close Strangford in its grip.

"Attacked by whom?" Kazi pressed.

"Not whom," Lily cut in softly. "What."

She raised her eyes to where Strangford hunched in the prow.

"You called them monsters."

"I don't understand," Kazi admitted, a note of helplessness slipping into his voice.

"Nor do I," Strangford returned. "Not without more to go on."

Kazi grasped the oars, mouth firming.

"Hume took no undue notice of you, though the story we gave him will only hold so far. Perhaps if we—"

"No," Strangford cut in. "There is nothing more to get from the lieutenant."

"Then what do you mean?" Kazi demanded, exasperated.

The answer dawned over Lily with a terrible certainty. It made her want to scream, to shout him into silence before he could give it voice.

She knew in her bones it was futile, and so she spoke it herself instead, the words tumbling from her lips like stones.

"You want to go to Bormio."

Kazi stilled, sharpening with sudden interest.

Strangford's face was pale but resolute even as his gaze held a tired apology.

"It's important, Lily."

She took a panicked breath—and then realized they were waiting, both of them, the two men watching for her response.

What she wanted was painfully clear. Had she any choice in the matter, she would stop it all and whisk them back to the safety of England that night.

If she did, she would be asking Strangford to walk away from what he clearly already considered his responsibility, a grave and terrible opportunity to make a difference.

She let out the breath she had been holding and gave the only answer she could.

"Then we'll go."

Kazi's expression eased into one of relief. Beyond him, Strangford remained grim.

Like a breeze from across the water, a tingling awareness shivered across her skin, tainted with the unmistakable scent of her onmyōdō.

Yes, it whispered down her bones. *Yes.*

SIX

Sunday, April 14
Ten o'clock in the morning
Bormio, The Italian Alps

ℱROM THE WINDOW OF Lily's hotel room, the Alpine village of Bormio spilled along the valley in a river of tidy whitewashed houses and church spires. To either side of the clustered settlement rose the mountains, soaring and snow-dusted peaks with steep gray crowns that thrust up into a thin blue sky. As Lily looked out over the scene in the bright morning sunshine, it felt as though she had woken up in another universe.

The mountains had not been visible when they arrived in the village late the night before. The train ride from Paris had taken the entirety of the day, the journey made more uncomfortable for Lily by an unexpected bout of motion sickness. It had been nightfall when they reached the end of the line and truly late by the time their hired carriage deposited them in Bormio's central square.

In the light of the day and after a full night's much-needed rest, she was able to appreciate the view.

Bormio did not feel like a place at war. When she had arrived last night, unshaded windows had glowed with lantern light. The Austrian air force was exponentially weaker than that of the British or Germans. Coupled with the inhospitable terrain and weather, it made the risk of an air raid here virtually non-existant. Only the very real presence of the Italian Royal Army signaled that the front lay just a couple of miles away. Military lorries rattled past her on the street below, soldiers crowded into the rear compartments. The uniformed men posed a marked contrast to the women in their full skirts and aprons chatting over their market baskets.

The headlines of yesterday's newspapers had blazed out a quote from General Haig, the leader of the British forces in Europe—*Our Backs are to the Wall.* As the Germans advanced a further three miles and captured Messines, Haig had issued a grim and unprecedented order that every soldier holding the line must ready himself to die before retiring a step further.

Though the quiet Alpine village in front of her appeared immune to change, the war was thinning to a breaking point.

Behind her in the hotel room, Strangford continued to sleep. He had said little more on their journey about what he had experienced during his contact with the catatonic lieutenant. Lily was painfully conscious of the many questions that remained unanswered—but then, that was why they were here in this remote and beautiful place—for answers.

She slipped out, taking her walking stick with her. The windows along the stairs were cracked open to let in the spring air. It was thin and crisp.

Down in the breakfast room, Kazi sat at one of the tables, relishing a steaming cup of dark liquid. There were only a handful of other guests scattered among the worn wooden tables. Lily suspected this inn bustled with winter skiers and summer hikers when there wasn't a war on.

She took a seat across from the inspector, leaning her stick against the table.

"The French line is holding." Kazi tossed down an Italian-language newspaper. "I can't make out any more than that."

Being cut off from his usual reliable and immediate sources of information was clearly bothering him. As he looked up, his gaze caught on the trousers she had put on that morning. He frowned as though weighing the difference between impropriety and practicality. Practicality won out as he gave her a brief nod of approval.

"You should be warm enough. The two remaining platoons of

the 137th Alpini are currently sharing responsibility for holding the pass, operating at roughly half strength. I couldn't find a carriage, but the hotel manager knows a local farmer who has agreed to bring us up by mule. We'll have to see if any of the fellows at the line speak English, or perhaps one of them has a bit of French. I don't believe we have any Italian between the three of us."

"No," Lily concurred, eyeing Kazi's breakfast. It appeared to be a porridge of barley and milk.

"Of course, none of these men were witnesses to the attack," he continued after taking a neat bite. "At best, they might have been present for the aftermath. Still, even that could be useful. The initial investigation was done by Italian military intelligence who unfortunately did not bring a camera to the scene until it had been largely cleared up. Shall we order you some breakfast? The porridge is very good."

Lily was a bit startled by the abrupt turn of his question. At the thought of food, her body sounded a note of unpleasant rebellion.

"Thank you, but I'm fine," she replied, grimacing.

The flow of the inspector's words was interrupted as he studied her.

"Forgive me if I'm overstepping, but I think you might feel better if you ate something."

"Pardon?" Lily replied, surprised by the suggestion.

Kazi set down his spoon, looking at her from under his dark brows.

"I am a father of three, Lady Strangford. I have had some opportunity to learn a thing or two about these matters."

Cups clattered softly against saucers at the back of the room. An older couple by the window chatted quietly in Italian, oblivious to their conversation. Outside, a donkey cart rattled past, the sound followed by the bright note of a woman laughing.

Lily's world tilted dangerously.

"That's not ... " she began, her voice suddenly hoarse. "You couldn't possibly ..."

But of course, he could. He was the most observant man she had ever met. It was his job to notice the things other people overlooked.

Things like how meat had been tasting strange to her, and how ill she had been in the mornings since they arrived in France.

... a father of three ...

He was observing her even now, and upon seeing her reaction, Kazi's expression shifted from one of mild concern to mortification, the blood draining from behind his skin.

"You didn't know ... I never would have ... Ei morechhe," he stammered, tripping into Bangla.

Lily didn't know the phrase, but it rang in her ears very similarly to *bloody hell.*

Shock swirled around her, threatening to shatter into something she was not entirely sure she could handle, a maelstrom of hope and terror and grief. She clenched her hands into fists on the table, resisting the urge to put her fingers to her abdomen as though she might be able to touch it and know whether what Kazi guessed was true.

Kazi raised his eyes to the ceiling like a man praying for strength. He took a breath, forcibly gathering his usual self-possession.

"I must beg that you forgive me for overstepping myself, my lady." he said, each word careful as glass.

"Of course," she murmured back automatically. "You mustn't ..."

Language abandoned her, leaving her flailing. She swallowed against a dry throat, closing her eyes.

Was it possible?

Her brain stumbled involuntarily through memories of past appointments, scrambling at numbers and days of the week until it finally spat out a conclusion. She tripped through the calculation twice before she accepted it.

Yes, she thought numbly. It was entirely possible that she was pregnant.

Bloody hell, she thought quietly, desperately. *Ei morechhe.*

Kazi rubbed his hand across his face as though he could wipe away the unspeakable awkwardness of the situation.

"The coffee," he said numbly. "It's real. You should have some."

"I ... I'm not ..." Lily tried, struggling to work through the terrible muddle in her brain to a coherent response. What should she be feeling right now? Was it joy? Excitement? The dread of disappointment, her hopes raised and dashed again as they had been so many times before?

Or perhaps it was the terror of another unspeakable grief.

The blood drummed against her ears, the ordinary sounds of the breakfast room crackling around her like flames.

Across the table, Kazi finally pushed through his own embarrassment and took a more thoughtful look at her face. What he saw there shifted his expression to one of startled concern.

"Is something wrong?" he asked.

"What a splendid morning," Strangford said from behind her, joining them at the table. "Stone me—is that real coffee?"

He sat down in his brushed and pressed Navy uniform, picking up Kazi's cup in his gloved hand and giving it a delighted sniff.

Lily took a breath, steeling herself, and turned to her husband with a smile.

"It would appear so," she calmly agreed.

~

The road wound to the pass in tight switchbacks, forcing them into a pace that would have felt maddeningly slow if it hadn't also been so difficult. The way was steep, the air cooling and thinning with each turn. Lily was grateful for the mule, even though she had never ridden on one before. It was very different from a horse. Though in reasonably good condition thanks to her kali practice and Strangford's insistence on walking everywhere, climbing the mountain on foot would have quickly exhausted her.

She wondered what that said about the men who held the thin air of this outpost for weeks on end before they were relieved.

Their guide was a white-bearded sheep farmer. He wore simple clothes accented with bright embroidery and spoke not a word of English. Even his Italian seemed to be some dialect that occasionally rang more like French in her ears.

Kazi rode in front of her. He seemed slightly too tall for his mule, but he held his seat with an approximation of his usual cool professionalism.

They had not spoken much since breakfast. Kazi kept his distance, even providing her with a fairly obvious opportunity to talk to her husband by offering to go ahead to meet the guide and ensure that everything was ready for their journey. Like an acknowledged coward, Lily had jumped up after him and insisted they might as well all go together to save time.

She wasn't ready to have that discussion with Strangford.

From the look he had flashed her, Strangford wasn't clueless. She could feel his quiet concern as he rode behind her, though he hadn't pressed her for an explanation.

She had to provide it at some point, of course. Even if he weren't going to get it out of her the next time he took his gloves off, he deserved to know. The matter concerned him just as much as it did her, but it was not something she wanted to reveal on an excursion to the Alpine front.

She would have to avoid contact with him until they returned to the village. Then she would share the news—and what exactly would that be? A taciturn police inspector suspected she might be pregnant. Her own calculations showed that her cycle was late, but only by three weeks, and she had never been very regular to begin with. There were any number of reasons she might feel ill in the mornings, travel itself being one of them.

Nothing was certain.

She found herself thinking longingly of what could change that. Gardner might have resolved the question with a brush of his hands, but Gardner was far away, stationed at a field hospital near Hazebrouck. An excursion there was hardly a simple jaunt from Italy, and it lay close to where the Germans were currently harrying the front line . . . a front line that felt far more dangerous to her than the Alpine outpost they currently approached.

This snowbound mountain landscape was very clearly not the one she had seen in her vision of Strangford's fall. But Hazebrouck? That was another story.

She still found herself aching a bit at the idea. It wasn't just certainty about her pregnancy that she desired. It was also the warm presence of her friend—his steady and compassionate common sense that might help her see her way through the morass of emotion clouding her thoughts.

Lily pulled her coat closer against the chill as the road zigzagged again in its manic rise up the face of the mountain. The air was exceedingly bright, and she found herself grateful for the broad brim of her hat. A pair of army lorries rumbled past as they climbed. Lily eyed them with envy even though their engines were obviously straining.

Patches of snow began to dot the landscape, intermingled with small white alpine flowers and short spring grass. It seemed counter-intuitive that the mountains would appear taller when she was more than halfway to the top of them, but they did. The peaks loomed to either side, jagged faces covered in shelves of ice big enough to crush her.

Looking back the way they had come, Lily felt almost dizzy. The road zippered down the incline to the valley in tight jigs and jags. More mountains were visible beyond the irregular cluster of pale buildings that was Bormio.

"It's awe-inspiring, isn't it?"

Strangford had ridden up beside her, Kazi and their guide drifting a little further ahead as she paused to stare.

"I've never seen anything like it," Lily admitted.

"Something happened at breakfast."

It was not a question—he knew her too well for that. Lily took a breath of the thin mountain air, steadying herself.

"Nothing is . . . wrong," she offered carefully. "I just . . . don't think this is the place to talk about it."

"I see" Strangford said, looking thoughtful. "But I'm here—when you're ready."

Lily nodded, feeling a clench in her chest at his words. She tapped her heels against the mule. It jogged to catch up with Kazi as though loath to be left behind, bouncing her against the saddle.

~

The Alpini base at the Stelvio Pass was an odd growth in the land-scape, like a lichen crusting the top of the road. The whole of it was snowbound, metal huts crammed into little spaces where the ground was flat enough to support them. An old skiing hostel perched by the side of the road, slightly ramshackle and obviously repurposed into a barracks.

To either side rose the peaks, sheer walls of stone and ice that towered over them. She noted the presence of a pair of artillery cannons dug into the mountainside and wondered with vague alarm how the Alpini had managed to get those half-ton piles of metal up the face of a twelve-foot cliff.

A wall of sandbags cut the road off near the hostel. The space around it was busy with men wearing the uniforms of the 137th Alpini.

At the start of the war, the pass would have been held by men recruited from Italy's champion skiers, mountaineers, and hunters. Like every other regiment, the war had thinned their ranks. The more seasoned mingled with others who looked young, fresh, and a bit softer. They were dressed in layers of soft gray wool over boots and puttees, some with short capes for additional warmth. Most of them wore quaint hats accented with feathers. The accessory looked almost festive until Lily got closer and noticed their color.

The feathers were raven black.

The lorries that had passed them earlier were parked at the hostel, their cargo holds now empty. Skis were lined up against the sides of the old building, along with coils of rope and other climbing gear. A pair of soldiers were carefully examining one of the ropes. The older of the two eyed every inch of it for flaws as the younger neatly recoiled it by his side.

A cookfire in the yard served as the kitchen. The men gathered there looked with interest at their little party as they dismounted, Lily plucking her walking stick from where she had strapped it to the saddle.

These were the men of the surviving platoons of the regiment, the ones that had been on relief rotation in Bormio when seventy-five of their fellow soldiers were wiped out in a single night of mysterious violence. They had been holding this snow-covered eyrie without relief now for over a month.

One of the older soldiers by the fire sheathed the knife he had been sharpening and rose to approach them. From his weary air, Lily gauged he had been charged with chasing off any civilians who found their way up to the pass. His look shifted to one of curiosity when he caught sight of Strangford's uniform.

Kazi didn't miss the significance of that glance. As their guide led the mules away, Kazi took a subtle step back. The move put

Strangford at the forefront of their group, quietly positioning him as their leader.

"Have you any English?" Strangford tried as the soldier arrived.

"No," the man replied.

He was short but solid, the hair of his mustache tinged with gray.

"Parle vous Francais?"

"No," he repeated. "Sei francese?"

"Inglese," Strangford returned.

"Bu eh eff." the man asked a bit skeptically.

Lily realized he was not speaking Italian but a set of initials—BEF, for "British Expeditionary Force."

"Navy." Strangford replied. He searched for a word, settling on French. "La marine?"

"La Marina," the soldier replied, eyebrows drawing together with puzzlement.

He glanced over at Lily and Kazi. Their appearance seemed to do little to reassure him. He shouted back to the men at the cookfire.

"Que, sergente?" one of them called back.

The sergeant rattled off his response, and a man was sent jogging into the hostel. A moment later, he emerged with an officer on his heels—a younger, taller man with a slightly receding hairline apparent under his hat.

"That's a tenente," Kazi reported from beside her, keeping his voice low. "Their equivalent of a lieutenant. He'll likely be in command here."

Taking a few steps away, the sergeant exchanged quick words with his commander. The lieutenant turned and called up to one of the gun posts overlooking the road, his voice ringing across the clear air.

"Soldato Sala!"

The soldato—or private—detached himself from the men perched by the gun, scrambling down the rock face with the nimbleness of a goat. He sprinted over to meet his superiors with youthful enthusiasm. There was another burst of Italian, a startled look at Lily's trousers, and then the private crossed over to present himself to Strangford.

"You speak English?" he asked.

"Indeed," Strangford returned, his eyes brightening a bit at the boy's obvious enthusiasm.

Sala could not have been more than nineteen, with charmingly crooked teeth and a reddish glint to his brown hair.

"I speak very good English. I translate for you." He hitched a thumb back toward the senior officers standing behind him. "Tenente Damasio asks what is your business here."

"I have been charged by my superiors to look over the scene of the March 15th attack," Strangford replied.

The boy paled a bit, eyes widening, and Lily wondered with quiet dismay whether any of his friends in the company had been stationed at the pass that night. He looked too young to have been at the front for very long, but the attack had taken place only a month before. It took little time in war to form the sort of bonds that hurt when they were severed.

Sala glanced back at his lieutenant, clearly hesitant to translate, but in the face of the officer's obvious impatience, he quickly rattled off an explanation.

The sergeant's jaw tightened.

"Hai documenti?" the lieutenant demanded.

Strangford reached into his jacket and produced a neatly folded packet of his Naval identification and the travel documents Kazi had acquired for them. The lieutenant examined them, eyeing each page carefully.

The sergeant's look had become distinctly hostile. He spoke again to the lieutenant. Lily picked up on one of the words.

Austriaci.

She could guess well enough at the meaning—Austrian. It seemed the sergeant was accusing them of being spies.

His superior made a short response.

"He says you are not Austrian because there are no Indians there," Sala offered helpfully.

The boy had come to stand beside her, taking the opportunity of his superiors' distraction to get a better look at her and Kazi.

Kazi arched a dark eyebrow but refrained from further comment.

The lieutenant handed his sergeant back the papers. The older man glowered a bit, obviously displeased by his commander's decision. What he said next had a distinctly unflattering air, the nature of the comment confirmed by the blush that rose to Sala's cheeks and the awkward look he flashed at Lily and Kazi.

Lily imagined it had something to do with the British military using women and foreigners to do its work.

As the lieutenant walked away, the sergeant summoned Sala with a flick of his wrist. Handing the young private Strangford's papers, he made a sharp declaration in Italian and stalked away.

Sala brightened, flashing Lily a grin—and for a moment, she was looking at someone else. Not a freckled soldier in a feathered cap but a raven-haired boy in an attic window making friends with a flock of mourning doves.

A man in a green uniform she said goodbye to on the platform of St. Pancras station.

That was my fight, Lily.

The thought of Sam put a hitch in her chest.

"The tenente say I show you whatever you need." Sala was clearly pleased with the assignment.

"Where did it happen?" Kazi demanded.

Sala blinked at him, confused by the question.

"Here," he replied.

Lily glanced around the base. The men seemed relaxed, a few of them playing cards or drinking steaming cups of coffee. An older soldier lay against a stone wall, his cap pulled down over his eyes, obviously grabbing a nap.

Other signs rose into her awareness—the fresh planks in the wooden door of the hostel, a long scrape in the rust on the corrugated iron side of a Nissen hut.

On the upper floor of the wooden building, two broken windows were covered in hastily tacked canvas. Faint, ruddy stains marred the walls beneath them, smeared by an attempt at washing.

"The hostel?" Kazi pressed, confused.

"No, no," Sala replied. "All of it."

He waved his hand, taking in the whole of the base, from the artillery nests to the fortifications of the front line that lay at the top of the rise, beyond the roadblock.

Kazi let out a low, frustrated breath, obviously looking for a way to better focus their search. He glanced to Strangford, who was staring down at his boots with an uneasy tension.

"Where did they find the dead?" Strangford asked.

Sala became solemn. It was a state Lily could already intuit was rare for him.

"Everywhere," he returned quietly.

"We'll start with the hostel, then," Strangford determined.

Without waiting for the rest of them, he set off for the building.

Sala hurried after him. Kazi paused to glance back at Lily, but when she made no move to follow, he turned and continued on his way.

The presence of a woman in the building would only draw more attention from any men still inside. Lily couldn't know what horrors Strangford might have to experience when reading any impressions lingering in the wood and stone, but the less notice he drew while doing it, the better.

Left behind, she found her attention drifting up the road. The front line would lie just around that bend in the pass—the place she had been reading about in the papers for four years. It was not the mud-thick barrier dug into the earth that haunted her nightmares, but she was abruptly overwhelmed by the urge to see it.

Lily set off up the remainder of the pass. The two artillery posts guarded the way, their massive guns set into the rocks nearly a dozen feet above the road, aimed out over the mountains. Looking up, she could see that hoists had been bolted into the stone. The men to one side of her were using the device to haul up crates of shells, presumably the supplies delivered by the lorries.

The road could not have been clear of snow and ice for long. Ammunition would have been carried in by mule or foot before then. She wondered if the clear roads would mean more skirmishing. The front had been more or less stable in this area since the outbreak of the war, save for a slight Austrian advance here and there quickly followed by forced retreat.

Noting her interest, the men at the gun called down to her, offering waves and at least one kiss blown into the air. Lily waved back, happy enough to accept the gallantry, knowing they must rarely have a woman here to offer it to.

She looked for more signs of the attack and found them with

gruesome subtlety. Splashes of blood were frozen into the snow on the high stone faces that lined the road, places too difficult to reach and clean. They would be there until the thaw.

A flagpole was embedded into a crack in the face of the rocks, driven there with what must have been immense force. More blood-stains were splattered around it.

An enormous stone by the roadside looked freshly split in two, the interior yet unstained by lichen or weather. The remains of a machine gun lay beside it, the thick steel barrel bent into a distinct curve.

The signs tickled at the back of her mind, leaving her uneasy.

Just beyond the top of the pass lay a solid wall of stone, sandbags, snow, and ice. It had been piled up high enough that a man could walk behind it without showing his head. The soldati stationed here had replaced their feathered caps with metal helmets. One of them handed out packages of cigarettes from a crate at his feet with an air of obvious celebration at the arrival of fresh supplies. Others tore open their mail, leaning against the wall as they read their letters.

She stopped at the wall beside a green-eyed young private relishing the taste of a square of chocolate.

"Is it safe to look over?" she asked.

The private pushed back the rim of his helmet, setting it at a more roguish angle, and flashed her a charming smile. Lily put his age at perhaps twenty-one.

"Ciao, Bella," he replied.

Lily could not resist a smile in return. She gestured from her eyes to the top of the wall.

"Is it safe?" she repeated.

The private shrugged.

"Sì. È tranquillo." He shouted down the line. "Rossi! Elmetto!"

One of the other soldiers tossed a metal helmet over, which her guide easily caught.

"Per Lei, Signora," he said, offering it to her gallantly.

She pulled off her wool hat and held it out in exchange. The private accepted it with another grin, and she tugged the helmet on over her hair. It was heavy. Hopping onto a step built for the purpose, she peered out over the pass.

The view was extraordinary. Snow clung to the peaks, creating geometric textures on the faces of the cliffs. The road continued to wind to the east, down into a valley and up another rise. The surface of it was pitted with old shell holes and still half-covered in snow.

On the high ground of the opposite side, she could see the darker line of the Austrian fortifications. They had also built a wall of sandbags and rock. Dark scorch marks blemished the snow beneath their position, showing where the Italian artillery had attempted a few strikes. She imagined the lines had quite deliberately been established just out of range of the guns but did not put it past the bored men manning them to take an occasional shot just for the fun of it.

The two lines were a perfect and impenetrable stalemate unless a raid could successfully navigate the treacherous ground below, exposed the entire time to artillery and rifle fire from above.

Whoever had attacked the base had done so by crossing that valley in the darkness of the night. In March, it would still have been bitterly cold and buried in snow. That a team of Austrian soldiers presumably managed it and then returned, carrying their dead with them, seemed an effort verging on the impossible . . . and they had not even stayed to hold the land they had won.

Why would a raid retreat after successfully slaughtering the two platoons encamped here? The sense of wrongness lent a sinister air to the panorama.

The front line extended to the south of the pass. It quickly declined from a solid wall to little more than a track skirting rocks and cliffs, punctuated by fortified defensive nests packed with rocks and snow to make them look like part of the mountain. Lily could see a machine gun and its crew lounging inside the nearest of them, with others strung out into the distance until it connected with the company holding the rest of the line somewhere to the south.

Between two of the outposts lay another rough pass. A strange mass, cobalt-tinged and snow-frosted, roiled along the low ground. It was a glacier, she realized with a dawning sense of awe, a river of ice frozen against the mountain for thousands of years.

The sight of it tugged at something in her chest like the jerk of a fishing line. Lily had just enough time to recognize it for onmyōdō before it swallowed her.

Her breath frosts in dark air.

A staff of wood in her hands, the weight of it strange. A splash of something hot and thick across her skin.

Strangford watching her through an unmelting snow.

The ground shaking beneath her feet.

Lily grasped the icy wall, holding herself upright against the sandbags, her heart pounding with fear.

The river of ice to the south pulled at her with an ache like desire.

Her green-eyed companion shook a cigarette from his pack with a neat flick of his wrist.

"Sigaretta?"

"No, thank you. Grazie," she replied, putting one of the three words she had managed to learn in Italian to use.

He shrugged, still with a smile, and lit his own. The smell of burning tobacco filled the air as she looked down the road to see Kazi, Strangford, and the young translator, Sala, approaching the front line.

Strangford was drawn with exhaustion. It signaled that their excursion had been successful. He had seen something about the night of the attack.

It didn't look good.

She walked over to meet them, shivering under the wool of her coat.

"Sala, ask the men if it is safe to view the pass today." Kazi ordered. "We'll join you in a moment."

Sala opened his mouth to object—undoubtedly to assure them that he already knew it was safe—but at a look from Kazi, he refrained. With a shrug, he loped off to the wall, where he was greeted with enthusiasm by his colleagues.

"Well?" Kazi prompted.

Lily bit back the urge to snap at him. He had no idea what he was asking—what Strangford had offered him by coming here.

"The men in the barracks woke to the sound of defensive gunfire from up here," Strangford said, nodding towards the wall. "Armed themselves—quickly. In the dark."

Lily found herself picturing it—the abrupt rise from sleep, the hurried movements in the gloom to the sound of the panicked breaths of other men.

"They heard metal clashing. Screams from outside," he continued, pushing out the words. "A party ran out to cover the far side of the road. Others took up positions at the windows on both floors. What they had drilled for."

He stopped there, hesitating.

"What is it?" Kazi pressed

A cold wind blew down from the high ground of the pass, pulling at the fine threads of Lily's hair under her helmet.

"You must understand," Strangford explained with careful patience. "The impressions I draw from the world are not left there by the events themselves but by the minds and souls of those who experienced them. What I see of the past, I see through them. Feel through them."

Kazi absorbed this, his agile mind filling in the rest.

"You are warning me that you cannot know how much of what you saw was real and how much was tainted by the imaginations of those who left your . . . impressions," he finished, borrowing Strangford's word.

Strangford offered a curt nod in return.

"Your caveat is acknowledged," Kazi said.

There was a burst of laughter from the front line, a rise of quick voices speaking in cheerful Italian. Sala grinned in the midst of it, accepting one of the newly-arrived cigarettes.

Strangford closed his eye, the stolen memories still sharp enough to bite.

"They came up the walls."

Kazi frowned.

"You mean they used grappling lines?"

"I mean," Strangford returned painstakingly. "That they came up the walls, bare hands on stone, like things out of nightmares."

Lily had seen Kazi truly surprised only once before. That had been four years earlier when she told him the words of a ghost.

His abrupt stillness was the same now.

"Some of the men who died saw blades flashing in the dark, others pale skin drenched in blood. Teeth like wolves gleaming in the moonlight, or simply shadows flooding over the windowsill, doors blasting from their hinges.

"Those are dreams, not memories," Kazi protested.

"Bullets passing through flesh like air, or blowing off bloody pieces, and they still keep coming. They just keep coming."

Lily did not miss his slip into the present tense. His voice broke on the words, a still-fresh terror setting its hooks in him.

Heedless of the wide-eyed inspector, Lily went to him. She slipped her arms around Strangford's body and held him firmly. Pressing her bare hand deliberately to the heavy curve of his neck, she let her touch ground him.

She glared at Kazi over his shoulder, feeling acutely all his responsibility for plunging Strangford into this nightmare.

And yet . . . something truly terrible had passed through this place—something that filled her with an ice-cold dread.

Then Strangford abruptly straightened, looking at her with surprise, and Lily realized her mistake.

The breakfast room that morning—black coffee, white porridge, and Kazi's cheeks reddening with embarrassment.

She said nothing. How could she? They were clustered on a mountain pass wreathed with echoes of terror.

Strangford seemed to know it too. His silence had weight as she released him, stepping to a distance.

Kazi frowned down at the dust of the road, his thoughts too consumed with the puzzle of Strangford's story to notice what was passing before him.

"You did not mention any enemy gunfire," he noted.

It was an odd observation, but as soon as he had voiced it, Lily's mind caught against it as well. From Belgium to Egypt, this war had been fought with guns.

"The enemy did not shoot," Strangford agreed.

His voice was stronger now, some of his color returning. Whatever the unintended consequences, Lily's touch had done its work, granting Strangford a bit more distance from the horror of what he had experienced in the hostel.

"Bayonets, then?" Kazi pressed.

"Swords," Strangford returned.

"Swords?" Kazi echoed with disbelief.

Lily shared it. No one fought with swords anymore. What good was a sword against a machine gun? Hearing Strangford say the words was like stumbling across a medieval knight in Hyde Park.

"For some of them," Strangford confirmed.

"What about the others?" she asked.

Strangford's eye was bleak.

"Hands. Or teeth."

Mountain wind, thin and clear, whipped at the little scraps of brush struggling for life at the roadside. Sunlight glinted off the snow icing the gray peaks that towered over them.

"That's ..."

She trailed off, not knowing how to finish. Impossible? Who was she to claim to know the limits of what was possible?

She closed her eyes, pushing her mind to move past the shock and find some sense in what Strangford was telling her. She found herself recalling Paris, the cherry blossoms falling onto the sparkling waters of the Seine.

"You called them monsters."

"Now you know why." Strangford replied.

Kazi paced beside them, his long legs eating up the ground as though physical movement might prompt his brain to spit out an answer to the questions twisting around inside of it. He halted with a hiss of frustration.

"Could you manage any more of it?" he demanded, whipping back to Strangford.

"Yes," Strangford replied tiredly.

Lily fought the urge to protest. He was already wrung thin by what the readings at the ski hostel had demanded of him. Could he manage more? Perhaps, but that didn't mean he should.

"But not indefinitely." she snapped out. "If we are to ask more of him, we should focus our efforts."

Kazi frowned, casting an assessing look at Strangford's pale face.

"The wall at the front, then," he offered. "Where the attack was likely launched."

It was an entirely sensible suggestion. It was also wrong.

Lily knew it in her bones—in the sudden, blaring song of her onmyōdō.

"Not the wall," she blurted.

The two men were suddenly paying very close attention to her. Strangford's look was one of mild concern—Kazi's of a sharp and dangerous curiosity.

She was paralyzed by the opposing tension between the urge of her onmyōdō and the knowledge that what it required her to say had no reasonable explanation . . . not for a man from whom she was determined to conceal the truth of her nature.

Kazi was far too clever. How could she have been so foolish as to think she could travel with him and not provide him with the clues he required to piece her own secret together?

She flailed for an escape and found it in the form of the auburn-haired soldier at the top of the road.

"Sala!" she called.

The young soldato perked up, deserting his companions to jog down to where she stood.

"What's at the glacier?" she demanded.

Sala brightened.

"Oh! You want to see the tunnels?"

She could feel Kazi's focus shift, the sharp weight of it moving from her to the soldato and past him to the landscape that lay beyond the wall.

"Yes," Strangford replied carefully. "I think we should like that very much."

"Va bene!" Sala agreed cheerfully.

He turned to bound back up the pass. Kazi strode after him.

Strangford held back, his tired face drawn with a new concern as he looked at her.

"Later," Lily managed, choking out the word before she hurried after the others.

SEVEN

$\mathcal{T}$HE YOUNG ALPINI SOLDIER scanned the stack of supplies by the wall.

"We need ... Ah! These."

Sala held up a pair of roughly foot-shaped metal frames lined with spikes and dangling leather straps.

"Climbing crampons," Strangford offered.

"Crampons!" Sala echoed happily, pleased to acquire a new word.

The devices strapped onto Lily's boots. She could immediately feel how they provided her with more traction.

Sala picked up an unlit lantern.

"If the Potato Mashers shoot at us, you go down behind the rocks," he instructed them cheerfully. "They cannot see you so good in the day with the sun on the snow."

Lily gathered that she had just learned the English translation of a derogatory Italian term for the Austrians across the pass. The notion of being shot at as they made their way to their destination, even with a poor line of sight, was far from comforting.

Sala led them through a narrow opening between the sandbag wall of the front line and the great, jutting rise of rock that bordered the road. Beyond the barrier, Lily found herself picking her way along a narrow track etched into the side of the mountain.

The side of the path dropped away in places, becoming just a thin shelf of stone overlooking a sheer plummet to the valley below. She found herself very glad of both her trousers and her walking stick.

They passed a machine gun blind set into a rock outcrop, their guide exchanging a greeting with the men stationed there. They looked both cold and bored. Beyond them, Lily could see how the long, winding track continued along the mountains until it folded into the distance, marked by more sentry points at what seemed like far too distant intervals.

The notion that these men had been stationed for months or even years in this inhospitable, desperately rugged place was humbling. How could a war be fought in this alien world where the air was thin enough to make her head pound and the cold still bit the skin of her cheeks, even this close to summer?

Sala veered from the front line, taking them instead down a faintly delineated track that curved around one of the peaks framing the other pass.

Lily realized she had only been seeing a sliver of the glacier before. The mass of ice below filled the entirety of the valley, framed by ridges of stone. The surface of it was still largely covered in snow, but here and there, places had cleared enough to reveal patches of a strange, deep blue.

The wind tugged steadily at her hair under her borrowed helmet. There was no other sound save the scrape of their crampons against the icy rocks of their descent. The sound was harsh against the otherwise timeless silence of the landscape before her.

Sala broke it with an enthusiastic monologue.

"More early in the war, all this was Austria," he explained, waving a hand over the valley. "They advance in 1916 and take the glacier, but we Alpini take it back."

Sala was clearly quite proud of this achievement, though based on his obvious youth Lily doubted he had been present for the occasion.

"It is not high ground, see?" he noted, gesturing. "We carry our big guns to the mountain and shoot at them. Boom, boom, boom."

He mimicked the fall of the artillery.

The narrow, icy ridge he pointed out was not marked by any path. As far as Lily could reason, the artillery in question would have to have been hauled over the top of the mountain from the pass to be positioned there, likely during the night to avoid sniper fire from the glacier. It seemed an impossible feat, but so did building a defensible front line across the Alps on what probably started out as a goat path.

"They hide in the tunnels like rats, but sometime they must come up, and then we kill them," Sala said. "Come! Follow me. The way I show you, we are safe. The rest? Who knows."

The young Alpini gave an illustrative and slightly terrifying shrug, then set off across the glacier with easy confidence.

Strangford followed after him without hesitation. At his home in Northumberland, it routinely got cold enough for skating. Kazi looked less excited about walking on the ice but took a breath and forced himself forward. After a few more careful steps, he gained some confidence in the crampons and stalked ahead with more of his usual grace.

They were safely out of sight of the Austrian line in the valley. Lily tugged off her borrowed helmet, the absence of the weight of it a palpable relief. She set it down on the ground and followed, moving carefully until she had a feel for how the metal spikes strapped to her boots gripped the glacier.

Their silent procession moved along a slender line of ice cleared of all but a light, blowing snow. Stillness descended around them once more. The glacier felt ancient, as though it had ruled here for thousands of years and did not readily tolerate intruders.

The wind gained a deeper chill as it blew across the ice. Mountains soared up splendidly to either side. Below her boots lay the unmoving mass of ancient water, tinted its uncanny blue.

Sala led them to a splinter of stone that protruded from the surface of the ice. From the heights of the path across the mountain, it had looked insignificant. Now that they approached it from the ground, the stone grew in scale, revealing itself to be at least forty feet in height. The glacier cracked around the obstacle, splitting into a narrow crevasse.

With startling incongruity, at the base of the stone lay a set of wooden steps descending into the ice. Boards were set onto carved shelves, already warped and uneven from the imperceptible momentum of the frozen river.

The stairway descended into a narrow, azure-tinted gloom. Lily's onmyōdō echoed up at her from below, drawing her on like the call of a siren.

"We go down! You love it. It is smashing."

Sala was clearly delighted at the opportunity to use this bit of slang he had acquired somewhere. Without further delay, he bounded down the steps.

The confidence was undeserved. The stairs were warped at uncomfortable angles and glazed with a layer of ice. Bolts in the walls at waist height peppered the way down, indicating that a rope must once have served as a banister. There was no longer anything to hold on to.

The way was too tight for more than one of them to advance at a time. Lily stomped her crampons into a firmer grip with each step, testing it before she lurched forward to the next.

Ice rose up behind and beside her, swallowing her as she descended deeper into a still, frozen twilight. With the loss of the wind, the silence grew until it, too, felt like it was swallowing them, smothering the little cracks and scrapes of their crampons against the boards.

The tunnel was not man-made but rather adapted. That it belonged to the glacier itself was evidenced by the strange formations that warped the walls overhead. Here and there, the path dropped too precipitously for stairs. Instead, wooden ladders were bolted into place.

Overhead, the patch of visible sky closed to a thin, jagged line, the glaring light of a mountain afternoon fading into an eternal gloaming.

"Stop one moment," Sala ordered, crouching on a landing. He put a match to the wick of his lantern. Lily, suspended on a ladder above Kazi, paused in her descent. There was a whiff of paraffin, and the eerie blue dimness was pushed back by a sturdy little burst of yellow light.

"A little further," Sala promised, carrying the light forward.

Lily hurried the rest of the way down the ladder to follow him. The presence of the light had made her sharply aware of just how dark it had otherwise become here in the heart of the ice.

They ducked through a low arch, this one clearly chipped away by men to allow easier passage through the tunnel. Another scramble of veering steps brought them to the bottom.

The space was too large to have been carved out, the ceiling rising from twelve to twenty feet overhead. The walls were smoothly uneven, undulating like the body of a worm. Only part of it was revealed in the glow of Sala's lamp, the rest lost in an artificial night.

Kazi stopped in front of her.

"This was done by melt," he said wonderingly, eyes moving over the strange contours of the space. "A river forming within a river."

A soft breeze gently tickled the hairs at the back of her neck. Lily turned, discovering with an uncomfortable chill that the tunnel extended not just before but also behind them, continuing on into an impenetrable darkness long and deep enough to coax out a thread of its own wind.

Sala and the others continued forward. Lily hurried after them, feeling no desire to explore where that black, silent mouth beyond the end of the stairs might lead.

The tunnel was cluttered with signs of a hurriedly abandoned occupation. Metal bunks lay against the walls, stripped of bedclothes and haphazardly disassembled. A gas-powered heating stove was tipped over on its side, the gas canister missing. A pile of refuse filled a hole cracked into the floor, forming a small mountain of empty tins and bottles. Someone had left another lantern beside an abandoned boot.

The space seemed suspended in time as though the stove, when touched, might still be warm, the beds only just deserted. And yet with the chill and the silence, the whole of it had the feel of a tomb.

"Anything here you think might help us?" Kazi quietly asked Strangford, coming close and pitching his voice low.

Strangford scanned the tunnel.

"All of this must have been abandoned two years ago," he said. "There would be nothing related to last month's attack."

"Then why are we here?" Kazi demanded.

The question echoed in Lily's own mind—why were they here? What about this place had woken the voice of her onmyōdō, compelling her to come?

No—not her. It was just as important that Strangford was here. She knew it the way she knew the ice she walked upon descended for fathoms, the captured dust of millennia suspended under her feet.

107

"Is there more to it?" Lily called out.

"Come, I show you," Sala replied.

He marched down the length of the tunnel, taking the light with him. The darkness pinching at her back, Lily scurried to follow.

Natural lacunae in the ice alternated with spaces carved with chisels and axes. In places, the floor was packed with snow to level the way.

One narrow bridge, made up of little more than a few planks thrown down over the ice, crossed over a gap of perhaps six feet. The planks had warped since it was built, but Sala marched over it without hesitation.

"The officers are here, I think."

He pointed to a cluster of small alcoves. A broken cot lay in one of them, alongside a trunk with a snapped hinge.

A mirror was bolted to the wall above a shelf cut into the ice. Lily could picture an Austrian captain shaving there by the light of his lantern.

She looked back to the tunnel and realized that there was no more of it. The bore in the ice through which they had been passing broke away ten feet past the captain's room, ending in a black canyon.

She edged closer for a better look. The gap was perhaps fifteen feet across and descended to a depth that was lost in the darkness. A cold breeze rose softly from the bottom, smelling of damp and earth.

Another hole was split into the wall that faced them across the chasm. Lily corrected herself—the tunnel did not end here. It was only broken in two by some fracture in the glacier.

Onmyōdō tugged at her, unmistakably pulling her towards the black mouth on the other side of the gap.

Cairncross had told her once what the word meant in Japanese— the way of yin-yang, of divining the paths that lead to good or evil fortune.

Nothing about the way in front of her looked fortunate.

A bridge would have been too much to hope for. Instead, only a pair of ropes breached the gap, anchored at either end by thick metal stakes pounded into the walls of the crevasse.

"Ah yes! You find the way to the Devil's Altar."

Sala's voice made her jump. Lily had not realized the soldato had come to stand beside her.

"Devil's Altar?" Kazi demanded, joining them.

"Where the Potato Mashers worship the devil." There was an edge of delight in Sala's voice at the opportunity to share such a juicy horror. "Not an altar above the ground like good Christians. They cut it out of the ground and stand over the hole, I guess. I don't know. Austrians are crazy."

A wind that smelled of time danced over her skin. The dark mouth on the other side threatened either to speak or to swallow her.

The onmyōdō yanked at her as though it would drag her over the edge.

"I think we should hazard it," Kazi declared, slipping past her to stare out at the dark mouth on the far side.

For a horrified moment, Lily wondered if the onmyōdō had gotten to the rational inspector as well, turning him into its instrument in a conspiracy to tear her into pieces.

"Certainly. It is perfectly safe, yes? Just needs … " Sala paused, casting a guilty glance at Lily as he lowered his tone. "Un po' cojones, sì?"

"Lily."

Strangford stood behind her, his gloved fingers gently touching her sleeve.

How could something that felt so horrible also seem so undeniably right? Lily closed her eyes against the impossible pressure of it and then finally broke.

"We'll go." Her voice sounded more sure than it deserved to be.

Sala removed his hat and slid off his crampons, tying the straps to his belt, then stepped out onto the rope. It was strung taut between the two stakes, the second line set at shoulder height above the first. The soldato gripped the upper line and set both of his boots on the lower, sliding himself out a step or two.

He proceeded to jump up and down.

"Very strong? See? The Potato Mashers cut the old one. We make this ourselves."

Kazi watched, his confidence visibly faltering.

"You come? Yes? One at a time, please," Sala ordered. "Push down with the legs. Not like this."

He demonstrated letting his legs swing the rope out from beneath him, turning him horizontal, and laughed.

Kazi muttered something under his breath in Bangla.

With an admirable show of strength, Sala easily pivoted back into an upright position on the ropes. He worked his way along, sliding his gloved hands and feet until he reached the far side.

"Very good! I made it! Now you."

It was not so far, Lily assured herself—no more than fifteen feet.

The drop below was black, the extent of its depth concealed by shadows, but surely it could not be that terrible. Not if the Alpini had managed to climb down, cross over, and ascend to fix the ropes.

Then again, the Alpini were mountaineers capable of hauling a few tons of artillery up a cliff face.

"Would you rather I went first?" Strangford asked, removing his crampons.

"No, I would not," Kazi retorted, slinging his own crampons around his neck.

He removed his hat, exposing the dark waves of his hair, and set it on the ground. With an obvious force of will, he stepped out onto the line.

Wind tugged at the flaps of his coat, clearly stronger once out of the shelter of the tunnel mouth. Kazi wobbled slightly on his third step out and gripped the line more tightly, teeth gritted as he searched for balance. Finding it, he continued down the rope with grim determination before stepping off onto the opposite ledge.

"I'll follow you," Strangford promised.

Lily propped her walking stick by the wall and set her hands on the rope, looking down into the abyss.

It was a mistake. There was nothing below but darkness and an impossible wind. The sight of it sent a thrill of primal fear through her.

The onmyōdō danced gleefully in her chest.

She stepped out and was hanging over nothing.

The rope under her boots wanted to swing out from beneath her. Lily fought it, an effort that required a surprising amount of strength, managing to hold herself straight. She paused to breathe, then slowly, painstakingly, slid forward another step.

110

Her movements were small, her focus on them complete. Slide, grip, slide until abruptly Sala's hands were on her waist, the soldato neatly tugging her back onto solid ice.

"You are almost Alpini," he declared as he released her.

Lily found herself waiting beside Kazi, his usually neat hair a bit disheveled by the wind, as Strangford made his way across.

"A curious expedition you have led us on, Lady Strangford," he noted quietly.

Lily started with alarm.

"But it wasn't my idea," she protested. "I only wondered what was here."

"Was that all?"

The reply was casual, but something in it set her nerves tingling.

Strangford reached them, landing solidly, and they turned to the tunnel.

Sala's lantern illuminated the walls as they proceeded. Unlike the paths through the Austrian encampment, the floor here was not leveled, the uneven curves sloping sharply upward. Lily was glad she had put back on her crampons, the spikes allowing her to grip where otherwise she would have slid back down the length of it, falling out into the chasm.

As they climbed the slope of the tunnel, the hue began to change. Sala's lantern was no longer the only source of light. The walls themselves began to glow with a distorted and distant illumination.

It brightened as the tunnel ended, and Lily climbed out into a chamber the size of a ballroom. The enormous, shallow cavern sprawled through the interior of the glacier. Like a proper cave, there were ripples and strange formations which glowed a muted blue she deduced was actually sunlight filtering its way down through several feet of ice. The space extended for at least the length of a cricket pitch.

The floor beneath her boots rose and fell like waves caught in time. Further ahead, she could see areas where the ground had frozen flat and smooth as a skating rink.

This close to the surface, Sala's lantern was no longer strictly necessary. Lily found herself glad for it anyway, the glow providing a spark of warmth against a place made of eternal cold.

Sala led them into the cavern. They followed in an unconscious line like schoolchildren. As Lily picked her way across the floor, ragged objects became visible here and there under the surface.

She paused to take a closer look at one of them. Were they stones? A spill of some other debris?

"Ah, yes!" Sala said, noting her interest and coming over with the lantern. "You found one of them."

"One of what?" Kazi demanded from behind her.

"The dead," Sala returned.

The lantern light made it clear. Lily was looking at the bones of a human arm and hand. The ice that encased them was remarkably clear, revealing little scraps of tanned skin still attached to the fingers.

"Bring the light closer," Kazi ordered, crouching down for a better look.

Lily half expected to see him pull out one of the slender notebooks he had used to such damning effect in his investigation four years ago, but this was not a murder scene. The arm had obviously been there for a very long time—centuries, at least. Maybe even longer.

"Where did the rest of him end up?" Strangford asked curiously.

Lily swept her gaze across the floor. She could make out more dark patches scattered across the room.

"Are those all bodies?" she asked.

"Oh yes. Not the whole bodies. The pieces of them. They were sacrificed for the devil."

Even though she was skeptical of Sala's obviously imaginative explanation, she still felt both fascination and horror at realizing she was standing on top of a frozen field of the very ancient dead.

"What devil?" Kazi asked.

"The one they worship from the altar. There."

The soldato pointed. Kazi picked up the lantern, and the glow spilled across a dark hole. He moved closer, Lily following.

She found herself beside the bareheaded inspector, staring down at a ragged wound in the floor near the center of the grand, softly glowing chamber.

Kazi studied it thoughtfully, then swung the light onto a jumbled pile of broken chunks of ice shoved up against the wall a few yards away.

"This isn't natural. It was cut. They drove the stakes in right here."

He pointed at the marks in the surface, rose, and strode to the debris, examining it in turn.

"You can see where the waste pieces were broken here but sawed on the other side." He eyed the debris, calculating. "There isn't enough of it."

"They cut something out," Strangford offered.

The two men locked eyes across the dim, ice-bound room.

"Perhaps you might take a closer look," Kazi suggested, deceptively casual.

Sala was the only one in the cavern ignorant of what Kazi was truly asking.

After a brief, telling hesitation, Strangford answered.

"Certainly."

He removed his gloves, tucking them carefully into his pocket, then knelt at the side of the scar in the cavern floor. He ran his hands over the jagged edges, frowning distantly.

Lily eyed Sala, wondering what the young soldato would make of it. He appeared happily oblivious, pleased with his role as guide.

She imagined the cold seeping up into Strangford's fingers and shivered. It seemed too much to think his efforts would be worthwhile. The men who moved that ice would have used tools to do it, not their hands, and even those would have been gloved.

Kazi circled the hole with his lantern—and then she saw it, an odd striation discoloring the cut side perhaps twelve inches down. The dark horizontal line was thin as a bootlace and deep brown in hue.

"What's that?" she said before she could think better of it, pointing to the scar.

As she did, her onmyōdō brightened, humming inside her with a happy anticipation that left her colder than the glacier.

She fought the urge to take it back. She couldn't—not with Sala watching, with Kazi here. Not unless she wanted to reveal her own secret, and even then, what could she say?

My power to shape the future wants you to touch that line. Therefore, I think it is a terrible idea.

There was nothing to do but watch, frozen as the dead under her feet, as Strangford reached out and brushed his fingers across that ancient stain.

His shoulders tensed, hand going still as a deep shudder went through him.

Abruptly, the onmyōdō snapped, releasing her from a tension she hadn't fully known she was feeling.

There was only one explanation for that. Whatever pivot between futures she had been moving towards had passed. What came next was no longer a mere possibility.

Lily had chosen it.

"Anthony." she called, her voice weak from that unsettling realization.

Strangford drew back his fingers, taking a deep, slow breath as he collected himself. Slowly, he rose once more to his feet. As he tugged his gloves back over his hands, Lily could see they were shaking.

"I believe we have seen enough." Strangford's voice rasped from a dry throat.

~

Sala kept up a merry flow of chatter as they exited the long, grave-quiet tunnels. He had taken to Kazi, quizzing him on whatever popped into his head—where he was from, how he liked London, and the meaning behind all manner of English slang terms. Kazi offered his responses with perfunctory accuracy between casting thoughtful glances back at Strangford, who had quietly insisted on bringing up the rear of their climb. Lily would rather have walked beside him, but the narrow passageways and stairwells did not allow for it.

She made good practical use of her walking stick, which she had retrieved once they crossed back over the rope bridge. The climb up the mountainside from the glacier felt far steeper than it had on the way down. The combination of the exertion and the thin air left her breathless. Only the apparently indefatigable Sala seemed immune to it.

The sun had advanced far along its path to the horizon by the time the fortifications of the pass came into view. The strange, startling notes of someone singing floated across the air, the melody as haunting as the peaks that surrounded them.

"What is that?" Lily asked.

"He sings how the village sleeps, but the Alpini does not. And when he falls, he falls into the flowers," Sala explained with a shrug. "It is just one of our songs. We pass the time."

The melody broke off as she and the others rounded the path and the machine gun nest came into view. One of the men stationed there shouted down to the front line. The meaning of the response became clear when they reached the sandbag wall to find the hostile sergeant waiting for them with barely concealed impatience. He rattled off a string of orders at Sala as they arrived that set the private blushing.

"Your mules are gone," he translated, glancing a little sheepishly between them and the sergeant. "The tenente sent them back. It is too late for the road by mule. Sergente Galliavola, he will drive you in the lorry."

"I see," Kazi replied shortly. "Very kind of him."

The dismissal was clear. Their excursion to the glacier with Sala had obviously been seen as an overstep. Lily hoped the young man wouldn't face too much trouble for it.

"Thank you for all your assistance today." she said, offering the soldato her hand.

He took it, giving her an enthusiastic handshake.

"You are welcome, Signora."

"The proper term would be Donna, I believe," Strangford cut in. "You have been shepherding around a baroness today."

Lily grimaced at him, but Sala's eyes brightened in a way that told her he would almost certainly be bragging about this to his friends in a few moments.

"Her father is an earl," Kazi added, earning himself a glare.

"It is my honor, Donna. I am very pleased to have met you. Er . . . and now I think you must be going." Sala cast an awkward look back at his scowling sergeant.

"Signora!"

The green-eyed private from before had moved to one of the artillery posts. As Lily looked up at him, he tossed something down. She caught it instinctively—it was her hat. With a nod of thanks, she tossed the helmet she carried back at him in return.

Galliavola gestured impatiently for them to follow and stomped the rest of the way to the encampment. Another soldato lounged there against the side of a single remaining lorry parked by the scarred hostel. He dropped his cigarette as the sergeant approached, the colleagues he was gossiping with making themselves scarce.

Galliavola barked out an order, and the soldato snapped off a salute, hopping into the driver's seat. The sergeant pointed them into the rear of the lorry, an open compartment lined with wooden benches.

"Andiamo," he said, slapping the side of the vehicle. The lorry lurched into motion, Lily gripping her seat to keep from bouncing out as the encampment and its terrible mysteries receded behind them, gilded by the light of the descending sun.

~

They rattled into the square at the heart of Bormio, startling a cluster of pigeons into the air. Their driver yanked the brake, the lorry jerking to a stop. Kazi and Strangford descended, her husband offering her a gentlemanly hand. The soldato, a fresh cigarette hanging from his lip, gave them a wave as he circled around and headed back up the pass.

The evening light turned the whitewashed shops and houses a soft gold. Somewhere nearby, a church bell rang out the hour.

Kazi waited with barely concealed impatience as a pair of grandmothers ambled past. There had been no opportunity to talk in the lorry with the wind and the engine rushing at their ears, their conversation easily audible to the Alpini driver. Lily knew he must be in a fervor to hear what more Strangford could tell him.

Before he could demand it, Strangford spoke.

"I believe Lady Strangford and I should take a bit of air."

A slight tightening of Kazi's jaw was the only sign he gave of his frustration. Whatever objection he wished to make, he held it back with an uncomfortable glance at Lily, one that reminded her awkwardly of their conversation earlier that day.

"Of course," he said shortly. "We can discuss matters further in the morning."

Strangford motioned towards the darkening road.

"Shall we?" he offered.

"I suppose we'd better," Lily replied.

It was warmer in the village than on the pass, even with the night descending. The air still felt like spring, tinged with the scent of mountain primrose. Windows sparked to life around them like fireflies against the growing purple of the descending twilight. Lily could hear the families inside laughing, the sound startlingly normal. It felt like a fairy secret set apart from the rest of the world, even with the soldiers smoking cigarettes outside the boarding house where they were barracked.

"Would you tell me?" Strangford quietly asked once they had passed the smokers, the road wending towards the countryside. "I would rather hear that way. The way you might have chosen to share it."

"I don't know that there's anything to tell."

Strangford stopped, sympathy darkening his gaze.

"Lily."

"Kazi noticed I had been feeling ill. He made a supposition. I think he was rather embarrassed by it, actually." she added, trying to force a bit of lightness into her tone.

"But you do not know he's wrong."

"I mean, it's possible ..." she began, then caught herself, taking a breath. "It's been seven weeks."

He slipped his hand into the crook of her arm, tugging her gently back into a walk. The houses thinned out along the road, the mountains rising behind them, gray teeth cutting into the rich pink sky. Under the brim of his cap, Strangford's dark hair and eye patch blended with the deepening shadows. He looked up at the peaks, turning his face into the flower-scented breeze.

He didn't ask any more questions, just held her arm and walked. In the end, that was what did it—because had he wanted to, he could have spelled it all out with terrible precision.

"I'm terrified," she confessed, offering the words to the mountain evening, to the thin curls of woodsmoke and the ice on the peaks picking up the last shimmering rays of light.

"You don't know that it would happen again," he said quietly.

"I don't know that it won't," she countered sharply.

Strangford's hand moved down her arm. Gloved fingers slipped between her own.

"No," he agreed. "We don't."

The gently spoken words were the blow that took the wall down, spilling all that she had been holding inside. The sob welled up like a geyser. It burst from her lips, and she flung a hand to her mouth to try to keep it back . . . then remembered who she was with and dropped the hand again.

Strangford's arms slipped around her as the grief poured out. She let that old and terrible sadness fall into his shoulder as he held her. It was terribly selfish, knowing as she did that when she finally looked up at him again, she would see marks of the same pain on his face, too.

The flood slowed after a while. She became aware of the startling beauty of the place where they had stopped—the ordinary stretch of Alpine roadway with its comfortable little houses and flower-dotted fields framed by the silent majesty of the peaks.

The pain had not gone, but for a moment, it felt almost manageable.

"Can you tell if it's true?" she asked, already knowing the answer.

"No." Strangford stroked a long hand along her back. "I'm sorry."

She let him hold her a while longer. The sun had disappeared completely behind the mountains to the west. Only its echoes remained, painting the sky with brush strokes of gold and violet. Swallows darted overhead, quick black shadows dancing along the edge of the night.

"Have you considered whether you ought to go back?"

Strangford's tone was careful. Lily still tensed against it.

"I have," she admitted. "It would be the safest thing to do—if Kazi is right. But so long as you are here in Europe, you are in danger."

She raised a hand, forestalling his objection.

"And don't try to tell me you'll simply avoid the front lines. We both know you have become intent on following this wherever it takes you, unless something comes along to convince you it doesn't really matter."

Strangford looked down.

"It matters."

A chill skittered across her skin at his words.

"Kazi is very capable," she continued. "But I don't know how far you can trust him … and he is not the one who can see what's coming for you."

The breeze set the tiny Alpine flowers dancing in the fields that surrounded them, carrying the scent of snow.

The words burst out of her.

"I feel like I'm being asked to choose between the man I love and a life I don't even know is real yet."

"You know which one I would tell you to choose," Strangford softly returned, brushing his fingers from her temple to her cheek.

"You could try to be a bit less predictable," she snapped back.

He let out a bark of laughter, then leaned in to kiss her. She let herself fall into the warmth of it, even though it was not a solution.

There wasn't really any solution.

He pulled back, resting his forehead against her own, and she felt the weight come back into him.

"I think I know what killed the men on the pass."

The admission startled her.

"What was it?" she demanded.

He shook his head, looking away to the north.

"I need to speak to James Cairncross."

It was not what Lily had expected to hear. That frightened her a little—more than she had been frightened by all of this already.

"But he's in England. Do we have time for that?"

"I don't know," Strangford acknowledged darkly.

Lily took a breath, steeling herself for what was to come.

"Then we shall have to get him to France."

EIGHT

Monday, April 15
Morning
Bormio, The Italian Alps

$\mathcal{K}$AZI EXERCISED REMARKABLE patience. He did not come knocking on the door of their hotel room, demanding more answers from Strangford. He restrained himself until they descended to the breakfast room the following morning to find him quietly sipping his coffee. Even when they joined him, he did not press for answers, instead politely inquiring whether Lily had slept well and then presenting her with a plate of toast slathered with berry jam.

Lily ate it and felt better. She was still not sure what to think of that.

Only then did he ask whether Strangford might wish to take a stroll. The two men departed together, leaving Lily to pack. She already knew what Strangford would tell him—that the object the Austrians had cut from the ice had been a very ancient corpse.

He had shared it with her the night before after they returned to their room, taking a cold supper there together. The body had been felled in an encounter that took place when swords were forged from brass, preserved for centuries inside the glacier.

Why the Austrians had gone to the trouble of hauling it away with them remained a mystery—one that apparently James Cairncross could illuminate.

Strangford sent his wire when they changed trains in Milan. They arrived in Paris after dusk. Around them, shades were being drawn, the streets emptying of vehicles as the city descended into a blackout. A reply was waiting for them when they reached their hotel.

The lines were neatly typed in English. For all that, they were as coded as any intelligence briefing.

Your convergence will take place 22 stadia west of the double aleph at dusk under Wodin.

"What is that?" Kazi demanded, peering at the slip over Strangford's shoulder. "A horoscope?"

"Not exactly." Strangford returned, tucking the message into his pocket. "Tell me, Inspector, what is our most direct route to Gravelines?"

That was how two nights later, Lily found herself standing with Strangford on a remote stretch of sand along the northern coast of France.

Strangford had explained it to her—how the aleph was the ancient root of the letter A, two of which spelled out the name of the River Aa. It ran through a hundred or so miles of Normandy before empty-ing into the sea at Gravelines. Twenty-two Roman stadia worked out to roughly two and a half miles, and Wodin was the God for whom Wednesday had been named in the original old English.

It was an exhaustingly arcane encryption, one entirely appropri-ate to Cairncross.

Kazi had not been pleased to be left behind at the farmhouse where they had found lodgings for the evening. The rambling stone building was located outside the old fortified port of Gravelines, where all the proper inns had been commandeered to house soldiers.

"Neither of you are trained investigators," he had noted irritably. "This source of yours might provide information you would over-look but that I would recognize as significant."

His tone had been sharp enough to alarm a pair of nearby goats, who paused in their chewing to glare at him suspiciously.

As much as Lily loathed to admit it, the inspector had a point. He was trained in interrogation, and this was his investigation.

Strangford was immovable.

"He won't speak to you."

There was nothing James Cairncross loved more than an opportunity to share his extensive knowledge of all things historical or supernatural with a willing audience. He would never be so thoughtless as to share anything personal about Lily and the other charismatics with a stranger, so what could Strangford possibly want to ask him about that Cairncross wouldn't want the inspector to hear?

Kazi hadn't liked it, but he had contained himself to one tense, careful objection.

"You realize how much depends upon this."

"I think perhaps I know even better than you," Strangford quietly returned.

Kazi had no response to that. After all, for all his skill as an intelligence agent, only one member of their party had actually experienced the horror of what had happened on the pass.

The place where Lily now stood was a deserted stretch of coastline about an hour's walk from Gravelines. There was not so much as a spark of light from any house or village, nothing but windswept dunes and soft sand meeting the quiet rush of the waves of the channel.

The sky was streaked with pink and violet fading into starry cobalt. Lily resisted the urge to ask Strangford for the time once more. Perhaps they had misunderstood Cairncross's message. Wodin might have referred to some obscure medieval battlefield or the aleph a Kabbalistic secret, and they might be waiting at the wrong place.

Then the gentle quiet of the coast was broken by the low thrum of a diesel engine.

The boat was nearly invisible coming towards them across the water, shadowed by the descending twilight. It was a small blue fishing craft and stopped a fair distance out. A lean, dark figure slid over the rail. The water he landed in reached only to his knees, and Lily realized that the decline of the shore must be long and shallow for some distance out into the waves.

He moved toward them through the quiet surf as the boat turned, pulling back out to sea.

James Cairncross had not changed much since Lily had met him four years earlier. His cropped silver hair and tidy mustache were relics of a long-past military service he never voluntarily spoke of, his tall frame only a little stooped by time.

"My lord," he said in greeting. "Lady Strangford."

"It is good to see you, old friend," Strangford replied, offering the former librarian of The Refuge his gloved hand.

"Shall we get to it, then? Adler will be back in an hour."

Eddie Adler was a former cavalryman who had fought with Cairncross in Afghanistan. He had once helped them rid the world of a batch of medical records soaked in the blood of murder. Lily had wondered then whether Adler subsidized his fishing income with a bit of light smuggling. She supposed now she had her answer. Only someone experienced in passing unnoticed through these waters would have attempted it now, with the channel crisscrossed by Royal Navy patrols prowling for rogue U-boats. Adler had risked both his life and his boat by coming here.

Cairncross could not have made it otherwise. Passports were required for passage on any regular boat, and they were very hard to acquire.

It would have been far safer to arrange to talk to him by telephone. Clearly, that hadn't been an option. Lily supposed that came down to the censors who monitored every communication from France. Whatever Strangford wanted to speak with him about, he didn't want the censors to overhear it.

Her old friend was barefoot, his trousers neatly rolled up to his knees. They were still well-dampened from his trek through the waves. The breeze tugged at the silver fringe of his hair above his weathered face.

"I am sorry to have put you to such trouble," Strangford said.

"When you wired me about an appointment in France I had no recollection of ever making, I assumed the matter must be important," Cairncross returned wryly.

Strangford's response was uncharacteristically solemn.

"It's about Afghanistan."

Cairncross went very still as Lily wrangled with her own confusion.

She knew Cairncross had served with a calvary unit during the war there forty years earlier. Adler still occasionally slipped up and called him "Sergeant." But what could Afghanistan possibly have to do with the attack on the Stelvio Pass?

She felt a thrill of warning that this conversation was not going to be what she had expected.

Cairncross was uncharacteristically slow to respond. Lily was surprised to realize that what she saw on his face as he looked at Strangford was anger—anger and a little fear.

"I assume your inquiry is prompted by something more than prurient curiosity," Cairncross bit out, each word edged with steel as he glared at the younger man.

"I would not ask it of you otherwise."

Some other conversation was taking place between the spare words her husband and the librarian exchanged, one that Lily was not privy to. Whatever they were truly discussing, Cairncross did not welcome it.

Lily found herself wondering whether perhaps she ought to have stayed back at the farmhouse with Kazi.

Cairncross's posture slid from one of stiff defense into defeat, his shoulders curling forward. He looked down the long, twilit stretch of deserted sand. There was no one in sight, not so much as a lone fisherman, only the whispering sea and the rustle of stiff grass along the dunes under a purpling sky.

"Let's walk," he said flatly and set off.

They fell into step beside him, Lily's pace quickening to keep up with the stride of Cairncross's long legs.

"How much do you already know?" he demanded after they had gone a little distance.

"I know what you are," Strangford returned bluntly. "And I know what that means to you."

Cairncross halted, drawn up short. He closed his eyes, his arms coming around his chest as though Strangford's words were weapons cutting loose the bonds of an old and terrible pain.

Lily had to work to conceal her own shock. This meeting wasn't about probing Cairncross's brain for arcane knowledge. It was about something Strangford had stumbled across with the relentless sensitivity of his hands—something Cairncross had not wanted to share.

I know what you are.

"Have you seen ... " he began, then stopped as the words failed him.

Beside him, Strangford's shoulders were heavy as he looked down at the sand. Now that she was beginning to understand, Lily could read his signals clearly.

He hated this—and of course, he must. Strangford took such pains to avoid discovering secrets, particularly those of the people he loved, and ferociously guarded any truths that managed to slip past his defenses. To bring up such a discovery now, like this, told her much about just how serious the matter must be.

"Only in fragments," Strangford replied. His jaw tensed with some deeper emotion. "I hope you understand I was not looking for it."

"No," Cairncross agreed wearily. "You wouldn't have been."

Lily's patience finally broke.

"I don't understand. What does that mean—'What you are?'"

"I'm a berserker, Lily." Cairncross replied.

A wind off the sea tugged at his coat. The waves rolled relentlessly from the sea as Lily stood numbed by surprise.

A berserker.

The word was a fragment of myth, of nightmare tales of men with the strength and viciousness of rabid beasts that peppered manuscripts like the one Portia Eversleigh had browsed one memorable evening in the library at Taddiford.

Except that it was Cairncross himself who had once told her that berserkers weren't just fantasy—that the world had once known warriors gifted with a form of khárisma that granted them extraordinary strength, indifference to pain or injury, and animalistic brutality.

She remembered the winter chill of the deserted garden at The Refuge as Cairncross gazed out over the high walls to someplace he clearly wished he could forget. His voice echoed through the back of her mind.

A berserker in full battle rage could tear a man in half with his bare hands.

Cairncross had listed it with the charismatic powers of history that had not survived to the present, whether by the will of Ash's Parliament of Stars or the mere mechanics of evolution.

Berserkers still felt like they belonged with tales of dragons and magic swords, not the very real and present fact of a dull old scholar she had known for years. Cairncross taught schoolgirls about the Reformation during the day and retired to his book-stuffed flat in the evenings to translate manuscripts from Medieval French for the fun of it.

"You said they were extinct," Lily protested.

"I told you they were no longer spoken of." Cairncross corrected her sharply. "That doesn't mean they're gone."

"But you don't even fight!"

"I don't fight," Cairncross returned wearily, "Because if I started, I would not stop until everyone around me was dead."

The words were not a threat or a boast but a banal reporting of fact. They were all the more terrible for it.

The shore still sprawled in untouched solitude for miles to either side. Against the dark cloth of the sky overhead, the stars began to blink into life with a small and indifferent gleam.

Nothing had changed except that Cairncross was a monster. He had always, quietly, been a monster . . . just like the rest of them.

"Why didn't you say anything?" she demanded.

"Because I have done all I could these past four decades to forget it," he admitted, voice hoarse.

"How much can you tell us?" Strangford prompted.

The gentle consideration in his voice spoke volumes, reminding Lily that Strangford would have absorbed more than just the fact of Cairncross's monstrosity from whatever accidental contact had revealed his secrets. He would also know how he felt about it. What it meant to him.

"I can tell you all of it," Cairncross returned. "But it won't be pleasant."

Strangford didn't press him, waiting with solemn patience for him to continue. When he finally did, Cairncross's voice rang of defeat.

"There was a mutiny in 1879," he began, shoving his hands in his pockets as he looked down the deserted shore. "The British Resident of Kabul was slaughtered by his own troops. There were a series of executions, of course, once the mutineers were overcome. They had the unfortunate side-effect of uniting the Afghans against us. My regiment was stationed at an unfinished encampment in Sherpur, just outside the city, when we received word that an army of roughly ten thousand had massed for an attack."

Behind his craggy profile, the sea was nothing but a dark line merging with the horizon.

"If they came at us in force, we would be overwhelmed. The regiments needed time to mount our defenses, and so the decision was made to send a detachment of cavalry out to attack."

"How many." Strangford. asked.

There was an odd weight to the question as though he already suspected the answer.

"One hundred and seventy." Cairncross replied.

The number staggered her.

"One hundred and seventy men against ten thousand?" she exclaimed. "That sounds like suicide."

"We were better armed and mounted," Cairncross countered tiredly. "But yes. It was understood we were to hold to the last man to buy those at the fort as much time as possible to prepare."

The casual sacrifice of it struck her cold—living men turned into an expendable calculation.

"How weren't you killed?" she demanded.

"Most of us were," he snapped.

"But not you," Strangford cut in carefully.

"No," Cairncross affirmed with a sideways and unhappy look. "When the attack was called, and we met with the enemy, I . . . changed."

There was a pain in him Lily had never heard before, not even in the moments where his grief for Ash had been revealed.

He returned to walking across the sand. His tone slipped deliberately into the mode of a lecture in a clear effort to distance himself from what he described.

"When berserkers are described in history, we often hear of a dramatic physical transformation that occurs when their charismatic ability is active. The Irish called it the *riastrad*—the distortion. A dramatic shifting of muscle and hair and tissue that turn the warrior into something no longer recognizably human. The Woden's Men of Scandinavia raged like dogs and were impervious to iron and fire, stripping themselves naked and dancing on the eve of battle. There are similar stories in China, Thrace, Assyria, even among the Aztecs, of men with the heads of beasts who howled like the damned as they charged. My own transformation could not have been so dramatic, or the men would have noticed. But I do know that I screamed."

He halted there, the awfulness of that memory fracturing the facade of academic distance he had been clinging to. It took him a moment to rebuild it, but the truth of what he felt about this history continued to bleed in through the cracks.

"I studied the way of the Tao. Not so well as Robert," he noted with a flash of grief. "But I have wondered before how the concept of shén might apply to certain charismatics."

"Shén?" Lily asked.

"Shén is . . . that part of ourselves which transcends the physical," he explained. "The substance that makes up the forces that move the universe."

"The Parliament of Stars," Lily filled in.

The words felt like a curse. It was as though by speaking them, Lily summoned someone or something that must now be listening to this terrible conversation on the beach—lending uncanny weight to a moment that blinked as the merest spark in an endless expanse of time.

"In the mythos of the Tao, there is an understanding that some of the gods were once men. That they . . . transcended through endeavor or the long accumulation of wisdom. But many of them are also described as having possessed extraordinary abilities when still in mortal life."

"You think they were like us," Lily offered, remembering Cairncross's other stories of saints, witches, and heroes.

"I think they may once have been like us," Cairncross confirmed. "And upon reaching the outer limits of the potential of their power, they became . . . something else. Something no longer entirely human. Something that might not recognize the life it once lived. The people it left behind."

The breeze picked up, setting the waves of her hair into a dance.

The air carried with it the breath of the sea and a memory of salt and grass, of endless twilight and the call of a carrion-eater.

"I cannot tell you how many men I killed in front of the Sherpur cantonment," Cairncross continued. "I can't tell you because I was not myself anymore when it happened. I was not James Cairncross. I had evolved into something else, something that cared nothing for the consequence of a single mortal life—what it meant. Whom it would leave behind. I cared only for destruction—the sheer principle of it—and for the taste of blood on my tongue."

"Taste?" Lily echoed.

The word was terrible on her lips.

"I was armed with sword and pistol—a Colt revolver. When I checked it after the battle I had only fired one round."

"You didn't ... " Lily swallowed thickly, forcing the words out. "You didn't use it?"

"No." Cairncross's blue gaze was pale and haunted as he looked at her. "I used my sword. My hands. My teeth."

He contained himself, fighting for distance, but it did not feel distant to Lily. Nor would it have been so for Strangford, who must have touched echoes of these memories at some point in the past. Brushing up against the wrong book in the library, perhaps, or on the night they spent together once in Cairncross's old bed in the deserted heart of The Refuge.

"They thought I was a hero," Cairncross continued bitterly. "I couldn't buy a drink for myself for months after. The man who held back the Afghan horde. They had to issue me a new uniform. They couldn't get the blood out of the old one."

He looked down at his weathered, ink-stained hands, then slipped them back into his pockets. He turned back to the sea as though seeking solace in the regular motion of the waves.

"We were sent to Lahore on leave. I sought company. Found it in a dashing glassblower from Amritsar."

Lily could read between the lines of the story. She found it did not shock her.

"We became rather intoxicated over the course of our evening together. Then as I was stumbling back to my inn, I was set upon by a group of thieves. There were eight of them. I was unarmed."

Dread crept in. She cast a glance at Strangford, but his face was impassive. That was enough to tell her he already knew something of what Cairncross was about to share.

"The next thing I remember is being covered in blood in the alley, the eight of them torn apart around me. Some had been grown men. Not all. Two could not have been more than fourteen—mere children."

His voice cracked on the word.

"And that is where Robert found me."

"Ash was there?" Lily blurted.

"Our first meeting," Cairncross confirmed with a bitter smile. "He was clever enough to be carrying a pistol and lucky enough to arrive just after the ... episode had ended. And so I begged him to kill me."

Beside her, Strangford muttered a curse.

"He refused," Lily guessed.

Cairncross laughed. It was a terribly sad sound.

"Well. You know how he was."

Lily did. The thought of it filled her with an old grief and resentment.

"He suggested we might find a cure for it," Cairncross said. "We couldn't, of course. I accepted that years later, but by then, I had learned I could survive with it if I stayed clear of any possibility of a conflict. It seemed to me that I must be the last of them—the Ulfheðnar. If I could endure the rest of my days in the quiet of a library, then I and my kind might pass from the world without leaving any more terrible of a mark on it."

The words fell into the night air like a prayer, melting into the rustling of the seagrass before he turned to Strangford, his weathered face drawn.

"But that is not the case. Is it?"

"I suspect not," Strangford replied.

The chill ran across Lily's skin, even under the warmth of her coat. It all made sense now—Strangford's reticence after their visit to the pass and the need for this dangerous meeting on the coast.

They're screaming.

The monsters in the dark.

Strangford had dragged this wretched history out of an old friend because he suspected the true nature of the shifting, nightmarish impressions he had drawn from the catatonic lieutenant in Paris and the stones of the Stelvio Pass. The outpost had not been attacked by some new German weapon but by nightmares out of fairy tales, relics of an ancient and best-forgotten past.

The Ulfheðnar. The wolf-men. The unstoppable warriors who bathed in the blood of their dead.

"Who?" Cairncross demanded, rigid with urgency. "Where?"

"They attacked two platoons of Alpini on the Stelvio Pass, outside Bormio," Strangford replied. "Most of them wore nothing, but at least one of the victims saw pieces of a German uniform on the man who killed him. The pass is held by Austro-Hungarian forces, but this . . . unit must be organized out of Berlin. I would estimate there are perhaps twenty of them."

"Twenty." Cairncross whispered.

A shudder went through him, an impulse of visceral horror.

Twenty. It should be a mere drop of water in a war that had cost the lives of millions of men.

It very clearly was not.

Cairncross pushed back his ghosts, gaining focus.

"Whether they physically transform or not, once they are engaged in battle, they will no longer be men," he warned urgently. "Wounds alone will not stop them. They won't feel the pain. They'll keep going until it becomes physically impossible for them to do so. They are far stronger than ordinary men. Some of the tales tell of skin that toughens like leather, becoming its own sort of armor. And they are fast."

His eyes closed, flinching against the pain of memory until he forced them open again.

"You must seize any opportunity you are given to kill them. Focus your damage on areas that make it impossible for the body to function. The spine. The head. A shattered knee might slow them, but they will not stop. They will keep dragging themselves forward until they have destroyed everyone in their path. Do you understand me?"

Lily realized his fists were shaking.

Her thoughts stalled in an alley in Lahore, in a moment of decision Robert Ash must have confronted as he faced a scene from Hell. He would have been entirely justified to pull the trigger, whether in self-defense or as an act of justice for the boys Cairncross had slaughtered. Instead, he had given him another chance and gained forty years of friendship.

"Isn't there some way to break them out of it?" she asked.

"Dying," Cairncross snapped in return. "Along with everyone around you. The only way I've kept from slaughtering more people is to avoid anything that looks remotely like a war."

He turned to Strangford, biting out his last words.

"I cannot help you with this."

"You already have," Strangford replied.

"You know what I mean."

There was no answer to that. Beyond the hush of the waves came the distant sound of Adler's engine.

"He's back already." Lily said.

"The moon is rising." Cairncross nodded towards the horizon where a fragment of the white orb had just peered over the line of the sea.

It made sense, of course. An old smuggler like Adler would know how long he had before the light would reveal him.

The boat itself came into view. It slowed thirty feet out, waiting in the long shallows of the beach.

Cairncross hesitated.

"I have been watching for signs of another berserker for forty years, and you must know that I am a very careful watcher. I have never heard so much as a whisper of their existence. To have twenty suddenly appear in the ranks of the enemy ... " He let his voice trail off. "There is something unnatural in this."

"Thank you," Strangford replied, the words as solemn as the blessing of a priest.

Cairncross stepped into the water, then glanced back, his eyes on Lily.

"You must not hope that you can save them. If you choose to face them, you must accept that you are there to kill or to die. You must hold nothing back. If you are not prepared to accept all that might cost you—"

"What do you mean?" she demanded, the feeling of sudden urgency laced through with something colder.

He was silent for a moment, considering as the sea swirled around his ankles.

"Your khárisma, Miss Albright," he began, reverting to the habit of her old name in the tension of his thought. "Your onmyōdō. I believe there may be . . . more that it might do. Something against which the wrath of a berserker would break like the tide. But I do not know what reaching it might cost."

"I don't understand," Lily replied—and yet something inside of her hummed with recognition. She found herself recalling the gloaming place between life and death, the one part of her Strangford could never touch. There had been a moment when the birth of a new power had threatened to spill further, farther, remaking her into something she did not think she would have recognized—as though the woman she knew herself to be was a shell that could only contain so much before it shattered.

She thought of the gods that marched across Evangeline Ash's ceiling in The Refuge, hidden behind a door walled up with lathe and plaster like the entrance to a tomb. It had been years since Lily had seen it, but she could still recall with painstaking detail the gilded profiles suspended among the stars, indifferent to the struggles of those that moved below.

Cairncross's face was bleak, aged by old heartbreak.

"Stay away from them. If you possibly can," he urged.

"And if we can't?" Strangford pressed from beside her.

"Then pray to whatever gods hold your favor," Cairncross replied. "And I will do the same."

He did not wait for an answer. He waded the rest of the way out, accepting the hand of the man in the boat who believed him to be a hero. The craft turned in near silence and faded into the darkness over the sea.

NINE

Wednesday April 17
Night
Outside Gravelines, France

"Berserkers," Kazi said slowly, leaning against the mantel and gazing down into the fire.

They were gathered around the hearth in the low, stone-walled farmhouse. It was old and solid, the furnishings well-maintained but obviously aged. Lily nestled into a sofa softened by layers of quilts, finishing a cold bowl of beans and leftover winter root vegetables brightened by a few spring herbs. It was her second of the evening. She caught Kazi glancing at her as she ate and flamed with a quick embarrassment, knowing he must take it as further confirmation that she was indeed pregnant.

They had been traveling. Traveling made one hungry.

The mistress of the house was washing dishes in the kitchen. Her husband had been killed in an earlier war. Her grown sons now fought in this one. So far, they were both alive. Lily knew she considered herself lucky.

Kazi had taken all of it far better than Lily had thought he would.

It was still odd to see him with his hat off, his thick brown hair revealed as though he were a friend paying a call and not the formal police inspector with whom they were forced to collaborate.

Strangford had told him everything they knew about berserkers, save for the fact that Cairncross had been one of them. She still had a hard time imagining the old librarian as a killing machine.

Though he refrained from dismissing Strangford's story out of hand, Kazi was far from comfortable with it. From her spot on the sofa, she watched him probe at it, torn between his skepticism and his logic.

"Is it a disease? Some sort of mental disorder?" he asked.

"I think it's rather more than that," Strangford replied.

"A hereditary condition, perhaps?"

"There is no evidence to indicate that it is hereditary."

Kazi continued to press, searching for more facts he could set his intellectual teeth into.

"What about weaknesses? Vulnerabilities?"

"None that we are aware of."

Kazi's fingers drummed restlessly against the ancient wood of the mantel. When interrogating a suspect, Lily knew he was relentless, seeking out different angles or ways to trip up his subject and manipulate them into revealing more than they intended to. Strangford was a collaborator this time, but Kazi still sought more comfortable ground as he shifted tactics.

"Your friend," he pressed. "How does he know so much about this?"

The question cut rather too close for Lily's comfort.

"He is a scholar who has extensively researched the subject," Strangford replied.

"A scholar?" Kazi echoed skeptically.

"He knows what he's talking about," Strangford returned deliberately.

Kazi's eyes narrowed thoughtfully, and Lily felt a kick of alarm. Still, it would be a long way for even Kazi's quick-knitting mind to leap from scholar to frenzied rage warrior out of myth.

"They took no advantage out of their victory." he noted. "They wiped out the opposition. The pass was theirs, and they did not claim it."

The fire crackled softly behind him, footsteps creaking on the floorboards upstairs as the old widow went to bed for the night.

"A weapon may be made of flesh as much as steel. It was a test." He leveled his gold-tinted gaze at her.

"It would appear it was successful," Strangford added.

Faced with that, Lily finally voiced the question that had been haunting her since their conversation with Cairncross.

"How did they find so many of them?"

Her words cast a sinister pall over the warmth of the fire and the whistle of the wind against the solid, ancient walls. Even the bric-a-brac in the cabinets and the worn carpets on the floor seemed to be waiting.

The light glinted off the silver threads in Strangford's hair. He looked tired. What he had seen on the pass still haunted him.

Kazi straightened.

"We need more information," he concluded. "Whether there have been any rumors of these berserkers. News on the German side of an Austrian victory in the Alps in March. Unusual recruitment efforts. Do you have a secure way to contact NID?"

"If I'm shipboard," Strangford replied. "The Relentless was docking in Calais when we passed through this morning. I've traveled with Captain Hawthorne before. He should grant me permission to use his signals room. You?"

"I can send a telegram from the civilian office in Calais."

Lily felt certain that Kazi's civilian telegram would be written in cipher and sent to a mock address before it found its way to the secret location where the SSB had its headquarters.

"There is one other potential source of information we might query." she offered.

She didn't need to elaborate. Both Kazi and Strangford knew exactly whom she was talking about.

"Can you contact him safely." Kazi demanded.

Lily considered the problem. She didn't have a scrambled wireless network like Strangford or a clever encryption like Kazi. Then again, she and her source had another sort of code, one based on their own unique shared history.

"I can," she said.

~

The next morning found them in Calais. The port city felt busier than it had when they landed a week before. But a week before, the Allies had still held Armentières and Messines. Now the front was reduced by miles, thousands more men were dead, and the Germans showed no sign of relenting. The troops landing here were clearly mobilizing as the new arrivals were rushed to reinforce the front.

The wounded waiting on the docks had increased both in number and in the severity of their injuries.

The ship Strangford sought was still in port. It was a destroyer painted gray with its bold white designation numbers on the side. A tall signals antenna was framed by the three diesel stacks.

Strangford approached the gangplank, exchanging a few words with the sailor on duty there. He had deliberately worn his uniform, a calculated move to prevent him from being tossed out on sight.

A few moments later, an officer appeared. He and Strangford shook hands before heading up toward the bridge.

With Strangford safely off, Lily and Kazi joined the queue in front of the telegraph office.

She found herself hesitant to strike up a conversation as they waited, which she knew wasn't entirely fair. She was still far from happy about being blackmailed into this expedition but had to admit that Kazi hadn't been wrong about the urgency of the situation. In fact, it seemed that the matter was even more specifically suited to Lily and Strangford's history and skills than he could possibly have suspected. Since their arrival, he had been nothing but even-tempered and professional. He had held good on his promise to keep his knowledge of Strangford's peculiar talents to himself, even though it must cause him some conflict with his superiors and with other intelligence agents like Captain Hume back in Paris.

She was wondering if perhaps she ought to take the opportunity to apologize to him for her simmering hostility through the early days of their trip when he spoke.

"You should consider returning to England. There's a passenger steamer docked at the Bassin Carnot leaving for Dover on the outgoing tide," he continued. "Your passport has an open return date. They should permit you on board."

Her fury was quick. She bit back her first retort, conscious that they were in a line of people. Even speaking English, the nature of what she wanted to say would have been discernible by the tone.

"We aren't done," she seethed lowly instead.

"Your circumstances have changed."

She did not need to ask what circumstance he referred to. For a moment, she considered it. If she truly was pregnant, did she have any right to stay? She had lost one child and nearly given up on the possibility of another. She should be doing everything she could to protect this one—if it was even real.

And if it wasn't, she might run back to England and lose her husband in the process.

Like an unwelcome bird tapping at the window, Cairncross's words continued to haunt her.

Your onmyōdō. At the extreme end of what it promises—of what it might allow . . .

The telegraph office clerk called out, and the line shuffled forward. The man behind her coughed into his handkerchief as Lily was wrenched between dueling obligations—to the child that might be. Her husband. Her heart.

And the power that simmered under her skin, whispering of terrible possibilities.

She felt as though she were quietly drowning.

Kazi moved forward another step, her feet drawing her after him of their own accord.

"Unless, of course, there is something else you might offer this expedition that has not yet been made clear," he added casually.

Her head whipped around to meet that careful, assessing gaze as her pulse pounded, rabbit-like.

He knows, she thought desperately, then caught herself, aware he must already be measuring the significance of every nuance of her reaction. He could not possibly know.

He suspects.

It was threat enough. What response could she make him that would not give her away? A denial could be just as revealing as a confession to this man.

She was saved by the call of the telegram clerk.

"Suivant!"

Kazi turned to the window to send his message. He walked out after paying, not bothering to look back. Propelled by the inexorable momentum of the queue, Lily took her place at the clerk's window.

She realized with a start that she hadn't yet determined how to send her own question without alarming the censors.

"Oui?" the telegram clerk prompted her with routine impatience.

The solution snapped into her head. She picked up the pencil and scribbled out a single line.

Has our mutual friend from Limehouse made any mention of monsters?

The addressee was neatly printed at the top of the page.

Ld. Torrington, St. James, London

She handed the slip to the clerk. The girl scanned the text, raising a plucked eyebrow.

"Monstres?"

Lily forced a thin smile.

"Oui."

"C'est fou," the girl concluded and passed the message back to her colleagues.

~

Lily found Kazi lingering on the pavement. As she emerged from the telegram office, he handed her a cone of newspaper stuffed with hot chips.

"Frites," he said as though they required explanation.

She recognized it as a peace offering, however humble and tersely presented. It would have been poor compensation for being shunted onto a boat back to England . . . but she was also hungry.

She took the chips. They were crisp, oily, and delicious.

"Aren't you going to have any." she thought to ask after a few bites.

There was just a hint of longing in Kazi's eyes as he glanced over at the cart of the frites vendor.

"He's using lard," he replied.

"Ah. They're not halal."

Kazi raised an eyebrow.

"You're familiar with the laws of the Islamic diet?"

"Er ... not exactly." Lily managed.

She was searching for an excuse for why she would know more about the subject of halal butchery than most other Christian Englishwomen when she recalled that she didn't need it.

"It's Anthony's wardrobe," she explained. "It requires certain ... considerations when sourcing materials."

"Oh," Kazi replied automatically—then paused, his eyes widening with something almost like excitement as he solved the puzzle. "*Oh*. Because the humane methods of slaughter required by the Faith would minimize the amount of pain impressed into the skin."

He shot Lily a look of admiration.

"That is fiendishly clever of him. I suppose I must know the butcher. There are only two in the city that follow halal practices, and Lord Strangford's gloves are of kid leather ..."

Lily stared at him, a chip forgotten halfway way to her mouth.

"You really can't help it, can you?" she said wonderingly.

"What?"

"Trying to understand everything."

He looked a bit uncomfortable.

"I'm not sure that I—"

Lily cut him off as more pieces clicked into place.

"You didn't go digging for Anthony's secret because you thought you could use it. You couldn't help yourself. There were questions, and you had to answer them."

A quiet surprise softened some of the hard, determined lines from his face. He appeared to be struggling a bit for a response when the telegraph clerk popped her head out of the door.

"Madame Strangford?" she called.

"Oui?" Lily replied, not bothering to correct the misuse of her title as a surname.

The girl handed her a folded piece of paper. She had received a reply.

It had never occurred to her that it might come so quickly, but of course her father would have set up a system to ensure he received prompt word of any messages. No lesser efficiency would suit a man who quietly manipulated the strings of the entire British government.

She thrust the frites at Kazi. He held them with barely concealed impatience as she opened the missive.

It took only a moment to read.

He snatched the page as she extended it to him, scanning quickly over the single line typed across the top, four words Lily had already memorized.

See George Montreuil Sunday

"George?" he asked as he looked up at her.

"My brother," Lily replied. "Shall we go fetch Anthony."

~

Despite its name, Montreuil-sur-Mer lay inland a few miles southeast of the port of Etaples. Four years ago, it had been a quaint town ringed by a fine medieval wall, largely dominated by the long dormitories and classroom buildings of France's military academy. The town had been expanded by the war with a sprawl of muddy encampments, while inside the walls lay the General Headquarters of the British Army, the brain that oversaw the entirety of its operations on the continent.

The train did not go as far as Montreuil. Lily, Strangford, and Kazi reached their destination by way of a dairy cart driven by a pair of oxen. Lily sat up front with the driver, Strangford and Kazi folded into the rear between clusters of milk tins.

The road to the town was lined with hospital tents buzzing with activity. Doctors barked urgent orders, their surgical smocks splattered with blood, the facilities crowded with casualties from the recent German attacks. One of the tents was hung with painted signs that designated it a quarantine area for the terrible flu that had begun to crop up that past winter.

Amid and between it all were the refugees. Women, children, and the elderly fleeing the advance made their way here, lining up for rations or medical care at the Red Cross tent. Some were ragged, others well-dressed and guarding wheelbarrows loaded with their valuables. It was curious what people would not leave behind, clothing and livestock sitting side-by-side with a rolled-up rug, a painting, and even a brass chandelier.

The traffic slowed to a snarl at the approach to the gates of the town, where a cluster of soldiers guarded the entrance. Some were positioned on the walls with rifles and machine guns ready, a disconcerting sight somewhat mollified by their obvious boredom. A sergeant marched up and down the line of carts, couriers, and tradesmen, shouting with authority for everyone to queue up and be patient.

Two young privates flanking the gate reviewed the credentials of everyone who wished to go inside.

Lily hopped down from the cart as Strangford pushed a few coins at their driver, which were accepted after a token refusal.

"Your business, please," droned the straight-backed, long-nosed private at the gate.

"Lord and Lady Strangford to see Captain George Carne," Strangford announced. "Accompanied by Inspector Tariq Kazi of Scotland Yard."

"Scotland Yard?" the private echoed, looking up at them skeptically. "What's he doing out here? Or a lady, for that matter?"

"The list, dolt," hissed the soldier beside him, nodding to the clipboard the long-nosed lad had momentarily forgotten he held in his hand.

"Yes. Right," he said, recovering himself. "Adams! Open a line to Captain Carne and let him know his guests are here. You may wait over there."

He pointed them to an open area inside the gate.

They passed through the solid stone walls into the bustling town. The streets were busy with a mix of townspeople and a great many uniformed officers. A Daimler with a general zipped past as a baker set out a new tray of rolls and a housewife shooed a few chickens back into the narrow yard of her home.

"Lord and Lady Strangford? I am Lance Corporal Lewis."

The announcement came from a lean, ginger-haired soldier of perhaps thirty. He held himself with a visible self-possession amid the busy foot traffic by the gate.

"I am Captain Carne's batman. I shall see you to his office. This way, please."

They fell into step behind the lance corporal as he plunged them into a twisting warren of streets he clearly knew well. A few supply lorries rumbled past. Lily stepped aside for a young lieutenant clutching a box of file folders, the man all but sprinting down the pavement.

They reached a part of the town dominated by long institutional buildings of pale stone framing a green exercise lawn. Lewis stopped at a door set in one of the structures and motioned them inside.

It was like entering the heart of a complex and noisy machine. The hall seethed with activity. Runners hurried past with bundles of papers, trolleys zipping along. Half-drunk teacups with a skin of milk on top balanced on crates of papers stacked in the hall. Through it all was a pervasive smell of cigarettes.

A racket of voices mingled with the clatter of typewriters and ringing telephones. Men in uniforms gathered in clusters that pressed against the walls with easy instinct to make way for the constant rush of traffic up and down the tiled floors.

Strangford was less than perfectly comfortable with diving into the close-packed chaos. He braced himself against it with a breath, moving neatly out of the way of a barreling private who could barely see over the top of his overloaded tea tray.

Lewis finally stopped at an open doorway, making two crisp raps against the frame.

"Lord and Lady Strangford with Inspector Tariq Kazi for you, sir," he announced formally.

Far less formally, a blond head poked out from the doorway and was immediately split by a blinding grin.

"Sister!" Captain George Carne exclaimed.

He bounded forward and plucked Lily from the ground in a hug so fierce it nearly made her drop her walking stick.

The term still sounded strange to her ears, as though Lily couldn't quite believe she deserved it. After all, for much of her life contact with her father's other children had been as forbidden as a dream. Her four half-brothers had been nothing but names in the society pages to her.

It had been four years now since George had apologetically thrust himself into her life. The start of that nascent relationship had more or less coincided with the rise of the war. Since then, George had made it a point to see her every time he had been granted leave, usually over a curry at a favorite house of his in Holborn. George always ordered his dinners as hot as possible and spent half the meal happily wheezing.

It still surprised her to have family who went out of their way to be close to her, but there was no room for doubt in the warmth of George's affection.

After a healthy squeeze, he transferred his enthusiasm to Strangford, pumping his hand up and down like the handle of a well, the dimple showing in his left cheek as he smiled.

"Good to see you as well, Strangford. I see you're looking as dastardly as ever."

George's gaze then moved to Kazi. He blinked, momentarily taken aback.

"Hold on, then. Aren't you that policeman?"

"I see you remember Inspector Kazi," Lily noted, feeling a little awkward. She had nearly forgotten that Kazi had interrogated George in the aftermath of the murder at Taddiford.

"Hard to forget," George returned. "He isn't investigating you for something?"

"Not at the moment," Kazi replied dryly.

"Well, that's alright, then. Sorry it's such a hubble-bubble about the place. The Germans hit Kemmelberg two days ago. We managed to hold them off, but they took a ready chunk out of the line, and we've nothing to reinforce it with, not after the attack on Bethune the night before. It's like hens pecking all up and down the front, looking for someplace rotten. The Boche have got to try for a major hit before long, muster the Eastern troops and all that, but the reports from our intelligence networks are all a regiment here, a battalion there. Can't know where to send what few reinforcements we've got because the big one could come from anywhere. Every time we fall back, supply lines have to be re-established and new fortifications built, which means wire, sandbags, concrete . . . Have you any idea how hard it is these days to find concrete? And don't get me started on the timetables. Do you know I've revised the fuel transport schedule six times in the last week alone?"

George delivered his monologue with rapid alacrity as though everyone standing in the hall understood perfectly what he was talking about. Her brother's specific posting at General Headquarters was in transport and supply logistics, the elaborate and constantly evolving calculations for how to get men and the supplies they required from one place to another on a shifting network of roads, rail lines, and available vehicles.

He had not been very pleased when first ordered to transfer from the Royal Sussex Regiment's sector of the front line to the relative safety of GHQ. Both he and Lily had scented their father's influence in the change, which had smashed his dreams of bashing the Hun beside his brothers in arms. Lily herself had been quietly relieved by her father's machinations as she no longer had to worry quite so much about George being gassed or blown to pieces. Yet he had ultimately taken to his work in administration with the same unstoppable cheerfulness he used when facing any other challenge life happened to throw at him.

He had even admitted to her once over a particularly piquant bowl of vindaloo that he'd come to appreciate his move to Montreuil.

"It's actually dreadfully important," George had noted enthusiastically after slogging back half a glass of lager and wiping a line of sweat from his forehead. "You can't fight a war without bullets ... and tins of beef, cigarettes, boots, rum rations, horses, spare gun parts— and loads of men moving about the place. One has to know where to find all of those things, only the farmer in Burgundy who was going to deliver you sixty gallons of milk can now only send you twenty because a Hun fighter was shot down over his barn, and then a flood takes out six feet of a critical rail line. The lorries break down and the horses get shot ... It's the most dreadful puzzle you could ever imagine, and there I am at the heart of it with enough paperwork to build a model of the Tower of Pisa."

The promotion George had received the year before was evidence of how well her brother had taken to the challenge, and lingering in one of the main arteries of GHQ to analyze resupply times was evidence that his enthusiasm for the work hadn't changed.

George stepped neatly out of the way of a file trolley and remembered himself.

"Dash it, I'm running on, aren't I? And we're crowding up the hall. Do come inside."

George's office would have been a room of reasonable dimensions had it not been positively jammed with file cabinets and papers. A single window looked out over the exercise green. Besides George's seat at his crowded desk, there was only one other chair in the space. Lily noted the presence of an ashtray by the window and the distinct smell of cigarettes.

"You haven't taken up smoking!" she protested before she could think better of it.

George grinned sheepishly beneath his neatly-trimmed mustache.

"I knew you would disapprove. But you've no idea what it's like around here! The work doesn't stop. It's five o'clock to midnight when the Boche are afoot and a fellow must find a way to keep his brain going. By God, this is a treat," he added, gazing at Lily with obvious warmth. "I thought I'd have to wait at least another six months to see you again. I was quite put out to find you were gone when I was home this past week."

"Will you be needing me, sir?"

George was surprised to recall that his batman was still standing in the doorway.

"Oh! Right. Yes. I mean—No. That will be all for now, Lewis."

"I'll see to acquiring the updated rail network reports, then," Lewis replied patiently.

He bowed neatly to Lily and the others, pulling the door shut behind him as he left.

"Well, then. Here we are. I'm sorry I've only the one chair to offer you. I'm not exactly flush with visitors, and it's all ..."

George waved a hand around, taking in the organized chaos of the room as though it were a word in itself.

"We're just chasing our own tails running after every new report out of Intelligence. They aren't saying where they acquire their information, but it's pretty obvious they've agents watching the railways on the German side of the line, reporting back on any troop transport trains they spot. But who knows what the Kraut logistics officers are muddling through? Or maybe they've gotten wise that we're watching, and the reports are bunk. We could be moving all our men to the wrong place, and we'd only find out when two hundred thousand Huns suddenly throw themselves at a different sector. But I'm rattling on. You didn't come here to talk about troop movements."

"No," Lily carefully confirmed.

"Is this an appropriate time for that *family business*?" George asked, putting an awkward emphasis on the words and following it with an even more obvious glance at Inspector Kazi.

"It's alright, George. Whatever it is, you can say it in front of the inspector. He'll learn it all eventually anyway."

"He will?" George asked, a little bewildered. "I didn't realize you were chums."

Lily had no idea how to respond to this. The notion that she was "chums" with Kazi bordered on the bizarre, but she found herself rather at a loss for an alternative way to describe their relationship.

"Yes, well ..." she replied uncomfortably.

George unbuttoned his uniform jacket, then reached into an inner pocket and pulled out an envelope, handing it to Lily.

"I've—errr—been wearing it for the last three days, so I hope it isn't too...you know. It just seemed the best way to keep it secure. It's still sealed," he added helpfully. "I didn't even try to steam it open."

Behind her, Kazi slowly lifted his gaze to the sky as though seeking the grace for further patience.

As Lily broke open the envelope, it occurred to her how terribly clever her father had been. For all that he was entirely unschooled in the ways of espionage, using George as a courier to get this message to France neatly avoided the vagaries and insecurities of the post as well as the eyes of the censors. Even the foreign office diplomatic bag, which was exempt from review by the censors, was still an obvious target for German spies.

Nobody was paying much attention to George.

Then again, Lily had asked her father for information related to his most closely-guarded secret. She should have expected nothing less. It was a stroke of fortune that George must have been home on leave when she wired.

"Come on, then," George prompted eagerly. "You know I'm dying of curiosity. You must tell me whether there's anything in there you can share."

Lily was saved from answering by a crisp double knock at the door.

"Come!" George called a little reluctantly.

Lance Corporal Lewis neatly revealed himself.

"Sorry to disturb you, sir, but the major is on the line."

"Dash it," George returned. "Excuse me for a moment."

He darted out, leaving them alone in the office.

"Well?" Kazi pressed, his own impatience only slightly better managed than George's.

Lily made a quiet and furious assessment of just how far she trusted him—and how badly they might require his assistance for what must come next.

"My father has a source behind enemy lines. One that operates separately from any official intelligence network."

Kazi's face dawned with understanding.

"Moonshadow," he replied with a note of triumph.

"Moonshadow?" Lily echoed.

"Your father has been quietly feeding information to the various services for years—and I do mean various. No one gets all of it, which amounts to a rather clever way of limiting how much deduction any one agency might be able to do about the nature of his source. He has refused to provide any details about where the reports are coming from. When he started, there were many who suspected he was in fact working for the Germans. A few still doubt his allegiances, but the information is too good, too uniformly accurate. If he was a German double agent, surely he would have fed us something false by now, something that compromised our forces. Nor does he use the stuff to try to leverage his way into deeper knowledge of our own intelligence operations. We finally gave his mysterious source a codename over at MI1c. It was simply too awkward to talk about it without one."

"Moonshadow," Lily repeated, feeling the name on her tongue, testing how it fit. She decided it was more appropriate than Kazi and his colleagues at the Secret Service Bureau likely knew.

"In my telegram, I asked my father whether his source knew anything about monsters," she continued.

She handed Kazi the letter and heard the sharp intake of his breath as he read the single line typed onto the page beneath the words *Inquire directly.*

Strangford stepped over to glance down at it, then raised his dark eye to her.

"It's an address," he said.

"In Luxembourg," Lily finished for him.

The single line directed them to a building on the Rue Sainte-Zithe in the heart of the German-occupied city.

There was no need to say more. Lily knew each of them understood perfectly well what Lord Torrington had not risked spelling out on the message he entrusted to George.

Moonshadow knew something . . . something they could only discover by contacting her father's source themselves.

Kazi carried the paper over to George's ashtray by the window. He picked up the box of matches, lit one, and set it to the corner of the page. In a matter of seconds, the paper had turned into a pale shell of ash. Kazi took the additional step of stirring it with the matchstick until the whole of it was broken into irredeemable fragments.

It was a prudent move, and Lily knew that the address was safely imprinted in all of their minds. What was far less certain was what they would do with the knowledge.

The door behind her popped open as George slipped into the room with a worried crease between his brows.

"I'm terribly sorry. I'm afraid I'm being called into an emergency meeting. It's all gone topsy-turvy, or I would have insisted on bringing you to lunch. The canteen's rubbish, but there's a decent little cafe outside the walls. Will you be around tomorrow?"

Lily exchanged a glance with the men.

"I'm afraid not."

"Oh. Right," George looked disappointed. "Well—I'll expect a full report from you at some point. And vindaloo in Holborn next I'm home. Promise?"

"Gladly." Lily replied and squeezed his hand.

Unsatisfied, he abruptly pulled her in for a hug, planting a kiss on top of her head. Lily accepted it, filled with unexpected warmth. Releasing her, he clapped Strangford on the shoulder.

"Give my love to your sister and her family, would you?"

"Of course," Strangford replied.

"Lewis will see you out," George finished.

He cast her a longing look, the wish that they could spend more time together written plainly on his face. Lily felt it too—after all, he was her brother. Then he was gone.

"This way, please," said the stiff Lance Corporal Lewis, stepping into the hole George had left in the doorway.

~

Roughly a mile beyond the walls of Montreuil sat a tiny ruined church. It lay in the center of a sheep pasture and had been abandoned long before the war. The thick stone walls were twined with ivy, enclosing a space no larger than Lily's old flat in Bloomsbury, punctuated by the empty holes where windows once were. Roofless, it opened to a sky that had slipped into gray since they left the town, the air kissed with a breath of imminent rain.

They disturbed a family of sparrows when they entered, the birds fluttering out through the roof, chirping with quiet alarm.

Lily laid her walking stick down on the ruined remnants of one of the pews. Strangford sat on the steps in front of the old altar, pulling off his hat as he glanced around with admiration.

"Twelfth century, I think," he said.

Kazi paced the floor, his shoes rustling through the dried, paper-thin leaves of last year's ivy.

"We need to find a line of communication with Luxembourg," Lily said.

"Does such a thing exist?" Strangford asked, eyes on Kazi.

"It exists. Army Intelligence has a network there," Kazi replied. "But it would take days, at least, to acquire permission to send a message, and another week for any communications to reach one of their agents. Then as much time again for a reply to come back."

"Too long," Strangford concluded grimly.

"And it would expose Moonshadow to their network," Kazi added. "More people would know the source exists and where it could be found . . . more people who could be caught by the Germans and interrogated."

They absorbed the conundrum of it in the hallowed stillness of the church. Lily could sense Kazi buzzing with barely-contained frustration, his need for logic and action stymied by the muddle of the circumstances.

Then Strangford spoke.

"I may know a way in."

"You mean a way *in* to Luxembourg?" Kazi demanded with surprise.

"The Navy's Heavier Than Air department developed a ... contingency plan. It is purely theoretical at this point. No one has actually put it into practice. But if successful, it might make it possible to deposit agents behind enemy lines without being detected."

"You're talking about the balloon," Kazi exclaimed.

Lily's skin crawled with alarm. Hot air balloons were already used routinely at the front for observation purposes. It was dangerous work as the balloons posed juicy targets for any German fighter planes that managed to make it across the line. And of course, the Germans had used the hard-sided hydrogen-filled orbs of zeppelins to make long-range bombing runs against England in the earlier years of the war. They only stopped because the RAF's own planes became rather too skilled at shooting the things down.

Zeppelins were driven by engines and could be steered but could be heard and targeted from the ground. A hot air balloon was dependent on the direction of the wind, but it was also silent. If it were to travel at night, it would be virtually invisible to those below—a silent, nearly undetectable means of transportation.

Kazi renewed his pacing with energy, already puzzling out the details.

"What's the range?" he demanded.

"No more than fifty miles if you want the balloon to continue on after dropping the agents."

Kazi stopped short, brightening.

"Because you could time the ballast. Release just enough as you approach your target landing area to descend to the ground, and then the loss of the weight of the passengers would lighten the balloon enough to rise again and continue on in the direction the wind was blowing."

"Until it ran out of fuel," Strangford finished for him.

"But it eliminates the need to conceal any wreckage," Kazi pushed back. "And when the grounded balloon was discovered, the Germans would be searching the wrong area for any spies. But where would you launch? You would need to be as close to the border as possible and in the prevailing direction of the wind."

"The equipment is loaded onto a submarine. Last I heard, the program had been stationed at Le Havre for testing." Strangford replied.

"Somewhere off the Belgian coast, then. Even from there, we couldn't reasonably expect to land much further inland than Ghent," Kazi calculated. "We'd have to make our way overland, but the Belgian frontier isn't nearly as closely watched as that of the Netherlands. It's already occupied territory. And with the excellent quality of your German ..."

"How many can it carry." Lily cut in coldly.

She could see the answer in Strangford's face even before he spoke. "Two."

The ground shifted beneath her feet, falling away from her as the situation turned to oil and slipped from her control.

"I think I'll stretch my legs for a spell," Kazi offered after a glance between the two of them.

Without waiting for a response, he strode from the church, granting them a shred of privacy for what must come next.

Lily faced her husband across the rotted remnants of old pews and dried leaves. A few soft, misting drops of rain begin to fall, gently dampening her skin.

"You're taking him."

It wasn't a question. It was a statement of fact, one they both knew to be true. Strangford didn't even try to deny it.

"He will insist on going," Lily pressed, needing to say it all aloud. "And, of course, the Navy wouldn't allow you to bring your wife with you on such a journey instead of a trained intelligence agent. They wouldn't let you bring a woman at all."

"You know I wish it wasn't like that," Strangford returned.

"Why did you even suggest it?" she snapped.

"Because it's the only way I can think of to reach your father's source. And we must, Lily."

His face was drawn, the tension and fear in him rising to the surface.

"How do you know?" Lily retorted, her own fear smothered by

rising anger. "You aren't the one who sees the future."

"No," Strangford agreed. "And you have shared nothing about what you've seen coming for us."

The bluntness of it cut her short. Strangford so rarely mentioned the information he unwittingly pulled from her skin. Through some accident of intimacy over the last few days, he must have gathered fragmented whispers of what her onmyōdō had shown her.

The blood on her hands. The monsters racing through the dark.

She had no response to it. Any words she might have offered were tangled up in a terrible muddle of anger and fear as the soft, soundless rain continued to drift gently down around them, dampening the ancient stones under her feet.

He rose from the step and crossed the aisle to join her.

"I can't pretend that I don't want you out of this. Do you know what they do to spies, Lily."

The words almost choked him.

"They shoot them," Lily replied.

She sounded far calmer than she should. It was as though what she felt were too large to fit into such simple syllables. The fear pressed up underneath that façade, filling her to the skin.

"Can't it be somebody else?" she demanded desperately.

"You know who we're going to see," Strangford returned. "How willingly do you think she would give her secrets away to a pair of strangers?"

Lily knew.

"It's not fair," she gasped, the tears finally breaching her defenses to slide down her cheeks.

"I know, Lily." Strangford closed the distance between them and pulled her to him. "God, do I know."

He paused for a moment.

"At least you've never foreseen me getting shot," he offered.

Lily let out a desperate laugh, one that collapsed into a sob.

His grip on her tightened, revealing its own edge of desperation.

"Don't ask me to stay. Please. I'd ... I would have to say no, and I don't ... I *can't* part from you like that. I don't want to go—I don't want to leave you like this. But I've seen what they are. I've felt them ..."

His voice choked off at the remembered horror of it.

"We're not safe, Lily. It doesn't matter who goes back to England. None of us are safe."

He was shaking, the words edged with desperation by the nightmare he had lived through in the stones of the Stelvio Pass.

In the face of it, her fears shriveled, revealing themselves to be tiny, selfish things. A remembered phrase rang down her bones, the words like an incantation. She spoke them aloud as she brushed her fingers along the newly-dampened line of his hair. In the elegant ruins of the humble church, they had the feeling of a vow.

"This is about more than us."

He kissed her then like a man seeking water, his leather-gloved hand pulling against the small of her back, drawing her firmly against him. She tasted him back, soaking up every desperate nuance of him—the smooth-shaven skin of his face, the wool of his uniform. His smell, his heat, as familiar to her as her own blood and yet never fading in their intensity.

He tugged at the cropped auburn waves of her hair, pulling her head back to meet her eyes.

"I will come back to you," he vowed.

Lily's heart skipped, her hand still resting on his cheek.

"You can't . . . You don't know—"

He cut her off, his grip on her tightening as the rain danced lightly against her skin.

"*I will come back to you.*"

Her power flared. Onmyōdō rose, swelling up to blind her.

Plaster and incense. A breath drawn in against the silence of a dim and cavernous room.

The screech of beasts in the dark.

The hot, thick splash of blood on her skin.

Strangford on the far side of an impossible, slow-drifting snow, mouth forming words she cannot hear.

"Lily." he asked.

He held on to her tightly, holding her up after her knees gave way, threatening to drop her to the floor of the church. She forced her muscles to answer, commanding them to work.

"I'm fine," she promised, the words so weak she felt compelled to repeat them. "I'm fine."

She succeeded in standing, placing her hand against his chest as though to brace herself.

"We should go find Kazi," she said, picking up her stick.

Strangford looked as though there were a thousand things he wanted to say. In the end, his mouth firmed, the line of it tinged with regret. He nodded, then followed her back out into the wide gray fields.

TEN

Sunday, April 21
Five o'clock
Boulogne, France

$\mathcal{L}$ILY STOOD AT THE RAIL of a converted collier ship and watched Strangford walk away. He and Kazi had seen her safely on board the Abercraig and were now headed back to the train station to arrange travel to Le Havre. The rain was threatening again, the sky over the port of Boulogne so low and gray it seemed the clouds must brush against the stacks of the crowded and eccentric assortment of Navy ships and requisitioned trawlers.

Their final farewells had been brief, truncated by the blare of the ship's horn as it prepared for departure. It was only because of the imminent need for the Abercraig to return to England for a further load of ammunition destined for the front that Lily had so quickly found a place on it—there had not been time to load in more wounded. Nor had there been any privacy, the dock crowded with workers hauling and arranging incoming cargo.

She had wanted to throw herself at Strangford, to beg him to stay—drag him onto the safety of the boat or slap him across the face. There had been time for none of it. She had contained the maelstrom of emotion inside her with walls of iron will as she said goodbye, conscious the entire time that it could well be the last moment she spent with the man she loved.

The fact of it raged inside of her as she watched the Abercraig's captain make his last arrangements with the harbor master. She tried to pull up the feeling of Strangford's arms around her back—his smell, his warmth. They slipped from her grasp, leaving her only with panic.

What was she supposed to do?

The question swelled up inside her like a wave, threatening to drown her—and something answered.

Lily slips from the deck of the ship with a whisper of salt and grass ... and is somewhere else.

Sheep dung and gasoline. The scrape of a match, a spark against the darkness.

A frozen and indifferent glitter of golden stars.

A door cracks open, revealing the sparkle of sunlight on the rippling waters of a familiar river. Soaring townhouses. Falling cherry blossoms.

The elegant form of an iron tower pierces the sky.

She lurched back to herself at the rail of the collier, knuckles white where she gripped it. The certainty rang through her, deep as bone.

She knew where she had to go next.

It made no sense. There was nothing there for her.

A call rang out from below as the deckhands moved to release the gangplank. She sensed the future swing, balanced on the edge of a blade.

Lily snatched up her bag and ran.

One of the sailors threw out an arm to stop her.

"Hold on there, miss. You can't disembark now—the boat's about to leave."

Lily turned on him, eyes flashing.

"I am not going to England. I am going to Paris."

Lacking any response to this unexpected announcement, he simply stared after her as she stalked back down into France.

~

Lily woke to the sound of someone gently snoring. It came from the woman in the other twin bed at her shared room in the boarding house near the Gare du Nord.

She had arrived in Paris after dark, exhaustion rapidly catching up with her, and stumbled into the lobby knowing she would accept whatever accommodation they had left for the evening. She was simply too tired to go any further, worn through by the miles of walking the day before and the emotional tumult of Strangford's departure.

She had no idea whom she was sleeping next to. She didn't particularly care. She felt hollow inside, empty of everything but her perennial nausea.

It was the nausea that forced her from bed. She stumbled past the snoring woman out into the hall, finding the shared bathroom a few doors down. She vomited into the toilet as someone knocked impatiently at the door, rattling off a stream of angry French.

Lily ignored it. She sat down on the cracked tile floor, taking a moment to make sure she was through, her mind as blank as the whitewashed walls. In a way, she welcomed the blankness. It was more comfortable than lurching to and fro between the same unanswerable questions.

Finally, she crawled to her feet, pushing out past the irritated young typist waiting her turn.

Back in the room, she hesitated over her valise, then pulled out her trousers. It was easier to run or fight in them if she had to.

She paid her bill and stepped out into a bright Parisian morning.

The city was already awake, bustling with early commuters and street vendors. A girl whizzed by on a bicycle, also clad in trousers, while a cluster of soldiers, clearly still out after a night's debauchery, laughed as they crowded around the door of a cafe.

The traffic flowed around Lily as she stood on the pavement, unsure of which way to go. Why was she even here? The onmyōdō had driven her back to the city, but it felt like a mad impulse, lacking any sense. Was she simply delaying her inevitable return to England?

All that waited for her there were the long nights of fear as she wondered whether Strangford would ever come home. Paris was admittedly better than that.

She started walking, carrying her stick at her side. She was free of her valise, having paid a few extra pennies to leave it at the boarding house until she determined what to do with it—and with herself.

The district of Montmarte unfolded around her, vibrant even through the weight of the war. Past the shops and a brothel or two, the road she had chosen more or less at random opened up into a steep park, built in tiers against the hillside and lined with flowering trees. At the top of it rose the elegant domes of the Sacre Coeur. The newly-constructed Catholic basilica was monumental, set in an odd lacuna in the close-woven and busy streets of the city.

Lily recalled hearing that construction on the church had been nearly completed when the war broke out. It had not yet been consecrated. It sat empty, a beautiful shell lacking worshippers.

She had not been to church in a while, and when she did, she attended a far more humble establishment than this gleaming confection on the hilltop. Still, she found her footsteps turning towards it, carrying her up the steep flights of stone steps to the summit.

At the top, she passed a group of students lounging on the stairs, eating hard-boiled eggs and gossiping about the plight of the working classes. Turning, Paris unfolded before her.

The city was painted with morning sunlight. It looked so much broader than London, a low sprawl of gray rooftops and glittering windows stretching as far as she could see.

Behind her, the new church loomed high and grand, an ornate tribute to God. It was separated from the people of Montmarte by a low wrought-iron fence.

The impulse that had driven her to the top gained a focus that surprised her, one that presented itself with an aura of need.

Lily glanced around. It was still early enough for the sunlight to have a gilded cast. The landing before the church was hardly on the way to anywhere. Those who bothered to mount to the top of the hill did so for purposes of their own and had little interest in what anyone else was up to.

She reached for the simpler of her powers—the mere foresight that might give her a glimpse into the nearest future. It answered her like an eager pet, offering up the imminent arrival of a police constable and a backfiring motorbike on the street below that would soon capture the attention of the students on the steps.

Lily fell into it, feeling the rhythm of what was to come pulse naturally through her skin.

One … two … three …

A crack sounded from the square, drawing the gazes of the students. The passing constable noticed the movement, ambling over to scold them for loitering.

Unobserved, Lily vaulted easily over the low iron fence that separated the church grounds from the hilltop, landing on a combed gravel path. Turning up her collar to cover the fringe of hair visible under her hat, she adopted the slouch and easy gait of a workman and crossed the open space of the yard as though she belonged there.

Another iron gate surrounded the entrance to a narrow stairwell that descended into the ground beside the building. Lily hopped it, her boots landing soundly on the top step.

The stairs ended at a low wooden door set in an arch of stone. This was a practical entrance, humble and unremarkable, set below ground level.

Lily took a pair of hairpins from her pocket and set to picking the lock.

It was a skill she had learned from Sam Wu in the gloom of the carriage house at The Refuge years before. She had practiced a bit since then, though her skills were admittedly rudimentary. Thankfully, it was a rather simple lock. Lily managed it in just a few minutes. With a satisfying click, she opened the door and stepped inside.

She found herself gazing into a dim hallway that smelled of cool, clean stone. It was the crypt, as yet unused and waiting for its crop of the dead.

Thankfully, the darkness was not complete. High, narrow windows here and there in the vaults that lined the exterior walls let in slender beams of illumination. It was just enough for her to make out vague shapes and openings in the gloom after she had closed the door behind her.

The ceiling over her head was low and vaulted, the hallway branching off into underground rooms and chapels.

She moved forward. The dull light from the thin windows faded as she pressed deeper into the bowels of the church until she was more or less blind.

She fumbled in her pocket for a tin of matches. Pausing, she lit one and gasped as it revealed a pale figure holding its severed head in its arms.

She took another breath, recognizing it as a marble statue of some martyr.

The flame reached her fingers. Lily shook it out with a curse, but the burst of light revealed a glimpse of a staircase a few yards ahead. Lily reached it by trailing a hand along the wall until the toe of her boot met solid stone. She climbed without seeing, the stair turning beneath her boots until her outstretched fingers met the rough wooden planks of a door.

She found the latch and slipped through into the nave of the basilica.

It stunned her. Soft morning light filtered in through stained glass roses. The massive dome overhead was ringed with windows that poured a gentle illumination down over the marching lines of wooden pews. The space was strikingly unornamented, just a quietly awe-inspiring sprawl of soaring stone pillars.

Pigeons fluttered overhead, letting out a startled cooing. Lily walked up the aisle, her boots echoing hollowly off the floor.

The altar stood under a further dome in the heart of the church. As Lily approached, she realized the stone over her head was almost completely covered in a glittering mosaic.

Gold sparkled from a rich blue background against an image of Christ ascending. It felt like an ancient relic, but Lily could see it was not quite finished, a few spaces yet undone along the edges.

Something in its glittering beauty made her skin crawl with a chill that had nothing to do with the cool air of the dim church.

The Christ was framed by legendary figures—an angel bearing a pennant, a gold-crowned virgin. Surrounding him in a splendid array were saints and popes and heroes, all set against a sparkling river of stars.

She was uncomfortably reminded of the ceiling of The Refuge, of Evangeline Ash's dizzying sprawl of gods, mortals, and what lay beyond the sky.

Under the shining silence of the mosaic, a feeling crept over her like a gust from an unexpected storm, the rumble of distant thunder.

Evangeline Ash had not seen the future. Her power had

communicated with something else—with whatever wove the threads of influence that snaked through the world, bending it to an unspoken will.

There was something horribly indifferent about the placid face of the Christ that loomed over her head, an indifference Lily felt echoed in the vast unused space behind her. The dome and all it carried within it seemed to expand, and for a moment, she was pressed down by the weight of her own relative insignificance, ground like an atom between the gears of the great machine of fate.

The machine that had taken Strangford from her. That threatened to destroy him.

It sparked her anger to life. The church felt like an ambush. Every fiber of her rebelled against it.

Why had she come here? Had the onmyōdō done it? The thought made her want to walk away out of pure, contrary spite—but where would that leave her?

Her only remaining option would be returning to England to wait for whatever the stars had in store for Strangford.

No. She would not do that. She couldn't. There had to be another path . . . but how to find it?

Through the onmyōdō, of course.

The thought froze her with quick fear.

Since the moment the power had bloomed in her on the far side of life and death, the onmyōdō had carried her forward like a wave. It blossomed up when it wanted to, moved by some random breath of fate—but perhaps Lily was the one to blame for that. She had always resisted, suspicious of the onmyōdō's purpose.

What might happen were she to actually invite it in?

It was like contemplating opening the door to a hurricane. Lily didn't even pretend to think she could control it. It would be like trying to direct the motion of the sea.

But if she were to turn her face to it for once, raise her sail, then perhaps—just perhaps—she might be able to navigate those mad currents instead of simply being blown around.

In truth, there was no alternative. It was that or give up . . . and she could not give up.

Under the terrible gaze of the gilded figures on the dome, Lily shivered, lowering herself to the cold stones of the church floor. She set her walking stick down beside her, assuming the cross-legged posture Ash had taught her all those years before.

Her blood roiled with a terrible mix of fear, anger, and worry. Lily struggled to muster what Ash had always said she needed—patience and acceptance. She had to let her feelings wash over her like water on stone, releasing her own desires.

It wasn't working. What she felt was too strong, too desperate. She couldn't possibly smother it. She was too much a mess—and so as a mess, she threw herself forward, lurching into the onmyōdō.

The church jolted away.

Lily stands in a hallway lined with doors. It is infinite, gateways marching into impossible distance, each humming with possibility.

The floor is flooded with water. Waves crash roughly against her boots, unsteadying her, wind battering her skin.

The doors lie before her, behind her, identical and yet vitally different.

With an impulse of desperation, Lily grasps one of the knobs and tugs it open.

Possibility rushes at her like the tide.

Her mouth is full of mud. The sky is smoke and fire, the ground shaking under the whistle and crack of falling shells. A corpse on the ground lies just out of reach, tails of a long black coat tossing in an unearthly wind. A familiar voice screams her name, the sound abruptly cut short.

Lily staggers back, iron on her tongue. The door slams.

She forces herself forward, putting her hand to the next.

Voices shout in German. With a crack like thunder, blood splatters against the wall.

Another opening shines at her, humming with promise.

Behind it, leaves rustle in the night. Something darts through the ruins of the world-that-was. Beasts growl from the darkness, slavering with blind and unspeakable rage. Shadows detach from the fabric of the night and leap toward her, snarling with lust.

She fights back from it, then reaches for another, and another . . .

Howls of rage in the night, slick warmth on her hands.

Shattered buildings. Eyes that blaze like fire.

The possibilities thunder at her, crashing in from all directions as doors fly open, pouring outcomes across her mind. She must drown in them. They will tear her apart, pummel her until there is nothing left.

"Please," she gasps, spitting a lingering mouthful of salt water onto the dull tiled floor. "I can't . . . *Please.*"

It is a plea—a prayer—and suddenly all is silent.

Closed doors linger in the gloom. The scale of the hallway has changed. It is bigger now, more vast, expanded into something that reminds her of the nave of a cathedral—all of it lined with terrible potential.

It looks empty, but Lily knows she is not alone. Something breathes in the silence that surrounds her, ancient and immense.

Words echo distantly across the dim, hollow space that surrounds her like the memory of a dead dream.

Ask for what you want.

Her heart thuds with fear.

There is only one way this works. If Lily asks, she must be ready to accept whatever answer she is given, no matter what it requires of her. What it costs.

And there will be a cost. She is wrestling with the Leviathans of time, space, fate. To bend them around such a petty, mortal concern as love leaves no room for nuance, for control.

Terror floods her. She refuses to bow to it.

Under the indifference of a painted sky, Lily sets the question into her bones.

Show me how to keep him safe.

Doors flash around her. She is battered by a wind that tastes of the space between the stars. Clinging to her purpose in the face of the storm, Lily opens up her mind, emptying its pages, making them ready for whatever must be written.

A key takes shape in her hand. The weight of it is cold.

The door reveals itself. It is dull and gray, smelling of oiled steel.

Fear sings in her skull, sounding a low note of unending dread.

Lily sets her key into the lock, and her answer opens.

Gray fur slides past night-dark leaves.

Black wings rise from black wool, framing a face she knows as well as her own.

Why didn't you tell me?

Breath mists over a block of ice in a windowless room.

A gray sky splits with light, bright chrysanthemums of destruction.

Something runs towards her through the smoke, panting like a beast.

Strangford stands between walls of earth, gazing at her down the tunnel of them, aching with regret.

I'm sorry.

The world blows apart.

Lily landed hard on the floor of the unconsecrated church, a placid Christ gazing down at her from the shadows overhead.

The floor under her palms was cold and unmoving. She fought for breath, her arms shaking along with everything else.

The vision was impossible. It made no sense. How could the path she needed to take to save Strangford lead to exactly what she had been fighting for years to escape?

The answer continued to burn inside of her like a bow-light, refusing to fade even as she pulled herself up from the ground, fighting her way back to her knees.

Lily trembled, holding herself there, and wondered what exactly she had just done.

The decision waited, suspended in the still air that surrounded her. She had asked and received an answer. Would she accept it?

She picked up her walking stick, then pressed a boot to the floor. Pushing up, she forced her way back to her feet. The knowing ran over her skin, dancing across her nerves with an impersonal joy. She took one clumsy step forward, then another. Quickening from a stagger to a stride, she hurried towards her way out of the church.

She had a train to catch.

ELEVEN

Later that evening
Lorraine, France

THE VILLAGE OF OCHEY was a cluster of red-roofed houses set amid rolling sheep pastures and fields sprouting new green wheat and beans. The buildings were glowing with the last rays of the setting sun.

Lily had taken the train from Paris to Nancy, but reaching Ochey had relied on her boots and her walking stick. She had traded her leather valise for a simple canvas rucksack with a woman back at the boarding house who clearly thought she was getting the better end of the deal, but Lily was grateful to be carrying her things with her back rather than her hand.

Not that she packed much—just a change of clothes, a bar of soap, and a hairbrush. She had left the rest behind. She would have no need of it where she was going . . . if she got there at all.

A warm spring breeze tugged at the hair under her hat. A woman in a nearby house cast a curious glance at her as she leaned out to pull her shutters closed, cutting off the light from her lamp. Windows all around Lily were similarly blinking into darkness as the residents prepared for blackout.

She hesitated, torn for a moment. The sunlight was already faded to a deep peach and gold as the day rapidly descended into evening. A horn-shaped moon was visible in the sky, a pale curve over the distant line of the trees on the far side of the fields. The sensible action would be to look for an inn.

A few swallows darted overhead, the wheels of a cart crackling against the loose stones on the road. A wrinkled farmer drove it, bent over the reins of his mule.

"Pardon," Lily said, waving him to a stop. "Où est la base aérienne?"

"A l'est," he replied. "Trois kilomètres, à travers les champs."

Her destination was just across the fields. She was so close.

"Merci," Lily returned.

The farmer drove on, and Lily gazed to the east, where the sky already drifted toward a velvet purple. Adjusting the straps of her bag, she stepped from the road, setting off across the pastures with the gleam of the dying sun at her back.

She could just discern a path, a meandering ribbon of earth between the quietly grazing sheep. Wildflowers rustled around her boots, her walking stick tapping out a regular rhythm against the earth. The white curve of the moon granted her just enough light to make out her way.

Before long, a cluster of irregular shapes rose against the deeper back of the horizon, dark squarish buildings surrounded by open fields.

Lily stopped, taking a moment to listen. Through the low hush of the breeze rustling the grass, she could make out a bark of laughter and the dull clatter of metal. She caught a thin fragment from a gramophone, the tune familiar.

The further it is from Tipperary, the nearer it is to Berlin …

Yes—this was the place she was looking for.

The airfield was in blackout, a protection against the ambitions of German night bombers who would gladly feather their caps with a strike against a Royal Air Force base just a few miles from the front lines.

Lily's path merged with a road that led to a darkened gatehouse. A low barbed-wire fence extended to either side of it. Lily could easily have hopped over if she was careful about where she put her hands, which told her that its purpose was less defense and more to keep the neighboring sheep at bay. This far from the front, they weren't concerned about a ground attack, and spies were considered less of a real threat than livestock wandering onto the runway. After all, they couldn't conceal whatever was happening in the sky.

The guard startled at the sound of her boots crunching against the gravel. He fumbled the book he had been reading by the narrow light of a shaded lantern, then dropped it entirely. He yanked out a sidearm and pointed it at her.

"Halt! Who goes?" he demanded in Scots-accented English.

"I'm a visitor. May I approach?" Lily asked, stopping.

At the sound of an upper-class female English voice, the gun lowered, no longer actively threatening her.

"What's that, then? You lost, lass?"

"No," Lily replied, taking his change in tone as an invitation to come closer. She moved into the low gleam of his lantern. The guard was older, his neat mustache entirely gray. It gave him a bit of the look of a grocer.

"Is the 100th Squadron still stationed here?" she asked.

"Could be," he returned warily.

"I was hoping to see one of your pilots, Sergeant Wood."

The word—Wood—felt strange in her mouth, even though she had needed to use it for the last four years to address the letters she sent, thanks to a thoughtless error in the scribbled notations of an Army recruiter.

The guard's expression shifted to one of relaxed surprise.

"Aye, he's here. Have you any identification?"

Lily handed him her Wrens card and the travel passport Kazi had arranged for her.

She doubted the inspector could have guessed she would use it to access a Royal Air Force base.

"Sign in, if you would," the sentry said, handing her the papers along with a clipboard.

Lily scrawled her name on the next open line.

"He won't be in the lounge," the soldier explained, tucking the clipboard away again. "He keeps to himself, that one, but the lads there might know where you'll find him. Right at the hangar, fourth hut on the left."

It had grown still darker while she had been at the gate, the moon providing just enough light for her to make out the general shape of things. The blackout here was clearly taken seriously. Curtains were hung carefully, with only the thinnest cracks of illumination showing around the door frames.

It was dark but not quiet. Lily could hear the clanging of a mechanic at work, followed by a burst of laughter. A door slammed somewhere in the distance.

She found the hangar. It was bigger up close than it had seemed from a distance, the scale of it bizarre in the midst of a sprawling countryside.

The road branched on the far side of it. To her left, the buildings fell away into open fields lining the packed earth of a runway. To her right, the way extended past a line of smaller half-rounded metal Nissen huts.

A pair of men strolled past her toward the runway, chatting easily with each other, each of them carrying a shuttered lantern. Their uniforms were not up to regulation, the standard RAF trousers or jackets combined with wool jumpers and civilian scarves. The two of them barely spared her a glance. She placed their accents—South African.

Behind them came the cough and chatter of an engine as a plane sparked to life somewhere nearby. Others joined it, the sound coalescing into a chorus.

The South Africans moved into a jog. Just when their figures had almost blended into the gloom that cloaked the field, their two lanterns bloomed into light on either side of the runway.

Lily stepped back as the massive, insectile scaffolding of an aircraft jolted and bounced past her. Two rows of canvas-shrouded wings were woven together by hollow spruce bracers, the cockpit looking like a slender seed in their midst.

Four more planes followed. Each one turned at the signal lanterns from the South Africans, pivoting into the wide darkness of the field. The engines wound up, the dark shapes speeding as they raced across the ground and were then aloft, transformed into black shadows blocking out small patches of the stars.

Lily watched until they were gone, transfixed by the sight. The planes would not be doing an observation run in the darkness. It had to be a bombing raid, the night providing some protection from enemy fighters and anti-aircraft guns.

A few huts down the row to her right, a door slammed open, emitting a spill of yellow light and a chatter of voices. One rose above the others, hollering a reprimand at whoever had just neglected to pull closed the blackout curtain.

The culprit shouted back in an arrogant Yankee drawl, flipping up a middle finger before strolling down the road. Lily stepped forward to intercept him.

"I'm looking for Sergeant Wood," she said. "Do you know where I could find him?"

"You're after Wood? Didn't think the Blackbird had a girl," he replied, slurring the words.

"Blackbird?" she echoed.

The word sent a shiver of unease down her back.

"He'll be down at the back of the field."

The American nodded in the direction of the runway, gave her a comradely clap on the shoulder, and then staggered off, humming a tune under his breath.

The quiet clatter of the base faded behind her as she headed out into the field, the hulking buildings merging with the shadows. The air smelled of sheep dung and new grass. Small frogs chirped some-where nearby, a cricket taking up the song.

Ahead of her, a lucifer flared to life. The flame of the match bloomed then faded, replaced by a single speck of dull orange glow. Lily caught a whiff of cigarette smoke and moved closer, making out the darker shape of a tall figure in an RAF jacket and peaked cap standing by the fence.

Other shadows flittered around him, quick-moving patches of deeper darkness against the soft blanket of the stars. He flipped a hand at them dismissively, and the bats twisted away, arcing back up into the sky. Something larger followed them with a flap of great, lazy black wings.

In the flare of the ember as he inhaled, Lily finally saw his face. The lines she knew so well were changed into something firmer, harder, but still familiar in a way that sent an ache deep through the center of her heart.

"Hello, Sam," she said softly.

The cigarette stilled. She could feel his eyes shift to her through the darkness.

"Bloody hell. Lily." The sound of his voice stirred up more memories—those same eyes glaring at her from the doorway of a place that would become like home. The pain in a scream she could not hear as orange light bloomed over the Thames.

The look in his eyes when she betrayed him.

Lily didn't know what the last four years had been to Sam Wu—what the war had been. She had only heard of his promotion to pilot by way of his năinai, Mrs. Liu, and still wasn't sure entirely how it had come about.

There was a lean air of danger to him she had not felt before. The man standing in front of her was a cipher, a stranger wearing the face of someone she once loved.

A tumult of emotion rose in her, threatening to burst. She fought the impulse to put her hand to his chest and feel that he was really there. She clamped down on it, knowing it would not be welcome.

"What are you doing here?" Sam quietly demanded.

There was no welcome in his voice. She should have been prepared for that. Four years ago, they had not parted on good terms, and since then, Sam had given her no opportunity to mend things. He had rarely taken his leave in England, and when he had, Lily only ever seemed to find out about it after he was already gone.

"I need a favor."

The words thrust her back to the carriage house of The Refuge—to Sam with the awkward angles of a teenager still about him as she asked him the same question.

The memory hurt. She shook it off. Things were different now. He was different.

"Ochey's a long way from Bayswater. Mere thing wouldn't have brought you out here," Sam noted, taking another pull on his cigarette. "So what is it?"

That he greeted her with cautious tolerance was as much as she could have hoped for. She took a breath, pushing forward.

"Have you liberty with when and where you fly."

"Some. Practice runs or exercises, so long as I file a plan and avoid the line." His eyes had narrowed. "Why?"

"What if you went tonight? And something...happened to drive you over the front?"

The cigarette stilled in his hand.

"The latter wouldn't be unheard of. The former would likely earn me a solid telling-off. But I'd like to know why you're asking."

"I need you to drop me into occupied territory." she replied.

It was the only possible answer. Lily had recognized that as soon as the onmyōdō presented it to her. If she could not accompany Strangford, then she needed to forge her own path to Luxembourg. The front was an impenetrable barrier from the coast of Belgium to the mountains of Italy. The borders of the neutral countries were fenced and ferociously monitored. She could not cross, and so the only logical solution was to go over.

Sam threw the cigarette down with a sharp, angry snap of his wrist.

"That's a quick way to get yourself killed."

He was only voicing half the truth. What she was asking would be dangerous for Sam as well. What if they were spotted, even against the darkness? Targeted by some anti-aircraft battery? Was she trading the life of her friend for that of her lover? The notion sickened her, even as a bone-deep knowing sang to her that it was right.

"I have to get to Luxembourg," she pleaded. "Tonight."

"Is it that important? No—don't you answer," he added before she could speak. "Put it to that thing inside of you."

She flinched at the word—*thing*. It made her power sound like a monster that lurked under her skin.

"I already did," she replied. "Why else do you think I'd be here?"

"I see," Sam said shortly.

Lily flinched against a rush of shame.

"That's not what I meant." She steeled herself, closing her eyes and allowing the rest to tumble loose. "It's Anthony. He's in danger."

She opened her eyes again, pleading.

"Please, Sam."

He absorbed it in silence.

This wasn't how it was supposed to be. They should be grinning over a plate of stolen pastries before sneaking into someplace they weren't supposed to go or lingering in the garage of The Refuge as

Sam tinkered with the Silver Ghost.

The pain of the last four years, the betrayal and loss and separation, should simply fall away as things went back to the way they had been before.

The night air around them was still and calm, rich with the distant chirp of insects and the smell of fertile soil. This was a peaceful place, quiet and unchanging beyond the slow-spinning wheel of the seasons. The airbase, the war—Lily herself—felt like an intrusion here, a tumor that ought to be eradicated.

She waited for his answer.

The ember of the cigarette he had dropped was still softly glowing. He crushed it under his boot.

"Follow me," he ordered.

He led her back down the length of the runway. They passed through a small maze of buildings to the hulking metal box of another hangar.

"Stay here," Sam said.

Lily stopped, hanging back in the shadows as he crossed the rest of the way to an opening set into the metal beside the great hangar doors. He pushed inside, the light from the interior blocked by a fall of black curtains.

She moved closer, peering through the slender gap between the fabric and the frame. Inside loomed the delicate structure of another plane. The awkward block of the engine was mounted behind a rounded open cockpit, the propeller suspended inside the delicate cage of the body. Canvas-covered wings extended both above and below, followed by the fragile structure of the tail.

Men lounged around the aircraft, passing a flask. One was in shirtsleeves, another in a ragged jumper.

Sam picked up a wrench from a workbench by the door and banged it against the metal surface of the wall, the sound jarring.

The men startled, scrambling up.

"Start the checklist for the Fee," he ordered. "I'm going up."

The men snapped into action.

"Should I rouse the lieutenant, sir? The rest of the squad?" a lance corporal asked.

"No," Sam retorted shortly. "I'm making an exercise run. Alone."

She could see the lance corporal's skepticism, but he didn't object. It surprised her. A lance corporal outranked a mere sergeant—but then, Sam was the pilot here. This was his plane, and the RAF had its own hierarchy when it came to such things.

The four men swarmed over the FE2B, checking gears and connections, dropping oil here and there. One of them scrambled up a ladder to the engine and topped off the radiator, then set to work with a wrench, carefully tightening bolts.

"Reload your ammo, Sergeant Wood?" a private asked.

Lily found herself staring at the two black guns mounted on either side of the forward cockpit, then startled to realize that Sam was looking at her, eyes locked onto where she lingered in the darkness.

"Do it," he ordered. "And have her out front in ten minutes."

He pivoted, stalking to the door as Lily ducked back from the curtain. He collected her without slowing, hooking a hand under her arm and hauling her forward.

They wove through the clustered huts, Sam leading them unerringly in the gloom.

"Does it bother you?" Lily asked. "Being called by the wrong name."

"I've been called by the wrong name since I landed on your island. And it'd be a bloody nuisance to try to tell His Majesty's Army to fix it. Keep your voice down."

He stopped at a door in a long row of smaller Nissen huts. Inside the corrugated iron shell was a fairly cozy nest. Two beds were framed by little tables, a worn but once fine carpet warming the floor. A lamp burned low.

On one side, the wall was covered in pictures torn from magazines, and a few photographs tacked up with tape. The other side was more spartan, the bed neatly made with nothing personal save for an odd collection of objects on the nightstand—a quartz stone polished to a shine by a river, a jar of some tincture labeled in Chinese. Lily recognized the style of the vessel and knew it was from Sam's father's apothecary.

"What's this for?" she asked, picking it up.

"Supposed to help me sleep," he muttered from behind her as he yanked open his wardrobe.

"Do you need help sleeping?"

He didn't answer. He pulled out a thickly padded wool jacket and tossed it at her.

"Put this on. And this."

A fleece-lined hat followed. It had flaps to cover her ears.

"Now turn around," he demanded, his hands already on the buttons of his coat.

Lily whirled away, facing the more decorated wall. The magazine pictures were fading, yellowed depictions of soaring mountains and snow-crusted pine forests. Canada, she thought numbly, carefully tuning out the sound of Sam's boots hitting the floor, the rustle of his shirt and trousers as he stripped. His roommate must be Canadian.

She remembered the coat he had just given her and shrugged it on. She was immediately sweltering.

"It's too hot for this," she protested, the hat still in her hand.

Sam stepped to her side, buttoning his waistcoat. He had swapped his uniform pants with their distinctive loose cut to the thigh for a conventional pair of gray civilian trousers.

"Not where we're going," he replied shortly.

He plucked the flat cap she had been wearing from her head. Taking the fur-lined hat out of her hand, he tugged it on over her ears, then handed her a thick pair of gloves.

He pulled a bundle of leather straps from the wardrobe, slipping them over his shoulders. Lily realized uncomfortably that it was a shoulder holster. He flipped open the magazine of a Webley, spun it with practiced ease, and shoved it into the saddle. He shrugged into a jacket a hair finer than the workingman's gear he used to wear when not in his chauffeur's livery.

The attire didn't look any warmer than the thick khaki of his RAF uniform. She wondered why he had bothered to change.

Sam reached into the wardrobe a final time and pulled out a marvel—a thick black overcoat made of soft and durable cashmere that descended from his neck to his ankles. It was definitely not RAF-issue. Lily made a quick, instinctive assessment of what such a thing would cost. The answer was beyond even a pilot's salary.

"Where on earth did you get that?"

"Won it off a renegade Russian count when I was on leave in

Nice," Sam replied.

His mouth crooked into an echo of the grin she remembered, and for a moment, she glimpsed the Sam she used to know—the one who could pick any lock in London and was irresistible to flower-selling girls.

"Is that why they call you the Blackbird?"

He flinched, face closing like a book as he turned back to the wardrobe.

"They ain't very creative," he replied flatly.

The black wool hung on him elegantly as though made for his tall, lean frame. Wearing it, he looked like something very much other than a Limehouse gutter rat—something sleek and dangerous.

"Gloves," he ordered, and Lily obediently tugged them on.

Sam assessed her narrowly. He crossed to the other wardrobe in the room, the one that must belong to his roommate. He popped it open with a practiced bang of his elbow, obviously having learned the trick of the latch. He took out a set of goggles and a scarf.

"Tuck up your hair."

Lily pushed the short, auburn ends of her curls under the hat. The goggles felt strange and heavy as she tugged them over her eyes.

Sam wrapped the scarf around her neck, pulling it up to cover half of her face. Lily felt swaddled. She was starting to sweat.

"You'll do," he concluded.

He tossed his peaked field cap back onto the shelf and pulled out a leather helmet lined with fleece. He left the straps of it hanging under his chin, grabbed his goggles, and headed for the door.

"Wait!" she protested.

He turned back, looking impatient.

"What I'm asking of you. I know it's …" she trailed off, unable to quite speak the words aloud. "I just want you to know that—"

Sam cut her off.

"My neck's safer than you think. Come on."

Without giving her time to reply, he stalked back out into the night.

The plane was emerging from the hangar as they returned, Sam's crew towing it forward on well-greased wheels. The lights inside the building had been doused, but the thin moonlight still gave her a better look at it than she had been able to glimpse through the curtain. The Fee was huge—far larger here on the ground than it looked flying in formation over London. The cockpit was very high up, the whole structure like a delicate skeleton of wood and cloth.

Her stomach sank a bit at the thought of trusting it to carry her up into the sky.

"We won't be able to speak once we're in earshot of them, and the engine's too loud to hear anything in the plane," Sam said. "If you have questions, ask 'em now."

"How am I to get down once we're across the front? By parachute?" Sam scowled.

"You don't know how use a parachute."

"Surely it isn't that complicated," Lily returned.

"We'll land," Sam bit back, already turning for the plane. "And if we're lucky, we'll get back in the air again after that."

Suddenly the civilian clothes made a terrible sense. Sam hadn't dressed for the plane. He had dressed for an incursion into enemy territory.

The horror of it brought her up short. He could not possibly go with her. As an enemy pilot in uniform, he would at least be treated as a prisoner of war. An unpleasant situation, certainly, but one that came with certain rights.

Out of uniform, he was a spy—and spies were shot.

"No," Lily declared, stopping short. "You can't possibly."

He whirled on her, eyes flashing in the darkness.

"We both know you won't let this go. Not if that cursed talent of yours has its teeth in you. That's how it works, innit?"

She thought of the rage and pain she had seen in his face the night her power had driven her to take his place in front of Jack Cannon. Her protest dried up in her throat.

"You've a better chance with me than you know. Far better than any other mad way you might come up with to get across the line. So come along. Or don't, if it sticks that hard in your throat."

He gave her no further time to protest. He was already gone, crossing the packed earth to where the plane and his crew waited for him.

The decision tore at her. She had asked the onmyōdō how to keep

Strangford alive. It had given her the answer, pointing her to Ochey, where she was asking Sam to risk his life.

Risking even more than that, if Kazi was right about the reason for her nausea . . . Lily lurched away from the thought. It was too much, an even deeper and entirely uncertain complication in what already felt like an impossible decision.

Sam called out orders by the plane, his crew rushing into action.

It was dark. Though the plane could be heard, certainly it must be difficult to spot. The aircraft in front of her was a bomber. One didn't drop bombs on one's own side of the front. Sam must have done this run before. He just had to find an empty field somewhere beyond the front line. Land, drop her off, take back to the sky again.

The logic felt weak.

The onmyōdō thrummed in her, resonating with a low sense of rightness.

"Prime the blades," Sam called out, ducking under the shadow of the wing.

Lily followed.

Sam set his boot on a tire and and grabbed one of the cables that braced the enormous, fragile wings of the plane. He nimbly vaulted himself into the high perch of the cockpit.

She made a quick study of the frame, plotting a likely course to the gunner's cockpit, which lay in front and slightly below where Sam was sitting. Shoving her walking stick between her back and her rucksack, she hurried to the plane and scrambled up, trying to avoid using any of the wooden struts to brace herself. She was half afraid they would snap in two if she tried.

Her arms strained as she caught hold of the edge of the cockpit and tried to haul herself up. Scrabbling at the side of the plane, her boot found a hold. She half fell over into her place, the walking stick catching awkwardly against the side.

Her cockpit was just an empty cup. Instead of a seat, two leather straps were bolted into the walls. Lily felt a quick, blind panic as she wondered how to settle herself.

"Sure he ain't had a few too many." one of the crewmen shouted from below.

The others laughed.

Sam ignored them, hands flying across the controls in his nest above her.

"All switches off." he called.

Behind him, the engineer grasped the enormous blades of the propeller. He hauled at them, putting them through a few spins.

Lily frantically shoved her rucksack and walking stick into the narrow space that opened from her cockpit into the body of the plane.

"Clear!" Sam shouted.

The engine sputtered, caught, and then thundered to life. The prop whirled into a spin that soon made the blades invisible. The sound was a barrage against Lily's ears, her shoulders hunching instinctively against it.

"Pull the blocks," Sam roared, pitching his voice powerfully to be heard over the racket.

His crewmen hauled at the wooden blocks under the wheels, and then they were in motion, the Fee bouncing across the ground. How had Lily ever thought this machine was delicate? It lurched beneath her, enormous and heavy as it hauled around a wide, awkward turn.

They faced into the wind and an empty stretch of open field as Lily wondered how the devil she had come to be here—and then the plane was moving, building up a heavy momentum with a rattle that chattered her teeth . . . until it abruptly stopped as the Fee swept into the air.

TWELVE

HERE WAS A RUSH of acceleration, a thrust of altitude as the Fee climbed into the sky. With the nose set at a steep angle, Lily found herself staring up into nothing but pure, unadulterated night. Stars exploded out of the darkness with an immensity that threatened to overwhelm her.

Sam gradually leveled them out. The nose of the plane descended, the acceleration settling so that she no longer felt as though she was being pressed against the back of her cockpit. The black line of the horizon shifted back into view, and Lily found herself a thousand feet in the air, looking down at the moon-shadowed fields and forests of Lorraine.

She understood now why Sam had bundled her into the wool coat. On the ground, it was spring, but here the wind carried an icy chill, and she was completely exposed to it. She pulled her scarf up higher, covering the exposed skin of her face with it. At least the force of the wind had fallen now that they were aloft. She no longer felt as though she were being buffeted by a hurricane.

Her perch at the front of the plane was bookended by a pair of massive guns. One was mounted in front of her. The other was attached to the end of a thick steel rod that protruded from between her and the place where Sam sat as he piloted the plane. Seeing them, she realized why her cockpit lacked a seat. Whoever held this precarious spot needed to be free to pivot between the two weapons to fend off an attacker. Her range with the forward gun was fairly broad, but the one behind would have to be aimed more carefully or risk hitting the plane, the propeller—or the pilot.

Though she now understood the logic behind it, the lack of a seat was harrowing. She crouched down as low in the cockpit as she could, twisting her hands in the leather straps bolted to the sides. They felt painfully insufficient.

She risked a glance back at Sam in his cockpit behind and slightly above her, the propeller a blur she could just glimpse over his shoulders. The collar of his great black coat was raised and buttoned, and he had at last fastened the straps of his fleece-lined helmet. Behind his goggles, his eyes were resolute.

It shocked her—seeing the grease-stained boy from The Refuge's garage at the controls of an airplane.

Of course, the man in the cockpit wasn't that boy anymore. He hadn't been for a long time.

They could not speak. The engine was far too loud, and the wind would carry any other sound away before it could be heard—not that it mattered. It was clear to Lily that Sam had no interest in talking about the past, in digging out the pain that lay between them and finding some way to a resolution.

He had granted her a lift. She had no right to ask for anything more from him.

The Fee banked slightly to the left as Sam responded to the sight of a familiar landmark below. He would be finding their way by the silver threads of streams and rivers, the dark patches that might indicate a town or a forest.

A strange scar in the ground below came into view, marked by the low orange glow of scattered campfires and the odd, unshaded lantern. The sparks of light came in two roughly parallel lines separated by a black ribbon.

It was the front line.

There was a distant crack. They were being fired on from the German side. Sam banked abruptly, making Lily grip tighter to her straps as he changed course to foil the ambitions of any anti-aircraft artillery in the vicinity.

He righted the Fee again with a twist the other way, and then the front was behind them.

The dark, rolling landscape below was identical to the one they had left behind—except that this belonged to the enemy.

The ground below changed texture. In the thin light of the moon, Lily realized they were flying over a larger settlement. She pulled on her limited mental geography. It had to be Metz. The city was blacked out, depriving Sam and his colleagues of any way to easily identify their targets.

Did that hold them at bay, she wondered? Or did they drop their bombs anyway, regardless of whether they took out a train junction or a block full of sleeping innocents?

She felt Sam bank them gently to the left. They would be flying north now, she deduced. Luxembourg must be sixty or so miles ahead.

Metz fell behind them, replaced by dark woodland, and something shifted in the sound of the engine, almost like an echo.

Sam leaned down over the front of his cockpit, smacking her urgently on the shoulder. His mouth was tight with tension. He pointed to the leather straps grimly.

It was a message Lily didn't need words to understand.

Hold on.

The meaning of that echoed engine noise dawned over her. They were no longer alone in the sky.

She twisted herself in tighter, bracing her feet... and the plane fell away from beneath her.

Sam's dive left her rising an inch or two off of the floor of the cockpit, only her grip on the straps keeping her from flying out completely. The Fee veered into a turn that seemed like it should tear them to pieces. The sound of their own engine rose to an urgent whine, and Lily risked a glance back.

There it was—a winged shadow against the starry blanket of the night. The world narrowed to the sound of her own breath in her ears, the quick thump of her heart. Was it an enemy?

The answer came in a chatter of machine gun fire.

Sam dove, twisting. The shots went wide, spraying into the air across their flank. The Fee rose again, throwing Lily against the rear of the cockpit. She closed her eyes instinctively against the fear.

That had been a terrible idea. She forced them open again.

There was only the one plane. They must have stumbled across a solo patrol. Had it been an entire German squad, they would already be dead.

Sam banked again, hurtling the plane through the sky. The dark shape of the enemy followed, moonlight glinting off the silver body of the aircraft. It was a German triplane, smaller than the Fee and more maneuverable. It carried the weight of only a single cockpit.

The triplane loosed another volley of gunfire. A trio of holes punched into the fabric of the wing.

They would not be able to outrun it. Lily did not need her onmyōdō to tell her there was only one path they could take that might save them from being blown out of the sky.

Sending out a silent prayer, she let go of the straps. Pivoting around, she faced the rear gun.

She made a quick study of it. She had little experience with fire-arms, but her brother-in-law, Walford, had dragged her out into the field behind Taddiford a handful of times to teach her the basics of firing a rifle alongside his older daughters. Portia had turned out to be a staggeringly good shot so long as she was wearing her spectacles.

Lily had done well enough.

The gun in front of her looked entirely foreign at first glance. It was longer and bigger than Walford's rifle with a broad metal disc fastened to the top of it—the ammunition magazine, she deduced. The barrel was enormous, like something designed to launch mortars, but a closer inspection revealed some key similarities.

Bolt. Grip. Trigger.

The weapon was mounted on a tall metal pole. The only way to reach it was to stand.

Her heart pounded. It was madness.

Another barrage of gunshots assailed them from the enemy fighter. Lily heard one plink off the metal casing of the engine.

Forcing the movement past her own visceral terror, Lily shifted into a crouch. She felt her body steady, finding its equilibrium with the wind, and then pushed to her feet, grasping the machine gun like a lifeline.

Sam's eyes, now level with her own, widened behind his goggles.

The walls of the cockpit barely reached her knees. It had to be as close as anyone could come to actually flying, and it was terrible.

The tone of the enemy engine changed. He was gathering speed, preparing for another attack.

Lily braced her feet, finding her balance. The gun was solidly mounted and steady under her hands. There would be no recoil. She fit the butt against her shoulder, taking the pistol grip in her hand.

The shadow of the triplane came at them from below, slightly to the left.

She pushed up through her thighs, shoving at the butt of the heavy weapon to bring the muzzle down. She aimed as carefully as she could between the fragile wings of the Fee. Grasping the bolt, she yanked it back and pulled the trigger.

The rattle jarred her teeth, noise hammering against her eardrums. Instead of the single neat crack of a rifle, she unleashed a hailstorm of bullets, sparks flying out into the night air. Lily released the trigger out of shock, thrown by a sudden terror of hitting their own plane.

The German fighter veered away, sliding back as the pilot worked to escape her range.

Lily followed him, using her shoulder to force the gun to move with an effort she could feel through her core. Sam flashed her a signal—a pivot to the right. Swallowing a sick burst of fear, she nodded in response, bracing herself.

The world shifted, the Fee sliding down and right. Lily clung to the gun, trying to push past her fear to watch for the fighter.

She sighted it behind them and released another burst of bullets.

The triplane rolled, coming up from beneath them. Another burst of gunfire scorched through the air. The bullets punched into the base of the plane, and the timbre of their engine shifted, taking on an alarming rattle. The smell of gasoline tainted the air.

Releasing the gun, Lily dropped back into the cockpit, grasping the side and throwing herself half over it as she looked down.

There was a hole in the plane, and it was leaking.

She whipped back up, looking at Sam. The line of his mouth was grim. He pointed to the front of the plane, then down.

Lily read the message. *Get the front gun. And brace yourself.*

Lily turned, thrusting her legs into the forward cavity and grabbing hold of the bow-mounted gun.

The engine stopped.

The nose of the plane dipped down gently . . . and then not so gently as their left wing dropped as well. Lily gritted her teeth as Sam sent the Fee into a gut-churning downward spiral. The quick shadow of the triplane whipped past her as she fought the urge to scream.

Time stilled, the moment suspended with crisp, frozen terror.

In the rush of the wind past her ears, she could almost hear the brush of great wings.

The engine coughed to life.

The Fee rattled like a child shaking a jar of marbles. Lily's teeth jarred together with a tang of copper. She gripped the gun as acceleration once more shoved her backward, clinging to the stock of it to avoid being thrown to the back of her perch.

She smelled smoke and the bitter taste of burning oil as the triplane came once more into view. The pilot was already veering, realizing his mistake—that Sam's deliberate and reckless stall of the engine had put the Fee at his rear—but Lily was already yanking back the bolt of the Lewis gun.

She unleashed a storm of bullets into his undercarriage.

She did not let go. She held the trigger down with gritted teeth until the aircraft above her abruptly sparked . . . and then burst into a chrysanthemum of flame.

Sam jammed the Fee to the right, lurching Lily against the side of the cockpit and turning his wings nearly vertical.

The blazing triplane plummeted past them, barely missing the wing.

Sam leveled them once more, and she looked down to see the flames of the German aircraft shrink to the size of a match-light, then abruptly bloom with a soft thunder as the plane hit the ground.

The entire encounter could not have taken more than three minutes. It felt like an eternity.

Behind her, the engine took on an earsplitting screech, then coughed.

The Fee jolted downward.

Sam adjusted their angle, controlling their descent. The ground still grew rapidly closer. Lily could make out the distinct textures of it—the dark fur of a woodland, the flat line of the fields—as the plane continued to struggle.

A pale scar revealed itself amid the rich darkness of the forest. Sam aimed them at it, Lily's mind slowly identifying it as a sand pit.

It rushed at them, and then they were upon it. The Fee jarred against the ground as sand flew up around them, blinding her and stinging her skin. With a great, terrible wrench, they whipped around in a sickening circle, slamming to rest against a dune.

The engine ticked softly against the silence. Lily stared at one of their two-tiered wings, trailing scraps of canvas and splintered spruce where it had torn from the body of the plane.

Her ears hummed with a low tone that felt dull after the roar of wind, motor, and guns.

Sam threw off his goggles and helmet, jumping down to her level and twisting his hand in her coat.

"Come on," he barked, and hauled at her.

A telltale distant buzz cut through the ringing in her ears. With a bolt of fear, Lily realized what it meant.

Their firefight had not gone unnoticed. More German planes were coming. It would be the impulse of a moment for them to strafe a deadly hail over the wreckage of the Fee as they flew by.

She scrambled into action. Pausing only to grab her pack and walking stick, she bolted after Sam, half-sliding down the side of the Fee until her boots hit the sand. Then they were running, sprinting towards the dark promise of the forest.

Machine gun fire sliced through the air behind her, a staccato that cut through the roar of the motors. Bullets pinged off the body of the Fee—followed by the soft whoosh of an explosion as a lucky shot ignited the remaining gasoline in their tank.

Flames roared up, consuming all that remained of the aircraft. Lily stood transfixed by it, shocked by the nearness of their destruction. Then Sam was yanking her into the embrace of the forest.

She ripped off her goggles, tossing them aside as they plunged through the undergrowth. Branches snapped at her face, occasionally catching at the bag she carried over her shoulder. Her breath came fast, burning in her lungs.

Sam was just ahead of her, dodging through the trees at something just short of a sprint, only pausing to yank her forward when she began to fall behind. In the darkness, the forest was nothing like those she knew in England. It was thicker, older, like something out of a fairy tale.

They ran for what seemed like an age before Lily finally halted, gasping.

"Stop. Please."

Sam turned, glaring back at her.

"Just for a moment," she pleaded, slumping against a primeval pine. She shrugged out of the borrowed coat, the wool stifling her. She slid down to the dry leaves, legs sprawling out before her. Her muscles ached with relief, her heart still struggling to return to a normal pace.

Sam glanced back the way they had come, then did the same, dropping down to the ground across from her.

"We don't know where we're going," Lily complained.

"North."

Sam pointed up at the sliver of moon just visible in a gap between the leaves.

Of course he would know. It would have been one of the most rudimentary forms of navigation for a pilot trained to fly at night.

"Where does North even take us? How far did we fly."

"We're about ten miles northwest of Metz," Sam returned.

Metz—they were still in German-occupied France.

"It's another fifteen miles to the border of Luxembourg. A dozen past that to the city itself," Sam added flatly.

Those borders had been open before the war save for sleepy checkpoints on the more widely traveled roads. The Germans had no need to fortify them when they occupied both countries. The impenetrable line of the front was the only real defense they needed.

"We can't wait until morning," Sam pointed out mercilessly. "They'll expect us to have run into the forest. They'll set trackers to find our path as soon as it's light enough, and we'll have left an obvious one crashing through the undergrowth in the dark."

"Then we should change direction," Lily determined, meeting his eyes across the distance that separated them. "And pick our way more carefully."

Sam nodded a curt approval.

Lily leaned back, trying to rest, even though she knew it couldn't last. Roughly thirty miles lay between her and her destination, two days walk at a minimum across unfamiliar and hostile territory. She had no idea how far this forest extended into Luxembourg, but at some point, she would have to leave it and find her way through more exposed territory. Both she and Sam were in civilian dress, but Sam was going to stand out. There were thousands of Chinese workers on the Allied side of the front, but the Central Powers had no such force.

"We have to find a way to get you back," she said, gut sinking with guilt for having dragged him into this.

Sam crossed his arms, leaning back against his tree.

"Don't worry about me."

"This is no time for bravado," Lily snapped back.

His eyes narrowed.

"It ain't bravado."

It wasn't. Lily could hear that in the ice in his voice. For whatever reason, Sam was not afraid of being exposed and shot as they crossed enemy land.

"So what's his lordship after in Luxembourg?" he demanded.

Lily closed her eyes. There was no avoiding it now. She owed him the answer.

"Your sister," she replied.

It had been nearly four years since Lily had last seen Wu Zhao Min, the woman who had named herself Madam White after a mythical snake, a spirit of transformation. And Zhao Min had transformed herself, turning from a victim plucked from the streets of Limehouse and subjected to unimaginable torment to the quiet mastermind of a private intelligence ring. When Lily met her, Zhao Min had been ruthlessly selling her information, showing no loyalty or obligation to anyone. Why should she? She knew all too well the character of the men whose secrets she exploited—and that of the ones she did business with.

Zhao Min had looked out only for herself and the women who worked with her. Then, four years ago, the Germans marched into Belgium and slaughtered a safehouse of innocents Zhao Min had helped escape from the virtual slavery of London's whorehouses.

That violence had earned them a very dangerous enemy.

Lily's father had never said as much out loud, but she had long ago deduced that Torrington's unofficial and highly effective source behind German lines was Sam's older sister.

She didn't know how things had been left between Sam and Zhao Min when they departed to play their distinct parts in the war. She only knew that the history between them was complicated and rife with suffering.

"What is Jiějie doing in Luxembourg?"

"What do you think?"

Sam drove a fist into the tree, just hard enough to hurt, and then whirled on her.

"Your old man behind it?"

"I rather suspect Zhao Min approached him with the idea," Lily replied.

"You know where she is?" he demanded.

"I have an address."

As the words left her lips, she wondered whether Sam would assume that Zhao Min had shared it with her rather than her flesh-and-blood sibling—but no. For all their estrangement, he knew who his sister had become. She wasn't the sort to trust her safety to anyone. She almost certainly hadn't done so with Lily's father, either. It was far more likely he had quietly sniffed out the address himself. Torrington was not one to leave anything to chance.

"And what about his lordship? He got any notion you're following along behind him?"

Lily clenched her hands against her knees.

"I didn't form the plan until after he had left."

"Convenient, that."

Sam's words were biting. She could hear the anger in him and knew it had nothing to do with Strangford.

She rose to her feet.

"If you have something to say to me, Sam, say it now."

"It ain't like that."

Her own temper began to flare.

"It bloody well is. I won't risk bickering with you through thirty miles of enemy ground. So if you have something to say, say it now."

He didn't answer. Instead, his eyes moved into the darkness that surrounded them.

Lily gritted her teeth.

"I will not allow you to simply ignore—"

"Something's here," he cut in.

The trees rustled softly over head. Everything about Sam had gone quiet, as though he was reaching out with his mind into the darkness.

"What is it?" Lily asked, her voice instinctively dropping to a whisper.

His eyes snapped back to hers, sharpening.

"Wolves," he breathed.

A chill of fear slid down her spine.

Lily listened for it, tuning her own senses to the silence that surrounded them. There it was, a quiet crunch of dry leaves.

Something was moving towards them, stalking carefully through the shadows.

Another subtle rustle caught her ear, this time from the opposite direction.

"How much trouble are we in?"

"They're hunting us," Sam said.

Fear rose. It railed at her with a primitive urge to run as the sounds moved closer.

"Tell them to go away."

He glared sideways at her.

"What're they going to listen to me for?"

She bit back a curse. She knew that wasn't how Sam's power worked. He could not control animals, only communicate with them. Getting them to do what he wanted was a fine and delicate art.

"Then how do we stop them?"

"Convince them it's a bad idea," he replied dryly.

Her eyes went to the sidearm he wore under his coat.

"Shoot. Scare them off." she suggested.

"We ain't that far from the crash site, and that place must be crawling with Germans by now. I shoot, they're going to hear it, and they'll know exactly where we are."

There was a soft crackle of dry leaves as something darted through the underbrush to her left. In the dim, filtered moonlight, Lily caught sight of a gleam of silver fur.

"They're trying to flank us," Sam said, taking another step to put his back to hers.

His hand dipped into his pocket. With a flick of his wrist, a lean silver blade snapped into place. Lily knew that Sam was quite capable of using it... but against a pack of wolves?

"Tell them we're dangerous," she pushed as she glimpsed another sleek flash of movement through the trees.

There was no change in Sam, nothing but a fierce concentration as he held the knife ready in his hand and glared out into the shadows that surrounded them.

The soft noises paused for a moment. Lily could almost sense the pack absorbing Sam's warning, considering it.

The rustling returned, moving closer. A branch danced as another wolf moved into place. They were being carefully and thoroughly surrounded.

Her heart fluttered rapidly in her chest, her skin going over with a cold sweat.

This was what it felt like to be prey.

Behind her, Sam hissed, an instinctive and angry sound of disapproval.

"What is it?" she demanded, then pressed when he did not immediately answer. "Sam!"

"They're going after the female first. Think she'll be weaker."

A familiar heat coiled up at Sam's words, burning away the chill of the forest.

Weaker?

Her heartbeat steadied, her vision sharpening. The rage that filled her was calm, sure, and dangerously focused. Details became clearer—the rough texture of bark, the delicate curl of brown leaves covering the ground. She could taste the crisp clarity of the air on her tongue.

A pure, steady hunger electrified her limbs, promising victory. Promising blood.

This time, Lily didn't fight it. Instead, she slid off her motorcycle jacket, dropping it to the ground. The staff turned smoothly in her hand, the easy weight of it like an extension of her being.

"Step back," she ordered.

Sam whirled on her, shock mingling with disapproval.

"Bloody hell, Lily." he protested.

She glared back.

"You know perfectly well what I am capable of." she seethed, the words edged like knives.

He went still, and she could see in his face that he did. After all, he had been there the first time. It was not something he was likely to forget.

Sam moved carefully away from her. He put his back to a weathered oak, the knife still ready in his hand.

Her power slipped into place like another skin, her easy knowledge of the future merging with a guiding breath of her onmyōdō.

They would try to scare her into bolting. A young male waited to the east, his jaws ready for a throat, an ankle—whichever target best presented itself when he prepared to leap.

He would be surprised.

They all would be surprised.

Readiness coiled in her, melting fire into her hands, her calves. Lily blazed with it, the awareness of what would come and how she must meet it as sure and steady as the earth beneath her boots.

Left.

The male darted from behind a tree, rushing towards her, his powerful legs eating up the distance. When she did not run, he changed tactics, thighs coiling for a spring.

Rib height. Now.

Lily snapped her staff, the movement clean and strong. It connected with his jaw, the crack of it echoing through the high canopy of the midnight forest.

Shock staggered him. The wolf shook his head as though he could fling off the pain. He turned, snarling, for another leap.

It would be high, six stone of predator flying into her chest and knocking her to the ground. He would pivot then with animal grace, sinking his teeth into her neck.

The power that thrummed through her promised to play out a different tune, one laced with blood.

The wolf leapt. Lily thrust her staff, driving the end of it into his throat.

He fell hard to the side, sliding across the ground with a wheeze of pain, but the others were already coming.

Four of them charged from the forest around her, lean and strong. They were not winter-whittled but sleek with the flesh of fallen men and horses at the nearby front line.

There was no time for thought, only motion, a fierce and graceful dance of destruction that slicked through her veins, fueled by the black and luxurious cascade of her power.

Wood connected with fur. Slash, swing, return. A silver body slid across the ground, pushing up a wake of dry leaves. Another leapt back with a whimper, favoring a leg.

Two remained, one before and the other behind her. She faced the first, knowing what would come. The pain it entailed was irrelevant. The path before her blazed with rightness like a whip of fire through the smoke inside her mind.

The female pounced, slashing black jaws. Lily snapped a blow at her head as, from behind, a second set of teeth sank into her ankle.

She was already moving. Her staff drove down and back, powered by the return momentum of her swing at the female. The end of it slammed through the cavity of an eye and down into the earth.

At her feet, the dead wolf twitched, blood pouring over her boot.

The rest of the pack watched from their various distances, ears flattened, their tails dropping.

As one, they turned, darting back into the shadows, the soft patter of their footsteps rapidly fading into the distance.

The yearning to follow them tugged at her chest. She felt the primal thrill of it—the chase past tree and hill, the raw breath in her throat and hot muscle as she pounded forward. The warmth of blood on her hands, the fierce joy of destruction until all of them were gone.

"Lily."

The voice tugged at her brain, a nagging pull against the momentum of her desire. It repeated, stubborn and unwelcome.

"*Lily.*"

It registered at last, and Lily lurched back from that dark instinct. Her fingers clenched against the wood of her staff until it hurt, but she was here once more—in the present with Sam's hand on her shoulder as he gazed at her, calling her back.

Blood seeped into the dry leaves that covered the ground. The dead wolf already looked different, tattered and tawdry like a piece of refuse.

Sam released her, moving away. Lily bent down and tugged at her laces. She slipped a hand into her boot where the leather was punctured and felt where the blood had soaked her sock.

"I don't suppose you have any whiskey." she asked.

Sam wordlessly reached into his coat pocket and pulled out a flask. He removed the cap and handed it to her.

"Gin," he said.

Lily sat down beside the dead wolf, her staff rising like a flagpole from its skull. She pulled off her boot and rolled down the sock, then took Sam's flask. She tried to pour the gin over her wounds, but her hands shook, making her clumsy.

Sam knelt beside her, taking the flask. He poured for her, the alcohol spilling over the two neat places where the teeth had managed to puncture her skin, twin full moons on either side of her ankle.

The gin burned. Lily endured it with a grimace.

Sam took a gulp from the flask, wiping his mouth.

The chill came over her gradually, sweeping from her back down into her hands, the trembling aftermath of violence. Her bare foot looked pale against the ground, drained by the dim light of the stars. There would be blood on her staff now, and more. Things she would have to wash off. How could she wash it off?

"What am I, Sam?" she whispered, bringing her shaking hands under her arms and holding herself against the dread that threatened to choke her.

It was the question she had wanted to ask for four years, ever since the moment he had watched her nearly kill a man who should have pounded her into the floor.

She looked up to where he leaned against the ancient bark of his oak, expecting to see fear or disgust in his eyes. Something else lay there instead—dark, knowing.

Shoving the flask into his pocket, he stalked over and grasped the staff. Lily looked away as he yanked it free. He wiped it on the pelt and handed it back to her.

It was still stained. Lily wondered if it would ever come off.

"Put your boot on," he ordered. "We need to go."

THIRTEEN

Tuesday, April 23
An hour before dawn
Occupied France

$\mathcal{L}$ILY STOOD AT THE EDGE of a nameless river. The dark water foamed between moss-covered banks still swathed in the shadows of lingering night. Sam eyed the current, then spat.

"Ain't fording that," he concluded.

They followed the water until they reached a bridge that led into a little hamlet. Dawn was just brightening the eastern sky. They crossed in silence, moving swiftly back into the shelter of the trees.

A tavern squatted near the outskirts of the cluster of houses, the forest encroaching upon its tidy yard full of neglected flowers. A German Army officer sat at one of the weathered outdoor tables, devouring an early breakfast.

Lily slipped further back into the trees, intending to make a quick and quiet retreat. Sam's hand stopped her. There was a familiar gleam in his eye as he studied the man.

Sam's gaze shifted to the trees. He chirped, a bright and mischievous sound. A moment later, a pair of gray squirrels spun down the trunk of a neighboring beech, bounding across the ground to where they stood.

The animals sprang forward, climbing him like a branch and darting playfully across his shoulders. One of them reached up and gave his hair a tug hard enough to make him wince.

"Enough of that," Sam complained in a whisper, plucking the squirrel from his head and setting it on the ground again.

He crouched down by the animals. Though no words were spoken, Lily knew that a conversation was taking place.

It appeared only one of the squirrels was listening. The other had taken to trying to pounce on its own tail.

"On with you, then," Sam ordered with an exasperated wave.

The pair leapt away, dodging through the forest to the tavern. They made it roughly half the distance before they paused to wrestle with each other, forcing Sam to hiss them back into line.

Alongside Sam, Lily crept forward until the German hauptmann was just visible between the soft green veil of the underbrush. She watched as two gray bodies darted out across the lawn to where the officer munched on his toast.

Unnoticed by the hauptmann, one of the squirrels started to sniff at the satchel by the man's feet. The other turned from the bag to scour the ground for crumbs.

"Don't you even think about it … " Sam muttered under his breath, his eyes on the slightly more focused of the two creatures.

The first squirrel straightened, ears twitching as it looked at the woods—then dove into the hauptmann's bag. A fluffy gray tail twitched excitedly where it hung over the side. A moment later, the creature emerged with something clutched between its teeth.

It made it roughly halfway across the lawn before its partner pounced on top of it. The pair of them proceeded to wrestle.

"Bloody squirrels," Sam swore.

Finally, the two rodents untangled themselves and bounded the rest of the way into the woods. Sam was forced to engage in a brief game of dart and chase before he let out a hiss of irritation that had both animals flattening themselves against the ground. Sam snatched the object the first squirrel still held in its mouth, and then the pair were dashing away through the underbrush, crashing along with a sound like something three times their size ought to make.

Sam unfolded a packet of papers.

"Sixty francs and two hundred marks. Ain't much, but it might get us a bite to eat and a roof over our heads for the night. Let's keep hold of this as well, shall we? Could stack up nicely later on."

He flashed her the officer's identification papers, then tucked them neatly into his coat pocket.

"Best wait till the next village before we cash in, just in case Herr Hauptmann realizes someone's made off with his blunt," Sam determined, setting off again through the woods.

They reached another settlement after a two-hour slog through the forest. Lily took some of Sam's squirrel-thieved cash and braved the village's main and only street, using it to buy a few pieces of dried meat and some biscuits nearly hard enough to chip a tooth. Sam softened them in a bit of water. She was hungry enough that she managed to wolf down all of it under the shelter of a glacial boulder covered in moss.

She didn't realize she was slumping back against the stone until Sam spoke up.

"You should rest. I'll keep watch."

"You need rest, too," Lily countered. "We should keep going until we find someplace safer."

Sam shrugged, devouring the rest of his biscuit. Rising, he brushed off the crumbs.

"Come along, then."

~

They ran out of forest three hours later on the outskirts of Thionville. Lily and Sam lingered within the shadows of the trees, looking out across the fields to the clustered buildings of a town three times as large as the little hamlets they had passed on their way here.

Lily's exhaustion was a weight dragging her toward the earth. Her hunger had already returned with force, unsatisfied by the snack they had managed earlier.

"I'll go," she said tiredly. "See how things lay."

Sam didn't protest. When she glanced back at the forest, she could see no sign of him, not even the telltale black flash of his coat.

Within Thionville, Lily was hardly spared a look. Plenty of the other women here wore trousers, with earth-stained hands and tired eyes that spoke of farms struggling through the absence of their men.

They were also thin in a way that signaled the lean edge of

starvation. Life had not been kind to those living under German occupation. Not everyone here would be her enemy, but Lily would be a fool to trust that. She needed to find a way to make Sam attract less notice.

Her route took her past the train station. Lily glanced through the gates to the interior.

It was crawling with German soldiers.

Her breath came short, pulse pounding as she forcibly reminded herself that there was no reason for them to take any notice of her—unless she was foolish enough to run.

The men were smoking and stretching their legs. Their train must have stopped briefly to take on more fuel or supplies. It was clearly a transport run of some sort, moving men from one part of the front to another. Lily thought back to what George had said in Montreuil and wondered briefly it if would be worth trying to find out where they were going.

Perhaps if she wanted to be shot as a spy.

She pivoted, driven by an urgent need to get away, and bumped into someone.

Greenish-gray wool swam in front of her eyes, screaming threat. Hands caught her shoulders, and she found herself looking up at the awkward smile of a tall young German soldier.

"Entschuldigung, Fräulein," he said.

"Mais oui," Lily replied shortly, managing a curt nod.

He released her and moved past, rejoining his colleagues with a raucous burst of laughter that set her teeth on edge.

Lily hurried past the station. She did not breathe steadily until she had rounded the corner, stopping to lean against the wall for a moment.

Raising her eyes, she faced the window of an optometrist's shop.

Something like an idea took shape in her mind.

~

An hour later, Lily slipped back into the dappled shadows of the forest. The distant clatter of life from the town fell away with a rustling of leaves and the crunch of her boots on the ground. She found Sam with his back against a tree, eyes closed.

Lily tossed her purchases into his lap, and he startled into consciousness.

"You shouldn't have done that," she warned.

"Done what?"

"Fallen asleep. Anyone might've come across you."

"You don't need to worry about me," he snapped back.

Something in the words rang oddly in her ears. It reminded her of what he had said back in his room before they left Ochey.

My neck's safer than you think.

Sam shifted his attention to her haul. He examined the cap she had brought him. It was nearly identical to the one she had bought for herself—gray tweed, used but serviceable. He set it on his head.

The other item was a narrow case of waxed canvas. Sam shook out its contents, holding up a pair of tinted spectacles.

Lily had seen similar devices pop up in London over the last few years, created by optometrists to aid soldiers whose eyes had been damaged in the war. The darkened lenses helped them with light sensitivity while they recovered.

Sam raised an eyebrow at her.

"Bit obvious, innit?"

"Not to someone who doesn't know what to look for. Unless you have a better idea?"

"Nope," he returned comfortably.

He slipped on the spectacles. The tint was dark. It was impossible to make out more than the vague shape of Sam's eyes through the glass.

"I must look like a bloody beggar," he complained.

"Better that than a dead man," she returned. "Now, come along."

They passed through the town. Lily felt terribly vulnerable, even though she knew the Germans looking for the occupants of the downed aircraft from the night before could have no idea what the pilot looked like and whether anyone had been with him. They certainly wouldn't be expecting him to be walking with a woman. Sam still drew an unwelcome amount of attention. The spectacles were partly to blame, but Lily caught more than a few eyes lingering on his long black coat. The obvious quality of it was a problem. Thionville had been occupied for nearly four years. No one here possessed a garment like that.

The lodging house Lily had identified on her earlier pass through the town looked like a farmhouse, complete with a handful of scraggly chickens pecking in the yard. The shutters were sagging, the roof tiles cracked.

The woman behind the counter looked as weathered as the house and named an exorbitantly high price for the two rooms Lily requested.

Lily stammered a protest in French, managing not to mangle the words. The woman shrugged.

"Prenez-en une," she bluntly returned.

"C'est mon frère," Lily tried.

Even as the words left her mouth, Lily recognized it would be rather a stretch for someone to believe that Sam was her brother, even with his distinctive eyes concealed by the glasses.

"Alors vous pouvez la partager," she retorted, slapping a single key on the table.

It took Lily's exhausted brain an extra moment to translate.

Then you can share.

To argue would only have drawn more attention, and she didn't have the energy to seek an alternative. Giving in, Lily took the key and dragged herself up the stairs.

The room was small, tucked under the attic with walls that sloped steeply down. There was only a single bed.

"I'll take the floor," Sam said.

Lily mustered an objection.

"Just because I'm a woman—"

"Dry up," Sam cut in gracelessly.

He flopped down onto the threadbare, faded carpet, stuffing his coat under his head for a pillow and promptly closing his eyes. Lily had to admit he looked convincingly fine with it.

It was barely midafternoon. They had not had anything remotely approaching a proper meal. Lily could not muster the will to care.

Sitting on the bed, she cast a last tired glance at Sam on the rug.

"You'll have to lose that coat," she said thinly.

"No," he muttered back without opening his eyes.

"It's too fine," she mumbled as she fell to her side onto the creaking mattress, her own eyelids drooping. "People notice."

"Then I'll bloody well carry it."

Then he was asleep. It happened in a blink, the change clear to her in the subtle shift in the rhythm of his breathing. Her body aching for reprieve, Lily gave in to her own oblivion.

~

Lily woke to the sound of the innkeeper pounding on her door, shouting in French about the checkout time. Sam muttered an eloquent string of quiet East End curses from his place on the floor as he rolled over. Lily called over him to the door, blurting out a promise of their imminent departure.

She was both rested and starving. Her legs ached, her skin blooming with bruises she had not realized she had acquired during the crash. She felt it all as she descended the stairs to the ramshackle parlor that passed for a breakfast room. The bread tasted more of sawdust than flour. Lily set it aside. At least there were eggs.

They walked carefully past the train station. This time, it was empty of German soldiers.

"We're better off on our feet," Sam noted quietly from beside her.

Lily knew it was true. They would be more conspicuous on a train, and there was nowhere to run. They were safer walking where they could keep to less-traveled roads or simply hide if someone who might pose a threat came by.

At a stable just outside the town, Sam neatly plucked a piece of old rope from a fence post as the single weathered nag in the yard looked placidly on. He used it to tie his conspicuous overcoat into a bundle on his back, leaving him in his shirtsleeves and waistcoat. It was an admitted improvement. At least now, he looked like any other poor traveler on the road, save for the tinted glasses.

They reached the border with Luxembourg around two o'clock. Sam led them off the road and into another patch of forest, avoiding any checkpoint might have been posted. The only sign that they were leaving France was a rusted wire fence set up by some woodsman to mark the edge of his property. They climbed over it easily and had officially entered the Grand Duchy.

Afternoon was wearing toward evening when Sam stopped,

gazing across the fields at a run-down farmhouse. The road to either side was long, straight, and deserted. He pulled off his glasses.

"Let's have a nose about," he said.

The fields around the building had been left fallow for more than a single season. Saplings raised their slender forms here and there among the spring grass. Weeds grew through the packed earth of the driveway. The windows were empty except for fragments of splintered glass.

Several rails of the fence had fallen, the posts tilted at crazy angles. There were no animals in sight. Whoever lived here had either run or been taken by the war a long time ago.

The front door was rotted and pulling loose from one of its hinges. Someone else had shattered the lock long enough ago for the exposed pieces to have rusted. Sam pushed inside with a nudge from his shoulder.

The house was small, consisting of just two rooms and a sagging loft. Light spilled down through a trio of holes in the roof. Their entrance startled a pair of mourning doves who cooed and fluttered in alarm until Sam made a shushing sound. One of the birds swept down to land on the edge of a toppled, three-legged table beside him. Sam stuck out an absent-minded hand, and the dove hopped onto his arm.

There was more broken glass on the floor next to the abandoned nest of some animal. The whole place smelled of damp and rot.

"Let's try the barn," Sam said, lifting the dove from his shoulder and gently setting it down on the remnants of the table.

They made their way out into the evening light, shoving open the leaning door of the barn. It protested against rusted hinges. Above the ancient stone walls, the roof was still mostly intact, the interior of the building clean and empty save for a few dry leaves in the corner.

"This'll do for the night." Sam declared, dropping the sack of food they had bought with the last of their money onto the dusty floorboards.

He took off his cap, tossing it down as well and running a hand through his flattened black hair as he slumped down against one of the posts.

A pair of rats crawled out from a hole in the back of the barn, whiskers twitching curiously. Lily had long since ceased to be alarmed by the sight of them. They scurried up to Sam and tentatively sniffed at his fingers. He scratched one of them behind the ear.

He had disliked them more when Lily had first met him. The creatures must have grown on him since then. He owed them a degree of respect, at least, after their ilk had gotten him out of more than a few close scrapes.

The other rat worked its way over to Lily. They weren't city rats. They were cleaner, soft and sleek. A warm brown in color, they looked both healthy and well-fed.

The rat nudged her fingers. Lily relented, giving it a stroke. The animal's pelt was warm.

"Are they always this friendly in the country, or is it you?" she asked, half-jokingly.

Sam didn't answer. He rose to his feet, glaring down at her, as furious as she had ever seen him.

"When were you going to tell me?" he demanded coldly.

"Tell you what?" Lily returned, confused.

"That you're pregnant."

The words hit like darts of glass.

That. You're. Pregnant.

Lily froze.

"How did you ... " she stammered softly. "How could you possibly ..."

"They can smell it on you," Sam bit back. He nodded stiffly at the rat under Lily's hand. "She's a mum as well."

The female gave a last press into her palm before darting back into the hole in the wall. *Her nest,* Lily thought numbly. Her young must be hidden inside.

The air in the barn had turned thick, her thoughts moving as though through mud.

Distance unfurled around her—the terrible miles of trench and artillery, war and the dead that lay between her and home. Between her and Strangford.

The stone walls of the barn drew closer, stealing her breath as memory assailed her.

The terrible pain. The splash of blood on linen. The grief that set its teeth into her heart.

A damnable urge rose within her, her power lurching to life in a manner as unwelcome as it was involuntary.

Somewhere beyond that, somewhere outside of her, Sam was yelling.

"—let me take you up in a bloody aircraft where we were *shot at.* Bloody *crashed.* Marching through the damned Bochelands and do you have any idea what they'll do—"

"No," Lily gasped, her nails digging into her palms as she battled it—that flaring, uncontrollable impulse to thrust forward through time.

To see what was coming for her.

"*No.*"

Sam's anger dropped at the raw sound of her voice.

"Lily." he asked, kneeling beside her.

"I don't want to know. I don't want to see it. Sam ... " His name was a sob, one that choked out of her. "Please make it stop."

Arms came around her, holding her with a solid strength she could feel through her coat. The vision blooming inside of her pressed up against the warmth of an embrace that felt strangely like determination ... and then broke, washing back down like water through sand.

In its wake came a flood of emotion, everything Lily had so carefully dammed up, spilling out in a moan of animal pain.

"Shhh. Hey. It's alright. You're alright."

Sam's words were meaningless, a comforting noise, but they seeped through the place where his arms met her coat, warming into her skin. Lily felt them with something that went beyond language. It steadied her, pushing back the fluttering panic that beat against the walls of her chest.

She felt spring sunlight on her face. Laughter over a box of illicit sweets. The smell of horses and motor oil as a heart beat steadily under her ear.

A realization sparked. She voiced it aloud in surprise from where her head rested against his chest.

"Is that you?"

"What?" he retorted, stiffening.

"That ... feeling."

Sam looked embarrassed.

"A bit. Maybe."

"How is that possible?" Lily demanded.

He shrugged with his arms still around her, and for a moment, he sounded more like the boy she knew than the man he had grown into.

"It's just what I do," he replied.

Lily could still feel the echo of it, warm and steady inside of her. It was like home, or friendship, or love.

"But I thought it was just animals."

"We are animals, ain't we?" Sam returned defensively.

He glanced out toward the crack in the barn door where the last orange rays of the sunset were leaking in, still holding Lily against his chest.

"It works the same with people as it does anything else," he explained. "Their minds are just too busy to notice. It's how I used to hook so many pockets. Give 'em a little nudge—what's that over there? Or hey, everything's easy. Nothing to worry about here. Not like they know what I'm about—it's just a bit of noise in the background—but sometimes it helped."

"The rats, the other animals. They notice it. Understand that it's you," Lily filled in carefully, feeling her way through this surprising and uncharted territory.

"They pay it more mind than we do," Sam confirmed. "And I mean for them to notice. I'm not trying to ... slide it by, so to speak."

That immediate golden burst of Sam's power had faded now, but Lily still held to the afterglow, keeping it close inside of her.

"Thank you," she said.

"You lost one, didn't you?"

Lily nodded, her cheek brushing against his shirt. The tears welled up again. She let them come, feeling one slide across her skin.

"Why didn't you tell me?"

"It's not the sort of thing you put in letters," she softly returned.

He was quiet above her. In the stillness, Lily could just make out the peeping of the rat's nest nearby as the mother nursed her pups.

Light danced in the suspended motes of dust that floated around her.

207

"I've missed you," she confessed.

It felt safer somehow to speak the words aloud when she couldn't see his face—only feel the solid warmth of him beside her.

"So much," she added, her voice breaking on the words.

His shoulders tensed. Very gently, Sam untangled himself from her, standing and moving away.

"I'm not the same."

She shook her head. "That doesn't matter."

Something in him coiled up with a tension that drew at the shadows lingering in the corners of the room.

"You don't know what I've done," he said. "What I've become."

Lily pushed herself up to face him.

"Then tell me," she ordered.

There was something wolfish in the flash of his teeth.

"It ain't a pretty story."

"I didn't ask for pretty," she retorted.

He laughed. It was a dark sound like claws skittering against stone.

"I suppose you've a right to know what you're traveling with."

Outside the barn, the sun slipped below the horizon. The light shifted from gold to a violet-edged twilight. Inside, the darkness thickened. Something stirred in the rafters overhead. *Bats*, Lily thought absently. She didn't fear those either. Not with Sam around.

"I joined the Royal Flying Corps as a mechanic," Sam began, his tone deceptively easy. "They wised up quick enough that I was more than just some blockhead with a wrench. By my sixth month, I'd jumped to first class and was running a crew."

None of this surprised Lily. Sam had always been clever with machines. It was a natural talent, reinforced by his years of tinkering at The Refuge.

"In '16, they started running short of observers. Too many of them had been blown out of the sky. There's hazard pay for those that go up into the air, so beetle-brain that I am, I volunteered."

An observer would typically occupy the cockpit Lily had perched in two nights before, making careful notes about German troop and artillery positions while the pilot behind them flew the aircraft. It was a dangerous job, like anything else in the sky. The casualty rate for airmen was easily three times that of any other branch of service, even the famously expendable infantry.

Something about Sam's story began to fill her with a creeping sense of dread.

"Took me maybe a month up there to figure out how the pilots managed it. I had half the puzzle already, of course, knowing the nuts-to-bolts of the machine. The rest was easy enough. Throttle, lift, wind, altitude. Course I knew better than to think I'd ever be flying myself. They'd only just started letting regular blokes into pilot training instead of sticking to toffs. Posh lads got a bit thin on the ground once their old men wised up to the likely life span of dear Clarence if he took to the sky. But then, I ain't a regular bloke. Low-class and Chinese, that's me, whatever else it said on my papers. I knew better than to apply.

"I was on a recon run over Lille when we're suddenly swarmed by the Boche. Pilot was an Oxford chum. Real rotter. He takes a shot in the arm. Can't manage the stick. So I climb back there, bull him out of the seat, and take over. Land us safely home with nary a jolt. Well—they don't so much mind where I came from then, short on airmen and the schools delivering at half the rate the war was eating 'em up. More or less handed me my wings and tossed me back up in the air."

Outside, the late spring insects started up, buzzing softly. The barn grew dark, casting Sam's familiar face in shadows.

"I did alright. Helped some that I understood the plane well enough to take the bloody thing apart and put it together again if I wanted to. I knew exactly what it was capable of, so I pushed it a bit further than some of the other boys—but not so far as the pillocks who got themselves stuck in a roll they couldn't pull out of. I was mostly running observation missions. They partnered me with a Bristol lad, Nate Levinson. Decent sort. Bit of a square—fine family and all that—but we got on. Called me his friend. Who was I to argue?"

Nothing changed in Sam's tone, and yet Lily felt it coming—the darkness in his story creeping toward them like a fog.

"We went up on a run last August, and this Boche unit comes in from the southeast. Twelve of them to our five. Had the new triplanes like the one that sunk us night before last. Levinson took a bullet to

209

the head."

The implication sank through her, ripe with horror.

"He would have been sitting right in front of you," Lily blurted, remembering her own position in the plane. "You would have seen it."

"Different plane. But yeah. He was. And I did more than see it," Sam replied.

He said no more. He didn't have to. Lily could deduce the rest, and it was terrible.

"The engine was damaged. Coolant leak. I tied off the stick, climbed back, stopped it up with my glove, and refilled it with my canteen. Managed to limp back to base. Didn't even realize I'd been shot as well until we were on the ground and the medic was hauling me to a stretcher."

"Where?" Lily demanded, her throat dry.

Sam flicked loose the buttons of his waistcoat. Yanking his shirt from his belt, he exposed an angle of his flank. The scar was a thick white line against the warmer tan of his skin, carving along his waist.

He shoved the shirt back into his trousers.

"Missed my guts by a quarter-inch. Bought me four weeks of lying on my back. When I finally got up again, I had a day or two of moving about without feeling like my insides were going to fall out before my chief mechanic dropped by to warn me the unit commander would be ordering me back up. He wanted to make sure I was ready."

"Were you?"

He lowered his head. His voice, when it emerged, was harsh as the croak of a carrion-eater.

"No."

It took him a moment to continue.

"Turns out having Nate's brains on my coat put me off flying. The notion of going back up there . . . did things to me. Made my hands weak. Couldn't breathe right."

Sam stiffened, his voice hardening.

"I'd gone soft. Afraid of dying. The CO wasn't going to take that as an excuse. So I found another way to solve the problem."

A cold instinct crawled over her skin.

"What did you do?"

There was more of a demand in the words than Lily had intended. Sam didn't miss it, turning to face her. His eyes were a pair of deeper shadows watching her through the gloom settling over the barn.

"Made a deal with the birds."

There was only one bird Sam could be talking about. Lily knew the truth like a stab of ice to her guts.

"The ravens," she replied.

The word felt like an oath.

She had dealt with those black watchers in the past. One such bargain had saved her life—at the cost of two others. She had heard their cries echoing through the space between life and death. Even the fact that Strangford was somehow owed a boon by them after his sacrifice in the train wreck at Ludgate did nothing to endear them to her.

She had to moisten her dry throat before she could ask the rest.

"What sort of deal?"

"Told them to keep me alive," Sam replied.

Lily's world was quietly flipping over, twisting in on itself.

"They can do that?"

"For a price," he returned flatly.

"What kind of price?" she asked, already dreading the answer.

"What do you think?"

It was a handful of syllables, a bit of air and noise, and yet it felt like something inside of her was breaking.

"You've killed for them."

Sam flashed her a sharp, dark look.

"You found me in a uniform, Lily." he replied. "You think they give those out for show?"

The barn felt colder. Lily put her arms around herself.

"No," she said quietly. "It would have to be more than that. You told me once they don't just want blood. They want sacrifice. Doing what you already swore to do when you enlisted—where's the sacrifice in that?"

She raised her eyes to meet his gaze across the weathered floor of the barn.

"What did you give them, Sam?"

She saw it—the flinch, as though her question were a dart that struck its target. He shifted from it, looking away as he pressed on with his story.

"I'd been flying observation. I asked for a transfer to a fighter squadron. Anti-aircraft patrols. Trench strafing."

"Trench strafing?" Lily echoed.

"You fly low over the enemy position. Fire into the backs of their heads. Ain't many who'll volunteer for it—puts you within range of the Boche artillery. But then, I didn't have to worry about that."

"How is that possible?"

He closed his eyes, gathering himself.

"It's like the devil's own luck. A perfect updraft comes along. Guns jam. Engines stall. Triplane caught me by surprise one night. Took sixteen rounds in my wing. Four more ricocheted off the fuselage. Worst I got of it was a graze to the temple."

He tapped the vulnerable place under his dark hairline.

He made it sound almost straightforward. Lily knew it was nowhere near that simple.

"How could a batch of birds manage all that?"

He shrugged, the gesture sharp, his arms crossed defensively.

"I dunno how it works. But it's them, and it does."

"You know that for certain?" she pressed.

His gaze had a bleakness to it that stole any remaining breath from her argument.

"I know."

She might have pressed for more details. Lily found she didn't want to.

"So that's it, then. You keep killing, and they keep you alive?"

He shifted uncomfortably.

"Not exactly."

The dry, quiet space of the barn was cloaked with shadows. Something scratched inside the walls. Lily forced herself to think of a mother rat curled around her young.

"They keep me alive. I kill the ones they ask me for."

It was the revelation she had not known she was waiting for—something much more than simple slaughter, the duty demanded of every man thrown into the war with a gun in his grip.

"Ask you for?" she echoed with soft horror. "Sam, you're talking about murder. You aren't a murderer."

He was a thing of terrible contrasts across the room, of paled skin and shadow.

"You have no idea what I am anymore."

Lily stepped forward.

"No. Fear might've driven you to it, but you would've stopped, even if it meant your life. So what else is it? What else do they have on you?"

"What do you know about it?" Sam spat back.

Lily twisted her fist in the front of his shirt, yanking him closer as she glared up at him.

"*I know you*," she ground back. "Now lie to me again. Go ahead and bloody try."

She could see the moment his armor cracked. Beyond it lay all that he had been hiding from her with his empty postcards, his hard distance.

Terror. Guilt. Grief.

"They take the ones that matter to me." He shoved her back, stalking to a distance before turning on her like a caged animal. "I fail them, and they take someone I care about. A private who was kind to me in the canteen. Maybe a girl I'd had a bit of a flirt with. The big ones, I think they're saving so I'll keep thinking about it. Wondering who could be next. It don't look like murder, just rotten bad luck. But it's them, and I know it. They make bloody sure that I know it."

The horror of it rooted her to the floor, washing a sense of helplessness through her.

"Oh, Sam," she whispered, aching.

"Don't," he snapped back, violence in his tone. "Don't give me your sympathy. I don't want it."

Lily bit back the rest. She could not force it on him. She had no answer to this. There was nothing she could offer to make it better, and she knew it.

"You won't say the rest of it, so I will," he continued coldly. "You might think I could break out of it by knocking myself off. Ain't so simple as that. Cursed luck gets me there as well. Course, I've only tried it the easy ways. Haven't had the guts for more."

"You've tried to kill yourself." Lily demanded, aghast.

Sam's eyes were desolate.

"Wouldn't you?"

She had no answer for that. He wasn't expecting one.

Sam put his hand on the door.

"Get some sleep," he ordered flatly.

He pushed out into the night. Lily heard the scrape of a match and glimpsed the orange burn of a cigarette before he moved away.

Rats rustled in the walls, and a bat squeaked softly overhead before fluttering outside. Lily lowered herself to the floor, wishing she had Sam's ability to radiate peace and comfort. All she could offer him was the future.

She was pretty certain he wouldn't want to see it.

She shoved her motorcycle jacket under her head, the familiar smell of the canvas a thin comfort as the exhaustion crept through her bones. How could she possibly sleep?

Lily was only vaguely aware of when the soft wool of Sam's overcoat came to lay gently over her body a few minutes later. Then the night stole her away again.

FOURTEEN

*T*HE OUTSKIRTS OF THE CITY came into view around midafternoon, the neat rows of two-story houses echoing something Lily
might have seen in a London suburb. The bright hues that had once
graced their facades were faded now, shutters and plaster carefully
patched in places. Every scrap of land had been turned to growing
vegetables, little spring gardens that fought for sunlight. The dogs
were thin, as were the people.

There were German soldiers everywhere.

Luxembourg crawled with gray uniforms. Lily fought an instinctive terror at the sight of them, but the soldiers hardly spared her and
Sam a look as they merged with the foot traffic heading into town.

They had barely spoken. The conversation of the night before
loomed over anything else they might have talked about. Lily knew
Sam wasn't interested in any attempt to comfort him. Empty plati-
tudes were worse than silence.

The street they were on ended abruptly at a fence that looked
out over a deep-cut valley lined with trees. It wended right through
the middle of Luxembourg's urban sprawl. On a cliff on the far side,
relics of the old fortress loomed, its gray walls and towers framing
more colorful tiers of houses interspersed with church spires.

The hulking steel of the antiaircraft guns looked startlingly out of place mounted on those ancient stones. Signs on the walls nearby were written in three languages. Lily could read the French.

Air raid shelter. Blackout enforced. Rationing in effect.

The mention of rationing made her stomach growl. She had woken to a strange breakfast that morning—a tidy pile of carrots and parsnips, a little withered and lightly covered in earth.

"The rats," Sam had explained.

It was a gift foraged from some forgotten root cellar. Lily brushed the vegetables off and ate them raw. So far, Kazi's unwelcome advice had proved true. If she ate, she didn't feel sick.

A Luxembourgian police lorry rattled past. Lily forced herself not to jump at the sight of it. The carrots had long since worn off. She needed a proper meal, a bath, and a rest, ideally someplace she didn't have to share with rats.

"Well, we're here," Sam noted quietly once the lorry had gone. "But I've no idea where to find this Rue-Saint-What of yours."

They couldn't find Zhao Min's address on their own, but she would have to be very careful about whom they asked. Loyalties here were deeply divided. Lily was conscious that while French was widely spoken in the city, her lack of German or Luxembourgish could garner the wrong sort of attention.

They turned back to a busier street lined with shops. Lily carefully eyed the people who flowed past. Her gaze stopped on a patch of purple.

The silk gown had once been very fine, lined with lace, and would have been fashionable at the outbreak of the war. It was worn to a shine in places now and had been carefully taken in. The alterations spoke of a frame that had once been stouter than it was. The woman who wore it was perhaps fifty, her dark hair thick above a once-handsome face.

"What about that one?" She indicated the purple silk with a slight nod.

Sam considered it.

"Fine rags. Bit run down. And she ain't fattening up on black market bacon. High class on hard times—and they'd not be so hard if she were getting on with the Boche. Good choice."

Praying their instincts were right, Lily approached the stranger.

"Pardon, Madame. Où est Rue Sainte-Zithe?"

The woman eyed the pair of them, her eyes shifting thoughtfully to Sam's dark glasses.

"Au Nord," she finally said. "Un demi-mile, à l'ouest de la fontaine."

"Madame Rischard!"

The call came from a man who moved towards their informant through the crowd, giving her a cheerful wave.

"Allez. Vite!" the woman ordered sharply under her breath.

Go. Quickly.

Sam took Lily's arm, pulling her into a rapid walk.

"North," Lily explained, remembering that he wouldn't have understood the woman's French. "Look for a fountain."

They found the street where they had been told it would be. Rue Sainte-Zithe was lined with respectable houses and dotted with trees. Lily followed the brass numbers nailed to the gates and doorframes like a compass as they counted off the distance to their destination.

The house they sought lay at the end of the road, where it overlooked the deep green cut of the valley that divided the city. It was distinguished by a quaint tower, the glass windows sparkling in the sunlight. The front steps were neatly swept, the hedges trimmed.

Lily hesitated. There was little reason to believe they would receive a warm welcome here. Sam and Zhao Min had been bitterly divided before the war, their relationship shattered by a terrible history.

Nor would Zhao Min be pleased that the secret of her location in Luxembourg had been discovered.

It was also entirely possible that Torrington's information was dated and Zhao Min was no longer here. Some German general could be billeted in the house for all Lily knew. They might be knocking at the door of a straight path to their own arrest and execution.

None of these worries were new. Stewing over them made no difference. The onmyōdō had led her to this place. The only choice Lily had ever had was to ignore it and let fate take its course.

That wasn't an option.

Lily raised a hand and rapped firmly on the door.

It was opened almost immediately by a young, thin woman of around twenty. Her blue eyes were large and luminous, her skin almost ethereally pale. She wore a plain gray dress, her dark blonde hair pinned carelessly at the nape of her neck.

"Bonjour," she said in slightly accented French, eyeing the pair of them cautiously.

Lily was abruptly aware of how bedraggled they must look. She hadn't seen anything approaching a bath in days, her clothes filthy from trudging through the forest and sleeping on the floor of a barn. Sam was still wearing his odd tinted lenses, his black coat bundled on his back like a peasant's blanket.

She was searching for a response that would not get the police called on them when she heard a voice from inside the house.

"Lily."

Strangford stepped into the hall, his expression shifting to one of horrified surprise.

"Here we go," Lily breathed softly.

Sam glanced down at her.

"You didn't tell him?" he exclaimed, then caught himself. "Of course, you didn't tell him."

Strangford came to the girl's side. He was wearing one of his black suits, with no sign of the Royal Navy officer about him. Even his hair looked a bit longer than it had before.

Lily had always liked it long.

"Entschuldigung, Fraulein Elsen. Ich werde das erledigen," Strangford said, his German flowing naturally.

She did not understand the words besides *excuse me*, but she could guess the rest.

I'll take care of this.

The girl—Fraulein Elsen—gave them one more thoughtful look before moving gracefully back into the house.

Strangford took her place in the doorway, eyes locked on Lily with dark promise before shifting to her companion—and then widening.

"Sam?"

"Were you expecting the King of England?" Sam retorted, taking off his spectacles.

Strangford's face broke into a smile as he pulled the younger man into a hug.

"By God, it's good to see you," he said.

He pushed himself back from Sam, looking up at him.

"You've grown," he declared.

Sam shrugged, the gesture unconsciously boyish.

"I'm no taller than I was."

Strangford released him. He was still smiling, but the expression felt heavier now, as weighted with years as the silver threads in his dark hair.

"That isn't what I meant," he said.

He returned his focus to Lily, his expression tight with unspoken emotion.

"Let's not have this conversation on the doorstep," Lily said, stepping past her husband into the house.

The hall was clean, well-appointed, and almost conspicuously unremarkable. A slightly worn carpet covered the floorboards. A landscape painting hung over an antique side table. There was an umbrella stand, a well-tended fern.

A child looked down from the top of the stairwell. She was perhaps fourteen, with thick black hair and dark, curious eyes.

"Alles in Ordnung, Inês," Strangford assured her.

Fraulein Elsen appeared behind the girl, slipped an arm around her waist, and drew her away.

With a sick lurch in her stomach, Lily recalled Zhao Min's perennial project to liberate women from the virtual slavery of the brothels. The child upstairs seemed far too young to be a refugee of a place like that...but such things mattered little to some.

As Sam pulled the front door shut behind them, Kazi came into the hall. He was in his waistcoat, shirtsleeves rolled up to expose the warm brown of his forearms.

He arched one elegant eyebrow at the sight of Lily.

"Why are you wearing an apron?" she blurted, unable to move past the incongruous garment tied around his waist.

"The cook has an ague," Kazi replied flatly. "And none of the rest of them have any idea what to do in a kitchen."

"What're you making, then?" Sam asked with obvious interest.

"Potatoes. And how did you manage to get here?" he calmly demanded.

"I flew. With him," Lily jerked her head at Sam.

Kazi's eyes narrowed.

"I thought I told you to travel light," he said meaningfully.

"Wait—is he implying I'm the baggage?" Sam protested.

"I wasn't exactly flush with options," Lily snapped at Kazi.

"You're not making it better," Sam pointed out crossly.

"And how much does he know?" Kazi pressed, his tone rising towards something she might almost think was a loss of temper.

"Not as much as he ought to, apparently." Sam complained.

"Enough," Strangford cut in, uncharacteristically sharp. "Sam is useful. I would trust him with my life—and he's already here. Now, if the rest of you don't mind, I would like to have a conversation with my wife."

In the silence that followed, Lily's stomach growled audibly. She put a hand over it, slightly humiliated.

Kazi's golden eyes shifted from Sam and Lily to a now danger-ously quiet Strangford.

"I'll get back to the stove, then." He pivoted back into what was presumably the kitchen.

"Who's that bloke?" Sam demanded.

"That would be Inspector Tariq Kazi of Special Branch." Lily's voice was more level than her nerves.

"What—a Peeler?" Sam exclaimed.

He looked between Lily and Strangford, then took a careful step to the side.

"I'll just go . . . lend him a hand, then. See if there's any pickle about the place."

"Do that," Strangford ordered without taking his eye off Lily. "We can catch up in a little while."

The words were innocent enough, but something in the way he said them made them sound like a threat.

"Right-O, then," Sam replied, hurrying after Kazi.

Lily wondered if it was the first time Sam had willingly sought out the proximity of a police officer.

His escape left her alone in the conspicuously unremarkable hall-way with her husband.

"Anthony." she began.

"Not here," he cut in.

He stalked to the back of the house, leaving her to follow.

Strangford pushed through a door into a walled back garden. It was narrow, greenly shaded by a large chestnut tree. A weathered wooden bench beneath it was clean and free of cobwebs. It looked well-used. Lily could picture the two girls from inside drinking their tea and reading magazines on a warm spring morning. It would be someplace safe for them, a little oasis of peace for lives that had likely been far from peaceful.

The day was wending towards evening. The air had a chill she could feel through her motorcycling jacket.

"Why." Strangford demanded, turning to face her.

His anger wasn't a surprise. Lily had known it must be the price she would pay for all of this.

"I asked the onmyōdō," Lily replied. "This is where it took me."

"That's a damned fine excuse."

Her own temper flared in response. She took a step closer.

"I have as much right to be here as you do," she seethed, daring him to contradict her.

She prepared herself for his counter-assault, but whatever line wanted to lash from his lips, he held it back. Instead, he thumped the rough trunk of the chestnut with his fist, hard enough that Lily winced at the pain he must have caused himself.

He walked away from it, dropping down onto the bench, and put his head in his hands. His knuckles were red.

"I wanted you to be safe."

Lily crossed to him. She lowered herself to her knees on the ground at his feet, but didn't touch him. Not yet.

"Don't I have a right to want that for you as well?"

He raised his head. The lines of his face were drawn deeper.

"I wish you didn't. Or that you would have just . . . let it go for once."

"Once is all it takes," Lily replied, the words stripped bleak.

She rose, sitting down on the bench. The inches that separated them felt like yards.

"Talk to me," she pleaded quietly. "Please."

He made a helpless kind of laugh.

"We are in the heart of German-occupied territory. We have no

221

reliable way to get home. We are chasing a rumor of a threat that should have died a millenia ago. What do you want me to say."

Lily swallowed thickly.

"There is ... something else you need to know."

The lines of worry around his eye tightened.

"What is it?"

In answer, Lily extended her hand.

Strangford did not take it right away, looking down at it with a caution she had not seen in him for four years. The sight of it struck her like a shard of ice.

She wanted to draw back. She didn't.

He slipped off his glove, and finally she felt the warm slide of his fingers across her palm.

"Wolves?" he asked sharply, snapping to attention.

"No," Lily bit back, then caught herself. "Not that."

"You can't just ask me to—*Oh.*" His eye widened, his grip on her hand tightening ... and then softening. "Oh Lily ..."

It was his tone that undid her. Of course he had absorbed more than the mere fact of her pregnancy. He had felt everything else with it.

All her fear.

The next breath broke out of her like a sob as she felt her walls crumbling.

"How can I choose?" she gasped, starting to shake. "How can I possibly choose between you?"

"Lily ..."

He pulled her to him, slipping his arms around her back. She felt his lips brush against her hair as she held him back, clinging to him like the only solid thing in a storm.

"I asked the onmyōdō," she said again, echoing the words like a desperate mantra. "I had to come. I have to follow you. There has to be a way to keep us alive—to keep *all* of us alive."

She could feel his sigh against her hair. His arms tightened around her.

"I could tell you that it's not your responsibility."

Lily pulled back, glaring at him.

"That isn't an answer."

His smile was sad.

"No. I didn't think it would be."

He lifted his still-gloved hand, brushing her hair back from her cheek.

"Why couldn't you have just come home?" she asked, unable to keep a childlike plaintiveness from the words.

He leaned in until his forehead touched her own.

"Would it have saved us if I had?"

The lump rose in Lily's throat, choking off her reply.

She shook her head, knowing it was true.

At the house behind them, someone audibly cleared their throat.

The woman on the steps was slender as a whip, wrapped in a gown of green homespun fabric that managed to look elegant despite its simplicity. Her black hair was drawn back from a face that might have been carved from marble for all it revealed of what lay within.

"We have matters to discuss," Wu Zhao Min announced, then turned to the door, leaving Lily and Strangford to follow.

~

The parlor, like the rest of the house, spoke of a bland respectability—a brocade sofa, two overstuffed armchairs, scattered portraits on the walls.

Lily doubted anyone who lived here was related to those depicted.

The gold-framed mirror, brass candlesticks, soothing blue wallpaper . . . none of it was odd unless one knew that the mistress of the place was far from conventional. It was as though Zhao Min had designed these spaces to allay the suspicions of anyone who happened to call on her. They would come into this calm, inoffensive space, be served tea and biscuits, and leave wondering why they had bothered to call.

Zhao Min sat in a straight-backed antique dining chair that felt oddly like a throne, as though she were ruling over the room, the rest of them mere petitioners.

Which they were, more or less.

Sam's sister was thinner than Lily remembered. The lines of her face were more pronounced, the angles of her body sharper. There was nothing of fashion in it. She had been hungry. Though Lily had seen the same look on many others in the villages she and Sam passed through since crossing the front, observing it on someone she had known well before the war made the change more stark. Times had been lean in England over the last four years, but there had always been enough. It was clear that had not been the case on this side of the front.

Black curtains hung by the windows of the parlor, ready to be drawn against the dusk. Sam leaned beside one of them, his posture all unhappy defiance as he steadfastly refused to look at his sister. Lily wondered if he had ever been one of the pilots charged with unleashing bombs on this city in the dark. What did it mean to him to learn that Zhao Min had been hiding in one of those blacked-out houses below?

Kazi came in with a tray of potato fritters. They smelled warmly of spice, and Lily's stomach immediately started rumbling.

"Praise be, there was ginger," Kazi commented as he set it down and took an empty chair.

He had rid himself of his apron and slipped his jacket back on, making him look his usual impeccable self. It was a remarkable feat, given that he must have been leaping out of a hot air balloon basket the night before.

"We grow it," Zhao Min replied.

Sam glanced over at the fritters. His mouth tightened as he looked away.

Lily knew he had to be as hungry as she was, and he had never been one to stand on ceremony around food. That he did so now told her much of where things must stand between him and his sister.

It wasn't good.

Only the five of them were gathered in the parlor. The two girls, Fraulein Elsen and the younger Inês, had made themselves scarce upstairs.

"Please," Zhao Min said, gesturing elegantly to the humble meal.

Feeding this many extra people was undoubtedly a hardship on limited rations, which would only make refusing it even ruder. Lily picked up one of the small bowls on the table and filled it, digging in gratefully.

"That Lord Torrington was able to provide you with this address is frankly a gross betrayal of trust," Zhao Min said. "I will not pretend to be pleased by it or your appearance here."

"The matter that brought us is one of extreme importance," Kazi began.

Zhao Min waved a hand dismissively, tone as cutting as a razor.

"We are at war. It is all of extreme importance."

"We have reason to believe the Central Powers are in possession of a very dangerous new weapon," he pressed back.

"Oh?" Zhao Min asked archly. "Is it the long gun? The new aerial bombs?"

Kazi hesitated before answering. He glanced to Strangford.

"You understand the extreme sensitivity of this," he asked. "Are you sure your Mr. Wu should be here?"

It was Zhao Min who answered him.

"No one in this room is less pleased to see my brother here than I am, but extricating him from this situation would only entail an additional and likely dangerous complication."

By the window, Sam went even more still, like the stiffness after a blow.

"Say whatever you have to say." Zhao Min ordered. "Lord and Lady Strangford will only tell it to him anyway if they have not already."

"It is not a gun," Kazi continued awkwardly. "We believe it may be some type of... monster."

The word surprised Sam from his quiet defensiveness. He shifted a questioning gaze to Lily.

"And how have you heard of these... monsters?"

Zhao Min drew out the word, her tone dripping with disdainful skepticism. Kazi flinched against it. Even Lily felt a momentary embarrassment—but not her husband.

"I felt them," Strangford replied, meeting Zhao Min's eyes steadily. "At the Stelvio Pass."

No one in the room had any question as to what Strangford meant by *felt*.

Kazi's eyes narrowed on Zhao Min and Sam. Lily knew he would be calculating how much the siblings already knew about Strangford's powers.

Sam was obviously biting back his own shock at discovering Strangford had shared his most dangerous secret with a police inspector.

She could feel the other secrets in the room—the ones Kazi had not yet discovered.

Her secrets. Sam's secrets.

We're monsters chasing monsters, she thought grimly and had to resist a terrible urge to laugh.

"Well," Zhao Min said thoughtfully, sitting back. "That is something else, then."

Zhao Min moved her gaze from Strangford to the rest of them. Lily could practically feel herself being measured.

"If I did have information related to your investigation, why should I grant it to you?" Zhao Min demanded.

Kazi's jaw tightened. Lily felt sure his indignant retort was delayed only by the presence of a fritter in his mouth.

"You provided some hint of it to my father," Lily cut in. "But not the whole. If you had, he wouldn't have needed to send us here."

Zhao Min acknowledged her deduction with a nod.

"You know my father passes on the information you send to him, distributing it to contacts within the various intelligence bureaus at his discretion. You have trusted that discretion in the past, but not with this."

The rest of it clicked into place. Lily cast her die on it and hoped she wasn't making a mistake.

"Because you don't trust what any of the bureaus would do with what you know about this. And it is important enough that you believe my father would feel obligated to pass it along anyway. What you require is someone who can pursue the lead outside of any of the bureaus—someone you trust."

"But you are not entirely outside the bureaus. Are you?" Zhao Min evenly returned.

Lily burned a bit at the question.

"You know where Strangford's loyalties lie."

"And your inspector?" Zhao Min pressed. "Will you vouch for him?"

Lily hesitated.

"We will," Strangford replied, setting down his empty bowl.

Zhao Min's expression was a wall, revealing nothing.

"If you know of someone better suited to pursue this, Miss Wu, I would gladly leave it to them," Strangford added.

Lily reached across the sofa and gently squeezed his hand.

Zhao Min rose from her chair, moving to a window that looked out over the valley that carved through the city. The sky above it had turned a ripe peach with evening.

"There is a special project in Germany, scientific in nature. It is referred to as Wotanskunst."

"Odin's Craft," Strangford translated automatically.

Lily tried to recall what she knew of Odin, an ancient Norse and Germanic god of war and wisdom.

Ravens, she thought absently. *He had a pair of ravens.*

She shivered away a chill.

"Is this out of the Kaiser Wilhelm Institute?" Kazi demanded.

"What's that?" Lily asked.

"The German research institute in Berlin," Kazi replied shortly. "It's where they developed chlorine gas."

Chlorine gas. The mention of it made Lily ill. She had heard of how men died after simply inhaling it, the gas reacting with the moisture in their lungs to turn into an acid that ate them through from the inside.

"A place much like your Porton Down. Isn't it, Inspector?" Zhao Min noted.

Porton Down. Lily tried to place the name in her mind and failed.

Kazi darted a glare at Zhao Min, then caught himself.

"We have our own special projects," he acknowledged.

Lily knew all about British military *special projects*. After all, she had very nearly been part of one herself.

She recalled the neat file drawers in the office of Dr. Joseph Hartwell—remembered those same records drowning in the sea off the coast of Kent, drifting down into the murk where Hartwell's ideas could never hurt anyone again. The good doctor had been in communication with the War Office over the potential military application of his experiments . . . experiments that would have created a breed of soldiers gifted with powers stolen from the blood of those deemed less useful.

People like her and Strangford. Like Sam.

Her mind flew back to a basement lined with tile, housing medical tables with buckles to hold down the unwilling. The burned-out husk of the hospital in Southwark. The flames and darkness of a warehouse on St. Saviour's Dock as something stalked her through the shadows.

Strangford's blood on the end of a blade. An antiseptic hallway of locked doors.

The parlor shrank, the air growing thick. Lily was having trouble breathing.

She forced herself back from it—from the panic of those memories. Hartwell's research was dead now. Any hope the Army had of continuing it would have drowned four years ago.

Strangford's brow was creased with worry as he looked at her. Lily realized she was clenching his gloved hand. She forced herself to relax her grip.

Kazi was still speaking.

"We cannot afford to fall behind, and we must know how to protect the common soldier from the worst effects of a gas attack. But we go no further. No new weapon of such nature will come from a British laboratory."

Zhao Min laughed. It was quick, a clear tinkling sound like glasses coming together.

"Careful, Inspector. I might think you quaint," she said easily. "But then you are of reasonable intelligence. You must have deduced that your British laboratory is experimenting with every chemical and substance they can get their hands on. They have simply failed, thus far, to find anything better."

Her eyes narrowed.

"There are always men who will seek every possible advantage, and never more so than with the excuse of a war at their fingertips. That your Porton Down has not produced a new and better agent of death is due only to the inferiority of your scientists. Not their elegant morals."

The rebuke was whip sharp.

"What do you know about Wotanskunst?" Strangford asked,

cutting through the rising tension.

"I know that it is medical in nature, not technological," Zhao Min replied, settling back to the business at hand. "And that the work involves an object that was taken out of the mountains at the Austria-Italy border."

Kazi, Lily, and Strangford exchanged a look.

"What was it?" Lily pressed.

"They refer to it *das Relikt*," Zhao Min returned.

The German term was close enough to English for Lily to understand it.

The Relic.

"Odin's Craft," Strangford echoed again, his shoulders tense. "In Norse myth, it was Odin who granted power to the berserkers."

Zhao Min was watching him quietly.

"You mean to say they are . . . manufacturing them somehow?" Kazi demanded.

Lily thought of the destruction at the Stelvio Pass, written into the blood frozen on the stones. Of the haunted look in Cairncross's eyes as he shared the stories of his hidden past. Even at such distance, the violence was terrifying.

That the Germans might be creating it at will . . .

Strangford raised his eye, looking to Zhao Min.

"Are they." he asked.

Zhao Min's look was grim, the ever-present note of defiance she carried falling away.

"There are rumors of a special unit, something more elite than the Storm Troops. I know there was a recent field test that was considered successful and that there are plans to deploy them at a critical area of the front in the near future."

"Where?" Kazi rose from his chair, looking almost threatening for a moment.

"I do not know," Zhao Min replied.

A field test. She was referring to the Stelvio Pass.

Beside Lily, Strangford lowered his head, hands tightening on his knees. He was fighting off his stolen memories of that night of violence and terror.

"We have to find out," he said roughly. "And we need to stop them from making more."

Silence followed his declaration as each of them absorbed its implications.

"And you, Xiang?" Zhao Min finally said, turning to her brother as she called him by his Chinese name. "What is your part in all this? Or do you merely tag along like a dog at their heels?"

Sam leaned against the opposite window, the lines of his body casual and dangerous.

"Dunno, Jiějie," he slowly replied, raising his head. "But seems to me what they're about will take some killing. I've got rather good at killing these last few years."

He pushed from the wall, crossing over to the table.

"Pass us up a bowl, then," he ordered Lily. "I'm feeling a bit peckish."

She slowly handed him some of the fritters. Sam slouched into one of the chairs and shoveled one into his mouth.

Zhao Min's eyes followed him with a look Lily wouldn't even start to guess the meaning of.

"Wotanskunst is located at a facility inside a partially reconstructed castle," she continued after a moment. "It is secured, as you might have anticipated. We will need to examine our options for getting inside."

"We?" Kazi echoed carefully.

Zhao Min pinned him with a look.

"You will be there by way of my intelligence. Your very presence potentially exposes and endangers my sources—and I do not endanger my sources. I will accompany you to ensure that you do not approach the matter like fools."

Kazi's jaw hardened at the word *fool*, but he made no retort. He knew well enough how far they would get without Zhao Min's assistance.

The tension in the room and the food in her stomach combined abruptly into overwhelming exhaustion. Lily stood. It was either that or start nodding off on the sofa.

"I need to rest."

"As should we all," Zhao Min returned with cool grace. "Mila—Fraulein Elsen—has seen to your rooms and can direct you. I would ask that you keep to them till morning. My housemates do not take well to strangers wandering the halls at night."

Strangford rose.

"Thank you," he said meaningfully. "We owe you a great deal."

Zhao Min acknowledged him with a regal nod, then swept from the room. A moment later, the luminous Mila appeared in the doorway, speaking in thickly accented English.

"This way. Please."

FIFTEEN

$\mathcal{T}$HE DARK WOOD FLOOR ends in a river. The water froths, spring high, brimming at the edges and moving fast. It is broad, too far to leap, and too fast to swim. The room continues on the far side of that barrier, where Robert Ash stands.

Her mentor wears an impeccably tailored charcoal suit, the tone darker than the silver of his hair and beard. His feet are bare.

Lily knows the room. It is the sanctuary of The Refuge, the place Ash retreated to for meditation—and it is not. The sanctuary was distinguished by a clever channel of water that ran through the center of the floor, spilling out into the garden to fuel the fountain that glittered quietly there in the warmer months of the year, not this torrent that rushes past her feet. Nor is it the garden that she sees outside the elegant floor-to-ceiling windows. In fact, they are not windows at all. Instead of clear panes of glass, open space looks out over a landscape of richly forested mountains framed by the curved roof lines of other temples.

Even in the throes of a dream, Lily knows it has been a long time since she has seen the man who changed her world—who broke her open and made her into something new, something she still isn't sure she understands.

There are so many questions she needs to ask him, so much he left unanswered when he deserted her for death, but in the end, there is only one thing she can say.

"What do you want from me?" she blurts, the words carrying over the incessant hush of the water.

It appears I was mistaken.

Ash's reply floats to her in a delicate breeze of thought. Across water that churns like a sea, he remains still.

Lily smells salt and mud. Hears the whisper of long grasses in the back of her mind, a sound from another place.

Or perhaps not so very far away.

"Why?" she demands. Her own voice is rough.

There is more to you.

Her head hurts. She knows these words. She has heard them before. She recalls a day of fire, the acrid stench of burning paint.

It has been hiding inside of you, waiting for the right stimulus to emerge.

"No," Lily protests, hands to her temples. The roar of the water has grown louder. It rushes at her ears. "It's already happened. You're talking about the past."

More words, breathless, humming, relentless.

Call it fate. The Parliament of Stars.

A chase of fear, cold across her skin despite the temperate air of the room. Outside the window, over the impossible mountains, the sky is purple with twilight. It will only ever be twilight here.

"What about it?" Lily cries in response. The pain in her head is growing greater.

Fear the responsibility it entails.

They are nothing but echoes, fragments of history—pieces of her life fallen out of time. Islands in the current of Tottenham Court Road. The whispering quiet of the attic of The Refuge.

The bridge where it all fell apart.

Your charisma has only ever answered to one thing.

Ash's bare feet are pale against the ground. His eyes on her warm with something like pity.

I would not put that burden on you.

~

Lily woke in darkness, breath caught in her throat. She fought for air with a gasp, drawing it in like one drowning.

She was lying in a comfortable room in a house in Luxembourg.

The bed was soft, covered in worn but still beautiful quilts. Strangford slept beside her, arms sprawled, his bare skin just visible in the near darkness.

The blackout curtains were open, the window cracked to let in a little fresh air. Strangford had opened it after they snuffed the lantern for the night. The city outside her windows was quieter than the one she called home. But then, even in a blackout, there was still life in London at night. People walked through the streets to clubs and restaurants by the glimmer of shaded lanterns, laughing together as they stumbled through the darkness.

Luxembourg was occupied. The only thing out on the streets at night would be German patrols.

Sleep would not be back for her soon, not with the adrenaline racing through her bloodstream, her heart jangling from the nightmare. Lily pushed back the quilts, swinging her legs off the bed. The floor felt cool under her feet.

Strangford breathed softly, sunk into exhaustion. Lily wondered again what his experience flying into Belgium in an experimentally rigged hot air balloon had been. How he and Kazi had made their way across a strange country. She knew they had landed outside Bruges and taken a train from there to Luxembourg, arriving only a couple of hours before Lily and Sam showed up at the door.

She might have learned more from Strangford once they were together in the room, but Lily was overtaken by a more urgent impulse, one that temporarily thrust her exhaustion aside. It may not have been long since she'd seen her husband, but those days had been full of fear and uncertainty, leaving her desperate for contact— to know that he was here and that, for the moment, both of them were safe.

She studied him for a moment, her eyes adjusting to the near darkness. The starlight from the window touched the line of his shoulder, silvering his dark hair. His eyepatch was set aside, his scars exposed. They were familiar to her, comfortable.

Her stomach grumbled.

Lily weighed her options, then gave in, pulling on a borrowed dressing gown Zhao Min had left for her. It was a simple pale blue in a cotton that felt like silk and dragged just a bit on the floor.

She lit the lantern, closing the shutter down to a sliver that granted her just enough light to avoid bumping into the furniture. She slipped out into the blackout of the hall—only to raise her head and see a similar spark wink at her from the far end, clasped in the hand of another dark-robed figure.

Her first instinct was that she must be looking into a mirror...but then a cold pressure crawled rapidly up the skin of her arms, lodging itself inside her brain. Her ears began to ring, the false sound growing in intensity. Was it some new sort of migraine? Lily felt ill and filled with something that tasted like dread.

Through it came a whisper, a low voice speaking in accented French.

"Inês. Shhh. It is just the lady."

The ringing and pressure seemed to recede. Lily blinked to realize the figure at the end of the hall was not a reflection. It was Inês, the dark-haired child she had seen on the stairs earlier. Mila had joined her, slipping a comforting arm around the girl's shoulders.

Lily felt a pang of guilt. Zhao Min had asked them to keep to their rooms at night to avoid startling the other residents of the house, women who had likely been terribly abused in their previous lives. And here she was, lurking in the dark at the end of the hall.

"Je suis désolée," Lily whispered.

She could just make out the paler shape of Mila's head nodding at her apology before the woman guided Inês into one of the rooms that lined the hall.

Lily took a breath. Her head felt fine, the odd sensation likely a result of rising too quickly from bed. She considered giving up and going back, but she was still hungry. The girls would now know it was her who was wandering the halls—she might as well get something to eat so she could manage a bit more sleep.

She moved lightly and carefully down the stairs to the ground floor. As she approached the kitchen, she was called up short by the sound of low voices from within.

It was Zhao Min, her voice razor-edged as she spoke a tense and rapid Mandarin. Lily couldn't understand the words, but she could hear clearly enough that whomever Zhao Min was speaking to, she was coldly furious with them.

The reply came—short and sullenly defensive in the same Mandarin. It was Sam.

Lily's heart sank. She knew she shouldn't be listening, but as Zhao Min fired back a stream of dagger-like syllables—an accusation or an attack—she found herself rooted.

Sam parried, on the defensive. Something in his tone reminded Lily of when he was getting reprimanded by Mrs. Liu, his nǎinai.

Zhao Min was not Nǎinai. Her retort, clearly meant to wound, cut through the quiet air of the night. Out in the hallway, Lily winced at the impact, even though it was not directed at her.

Sam's reply came more softly, aching with feeling.

"I'm sorry. Bàoqiàn, Jiějie."

The meaning of the word sank into her understanding. *Bàoqiàn.* It sounded like regret.

Zhao Min snarled back her reply as though Sam's heartfelt apology was a spark to some long-dry tinder, bursting it into hot, terrible flames.

"Nǐ de dàoqiàn méiyǒu rènhé yìyì."

Her words rang like funeral bells—empty and resoundingly final. This felt like disaster, one Lily was clearly not meant to witness. She needed to go.

A chair scraped against the tiles. Sam must be standing up. Lily could picture him behind her closed eyelids as he spoke, his hands pressed to the table, dark hair falling across his narrowed eyes.

"You've made that clear enough. You'll be rid of me in the morning."

As Sam's footsteps approached the door, Zhao Min's chair scraped as well as she rose to throw one more sharp, expert weapon at her brother across the kitchen.

"Zhè bùshì nǐ jiā."

"We stopped being family a long time ago," Sam replied as hard as stone. "I wouldn't mistake this place for jiā."

Jiā. It made Lily think of the photograph Mr. Wu used to keep on his desk in The Refuge's potting shed, where a grinning boy and a defiant-eyed girl stood side-by-side, linked by blood, place and memory.

"Wu Gūniáng," Sam said, coldly taking his leave of her.

It was wrong. Zhao Min had always been Jiějie to him. Lily shouldn't have been hearing her surname on his lips with all the formality of a title you would grant to a stranger.

Lily slipped back as Sam emerged, letting herself fall into the deeper shadows at the end of the hall. She needn't have bothered. He wouldn't have seen her even if she had been right in front of him. He was too wrapped up in a tempest of both old and fresh pain.

Passing the stairs, he yanked open the front door, stalking out into the night.

Lily waited in the darkness, taking a breath to gather herself. She moved to slip up the hall again, determined to go back into bed even if it meant lying there with an empty stomach for the rest of the night.

At the soft brush of her footfall on the carpet, a voice spoke from within the kitchen.

"You might as well come in."

Lily knew better than to pretend. She stepped inside.

Zhao Min stood by the table in the glow of a low-burning lantern, wearing the wrapped shirt and loose trousers of her zhong yi. Her hair hung down her back in a simple braid. It made her look younger—but then, she was only twenty-eight or so. Remembering that was startling.

"I'm sorry. I didn't mean to overhear," Lily admitted.

Zhao Min looked up from the table.

"You're breeding."

It was not a question. Lily supposed she shouldn't be surprised. Zhao Min had spent years imprisoned in a brothel and had continued to haunt them since, albeit for very different reasons. The women in such places had more reason than most to know how to recognize the earliest signs of pregnancy, when the right tea might solve the problem instead of a butcher's wire.

"Yes," Lily confirmed, her hand slipping automatically over her womb. It was still flat, still motionless. Her last child hadn't yet quickened when she lost the pregnancy. She still wasn't sure what it felt like to have a life kicking inside of her.

Zhao Min moved to the pantry. She pulled out a bit of dried sausage wrapped in waxed paper, a hunk of cheese, and a jar of preserved apples, then set them on the table.

They were luxuries, almost certainly purchased on the black market at extortionate prices.

"I can't possibly."

"Eat it," Zhao Min interrupted bluntly. "If you go hungry, you'll lose the child."

The words hit far harder than Zhao Min could have intended.

Her expression softened. She pushed the food closer to Lily's side of the table.

"Take it. Please."

Lily sat down and started to eat. The sausage was cured and spiced. It covered up the odd metallic taste she had been getting from meat over the last week. The cheese was rich and creamy. She felt the terrible awkwardness of enjoying the gift as Zhao Min sat across from her, whittled down to bone.

She would not speak of what she'd overheard, however much a part of her wanted to intervene. Lily knew better than to think it would be well received.

"You're helping them," she offered instead between bites. "The women here. Like you did back in London."

Zhao Min was quiet.

"A few. When I can. It is a drop in the sea." She looked out the window, through the blackout curtain to someplace beyond. "It was not my intention."

There was so much in that phrase. Of course it had not been intentional. Zhao Min had come here to spy, to strike a blow against the Germans to revenge the women she had resettled in Belgium, women they had slaughtered during the invasion.

It was possible that Zhao Min had demanded recompense of some sort from Lily's father, or the government, in exchange for the information she gathered here—but money couldn't be delivered to her in Luxembourg. Her access to anything deposited back in England was necessarily uncertain. She might never make it back. The business motive was irrelevant here, but the instinct to protect the vulnerable clearly had deeper roots.

"None of you should be here." Zhao Min sank back against her chair.

It could have been a rebuke, but all Lily could hear was her exhaustion. She realized Zhao Min must have been feeling it since long before they arrived. She was simply very good at hiding it.

Lily couldn't disagree with her. It was what she had been thinking since all of this had begun.

"If there were anyone else ..." she started.

"But there is not," Zhao Min finished for her.

Zhao Min's words had an added weight. The woman across the table might not be gifted with supernatural powers, but there were few in the world who could do what she did.

Silence fell across the kitchen, the world outside cut off by the blackout curtains. The pool of lamplight was a quiet womb. Lily still tasted the ginger from the preserved apples, the spice of it warm on her tongue. For a moment, she could almost pretend the kitchen was somewhere else, in another time—safe back in England, perhaps— and that the pair of them were just two ordinary women caught awake, quietly and comfortably whiling away a bit of the night.

"Do you ever wish you could walk away from it anyway."

It was as though the question had been bobbing up inside of Lily, looking for a chance to spill out—one it finally found in this unexpected moment of quiet intimacy.

Zhao Min raised her head.

"Wash our hands of it. Let the order of things go as it will." There was a note of longing in her voice before it went hard again. "Order is not kind to women."

Lily considered the forms of order Zhao Min had known. The illicit institutionalization of slavery and prostitution. The mob authority of petty gods like Jack Cannon, carefully overlooked by the men who ruled from their gilded chambers in Westminster Palace. Cash and sin, power and abuse. The violent organization of war and all that it chewed to pieces in its maw.

"No," Lily quietly agreed. "I don't suppose that it is."

Zhao Min's hand clenched on the table.

"Do not think I serve them. Their nation. Their cause."

Her shoulders tensed. Lily read in the lines of them a hard-earned rage. She knew Zhao Min was talking about her father—about all that he represented.

"I serve no man," Zhao Min continued, dark eyes flashing at Lily from across the table. "I do not trust any of them."

Lily didn't question it. Zhao Min may have chosen Torrington as her contact back in London, but Lily was not such a fool as to mistake that decision for trust. Torrington had been the lesser of the available evils, one that would at least be prudent and expedient.

She wondered for a moment whether she entirely disagreed. Her history with her father was a difficult one, pockmarked by disappointments. She did not doubt his love, but she had never been entirely certain how far it would stretch.

Her thoughts drifted back to the dream that had woken her earlier—to the softly rushing water and the whispered voice of a man long dead.

There is more to you.

"What about fate?"

The question was out of Lily's lips before she quite realized she was going to ask it.

Zhao Min laughed. It was bright and sharp-edged.

"The Tao? The Great Path? Is that what woke you in the night? I do not trust it either. I make my own path."

My own path.

Lily's pulse jumped with a buzzing sense of potential as the glow of the lantern danced light across the polished surface of the kettle on the stove, the glass of the pictures framed on the walls.

She heard the echo of Robert Ash's voice inside her head, carried on a wisp of acrid smoke.

Then why can't you change it?

Memory lurched up of flames flickering around the sides of her face, blood dripping down her cheek.

"Do you think that's possible?" Lily hoarsely demanded.

Zhao Min's grin sliced through the darkness, a gleam of white against the shadows.

"We are two women returned from the dead. Who better is there to try it than us?"

The words sparked a strange and dangerous excitement, a whispering sense of belonging to some intimate conspiracy.

The feeling passed. The quiet mundanity of the kitchen settled back into place around her, leaving her only the odd sensation of being cocooned in unexpected ease with someone she had never thought to call a friend.

"If you could really do it … If you could rewrite fate … " Lily began tentatively. "What would you want?"

The lantern hissed softly, the glow highlighting the hollow spaces under Zhao Min's cheekbones.

"To be safe," Zhao Min replied. "And I was, for a time. I gave it up to help the others. It was not enough to simply have it for myself."

She closed her eyes, looking tired and pained for a moment.

"I cannot find joy in it until all of them are safe as well. Now you," she finished, drawing some of her hardness back around herself again.

Lily didn't let it intimidate her. She knew the honesty she had been granted was a gift and was owed a like response.

She searched for the right answer, drawing it up from an unspoken well inside of her.

"I never had a family." The admission twinged against an old pain. "Then I found one. Made one," she clarified carefully. "I want to protect them. To hold on to them as long as I can."

She wasn't thinking of what the words might mean to Zhao Min. Once she said it, she could see how the other woman stilled as though preparing for a blow.

Lily opened her mouth to apologize, then stopped. It would only make it worse.

"If you want to save them, stop running from what you are," Zhao Min said, her sharp edges back.

"And what is that?" Lily asked, certain she would not like the answer.

Zhao Min's mouth twisted into a narrow smile.

"You cannot hide from me, Lady Strangford. I have seen what you can do."

Her mind flew back to the hot rush of power on a Limehouse stage. The shock in the eyes of her enemy. The fierce, glorious sensation of her own dangerousness.

The blood of wolves on her hands.

"That's not who I am," Lily protested, reeling back from it.

"It is, whether you like it or not," Zhao Min retorted.

"But I'm pregnant."

Zhao Min lifted an elegant brow, eyes glittering.

"Ask my brother—what is the most dangerous animal to encounter in the wilderness?"

Lily didn't have to ask. She already knew the answer, even as a child of the city. It was simply understood.

"A mother," she replied. "Defending her young."

The words tasted like copper in her mouth, summoning terrible memories of the instinct for violence, the hum of wood on flesh, the crack of bone, the crimson spray.

It make her want to choke.

Zhao Min rose, clearly intending to end the conversation. It sparked a hot flash of anger.

"As you say, then. Lǎoshī," Lily snapped.

Zhao Min paused in the doorway, stiffening slightly at the sound of that title—the term Lily had heard Sam use to address the man who plucked him from the street and demanded he remake himself. The one that meant *teacher.*

Lǎoshī. The echo of the word hummed through her in a way that felt oddly like onmyōdō.

The woman on the threshold met Lily's gaze, offering her a careful nod in response. Then she was gone.

SIXTEEN

Friday, April 26
Morning
The City of Luxembourg

"ABSOLUTELY NOT," Kazi pronounced, back stiff. "I will not be staying in Luxembourg."

"You don't speak German, and you look like a foreigner. You are a liability." Zhao Min returned flatly.

They had gathered in the kitchen around the worktable, the aged surface carefully rubbed with wax. The blackout curtains were pulled back, allowing sunlight to stream into the room through windows that looked out over the small back garden.

"So does he," Kazi snapped back, pointing at Sam.

"What?" Sam complained. "I've got my specs. And I thought I might grow my beard out."

He rubbed at the bristle of his three-day scruff.

"No, you will not," Zhao Min countered neatly before returning her attention to Kazi. "And he is useful, whatever his other faults."

"Useful how?" Kazi demanded.

"He's a thief."

"A thief." Kazi echoed, his outrage rising up a notch.

"I'm bloody pilot, thank you very much," Sam retorted. "Ain't robbed anyone in an age."

Kazi straightened to his full height, looming over the slighter

245

figure of Sam's sister.

"I am a law enforcement officer with decades of training."

"That is not an asset to me." Zhao Min eyed the inspector thoughtfully. "What about that Webley you carry under your coat?"

Kazi's hand went instinctively to his jacket. He frowned under his dark mustache.

"Firearms are only to be used in situations of the utmost—"

"Sure they are," Sam cut in. "But can you hit anything with it?"

Kazi's eyes narrowed with a barely concealed flash of temper.

"I assure you, Mr. Wu. I am quite capable."

"I am more concerned with how any of you will be capable of successfully infiltrating a highly-secured German Army research installation." Zhao Min's tone was thick with skepticism.

"Maybe this'll help, then."

Sam threw a slender booklet down on the table. Lily recognized it as the identification papers belonging to the breakfasting German officer she and Sam had encountered on their first day after the plane crash. Zhao Min plucked them up, examining them for a moment before her gaze returned to her brother.

"Where did you get these?" she demanded.

"Squirrels," Sam returned through a mouthful of porridge.

"Come again?" Kazi said, frowning with confusion.

Sam flashed the inspector a shifty look and swallowed.

"Squirreled them away for a rainy day." he clarified.

Beside Lily, Strangford coughed in a manner that sounded suspiciously like suppressing a laugh.

Zhao Min narrowed her eyes at her brother, then turned her attention back to the identification booklet.

"This belongs to a hauptmann with the Zentral-Abteilung de Oberste Heeresleitung."

"The Central Division of the German General Staff." Kazi asked, his interest obvious.

"See? The Peeler does know a bit of Kraut," Sam cheerfully pointed out.

The remark earned him a glare from Kazi, but Zhao Min did not seem to hear it, her attention focused elsewhere.

"Could it help?" Lily prompted

"That depends," Zhao Min said thoughtfully.

"On what?"

"Your husband," she replied. "Xiang, tell Mila to fetch my laundry hamper."

Sam shot his sister a glare and strode from the room. He returned a minute later with Mila, who carried a wicker basket. She set it down on the floor, giving the group assembled in the kitchen a wary look before she made a quick exit.

Zhao Min knelt down on the floor beside the hamper. She took a few items of dirty clothing out and set them carefully aside before pulling free the muslin liner and tipping the now-empty wicker basket upside down.

A straight razor appeared in her hand, the gleaming length of it snapping out with an elegant flick of her wrist.

The last time Lily had seen Zhao Min's weapon of choice, it had been dripping with Jack Cannon's blood as the Lord of Limehouse crumpled at her feet.

With a neat movement of the blade, Zhao Min sliced through the reeds holding closed the base of the basket. She flipped the panel of woven reeds up, revealing a narrow compartment hidden in the bottom of the hamper.

The razor closed, disappearing back into a pocket of Zhao Min's skirt, and she carefully lifted out what she had taken such trouble to conceal beneath her laundry.

The bundle of cloth was an unmistakable greenish-gray, the fine wool offset by glints of silver braid. Zhao Min snapped the garment into unfolding, holding it up for them to see.

"That's the jacket of a German captain," Kazi softly pointed out in the silence that followed.

"It is," Zhao Min confirmed . . . and like that, Lily understood exactly what she intended.

Her stomach lurched with dread.

At Lily's side, Strangford had gone very still, staring at the jacket as though he expected it to lash out and bite him.

"The collar boards and shoulder straps will need to be changed," Zhao Min continued. "They do not match your hauptmann's regiment, but Mila is quite deft with a needle, and I know the designs we require. We would need to remove this at any rate."

She flicked her finger at a part of the silver braid that was marred by a rust-hued stain. It was a color Lily knew well—the hue of dried blood.

"Where did you acquire this?" Lily demanded, feeling cold.

"It was a gift."

"But where did it come from?" she pressed urgently, even as Strangford reached out a gloved hand and clasped it over hers, squeezing gently with silent caution.

"The battlefield, of course," Zhao Min calmly returned.

Behind her, Sam muttered an ear-burning curse.

Kazi was quiet, watching the exchange carefully. He did not yet understand where the tension in the room had come from.

It would not take him long to figure it out.

"For this to succeed, you must do more than wear it," Zhao Min continued. "My sources indicate that the facility at Vianden is over-seen by Abteilung IIIb, the German Army intelligence division. A IIIb officer will not be fooled by a simple uniform and passable German."

"You need me to find his thoughts. His memories," Strangford replied.

Lily wondered if anyone else could hear the quiet fear in his voice. In the distance, a church bell tolled.

"Your uniform didn't belong to a General Staff officer," Kazi pointed out.

"Attitude. Culture. Protocol," Zhao Min listed. "That is where he cannot fail. The rest must be invented, and then we hope that the officer directing Vianden is not deeply familiar with the details of personnel at the Oberste Heeresleitung."

"He will still need more than rank and papers to get inside," Kazi pressed. "They're hardly going to show off a secret project to whoever presents himself at the door."

"He will not ask to see the project," Zhao Min replied, her eyes still on Strangford. "He will ask to tour the castle. His Swiss wife has an interest in medieval architecture."

"Wife?" Lily echoed uncomfortably.

"We will need to work on your accent," Zhao Min noted, then

pressed on. "I will provide you with a letter of introduction. I have an excellent forger. Whom should it be from?"

She directed the question to Kazi, throwing it across the room like something he must catch by instinct.

"Von Müller. He's chief of the German naval cabinet. Lord Strangford could pose as an army liaison with his office."

"Because he knows far more about German naval operations than he ought to," Zhao Min agreed. "Do you not?"

"Yes," Strangford grimly confirmed.

"The trousers and cuffs will need to be shortened," she finished, apparently satisfied. "Mila can make those adjustments."

She was folding up the jacket when Lily asked the most important question—the one no one else had bothered to voice.

"How was he killed?"

Zhao Min paused, then raised her eyes to Lily.

"I suppose we will find out."

Her answer made the room feel small, the air thin. Lily bit back her protest. Zhao Min was right. A German intelligence officer might anticipate a spy but could not possibly imagine one who could draw on memories of life in the German army through the uniform he wore against his skin. Nor did the Germans realize just how much of their naval operations had been deciphered by the codebreakers in Room 40 at the Admiralty.

It was the best plan they could hope for—and it only required that Strangford live through the unknown horror of a stranger's death.

Strangford ran a gloved finger over the lapel of the jacket, staring down at it like a cobra he had been asked to tame.

"I will do it."

Zhao Min considered him critically, her eyes roaming from the dark circle of his eye patch down to his shoes.

"We must cut your hair," she concluded.

Lily smothered the urge to scream.

~

Their carriage arrived promptly at eight the next morning. The unassuming conveyance was pulled by a pair of aging, bow-backed horses. Zhao Min must have called in quite a favor to acquire them—horses were not easy to come by in occupied Luxembourg. The German Army, like the British, had an insatiable appetite for the animals. This pair had probably only been spared because they were clearly incapable of hauling artillery.

Strangford greeted the horses like old friends, his face lighting up with boyish happiness. His family's breeding stock at Allerhope had been similarly gutted by the war, along with his own horse. Beatrice had been requisitioned in 1916 and destroyed within a year.

He ran a gloved hand along the silken hair of one of the animals' necks.

"She'd rather have her ear scratched," Sam muttered from beside her.

He had stubbornly resisted Zhao Min's order to shave, still sore about her announcement that Strangford would be driving the carriage.

"But I've the spectacles!" Sam had protested.

"And he has the German," Zhao Min retorted. "Be glad I don't put you in the box."

The box in question was a surprise—a secret compartment built under the floor of the carriage, just large enough to fit a man if he didn't mind traveling in something smaller than a coffin. It was where Zhao Min stashed the now-altered German officer's uniform, the silver braid on the collar boards replaced by dark green with red piping. Lily knew that Mila had worked on it late into the night.

The boots that went with it were too big for Strangford, but there was nothing to be done about that.

He would not be traveling in uniform. A lone German officer with such an odd assortment of civilians would only attract more attention, and they wanted as little of that as possible.

Sam left her to check on the rigging for the horses. Back at the house, Zhao Min, dressed in gray half-mourning, spoke quietly with Mila and the younger girl, Inês, who looked pale and a little scared. As Lily watched, Zhao Min gave her a hug.

The gesture was surprising. Lily had somehow assumed that Zhao Min was incapable of showing that sort of affection.

"She's a charismatic."

Lily started at the sound of Strangford's low voice. He had come to join her on the pavement. He looked harder-edged with his hair cropped short again, the eyepatch a starker monument on his face.

"Who?" she demanded.

"The girl," he replied, giving the slightest nod toward Inês.

"How? Why." Lily barely remembered to keep her voice low.

"It's a ... projection of sorts. Something like ... noise," he finished, searching for the right word. "She does it when she's scared. If she feels something is threatening her."

Lily recalled the strange sensation that had come over her in the hallway their first night in the house when she had inadvertently startled Inês in the darkness.

"I felt it," she admitted with surprise. "I thought I'd just risen from bed too quickly. How did you ...?"

"She helped Mila with the wash," Strangford replied. "Zhao Min told her not to, but she doesn't like leaving Mila to do all the work."

"And of course, Zhao Min couldn't tell her why—not without giving you away." Lily filled in, putting the pieces together. "But that means Zhao Min must know about it."

"She knows," Strangford replies.

Lily's head spun.

"What about Mila? Or Zhao Min's cook?"

"It's just the girl," Strangford replied, anticipating her question.

Just the girl—just a single charismatic living in the refuge that Zhao Min had built behind enemy lines.

Something about it hummed with potential.

"That makes me feel ..."

Lily trailed off, not knowing what word would fit. Strangford squeezed her hand.

"Me, too," he replied.

~

Five hours later, Lily woke with her face plastered to Sam's shoulder, jolted by a bump in the road from a sleep she hadn't realized she'd fallen into. She sat up abruptly, blinking as she reoriented herself.

The upholstery of the carriage was worn, the floor dusty. Through the half-opened windows, she could see the fields of Luxembourg, green with new spring wheat.

251

Outside on the driver's seat, Strangford kept up a slow and steady pace. The horses pulling the carriage wouldn't be able to handle anything more, not with a full day's journey between them and Vianden.

On the other bench, Kazi and Zhao Min stared out opposite windows. The air was close and stuffy.

Lily glanced up at Sam, mildly embarrassed at having used him as a pillow. She realized with horror that there was a wet spot on his shirt where her face had been.

Sam grinned.

"Bit sticky in here," he noted, flapping the damp fabric.

Kazi looked over, frowning. Lily hoped her cheeks weren't flaming. She considered jabbing Sam in the ribs with her elbow, but the inspector would almost certainly notice. She resolutely pointed her eyes outside the window instead.

"Who's up for a game of Spot the Animal?" Sam asked. "We can put a little stake on it."

"He cheats," Zhao Min announced.

"Hey." Sam protested.

"I don't gamble," Kazi replied.

The carriage settled back into a stuffy, dull silence. Sam began humming the tune to a particularly raunchy music hall song under his breath.

"Stop that," Zhao Min snapped.

"Stop what?"

Zhao Min rolled her eyes and looked away, resolutely ignoring him.

"You must be imagining things," Sam cheerfully lied.

"Shǎguā," Zhao Min muttered.

"I heard that."

"That was the point."

"Does anyone have a newspaper?" Kazi cut in tiredly.

"They're in German," Zhao Min said.

The inspector let his head fall back against the wall of the carriage. It bounced as the vehicle hit another pothole. He winced, and Lily recalled why she used Sam as her pillow instead.

"Are we there yet?" Sam complained.

He was answered with curses in both Mandarin and Bangla.

Lily fought the urge to return to her nap as the carriage jolted and swayed past a slow-crawling landscape of scattered farmhouses and distant lines of trees.

Then the trees slipped away from her, swimming into darkness.

The darkness shifted, taking a dangerous shape.

Grey-green uniforms. An oiled rifle barrel.

Small stones under her knees.

Blood splattering across the dirt.

The carriage lurched, Lily's head striking the wall. Nausea swelled up.

"Stop it," she demanded. "Stop the carriage."

Sam pivoted, sticking his torso neatly out the window and calling up at Strangford. Lily was already scrabbling at the door, wrenching it open and spilling out onto the road. She collapsed at the verge with her hands and knees in the soft spring grass and promptly lost her breakfast.

There was a thump behind her as Strangford's boots hit the ground. He crouched down, handkerchief in his hand.

"Water, Sam," he called back.

"Is this a baby thing?" Sam asked from behind her as he handed Strangford the tin cup of water.

"Checkpoint," Lily rasped urgently, her voice like sand in her throat.

Strangford's glove tightened on her arm, and Lily realized what she had done.

Kazi stepped from the carriage behind Zhao Min, blinking against the noonday sun as he set his hat back on his head.

Lily took a breath, fighting a dizzying panic.

"What's that, then?" Kazi demanded.

"She's just a bit green, is all," Sam called back to the two of them. "Yǒu jiǎncháshào."

He spoke the Mandarin phrase in the same easy tone of voice, but at the sound, Zhao Min's expression shifted, her eyes flashing from Sam to where Lily crouched in the dirt. The reaction was subtle but told Lily that Sam's seemingly casual words had been a warning.

"It is just as well," Zhao Min said. "There is a checkpoint ahead."

It wasn't enough. The danger could be anywhere. They needed to know more.

Conscious of Kazi's eyes on her back, Lily hugged her arms around herself tightly, pulling for any remaining threads of the vision.

Her power coughed up the answer in the smell of river water and a rainbow of steel.

She puzzled frantically over how she could possibly warn them with the inspector standing right there—and then she knew.

It was awful. She did it anyway. There wasn't time for anything else.

Lily coughed.

"Sorry." she said, touching her chest and flashing a pleading glare toward Sam. "Just a little ash in my throat."

Sam's face paled.

"Bridge," he blurted—then visibly gathered himself, regaining control. "Didn't you say it was by the bridge, Jiějie?"

"I did," Zhao Min confirmed flatly, managing to encompass all of them in a single swift glare. "By the bridge at Diekirch."

Kazi's mouth turned into a thoughtful frown. Lily realized she was holding her breath. She forced herself to release it.

"Won't they be checking papers?" Strangford asked.

"They will," Zhao Min confirmed.

"And none of us have got any." Sam pointed out.

"I have," Zhao Min countered.

"So what, then? Is it time for him to play the officer?" Sam asked, nodding to Strangford.

The suggestion made Lily feel cold despite the warmth of the afternoon.

Zhao Min didn't answer. She eyed their party carefully, her gaze stopping at Kazi.

"Can you swim?" she demanded.

"Pardon?" Kazi returned, surprised. "Yes—of course I can."

"How well?" Zhao Min pressed.

Kazi's eyes narrowed.

"Suitably well."

"There will be no uniform," Zhao Min determined. "Two women will attract far less attention than an officer or any other man of military age ... even if one of them has misplaced her papers. Your wallet, Inspector."

"Why."

Sam sighed tiredly.

"She's going to bribe them, mate."

Zhao Min waited with an expectant hand.

Kazi removed his leather billfold. Zhao Min opened it and plucked out a small bundle of banknotes.

"Take to the woods," she ordered. "Cross the tracks west of the station at Bitsdorf and find a place to swim the river."

"It'll be bloody freezing," Sam complained.

"Perhaps your beard will keep you warm," Zhao Min retorted. "Leave everything you can in the smuggler's hold—wallets, coats. There is a logging road that branches off a mile north of the village. I expect you can find us there?"

She directed the question to Sam, who scratched at the side of his nose, looking a bit shifty.

"Sure, we can manage it," he replied.

Lily wondered which woodland creature he would win over to assist with that, then suppressed a wince as she considered just how many secrets they were tossing around right under Kazi's extremely perceptive nose.

Strangford shrugged off his coat, handing it to Lily. He passed her his wallet as well, followed by his gloves.

"Are you certain?" she protested before taking them.

"I'd rather they not get wet."

Muttering a curse, Sam removed his waistcoat, tossing it at his sister. Zhao Min plucked it neatly out of the air with a grimace of distaste.

At last, Kazi let out an eloquent sigh and took off his hat.

"Ēi khēpā," he muttered, tossing it into the carriage and following it with his coat.

Zhao Min dropped the garments unceremoniously into the smuggler's box and lowered the black veil on her hat.

"Lady Strangford?" she prompted impatiently, her face shaded by dark lace.

Strangford squeezed Lily's hand.

"We'll manage. Go on."

"Don't yank on the reins," Sam barked at her, then set off toward the distant line of the trees, Kazi following after him.

Lily climbed up onto the driver's seat. It was uncomfortably high and even more uncomfortably exposed. The reins were foreign in her hands. She barely knew how to drive a carriage. Thankfully, it was clear the two tired old horses wouldn't have bolted had she kicked them.

Strangford turned back, offering her a tentative smile before he followed after the others.

Lily gave the reins a gentle tug. Nothing happened.

"Move, you beasts," she muttered, snapping them again with force. The carriage finally rolled forward.

~

Zhao Min had been right about the checkpoint. Offering bribes to ease one's passage appeared to be routine, and the German Army sentries had little interest in a veiled widow and her servant, misplaced papers or otherwise, once the requisite cash had exchanged hands. They were waved through impatiently as the soldiers looked forward to richer pickings or the excitement of a rogue deserter.

The bridge was small, but the river beneath it ran high, water foaming at the banks. Lily eyed it nervously as they crossed, thinking of the three men making their way through it somewhere in the forest that lay to the west.

Shortly after their stop, the broad fields had given way to a thick, dark woodland that covered the landscape, rising into dense hills. The road beyond Diekirch was lined by ancient trees like something out of a fairy tale where witches hunted for unsuspecting children.

The logging road was where Zhao Min remembered it, though it had clearly been some time since it had been used. The track was overgrown with grass, the ruts of old wheel tracks barely visible as it proceeded deeper into the forest. Following Zhao Min's directions, Lily drove them slowly along it past the dark-leaved trees until the road was no longer visible behind them.

The carriage door creaked as Zhao Min stepped out. She pulled off her hat and veil, tossing them onto the seat as she let out a sigh of relief. Lily climbed down from her perch, gratefully tying off the reins.

The forest was quiet save for chirping birds and the rustling of leaves in the breeze. The sounds soaked into her skin, unraveling the last coil of tension Lily had been holding in her gut.

"How much longer do you think they'll be?" Lily asked.

"Their route was more direct," Zhao Min replied. "Not long."

She took a seat on a graying stump, arranging the folds of her skirt around her.

The forest rustled, the air scented with earth and dried leaves. Patches of light danced across the ground.

"Will you go home when this is over?" Lily asked.

"If I survive?" Zhao Min prompted ruthlessly.

"If you survive," Lily forced herself to agree.

Zhao Min considered it, her slight gray figure like a punctuation mark against the soft brown and green of the woods.

"I am not sure where home is anymore," she finally replied. "It has never been London. And there is nothing for me in Hubei. I do not belong there any more than I belong here."

She waved a tired hand, taking in the ancient forest that surrounded them.

Lily leaned back against one of the trees, feeling the rough texture of it through the fabric of her motorcycle jacket.

"I know something of how that feels," she said, then caught herself. "I don't mean it's the same. But in my mother's flat, when I was a girl, somehow I only ever felt like a guest. Then there was school."

"Dreadful."

"Entirely." Lily confirmed. "A series of flats. Some of them tolerable. But I never really felt like I belonged anywhere . . . not until The Refuge. It's funny, isn't it? I never even lived there, but I miss that place more than anywhere I've ever known."

"It was jiā," Zhao Min replied simply.

"Jia," Lily echoed, trying out the feel of the word on her tongue.

Zhao Min cracked a hint of a smile.

"Close," she said.

The breeze tossed the loose tendrils of her hair.

"It wasn't given to me," Lily felt like she was navigating a forest without a path. "In fact, I nearly ran away from it. It found me, or I chose it. Maybe a little bit of both."

Across the clearing, Zhao Min closed her eyes. She looked tired.

"I know where you are going with this."

There was a gentle note of warning in the words, but Lily wasn't quite ready to let it go.

"You know my father."

Zhao Min nodded a careful acknowledgment.

"And you know what he did to me," Lily continued.

Memory cut her, a slash of remembered pain—the flashing terror of a vision. The crimson gown. Scattered jewels framing empty eyes staring up into the night.

The blue sky over a deep hole in the ground. A warm hand on her shoulder.

All will be well.

And the bitter loneliness that had followed.

"I do," Zhao Min agreed, meeting Lily's gaze.

"I have not forgiven him." Lily felt the truth of the words like a vow. "I'm not sure I ever could. But I let him back into my life anyway. And I am glad of it."

For a moment, it was as though another veil had fallen away from Zhao Min's face. Lily glimpsed something there she had never been privileged to see before.

A terrible pain. Sadness. Longing.

She was overwhelmed by the urge to cross the clearing and put her arms around the woman, to simply hold her against the onslaught of that hurt.

She didn't. She knew it would not be welcome.

Like a shifting of the clouds, the moment passed, and Zhao Min was herself once more.

"They are coming," she announced.

Lily heard them a moment later, the footsteps crunching against the dry leaves that papered the ground. The bright white of shirt-sleeves became visible through the gaps in the trees.

Kazi led the procession, his dark hair plastered to his skull. His still-soaked shirt had turned form-fitting. He plucked at the fabric as he caught sight of the women in an awkward effort to pull it loose again.

"If you will excuse me," he said stiffly.

He rounded to the far side of the carriage, where Lily heard him shuffling around in the boot for drier clothes.

Sam arrived next. He had foregone his shirt entirely, the wrung-out and wrinkled garment slung over his shoulder instead, leaving his chest exposed.

The sight of it made her cold.

The scar he had shown her before was where she remembered it, the pale, twisting white line curving around his midsection.

There were others. She could see them on his arms, his torso—a white slice here, another there. A scattering of little marks across his left shoulder.

They were peripheral, all relatively minor . . . but there were so very many of them.

It's like the devil's own luck.

The realization took the warmth from the afternoon. They were wounds that should have killed him, over and over again, deflected into something else. The evidence of his bargain with the birds was etched into his skin—of the life he had bought for himself at the cost of a great deal more death.

Sam turned to snap loose the damp fabric of his shirt, hanging it over the traces of the horses. The move revealed more pale symbols carved by war and dark magic into his flesh.

A pair of sparrows whirled around him. One landed in Sam's still-damp hair. He pulled a few seeds from his trouser pocket and offered them up to his visitor in thanks.

The birds fluttered away.

Kazi came back around the carriage, once more in a dry shirt, jacket, and tie, his hat neatly set in place. He looked desperately relieved.

"Don't suppose you packed another shirt," Sam asked his sister.

"Do I look like your valet?" Zhao Min snapped in reply.

"You haven't a spare?" Kazi asked.

"Not all of us had a chance to pack before getting our arses dragged into the Bochelands," Sam retorted.

"I have something for him." Zhao Min nodded to Strangford as he stepped into the clearing.

Water dripped onto the leaves around him. His shirt was molded to his shoulders, trousers close against his thighs. The damp did little to muss his short hair. Lily found she missed the way it would've curled in the past.

He pulled his eyepatch from his pocket, tying it back into place.

"Is it time, then?" he asked calmly.

"There is nowhere else to stop between here and Vianden," Zhao Min confirmed.

The air in the clearing seemed to thicken, but Lily made no protest. What could she say? They had agreed to this—Strangford had agreed to it.

Zhao Min opened the smuggler's box and removed a cloth-wrapped bundle. She handed it to Strangford. He glanced down at it as though he held a nightmare in his hands.

Without another word, he turned back into the words, carrying the dark package.

"What's the matter?" Kazi demanded, sensing the tension.

"We're putting a bloke who reads the past through his skin in a dead man's clothes," Sam replied. "What do you think's the matter?"

"You mean he ..." Kazi began, then caught himself as he rapidly put the implications together. "Of course he would. But that's—"

He cut off, his face falling into a mask of sympathy and horror.

"I'll go to him," Lily said thinly.

She found Strangford in a clearing. Squirrels scurried up the trunks of ancient oaks around him as the soft green leaves whispered overhead. The place he had found was idyllic, like something out of a story. In his soaked white shirt, Strangford looked like a lost knight errant—a ghost from another age.

He was staring down at the uniform, which now lay exposed on the unfolded piece of muslin.

Lily slipped her arms around his waist, letting her head fall against his shoulder. The damp linen of his shirt was cool under her cheek.

"You don't have to do this," she said.

"That's not entirely true," Strangford replied stiffly and began to unbutton his shirt.

~

The others were quiet when they returned to the clearing. The sun had slanted an hour lower, the light angling through the dancing leaves. Zhao Min still waited on the stump. Sam flicked pebbles at the trees while Kazi paced, his arms crossed stiffly over his chest.

Strangford was straight-backed and elegant in the German uniform. The pale sheen of cold sweat against his skin was almost unnoticeable.

Lily was fairly certain she had been able to muffle the sound of his screams.

It turned out the hauptmann had not died easily.

Strangford climbed back into the carriage without speaking. He sat there, looking down at his now-gloved hands where they rested on the gray-green wool that covered his knees.

"Can he use it?" Zhao Min demanded quietly.

"He will manage," Lily snapped.

A part of her wanted to rail at Zhao Min for possessing the damnable piece of clothing, but there would be little point in it.

Sam plucked his shirt from where it hung on the traces. It was less visibly damp. He slipped it on, pulling his waistcoat over it. Setting on his tinted spectacles, he climbed up onto the driver's seat.

"Entschuldigung," he muttered under his breath. "Guten Arbend—Abend. Bugger."

Sam's German practice was interspersed with East End curses as he took the reins.

The rest of them climbed inside. Kazi almost brushed against Strangford in the close confines of the interior. Strangford flinched at the near contact.

Lily resisted the urge to take his hand.

The carriage jolted into motion, rocking slowly as Sam brought it about.

~

The village of Vianden clustered along the curving bank of a river. The land to either side rose up steeply to tall, forest-covered hillsides. A plateau to the north was crowned by a once-elegant castle, the

261

walls and turret still showing signs of ruin. It looked like an illustration out of a book, kissed with the sunset as it emerged from beyond a bend in the road.

There were no obvious signs of the war. The houses nestled closely together, most of them painted a warm, creamy white. Window boxes already offered up little spills of greenery. The streets were clean, steps neatly swept as they drove slowly by, but a closer look revealed that the people here also had that whittled-down look of longstanding hunger Lily had seen in the city.

Beyond the clustered homes lay the forest, thick with the encroaching twilight.

She looked up at the castle. It loomed over them now that they had reached the streets of the town. The structure was more imposing up close, the stone walls rising flush from the jagged stone cliffs of the outcropping on which it was perched. Scaffolding was visible on one side of the inner keep, but it was the small, dark silhouettes punctuating the walls that held her attention—guards pacing easily with rifles in their hands.

This was not some gentleman's hunting retreat. The castle was much older than that, the site clearly chosen for defense. Those walls were meant to hold off armies and trebuchets. Were they really going to try to get inside? And if they did . . . how would they make it back out again?

The carriage rocked to a stop in front of an inn with a pale pink facade. It was slightly broader than the houses that lay to either side. Tidy shutters were open to the spring air, windows glinting light and warmth against the encroaching evening. Vianden was far enough from the front not to fear air raids. After all, they had very nearly reached Germany itself.

Zhao Min had assigned their roles during the drive.

"Wife." She pointed at Lily, then herself and the others. "Widowed sister. Valet—Turkish. They are quite fashionable."

Kazi visibly bristled.

"I look nothing like a Turk."

"They won't know the difference," Zhao Min replied. "And you can't be important enough for anyone to bother to speak to you."

He had bit back whatever retort he wanted to make, settling for sullen silence instead.

As the carriage stopped in front of the inn, Kazi let out an eloquent sigh, then climbed out, holding open the door for Zhao Min to descend, the dark fall of her veil obscuring the top half of her face.

"Are you certain you're up for this?" Lily quietly demanded.

Strangford's jaw tightened.

"I'll manage," he snapped, then crumpled a bit. "I'm sorry. I—"

Lily squeezed his gloved hand.

"You don't have to be kind right now."

He accepted it with a stiff nod, letting out a long breath.

"It will get easier. The longer I do it. I'll be ..."

"Accustomed," Lily offered.

"I need you to let go now," he said carefully.

She withdrew her hand and watched him pull on his power, his eyes losing focus as he pushed himself into the memories woven into the stolen uniform. Agony and fear twisted across his face, the spasms clenching his hands into fists.

She wondered with a jolt whether she would need to silence him ... but then he was past it.

He breathed in, straightening. The lines of his body lost Strangford's familiar grace. This man was harder, moving with arrogant ease. He exited the carriage, turning and offering his hand.

Looking at him framed in the doorway, Lily felt like she was seeing someone else. In the foreign gray of the uniform, with his eye patch and close-cut hair, he looked strange and dangerous, decorated with the colors of a dead man's rank.

She accepted the German officer's hand and stepped onto the pavement.

The innkeeper bustled out, his eyes immediately going to the uniform. He turned both bright and nervous, his welcome ringing with mildly desperate enthusiasm.

"Willkommen! Treten Sie bitte ein." He bowed, waving them into the building. "Bitte."

At the front desk, Strangford whipped out his identification papers. He made a joke in German that the innkeeper laughed at, forced and thin. A string of instructions was rattled off in a voice that sounded like it belonged to a stranger as the innkeeper continued to nod, flashing a nervous smile.

He handed over the keys to their rooms. Strangford waved a gloved hand in a brisk dismissal and turned away.

Upstairs, she and Strangford split from the others to step into their suite. As soon as the door was shut, he reached desperately for the buttons of the coat, his gloved hands impeding him.

"Get this off of me," he demanded, his voice strangled.

Lily hurried to him, her hands flying down the fasteners. As soon as she was finished, he tore off the garment, throwing it onto the bed. He stood there in his shirt, looking stiff with near panic.

A quick knock sounded on the door. Lily peeked out to see Sam standing on the threshold, his eyes still shaded by the dark glass of his spectacles.

"Here," he said quickly, pushing Strangford's small valise at her.

"Thank you," she replied gratefully, accepting it and shutting the door.

By the bed, Strangford ran leather-covered fingers through the cropped black of his hair.

"Do you need help with the rest of it?" Lily asked.

Strangford looked down at the green-gray wool trousers.

He let out a desperate bark of laughter, his voice breaking a bit. "Please."

SEVENTEEN

Ten o'clock that evening
Vianden

$\mathscr{S}$TRANGFORD WAS SLEEPING. Lily was grateful for it. Once he had freed himself from the uniform, Lily had helped him clear any lingering impressions of the dead hauptmann in the best way she knew how. He had passed out immediately afterward, exhausted by what even an hour in the German wool had required of him.

Sleep felt rather far for Lily. Rising carefully, she washed up and headed outside, moving quietly past the doors to the rooms where the rest of their party slept.

She found herself in a small garden bound by low walls. The night was cool enough that she was glad she had thought to bring her coat. The air smelled of the forest, which she could see as a dark, thick mass rising up the hillside behind the inn.

A flagstone patio was framed by a few tables that would have offered a lovely place to lunch on warmer days. Among the starlit shadows that cloaked the place, Lily made out an impression of dark green rhododendron leaves, perennials offering green shoots from their beds.

The castle loomed above her. There were lights from the evening watch on the walls, illuminating parts of the black facade. Even at this hour, the German Army patrolled there, guarding whatever was hidden inside.

Something Lily felt certain should never have existed were it not for the arrogance of an empire at war.

She realized she was not alone. A dark figure stood on the flagstones. Lily hesitated, keeping to the shadows as she waited for her eyes to adjust.

It was Kazi, and he was singing—or at least, that was what it sounded like, the low words tinged with a rhythm that wrapped around her like an old scarf, warm and comfortable.

She knew she ought to leave him to his privacy, but she found herself held up by curiosity.

Kazi bowed gracefully at the waist, like a dancer making an invitation to some unseen partner. He chanted the gentle rhythm of his words again and descended to his knees. Folding forward, he touched his forehead to the stone.

There was something noble in the gesture. It reminded Lily of a knight in a stained glass window prostrating himself before his liege.

Kazi sat back on his heels, gazing out into the forest.

"Have you need of me?" he asked.

He didn't turn, but Lily knew with a rush of embarrassment that the question was addressed to her. She stepped from the shadow of the inn into the garden where the darkness was softened by the bits of lamplight that slipped through the shutters.

"No. I'm sorry. I was lurking."

Kazi stood, neatly brushing off his knees.

"Were you praying?" Lily asked, mustering her courage and coming a bit closer.

Kazi sighed.

"The garden seemed a less distracting environment than a room shared with your Mr. Wu. And I have been rather rotten about practicing Salah this past week."

"How often are you meant to do it?"

"Five times a day." Kazi replied.

"That seems a lot," Lily remarked, a bit surprised.

He glanced over at her, a hint of a smile tugging at his mouth.

"If one is only accustomed to remembering God once a week."

Giving in, Lily sat down on one of the wrought iron benches.

"I can hardly claim to do it so often as that," she admitted.

Kazi took a seat beside her. They gazed out over the garden. She could hear the low murmur of voices from the neighboring houses—the sound of a door closing, someone calling a dog inside. It was a foreign place, far quieter and more forest-bound than the city she knew, but there was something peaceful in it, and Kazi's company felt rather easier than she had expected.

He raised his eyes to the profile of the castle.

"What do you think of our plan for tomorrow?" he asked.

They had discussed it further during the ride to Vianden. Zhao Min would drive the carriage that carried Lily and Strangford, in the guise of the German hauptmann, to the castle gates. She had assured them that with Sam's spectacles, she could pass for a boy, and her German was admittedly as smooth as that of a native.

It was their job to bluff their way through the gates. It would be up to Sam and Kazi to do the rest.

Sam had insisted he should be the one to occupy the smuggler's box inside the carriage, but Kazi had flatly refused, demanding to know why a pilot and ex-thief was considered a better partner in their invasion than a law enforcement officer and spy. No one had been able to answer him without giving away more than they cared to, but before it had become truly awkward, Sam had changed tactics and announced that he would strap himself to the underside of the vehicle instead, leaving the hiding place to Kazi.

"Just try not to bounce over any potholes," he snapped at his sister.

Their success still depended on so much—whether Zhao Min's forged letter of introduction would pass muster. Whether Strangford could tap into the memories layered into the hauptmann's uniform without breaking down from the stress of it. Whether Lily could successfully pass as his French-speaking Swiss wife. Would someone look under the carriage? Would it be watched once parked somewhere on the grounds? Would Sam and Kazi be able to slip away to search the castle?

They had no idea what they were looking for or where to find it.

"I think it's madness," Lily replied. "But I haven't anything better to suggest. And we have to try."

Kazi took a moment to respond.

"If I tell you something, will you try not to be alarmed by it?" he asked.

Lily startled beside him.

"That is a rather alarming question," she pointed out.

"I am aware. But I'm afraid I haven't any better way of prefacing it."

"Go on."

"The checkpoint we avoided this afternoon. That was you."

Lily kept herself very still as her pulse pounded, fighting the urge to run.

"I'm not sure I know what you mean," she carefully returned.

A breeze passed through the garden, ruffling Kazi's hair. It took him a moment to respond. It was as though he were picking his way carefully through treacherous ground.

"Four years ago, at the Eversleigh estate in Hampshire, I arrived to find a Royal Army Medical Corps doctor tending to a man who had been shot. Very recently shot," he added, flashing a glance at her before looking back to the woods. "I checked on the physician's credentials. A Captain Gardner, formerly of St. Bart's in London, assigned to the Fifth Southern General RAMC Hospital in Portsmouth. Mrs. Eversleigh stated that the gunshot that injured her husband was heard at roughly ten past seven that evening. I entered the house at seven twenty to find the doctor stitching up an incision made to relieve pressure on a punctured lung. Portsmouth is at least an hour and twenty minutes by train. When I asked Captain Gardner how he had come to arrive at the house so fortuitously, he claimed he had simply happened to be making a call."

Lily held herself very still, as though any movement might upset the delicate balance of this conversation and turn it into something more dangerous.

Beside her, Kazi sighed.

"Please, Lady Strangford. I am not a threat to you."

His voice was earnest. Taking a breath and trying to push past her near panic, Lily asked herself whether she believed him.

She found, to her surprise, that she did.

It shifted everything. The forest ceased to loom at her, the garden shrinking back to its ordinary size. The little noises of night in the village settled back in—a soft note of laughter, a woman somewhere singing a tune.

She turned on the bench to face him.

"Just say it."

He met her look without flinching.

"You are able—in some way, at some times—to see events in the future."

It should have been a blow... but it didn't feel that way.

She waited, letting him continue.

"It's how the doctor came to be at Taddiford. Someone called him there before Mr. Eversleigh was shot. I could not rule out that it was your husband who possessed the ability—perhaps some further complication of the power he carries in his hands. But on the beach that night . . . it was dark and terribly confused. But there was a moment when I swear I heard you call out to me before the bullets began to fall. And earlier, at Scarborough, when we were arguing in the street after that first shell hit Lt. Brockmeyer's house ..."

"I told you to get down," Lily finished for him. "Before the Germans fired again."

She remembered all of it, every detail of those early encounters when this man who had posed such a clear threat to Strangford, pursuing him with all the terrible impartiality of perceived justice. The noise and horror of the German bombardment at Scarborough, the desperate battle in the rain and the darkness on the beach below Taddiford. The night another charismatic had been riddled with bullets in front of her.

"You have known since then?" she asked.

"I ... wondered," he replied carefully. "But having traveled with you on and off for this last week, it simply ... fit."

His gaze sharpened, his voice becoming even more serious.

"I will not use it. I would not have mentioned it at all except that the madness we are attempting tomorrow may require any and all resources at our disposal if we are to have a chance of success. Resorting to the sort of awkward charade I saw executed this morning to conceal your abilities would cost us time and, very possibly, our lives. It seemed prudent to make clear such concealments are unnecessary."

"I understand," Lily acknowledged.

She should have been terrified. She was surprised to discover that she was not. It wasn't that she believed Kazi would never reveal her secret. She knew well enough there could be circumstances where he would feel compelled to share the information ... but she was quietly certain he would only do so in a time of the utmost need, like the one that had brought him to call on Strangford.

Given all they had learned since then, she could not entirely fault him for that.

They had all been so concerned with concealing what they were—with the threat exposure might entail—that they had curled up inside their shells when taking a greater risk might have seen them accomplish so much more.

Robert Ash's voice echoed in her mind, carried to her like a gust of wind.

You have a vital part to play in all of this.

She studied him—this man who was once her enemy, who had ferreted out all of her secrets.

"How did you end up in the Foreign Section of the Secret Service Bureau?"

It was his turn to stiffen, but even as he did, Lily saw him push past it—willing himself to lower his guard as she had just lowered hers.

"Are you familiar with the Ghadar Affair?"

"Revolutionaries," Lily said, the memory popping into her mind. "From India."

"A political organization advocating for independence from the British Empire," Kazi quietly corrected her. "But shortly after the outbreak of the war, the Secret Service Bureau received intelligence that the German Foreign Office had involved itself to further urge and support a rebellion against the crown."

"To force us to fight on two fronts," Lily finished for him.

She could immediately see the terrible potential of it. If war had broken out in India at the same time Britain was holding the line against the German advance in France and Belgium, it would have compromised their already overstretched forces—especially at that early stage of the war, when the new volunteers who flooded the ranks of the army had not yet been trained.

"I was with the Domestic Section at the time, assigned to a counterespionage unit. They tasked me with infiltrating the Ghadar cohort in London."

Something Kazi's careful tone set off a warning bell in her head.

"My race and background made me the natural candidate," he continued. "Though of course the community in London is small enough that I was already known to many of them. I could not assume a different identity."

"You had to join them as yourself." Lily filled in. "Under your own name."

He nodded.

"Did they know you were with the Bureau?"

"No. But they knew I was a policeman, and my Special Branch experience was seen as valuable to them. It did not take me long to penetrate their inner circle. There were plans to attempt an assassination of Lord Kitchener. A bombing in Liverpool. I was able to disrupt them without revealing my true allegiances."

"You would have had to pretend you were sympathetic to the cause of Indian independence. Quite convincingly." Lily noted.

"Correct," he returned with a conspicuous lack of further elaboration. "In January of 1915, I learned of efforts to incite and supply a mutiny in Bengal, supported financially by the Germans. The operation moved to Bengal and control was transferred to the Bureau's Foreign Section under Sir Mansfield Cumming. 'C', as they call him."

He stopped there, an abrupt abbreviation.

"But what happened?" Lily pressed.

"You asked how I came to be with the Foreign Section."

"And you have answered me," she finished for him, not hiding her disappointment.

His face fell, revealing dismay.

"It is not a pretty story."

"I have stood over the dead with you, Inspector," Lily replied. "You should not need to question the delicacy of my sensibilities."

He let out a dark and slightly pained laugh.

"Perhaps it is not your sensibilities I am worried about, but my own."

"I'm sorry." Lily hurriedly cut in. "I didn't mean to ..."

He cut her off with a gracefully raised hand.

"It was particularly difficult," he continued, each word careful as a shard of glass. "Earning acceptance from the revolutionaries in Bengal. They were almost exclusively Hindu, but the party in London had been more heterogeneous, and my references eventually won me entry. They were led by Jatin Mukherjee. He was . . . passionate. The sort of man who made you wish you were a hero. That was what he had collected around himself—a cohort of men who wished to be heroes. The cells he oversaw were organized, strategic. When there was flooding and sickness, they swooped in with relief and supplies while the British authorities did nothing. Unless the colonists were impacted, they hardly noticed."

"You respected them," Lily said.

"I respected their efforts on behalf of the population," Kazi corrected her. "And many of their grievances were genuine. But an armed uprising against the empire was only ever going to end in disaster."

He had not said that India was better off under English rule—an omission Lily did not fail to notice.

"An attempted mutiny by another cohort of Ghadar in Punjab Province was easily and violently suppressed. Eight hundred men were executed. And still, they pushed forward with plans for an uprising in Bengal. Mukherjee was to meet a shipment of German-funded arms being sent to India by a cell in the United States, but I reported the details of the rendezvous. The boat was seized, and the Bagha and his men were ambushed by the Indian police. He was shot. He died the next morning."

The words cut across the spring air, laced with quiet rage. Lily wondered who it was directed at. The revolutionary who brought medicine to the sick? The government who shot him down? Or at himself, the man who handed them the means to do so?

"Bagha?" she echoed.

"Tiger," Kazi clarified. "That's what we called him. Now you have the whole of it."

Lily wasn't entirely sure that was true. He had shared the facts, perhaps, but Kazi's story did not feel whole. She wondered if he honestly understood the rest of it himself.

"Is there anything else it might be helpful for me to know before tomorrow?" he asked.

The vulnerability of the moment before was gone. He was once again the man she was familiar with, poised and professional, but even in the near darkness, Lily could see the delicate lines carved around his eyes, the tiredness in the line of his jaw, a bit better than she had before.

"Just... trust whatever any of us are telling you," she replied at last, her own voice sounding a bit tired. "Even if it doesn't make much sense. And if a rat starts tugging at your trouser cuff, it's probably time to run."

Kazi absorbed that last bit with a curious blink, and then a nod of acceptance. He rose to go.

"Kazi," she called after him.

He paused, glancing back as she rose from the bench.

"Thank you."

He didn't smile. If anything, his eyes seemed to go harder— perhaps to hold back whatever within him might be trying to escape.

"I am just doing my duty, my lady."

EIGHTEEN

*T*HE ROAD TO THE CASTLE wound like the body of a snake, climbing the steep slope of the hill in a series of alarming switchbacks.

Lily sat beside Strangford in the interior of their vehicle, uncomfortably conscious of the Special Branch inspector concealed under the opposite seat and the enterprising former housebreaker cleverly harnessed to the undercarriage.

The walls of the fortress rose overhead, emerging from the green froth of the trees to an imposing height. The patrols were very much present, Lily near enough now to see the rifles in their hands.

She leaned back against her seat, fighting the urge to panic.

Strangford was stiff and silent beside her. He had been ever since he had put the uniform back on that morning, this time managing it without crying out.

The carriage rattled over an uneven stretch of cobblestones, jarring her teeth. She hoped Sam didn't get his head clonked as they jerked to a stop in front of an arched gate built into the outer wall.

"Halten Sie! Bitte anhalten und sich ausweisen."

Zhao Min rattled off a few quick lines of German in response to the challenge, her voice convincingly dropping to sound like that of an adolescent boy.

275

Lily risked a peek out the window. The gate into the castle grounds was crossed by a wooden barricade. An old iron portcullis still hung overhead. The soldier who had ordered them to stop stood beside it with a clipboard in his hand, looking up at where Zhao Min perched on the driver's seat.

Another German reclined in his chair in the gatehouse. Above them on the wall, two men huddled in a sandbag-framed machine gun nest.

Beyond the outer defenses, Lily could make out only the top levels of the castle. The upper floors were partially roofed, the tower still in ruins. Moss climbed up the northern side, and a few birds fluttered out of the roofless portion of the main building, black specks against the clear blue of the sky.

"Er möchte Ihre Papiere sehen, Hauptmann," Zhao Min called down.

Strangford flipped the lever that held up the glass of the carriage window, letting it drop. He pulled the stolen military identification and the forged letter from his jacket and handed them to the soldier.

The boy was awkwardly young. He took the papers and examined them in a way that made Lily question whether he had any real skill for identifying their validity.

He peered through the window, making a perfunctory scan of the interior. His eyes stopped and widened a bit at the sight of Lily. He clearly had not expected to find a woman.

"Gibt es ein Problem?" Strangford demanded, his voice uncharacteristically cold.

The private snapped to attention.

"Entschuldigung, Hauptmann. Einen Augenblick."

He took the papers to his reclining colleague in the gatehouse, who dropped the four legs of his chair back onto the floor. He picked up a telephone receiver and wound the handle. Lily could see a bundle of wires trailing out of the gatehouse and over the thick stone walls to the interior. Other lines hung from the exterior, disappearing into the trees.

A quick conversation was punctuated by barked acknowledgments in German. The private in the gatehouse tossed the papers back to his companion.

The younger soldier returned to the carriage, giving the documents to Strangford and snapping off a quick salute.

He shouted up at the men in the machine gun nest, who waved a couple of lazy fingers in acknowledgment. The wooden barrier swung open. With a snap of the reins, Zhao Min drove them into the passage through the thick bulk of the castle ramparts. The shadow of it fell across them with a breath of cool air.

Lily caught a closer look at the machine gunners as they entered, the heavy iron barrel of their weapon trained on the road. It felt like a great deal of security for a fortress located a hundred miles from the front lines.

Beyond the gate, the road wound tightly between walls and castle, high barriers of ancient stone rising to either side. Here and there, outcroppings of the rock plateau upon which the castle sat were visible, reminding her that beyond the walls lay steep cliffs that descended into the town on one side and the forest on the other.

Lily could barely see the top of the castle from this angle. It loomed over her, immense and threatening.

At the end of the drive, a row of outbuildings clustered against the outer wall, most likely the old stables and carriage houses. A half-dozen soldiers were lingering there, smoking cigarettes and laughing.

They did not make it as far as the men. A guard waited in the road, his hand extended to signal them to a halt by a steep, narrow stairwell set against the side of the castle.

The stairs showed signs of recent repair, the newer stone set flush against the older, weathered materials. An officer descended them. He was clean-shaven with fine brown hair which receded a bit from his forehead under his cap. Tall and thin, he wore a pair of round, wire-rimmed eyeglasses.

The indicators of rank on his uniform were the same as Strangford's, marking him as another hauptmann, though he had both a dagger and a service pistol strapped to his belt.

Lily wasn't sure if it was good or bad that neither of them outranked the other.

Strangford stepped out of the carriage without waiting for an invitation. He set his officer's cap neatly on his head, turning to offer a hand to Lily. She accepted it, allowing him to help her down even as her heart pounded with trepidation.

Her walking stick clicked against the stones under her boots. The entire place felt like a prison, one that could easily swallow them whole when this all went wrong.

"Herr Hauptmann Keller," the officer said, using the name from Strangford's stolen papers. "Ich bin Hauptmann Vogel. Wilkommen bei Schloss Vianden."

Hauptmann Vogel's greeting was courteously delivered, but the officer's eyes were not warm. They flickered from Strangford's uniform to his eyepatch and scars, then over to Lily. His gaze hitched for a moment on her walking stick.

Vogel extended a hand. Strangford took it. He had worn his gloves. They had decided earlier that the risk he might be thrown by an unexpected impression outweighed the possible advantage he might gain from reading the man, at least right away.

Hauptmann Vogel's eyes snapped to the gloves, then lifted to Lily's face with a cool smile.

"Frau Keller, nehme ich an?" he asked.

Lily tried not to panic, smiling sweetly at Strangford.

"Meine Frau spricht leider kein Deutsch," he apologized easily. "Sie kommt aus der Romandie."

"Ah," Vogel said, shifting languages fluidly. "But then we must speak French, of course."

Lily wasn't sure how to feel about his obvious facility with the language. Her French had improved over the last week, but she was far from a native speaker, nor had she had much time to practice the idiosyncrasies of the French of West Switzerland.

Not that it mattered. There was no turning back now.

Vogel's eyes rose to where Zhao Min sat on the carriage, noting the tinted glasses she had borrowed from Sam. She wore Lily's motorcycling trousers and coat, her hair expertly hidden under her cap. She looked like a bit of an urchin but was not obviously female.

"I hope you will forgive the intrusion," Strangford said, drawing Vogel's attention from their driver. "But as I am on leave here in Vianden to take the air, I hoped I might be able to show my wife the ruins. She is something of an amateur scholar of historical fortifications. We have a letter of introduction."

He handed Vogel the forged letter. The German officer accepted it, giving it a thoughtful study.

"You are with Von Müller's office," he noted.

"I am," Strangford confirmed.

He sounded comfortable, professional . . . even a little bored. Lily had to hide her surprise. She knew Strangford could put on an act when required, but he did not usually have to do so in the persona of a foreigner whose past screams were echoing somewhere under his skin.

"Then you must know Kapitän Altepeter," Vogel offered, his clear eyes focused on Strangford.

Strangford frowned.

"Isn't Altepeter with the Markgraff in the Baltic?" he returned.

Something shifted in Vogel's gaze.

"Ah yes," he replied. "Of course, you are correct."

Lily slowly let out a breath. She had no doubt the question had been a test, one that apparently Strangford had managed to pass thanks to the efforts of the Navy Intelligence cryptographers in Room 40.

"And you, Frau Keller—you are interested in castles?"

"I was raised in the shadow of Château de Tourbillon," Lily replied, parroting the story Zhao Min and Strangford had cooked up for her back in the city. "I have always admired fortifications."

"I hope our presence here is not an intrusion," Strangford added.

"Not at all." The light glinted off of Vogel's spectacles. "You are quite welcome. I would be delighted to offer you a tour."

The enthusiasm sounded genuine. It set Lily's hackles rising.

Abteilung IIIb, she thought. If Zhao Min's information had been correct, it meant that Vogel, for all his courtesy, was an agent of Germany's elite intelligence bureau.

Behind her, Zhao Min snapped the reins, the carriage pulling away up the drive. Lily could not help feeling as though someone was taking her life preserver away.

The interior of the castle was bare and shadowy. The air dropped in temperature an instant ten degrees, dancing a chill across her skin as Lily stepped inside. The vaulted stone ceilings looked old and solid, echoing with the tap of her walking stick. The floor had been swept, but there were still old stains that made her think of aher think of creeping moss, lichen and animal nests undisturbed for decades.

It was also empty. Both the lack of furnishings and the cool silence told her that the German garrison here must be based in some of the castle outbuildings.

A bundle of wires ran across the ceiling, bolted into the stone with brackets at regular intervals. Unlike her assumed persona, Lily was not particularly enamored with ruins but found she did not appreciate the Germans permanently scarring the stones.

"The oldest portions of the castle date to the 11th century." Vogel said, slipping comfortably into a lecture. "The counts of Vianden were among the most influential houses in the region. Expansion continued through the 17th century before the place was abandoned and allowed to fall into ruin. This way."

He led them deeper into the interior. They passed through a narrow hall with tall windows that looked out across the village to the river. From this height, the water looked like a gleaming silver serpent, houses clustered like anthills against the bank. Below her, in a broader part of the castle yard, a sergeant drilled a small group of soldiers. She heard a lorry engine backfire. A few of the men shouted colorful insults. The modern sound felt like an invasion, something that could not possibly belong to the graceful old stones.

Lily tried to make a quick mental tally. How many men had she seen so far? Perhaps twenty?

"An attempt at reconstruction began late in the last century but was constrained by funds, then abandoned with the war," Vogel continued, leading them to the next room.

She stepped aside to make way for a private wheeling out a crate of bullets.

The space they entered next was round in shape, the center of it dominated by a quartet of enormous stone pillars that still showed fragments of ancient, colorful paint. They framed a low-walled box in the floor, measuring perhaps four feet to each side.

The windows that lined the walls were tall and free of glass. As they entered, a few pigeons fluttered from their perches along the high arched ceiling, making a quick exit to the safety of the outdoors.

The space had an aura of a church but was clearly being used for storage. There were stacks of boards along one side, equipment for more scaffolding like what she had seen rising against the ruined tower. There were ropes, buckets, masonry trowels, and bags of cement, all relics of the renovations Vogel had just spoken of.

"This was the chapel, as I understand it," he said.

"Is that window authentically Romanesque?" Strangford remarked, his delight genuine.

Lily resisted the urge to roll her eyes, refraining from any comment of her own. She knew very little of the architecture of castles. To engage in conversation would only risk revealing her ignorance. Instead, she played the part of the quiet explorer, knowing that every minute they could keep Vogel occupied granted more time for Kazi and Sam to make their way into the castle to search out anything they could discover about the mysterious program supposedly hidden here.

Lily drifted to the pillars. The wall that linked them was waist high, and when she looked over it, she realized it encased nothing—just a hole in the floor looking down into blackness. She could barely make out a faint spill of light below, just enough to show her there was another floor beneath them.

"Curious, isn't it?"

Vogel's remark came from very close beside her. Lily suppressed a flinch.

"The Lower Chapel," he added. "The nobles would worship here with the family priest while the servants gathered below. They were able to hear the service through the opening."

Lily considered the idea and found it appalling.

"Below the floor?" she demanded before she could quite catch herself. "Like a sewer?"

"I expect it similarly served to contain the stench," Vogel returned easily.

Lily fought back a swell of distaste at the remark, covering it with a bland smile.

"Is there more?" she asked.

"Of course," Vogel replied, offering a slight bow and motioning her to another door.

They left the chapel for another hall, this one even larger than the first. It felt older, both grand and ancient. The windows looked out over nothing but the untouched forest, green and wild as it rolled across the surrounding hills.

The room was unfurnished save for a few antique weapons mounted on the walls, a cluster of pikes, and some rotting flags. Lily's gaze halted on a halberd, the cracked staff topped with a rusting combination of an axe and spearhead.

A breeze brushed her cheek, smelling of smoke and mud.

Lily blinked. The weapons remained dusty and unmoving.

"Where did you acquire your souvenir?" Vogel indicated Strangford's missing eye.

"Mortar blast. Outside Brest-Litovsk," Strangford replied, and Lily knew he was pulling one of the Eastern Front battle sites from his memory.

"I presume that it was this that saw you transferred to the Oberste Heeresleitung? It could not have done much for your aim."

Vogel's tone was lightly joking, but Strangford fixed him with an intimidating look that felt foreign to Lily.

"A strong shooter does not aim with two eyes," he coldly returned.

The German accent in his French had thickened. Lily found herself wondering how much of the response to the slight belonged to her husband and how much was the tone of a dead man.

A lower-ranking officer appeared in the doorway.

"Herr Hauptmann?" he called.

"Excuse me for a moment." Vogel politely detached himself.

As the two Germans spoke, someone else strolled into the hall through the opposite door. He was tall and remarkably handsome, with soft brown hair and bright blue eyes. His insignia marked him as an unteroffizier, the German equivalent of a corporal or sergeant. The colors accenting his uniform were black and gold rather than the pale blue Lily had seen on Vogel and the other soldiers staffing the castle, indicating he came from a different regiment.

He was happily munching on a ham sandwich. His eyes brightened with interest as he spotted Lily and Strangford.

"Guten Tag, Herr Hauptmann. Meine Dame," he said cheerfully. "Wie geht es Ihnen?"

"I am sorry. I don't speak German," Lily replied automatically in

French, her attention still nervously focused on Vogel and his lieutenant as they spoke quietly in the doorway.

"Ah! That is good. I speak also French," the unteroffizier said, his words thickly accented. "You are new? First time, yes? I am just here for ... Wie heißt es nochmal? Réviser."

The French word meant something like "overhaul." Lily wondered if he had chosen correctly. His French was clearly not the best.

He took another huge bite of his sandwich, talking through it.

"You are a little small for the Wulfstruppen, but you must be a good fighter. Ja? And they let you bring your frau? They did not give us permission. But I do not know that you are lucky." he warned.

Lily was no longer looking at Vogel. Her attention had sharpened on the unteroffizier.

"Oh? And why is that?" she asked.

"Well, they put needle in the spine," he replied, chuckling a little. "Not very pleasant to see. But the needle is not bad," he assured Strangford. "After—that is ... more bad, a bit. They did say to you— die Risiken? Err ... dangers? Nicht jeder überlebt's."

The switch to German felt deliberate, based on the man's sideways glance at her.

She could nearly make out the meaning in spite of it. The first part was the German for *not*. She tried to break the final word out. Überlebt's ... did she recall correctly that über meant *over*? Or was it *around*?

Lebts—that was something to do with life, she thought. Not all of us are ... around life?

The meaning clicked.

Survive.

The unteroffizier put his hand on Strangford's shoulder—the one that was not holding the ham sandwich—and looked solemn for a moment.

"It is a great thing you do for Germany."

He dropped the hand, looking both cheerful and a little sneaky as he switched once more to German with another glance at Lily.

"Wir sehen uns am Mittwoch. Bei Bailleul. Richtig?"

"So Gott will," Strangford replied in the lazy tone of a dead man.

From the corner of her eye, Lily caught a glimpse of Hauptmann

Vogel accepting a piece of paper from his lieutenant. She recognized the shape of it, the regular format that remained more or less unchanged across national lines.

It was a telegram.

With no small trepidation, she found herself thinking once more of the wires outside the castle.

"Herr Bülling," Vogel snapped. "Weiter machen!"

Their unteroffizier—Bülling—jumped to attention, flicking off a neat salute.

"Jawohl, Herr Hauptmann," he replied

He gave them a wink and strode from the room.

The lieutenant with the telegram was gone. It was only Vogel, and it seemed to Lily that his smile had grown a little broader.

"I apologize for the interruption," he said smoothly—and Lily's world slid forward.

A flick of the strap of his sidearm holster. The weapon snapping out, aimed at Strangford's head.

Pounding feet from the next hall with the harsh echo of shouted German.

Knowledge blazed through her mind—the wires draping from the walls. Vogel's easy agreement to a tour, whiling away the minutes with stories and casual questions.

He had been waiting . . . waiting for the message he had sent to German High Command with Strangford's stolen name to earn a reply.

They were exposed.

Panic roared, threatening to cripple her.

Vogel drew the pistol from his holster, his eyes on Strangford, the only threat he perceived in the room—but Lily was ready.

The walking stick twisted in her hand, leaping to her command like something alive. She whirled with it, legs braced, the movement as practiced as a step in a dance, and felt the singing vibration through the wood as it snapped against Vogel's hand.

The hauptmann barked out a curse as his pistol flew across the room, hitting the wall with a dull crack.

Strangford was already moving. He sent Vogel to the floor with a graceful sweep of his leg and a well-placed fist.

The next foresight blazed through her, quick enough to hurt.

"Take his voice," Lily hissed.

Strangford dropped to a knee, drawing back his arm. His palm connected with the officer's solar plexus, and Vogel gasped like a grounded fish as he fought for air.

"Now pin him."

Lily shoved up the hauptmann's jacket, yanking open the clasp of his belt and whipping it from his trousers. Her husband met her eyes over Vogel's prone body and raised a slightly wicked eyebrow, reminding Lily of precisely where she had learned that maneuver.

Bracing his leg, he forced Vogel into a roll. Lily thrust the belt into his mouth as he regained his breath for a scream. She pulled it tight, gagging him while he bucked, trying to rear off of the floor. Pulling the dagger from the sheath at the officer's side, Lily stabbed the fabric of her skirt, then tore off two long strips of wool, using them to quickly bind Vogel's arms and legs.

"Through the door," Strangford ordered, finally able to release his hold.

Lily dropped the dagger and grabbed Vogel's ankles. Strangford hefted up the other half of him, and they scurried toward the door Bülling had come through, the bound hauptmann twisting and thrashing against them.

The next room looked like a medieval pantry packed with crates of German goods sandwiched between cases of ammunition. They unceremoniously dropped Vogel behind a stack of cases of tinned beans as he made muffled threats at them through the belt.

Strangford had lost his hat somewhere in the struggle. Lily looked at his gloved hands.

"Should you—" she began.

"No time." He grabbed her arm.

She could hear the sound of quick-stepping boots and barked German orders behind them, and knew that Vogel's reinforcements had made it to the room they had been standing in a moment before. Strangford pulled her into a dash. Lily sprinted past the crates into the adjoining chamber—running straight into a solid male body.

NINETEEN

"OOF," KAZI GASPED AS LILY collided with his chest. The inspector instinctively caught her, immediately releasing her again and straightening his hat.

A pair of humble brown sparrows whizzed through the doorway behind her and fluttered agitatedly around Sam's head. He had foregone a hat, a practical choice given that he had arrived there strapped to the underside of the carriage.

"Bit late," Sam snapped at the birds, earning him a quick look from Kazi.

"Are we exposed?" Kazi calmly demanded.

"Rather," Strangford replied.

"We ain't found sweet Fanny Adams," Sam reported. "Just been wandering in circles dodging you lot."

He kept his voice low, flashing a wary look toward the sound of German soldiers two rooms away.

"I think we may have run out of time for further investigation."

Strangford's tone was wry, but Lily could see the pallor under his skin. The uniform was taking its toll.

"Best find ourselves an exit, then, before we get done in," Sam declared.

Emotions warred on Kazi's face, fury and frustration giving way to a tight resignation.

Lily couldn't blame him. It felt like a terrible waste to have come all this way only to end up right back where they started with less chance than ever of discovering the nature of the German Wotanskunst program.

With a jerk of his head, Kazi stalked back the way he and Sam had come. They moved quietly, with an ear to the German voices echoing from elsewhere in the castle, circling through the rooms until they reached the antechamber where Lily and Strangford had first entered the building.

Shouted orders resounded from just outside the exit. Other voices carried over from the way they had come. Two clusters of soldiers, inside and out, were closing in on them like the teeth of a vise with a bound and gagged hauptmann lying in between.

"Should we fight?" Sam asked.

"They have far more guns than we do," Strangford said. "I vote that we try the chapel."

"Right, then," Kazi said, pivoting on his heel.

They spilled back into the high, radiant space Lily and Strangford had toured with Vogel a few minutes before. Sam crossed to one of the windows, leaping to catch the sill and hauling himself up, boots scrabbling for and finding a slight toehold in the stones where the plaster on the wall had chipped away.

He looked out, then jumped back down, speaking quick and low.

"The carriage is still down there. Couple of Boche are combing it over, but there's no sign of Jiějie."

"She must have found somewhere to conceal herself." Strangford noted.

"Aye, and she's got her chiv. I wouldn't want to be the one to find her."

Sam made a quick assessment of the room.

"Could tie a rope to one of them pillars and shimmy down through a window, but like as not, the Boche outside would pick us off before we reached the ground."

Lily was only half listening. She drifted back to the strange well in the center of the chapel floor, the pillars framing the opening down into the darkness.

"Has anyone been down to the lower level?" she asked.

"I thought the castle was built on a plateau," Kazi replied.

Sam scooted over to join her after a sharp glance at the door, where they could still hear the distant voices of the soldiers. It was only a matter of time before they searched the castle more systematically.

He pulled a match from his pocket, lit and promptly dropped it into the well. It flared and then faded as it fell, but it provided enough light that Lily could see it was roughly twelve feet to the stone floor below.

The feeling rose up at her like a breeze, soft and salt-scented, whispering against her ear like long grass.

"We need to go down there."

In her mind, the words resonated like the aftermath of a plucked harp string. She raised her head to find Strangford looking at her, his dark eye sharp with understanding.

He was not alone. Kazi's focus had fixed on her as well.

"I don't see a stair," Sam noted.

Kazi stalked over to the pile of building materials, grabbing a coil of rope. He tossed the end of it down into the hole, then set about neatly tying it to one of the pillars with a sturdy boater's knot.

"They'll see it as soon as they come in," Sam pointed out. "They'll know exactly where we've gone."

"That is why you are staying behind to untie it and find your sister," Kazi replied, swinging his legs over the side of the wall.

"What? Why me?" Sam protested.

Kazi grasped the rope in his hands.

"Because Lord Strangford and I are best equipped to recognize whatever might be of value below. And you are best equipped to slip outside without being noticed. Or am I wrong?"

Sam's mouth firmed into a stubborn line.

"I still don't bloody like it," he retorted.

Kazi responded by raising an eyebrow and dropping down into the darkness.

He descended the rope with relative ease. Lily heard the soft slap of his boots striking the ground below.

"Clear," he called up softly.

Lily met Strangford's gaze across the black gap.

"After you," he said.

She bit back a retort. Whoever lingered there longest had the greatest chance of getting caught, and she could see the uniform was wearing on him—but there was no time to argue.

"Watch out," she barked into the lower chamber and tossed down her walking stick.

It did not clatter against the stones. When she looked, she saw Kazi had neatly caught it.

Lily climbed over the waist-high wall, slightly hampered by her skirts. If only posing as a German officer's castle-mad wife had been compatible with trousers. At least she had shortened the skirt when she cut off pieces of it to bind the intelligence officer they had left behind the beans.

She twisted the rope between her shoes, using the bend to take a good portion of her weight as she lowered herself down. The fibers burned against her ungloved hands. Lily felt a moment of gratitude for the callouses she had earned through her kali practice, however unfashionable they were.

She worked her way down into the cool darkness, muscles burning in her upper arms and shoulders, jumping the last few feet to the ground.

"Your weapon," Kazi said in greeting, extending the walking stick.

Strangford landed just behind her, startling her for a moment with the sudden appearance of his German uniform. The three of them faced each other in the deep gloom of the underground chamber.

The rope slipped up behind them, drawn into the circle of illumination above.

"Take 'em," Sam whispered overhead and tossed something down.

Lily reached up, catching it in her two hands, and realized it was the match tin.

It burned in her hands, hot to the touch with something more than the lingering friction of her descent along the rope. A whiff of smoke passed through her brain.

She pushed past it, slipping the match tin into her pocket.

The well of light above them was silent. Lily could feel the emptiness and knew that Sam had already dodged away.

The underchapel was low-ceilinged and dark. Two thin slits of windows let in just a little bit of light, enough for her to make out the general form of the space around her. It was the same breadth as the chamber above, only darker and less ornamented. The stones of the walls looked older. The air tasted of dust.

Two doors broke the monotony of the walls. The one to the left was walled up, the bricks used for the task obviously modern. By silent consensus, she and the two men passed through the other.

They found themselves in another chamber, low like the chapel and darker. Cobwebs hung in thick veils at the corners, decorating piles of decaying furniture. There were moldering tapestries, broken-legged tables, and splintered chairs, all slowly rotting.

A heavy door was set in a wall Lily deduced must lead to the outside. It was obviously old, the lock a mass of rusting iron, and clearly unused. The whole thing was covered in cobwebs. She caught a flicker of movement as spiders darted across its surface.

There was fresher wood in the room—another stack of crates labeled in German. One of them was open, the top set slightly back. Strangford carefully pushed it aside and pulled a single delicate glass vial out of the tightly packed straw inside.

Lily's pulse leapt. The vial wasn't a typical supply for an encampment. It spoke of scientific or medical research.

Kazi's gold eyes locked onto the tube of glass with avian intensity.

"We should search this floor," he declared.

Lily wanted to protest. The door in the wall promised a chance at escape. Every minute they stayed inside the castle increased their chances of being caught—but Kazi was right.

What they were looking for was close.

There was only one other exit, on the opposite wall from the door to the outside. It led into a narrow hall that ran parallel to the chamber with the crates.

An opening in the longer wall led to the base of an ancient, narrow staircase that ascended to the upper floor. It was largely free of debris and, therefore, regularly used. An entrance to it must have been hidden somewhere above.

At the end of the hall, heading back in the direction of the chapel, lay another door. It was distinctly modern, solid metal with a wheeled handle like the bulkhead on a battleship.

They faced it in silence, each of them knowing perfectly well what it must signify.

"I should go first," Strangford said, his face shadowed by the gloom.

He spun the wheel. It moved easily on well-oiled bearings. With a soft clank, the bolt gave way. The door swung open.

Strangford stood silhouetted in a perfect rectangle of glaring white light like a portal to another world—a place that should not exist inside the dank basement of an ancient castle.

The room was a long rectangle, its walls plastered spotlessly white. Electric lights glared down from the ceiling, banishing shadows.

At the far end, a pair of stainless steel tables were loaded with machines and equipment—lenses, motors, racks, and burners.

Both of the long walls were hung with wooden shelves, heavy with lab books, glassware, and trays of neatly labeled vials.

Lily recognized a centrifuge next to a stack of slides. A distillation apparatus bubbled quietly. The air smelled of rubbing alcohol, cleaning solvent, and something like musty old leather.

In the center of the room loomed a surgical table fitted out with thick straps.

The table reminded her, uncomfortably, of a similar device she had stumbled across in the nightmarish basement of a burned-out clinic in Southwark.

An plump older gentleman with a thick white beard sat at the back of the room with his eye to a microscope.

"Sie können das Mittagessen auf den Tisch stellen," he said absently, waving towards the desk in the corner by the door.

Then he looked up.

"Oh! Entschuldigung, Herr ...?" He ended it with a question.

"Hauptmann Keller," Strangford replied.

"Sie sind wegen der Wotanskunst gekommen? Ich habe Sie noch nie gesehen. Haben Sie sich der Blutprobe unterzogen? Ohne diese können wir nicht fortfahren."

Lily's mind buzzed at the rapid stream of German. Certain syllables leapt out at her, rising like bubbles to the surface.

Wotanskunst. Blutprobe ... blood probe?

"Ich habe den Blutprobe nicht gemacht," Strangford replied easily, slipping into his role. He stepped inside, coming fully into the light, and Lily saw the scientist frown a bit at the sight of Strangford's missing eye. The frown turned to a blink of surprise as he realized there were two more people standing behind him.

There was nothing to gain by lingering in the gloom of the hall. Hoping the tears in her skirt weren't too obvious, Lily entered, walking stick in her hand. Kazi followed behind her.

"Shall I close the door?" she asked casually in French.

"You are French, Frau?" the scientist asked, easily switching languages.

"From Romandy in Switzerland," Lily replied.

His face brightened above his beard.

"Die Romandie!" he exclaimed happily. "My parents, they had a summer house on Lac de Neuchâtel. It is very beautiful. I have many fond memories."

"I am from near the Tourbillon," Lily replied, keeping her voice level.

"Ah yes. The Chateau is most dramatic. But your accent does not sound quite right. You have also lived elsewhere?"

"In Paris. For school," Lily quickly invented, nerves jarred that this potential enemy was actually familiar with the place she pretended to be from. "This is your lab?"

"Yes! Of course, excuse me. Herr Doktor Hans Kirchweger. I am the principal scientist for Wotanskunst." His face fell a bit. "I am afraid we do not generally allow wives to attend the procedure. Or manservants," he added with a look at Kazi.

Lily was glad that Kazi didn't speak French. She could guess how well he would take to being presumed to be the help.

"I assure you that my wife is of an unusually firm constitution," Strangford returned, straight-faced, taking off his cap.

To her right, by the entrance they had just passed through, sat a plain wooden desk crowded with books and papers. At the far end of the laboratory, beyond the surgical and lab tables, hung another door. It was made of metal, like the one behind her, but with a simpler handle. A rubber seal lined the edges. There was condensation on the surface of it, the beads of moisture pearling in the light.

Lily found herself staring at the little pool of damp staining the concrete at the base of it. A low buzz rose in the back of her mind, a hum like a generator beginning to spin.

Something tugged her toward the door, smelling sharply of

salt and mud. Lily swallowed back the recognizable impulse of her onmyōdō.

"Would you mind explaining how it all works?" Strangford asked, running a gloved hand along the surface of the surgical table. "I have an amateur interest in the blood sciences."

Kirchweger perked up, clearly delighted.

"Then you must allow me to show you." He spoke with the enthusiasm of a boy who had just been invited to hold forth on his favorite subject. "The source material, of course, must be purified and properly separated. It is first ground with liquefied nitrogen and then further dissolved in an alkaline solution. I then use the centrifuge and a high-salt solution to isolate the precipitate, which is washed in alcohol."

Any concern about whether his three visitors really belonged there was gone, forgotten in his excitement over an interested audience.

Back by the door, Kazi lifted up a little steel pin that hung from a thin length of chain and dropped into the mechanism for the handle, locking it closed.

"The vehicle for transmission is a simple fungus—aspergillosis," Kirchweger continued. "A very common mold, but it has proven an excellent carrier for the transformative material once isolated from the source. Of course, it must be injected directly into the epidural fluid space to be effective. Other methods have proved useless, likely because the immune system of a healthy young male is able to neutralize the fungus before it reaches the brain."

Lily moved to the desk, glancing down at the papers there. She could make only a superficial study of them as most were written in either German or Latin. There were lists of names and dates alongside notes she could not translate . . . and then something familiar caught her eye.

It was a bit of handwriting, narrowly revealed amid the tumble of other documents.

Lily pushed them gently aside, revealing more. The dark, confident lines of the pen blazed up at her, and everything else in the room faded away.

Kirchweger rattled on in the background, Strangford listening with unfeigned interest. Kazi stared thoughtfully at the neatly labeled jars of chemicals that lined the shelf—*Sulphuric Acid, Ammonium Nitrate.*

Behind him, at the far door, moisture pooled coldly on the concrete floor.

Lily stared down at a script she knew, one that she had seen on a thousand pages as they drifted slowly into the eternal blue of the sea.

She spoke the name aloud like a curse.

"Hartwell."

Kirchweger turned to her with a start of surprise.

"You are familiar with the great doctor?" he asked.

"I know him better than you could possibly imagine," Lily replied.

She felt the cold of a winter rooftop on her skin. Heard the sound his body made as it slid over the edge and plummeted to the ground. Felt the absence of a scream.

"We met through the Rassenhygieniker," Kirchweger continued.

Rassenhygieniker. It was a term she had heard once before from her husband's lips as he read the single page of a lost letter shuffled into the final batch of Dr. Joseph Hartwell's papers. A term James Cairncross had neatly translated.

Race hygienists.

Lily didn't say aloud the word that leapt to her throat.

Eugenicists.

"I was privileged to correspond with Herr Doktor Hartwell before his untimely death," Kirchweger said. "Such a terrible loss to science. I owe almost the entirety of my current work to his unique genius. It was he who woke me to the possibility of transferring desired traits from host to donor through the blood. I am not ignorant of the irony that I must now use the doctor's work to defeat his own country-men in battle, but these are the dark times in which we live. And of course, I could not have completed the work without the support of the Kaiser. He has been most generous with his resources—not the least of which was successfully acquiring the prima materia."

"Prima materia," Strangford said. "Isn't that an alchemical term?"

Lily wondered if she was the only one who could hear the tension that had entered his voice. He also had memories of Hartwell—both his own experiences and those of the dead.

Kirchweger brightened again.

"But it is alchemy, is it not? The art of transformation. Turning dross into something greater. These men, these noble pioneers, they are our mercury, but when they emerge ..."

The smell of chemicals in the room seemed to intensify. Underneath it lay something thicker—something Lily finally recognized as rot.

The buzzing at the back of her head grew louder.

"Here," Kirchweger said, turning to a hole cut into the wall between two of the wooden shelves. It was a safe set into a space chipped out of the stone. The box was roughly two feet square and would normally be enclosed by a metal door with a combination lock. The door currently hung open. Someone had clearly wanted the doctor to take precautions he either found unnecessary or routinely forgot.

Kirchweger reached into it and pulled out a slender, wax-stopped vial. Lily could just see a rack of them inside the safe, twinkling in the gloom. The liquid inside was a dull brown.

"Unimpressive, eh?" Kirchweger said. "And yet when precisely administered, the effects of it are ..." He shook his head with something like religious awe.

The buzzing centered itself on the moisture-beaded door at the back of the room. It loomed in her perception, seeming to grow larger.

Hartwell had found his catalysts in the blood.

Something was missing here.

"What about the prima materia?" Lily demanded.

The doctor hesitated.

"Your constitution would need to be particularly firm, Frau," he carefully replied.

"I'll be fine," Lily said bluntly.

"We would be most interested to see," Strangford added, managing to play his part better than Lily was, though she knew the uniform must be wearing on him.

"It is quite fascinating," the doctor admitted, wavering.

Coming to a decision, he turned to the dripping door, unlocking it with a key from a ring in his pocket. He pulled the slab of metal back as Lily and Strangford joined him.

Kazi hesitated behind them, pausing by the open door to the safe.

Cold air washed over her. It smelled of straw, damp, and something else like a boot left out too long in the rain.

The space was roughly the size of a pantry. The walls were stone, save for the one on the opposite wall. A tall rectangle there was filled with modern bricks joined with hasty mortar. A quick calculation told her this must be the other side of the door they saw blocked up in the underchapel.

The walls were lined with more shelves, all of them packed with blocks of ice thickly packed with straw. A steel table took up almost the entirety of the remaining space.

On top of it lay a corpse.

It was little more than a twisted length of dry, desiccated hide. Yellow bones peeked out from under age-tanned skin, patches of which still clung to a skull lined with wisps of coarse black hair. Teeth, seeming longer than they ought to be, split the jaw into an unending roar.

It lay on a bed of ice—no, Lily corrected herself. It was *in* the ice. The body had been almost entirely chipped free, but the glittering pieces that remained made it clear it must once have been entirely encased.

It was a man, whittled to bone and leather by time. Even with the flesh stripped away, Lily could see he had once been massive.

Eyeless sockets glared up at the low ceiling.

She did not have to ask to know. It was the devil of the glacier, come to rest in this icy crypt.

"My estimates put it at the Late Bronze or Early Iron Age," Kirchweger was saying somewhere behind her, his voice running against her consciousness like the burble of a stream. "The state of preservation is, of course, unprecedented. I was able to extract dried matter from both the bone cavities and the brain."

The fleshless hand still gripped a length of metal, pitted and warped with rust.

A sword.

She remembered the dark, ragged shapes trapped within the ice of the cave. A severed arm. A mutilated torso.

The word blazed through her mind in James Cairncross's tortured tones.

Berserker.

As though the thought was a catalyst, the future spilled in.

Rough wood slides across her hands. The air stinks of burning flesh. A soft impact shivers up her arms, followed by a splash of hot liquid.

Then ragged screams. An unrelenting thunder. The earth groaning beneath her feet.

Beasts stalk through a forest thick as dreams.

Smoke plumes above the hollow shell of a church. Flies buzz over fields of the dead.

A breath whispers from somewhere else, scented with paint and dust.

What about the space between the doors?

Strangford crouched between walls of mud, his gaze dark with determination. With apology.

"Lily." he said.

His arm was around her waist, the only thing keeping her from collapsing onto the floor of the crypt.

"Ich bitte Sie um Verzeihung," Kirchweger stammered, waving his hands with dismay. "I am sorry, Frau. I should have realized the sight would be upsetting. Please, come. I will bring you water."

The horror roiled through her, stealing her breath. She let Strangford hold her as the doctor hurried over to a sink. Kazi had joined them, his eyes darkening with an unspoken demand from the far side of the mummy.

She trembled with the unexpected force of the vision, with the nightmare it promised. Knowledge sang at her from the corpse in the icebox, pulsing in the unwelcome tones of the onmyōdō. Lily spoke it aloud even as she knew it would raise the threat around them to a fever pitch.

"That thing. This place," she rasped, raising her head. "We have to destroy it."

She met the eye of her lover.

"All of it," she finished.

The line of Strangford's mouth turned grim. He released her gently, and Lily felt the tingling potential of the moment racing down her skin.

She did not realize she had unthinking spoken the words in her native tongue until the spell was broken by the surprised voice of the doctor.

"Sprechen Sie Englisch?"

TWENTY

$\mathcal{T}$HEY WERE LIKE FIGURES in a diorama.

Strangford still supported Lily in the doorway to the icy crypt. Kazi had taken a step back out into the glaring white light of the lab. He hovered there, his head swinging from Lily to the scientist a step away from him.

Kirchweger's mouth had fallen open, his cheerful enthusiasm replaced with dawning suspicion.

Lily's brain screeched with warning. Before she could act on it, Kirchweger's hand snapped out, slapping against a buzzer mounted to the wall.

There was no sound. It didn't matter. Lily knew that somewhere in the soaring stone chambers above, a bell was ringing.

With soldiers scouring the castle for intruders, there was only one way Kirchweger's signal would be taken—as an alarm.

A pistol appeared in Kazi's hand. It snapped out, the steel of the barrel connecting with Kirchweger's temple.

His head struck one of the nearby tables as he fell.

Lily rushed toward him instinctively, wondering with a sick panic whether they had killed him—and whether they would still need to kill him if they hadn't.

Before she could demand what they should do next, the far door clanked ominously.

The wheel of the lock jerked, coming up short against the barrier of Kazi's pin. Voices rose on the far side as someone began to bang on the metal.

They had been found ... and now they were trapped.

Lily pushed back to her feet, stalking past Kazi to the wall safe. She reached in and grasped the wooden rack of wax-stopped vials.

"What are you—" Kazi began.

Lily yanked. The rack flew across the room. Glass shattered, releasing an acrid stench.

She looked back through the door into the crypt where the dead berserker lay and felt the decision harden.

The jars that lined the walls of the laboratory offered a range of options. Lily was dizzied by them until Strangford joined her.

"What do you need?" he asked.

"Something that will burn."

He pulled out a nearly full gallon of pure ethanol.

The banging at the door intensified, taking on a heavier and regular rhythm. The German soldiers outside must have found something to use as a ram.

Lily threw the jar into the crypt. The glass shattered against the table, spraying the corpse and the packed straw with alcohol.

She pulled Sam's matchbox from her pocket, her hands shaking.

Kazi hurried over, looking from her to the rest of the jars on the wall.

"I don't think that's a very wise—"

Lily threw the match.

Flames whooshed to life, turning the damp cold of the room into a blistering heat. The mummy burned like a candle.

Something inside of her shifted like the turning of a clock. Relief washed over her with the warmth of the fire.

The door behind them shook in its frame as the battering ram struck again with a squeal of metal, more dust showering down.

"We're out of time," Kazi shouted.

He grasped the nearest of the metal tables and flipped it.

A distillation apparatus crashed to the floor in a shower of breaking glass as the table fell onto its side.

"Get behind it," he barked.

Lily dove into place beside him, Strangford following.

With another scream of protesting steel, the door flew inward.

Soldiers pressed into the room, guns drawn.

A smattering of bullets pinged off the steel surface of their shield as Vogel shoved in behind his men, his face furious as he shouted orders.

The other men startled, parting like a sea for something coming from the darkened hallway behind them.

The charming German unteroffizier, Bülling, stepped into the room. He took in the sight of the fallen scientist, the broken glass, and the smoke clouding the ceiling. His eyes widened with gentle surprise.

"Geh raus! Jetzt!" Vogel screamed.

The other soldiers scrambled back into the hall.

"They're leaving?" Kazi exclaimed, risking a peek past the table. "Why are they leaving?"

Vogel dragged the door closed with a clang. Only Bülling remained.

Something shifted under his skin.

Lily's hand clenched around her walking stick as she realized the answer to Kazi's question. It came to her with a wave of dread. Cairncross's words blazed across her mind.

If I started, I would not stop until everyone around me was dead.

"We need to get out of here."

"I can handle a single German. It's what's on the other side of the door I'm worried about," Kazi returned.

"No. Not that way." Lily replied thinly, her hands beginning to shake. "We need another way. We need it now."

Bülling began to change.

It started in his shoulders and thighs, the muscles thickening and bunching, ripping the seams of his uniform. His skin flushed an impossible red, the hair on his head rising as though charged by electricity. His eyes bulged, his lips pulling back in a gruesome parody of a smile. His grin seemed longer than it should be, sharper.

She told herself it was impossible. Teeth didn't lengthen.

The instincts of millennia screamed at her.

Predator. Threat.

Run.

The handsome unteroffizier roared. The force of it blasted off the walls of the lab, freezing her with terror.

Bülling grasped the edge of the surgical table. Instead of dodging around it, he simply jerked his arm. The metal slab spun through the air until it struck the wall, carving a scar into the plaster.

It was inhuman. Unstoppable. Deadly . . . and it was charging toward her.

Time slowed, ticking away like grains of sand. Flames smoldered in the burning crypt, curling through the last of the dried flesh and straw. Out in the lab, a shelf of notebooks collapsed to the floor.

Lily's fighting instinct sparked to life . . . and then spluttered.

She swings her staff.

Her body hits a wall, bones splintering.

A different strike, a different angle—iron claws rake across her skin.

Teeth penetrate muscle. Joints scream at an impossible twist. Bullets riddle her flesh.

The power stutters and chokes like a bad engine as attacks and reactions churn through her mind, choppy and abbreviated by an inevitable outcome of pain.

Lily collapsed back into the present, where panic hit like cold water. She realized what had just happened—what it meant.

There was no way to win.

Kazi was screaming at her. He had lost his hat. The sound was slow and muffled, distant like a dream. She saw him bolt from the table to the door to the crypt.

There *had* to be a way. This was what she was made for.

Lily pushed back. She tasted blood as she forced herself deeper, thrusting into the heart of her onmyōdō, focused on a single demand.

Conquer. Win. Destroy.

Doors whirl past her, flinging open like a pack of shuffled cards. Every one of them promises death.

She pushes back, pushes harder.

The doors begin to bend.

She feels the tension like a membrane stretching as she presses against it, her demand confronting the limits of what is possible until she threatens to break it apart.

For a moment, the familiar salt-scented breath of onmyōdō shifts into something else—a different wind, one that tastes of silence. Of what glitters in the space between the stars.

Fear swells within her, deep and cold as a tide.

No.

Lily fell back into herself with a force like a train collision—and looked up at the horror that was Bülling as he raised an iron bar in his impossibly thick arm and prepared to crush her skull with it.

His head snapped back. Lily felt something warm splatter across her face.

Behind her in the doorway to the crypt, Kazi held his pistol ready for another shot.

Strangford's arm locked around her chest. He hauled her to her feet, half throwing her towards the smoldering icebox.

They reached the door, and Lily looked back.

The berserker straightened. Kazi's bullet had struck him in the head, taking out part of his cheekbone. Lily could see bone and muscle, blood pouring down the side of his face.

The unteroffizier took a step forward, then another . . .

Kazi breathed something Lily felt sure was a prayer—then shifted his aim to one of the glittering jars on the wall.

He pulled the trigger, and the room bloomed with flame.

The explosion blew Bülling across the nearest table, taking out a centrifuge. Lily was thrown back, slamming to the floor next to the still-smoking remnants of the ancient monster from the glacier. She gasped for air, tasting blood, rolling to look back out into the lab.

The entire wall was destroyed, the steel tables shoved across the floor by the force of the blast. The ceiling was scorched black, the ground covered in smoking shards of glass.

Someone was screaming in German beyond the other door. Lily wondered if the smell of fire would draw them back inside.

Glass tinkled like delicate chimes. From behind the mess where Bülling had fallen, the burnt claw of hand rose up, clamping onto the surface of the table.

Kazi yanked shut the door, collapsing the crypt into utter darkness.

"Your staff." he shouted, urgency sharpening the words.

Lily shook her head, ears still ringing. A moment later, something thudded against the door.

She scrambled to her feet, shoes skidding on the wet floor. She collided with the solid warmth that was Kazi and felt her way down his arm. He was holding the steel lever of the door handle closed, and even as she touched him, she felt it wrench against his grip.

Lily shoved the walking stick against the handle, kicking it into place. The yew was old and strong. It would hold—for now.

The door shook with an impact that sounded like a cannon blast through the crypt. Standing next to it in the darkness, Lily knew with an animal panic what was trying to break through.

Smoking black flesh. Cracked skin. Feral teeth.

"We have to take down the wall." Kazi's breath was short.

"The table," Strangford said.

There was a sweep of Strangford's arm across the surface, and a sound like a dropped cloak as the last remnants of the mummy fell wetly to the ground.

"Get into the corner," Kazi ordered.

In the utter blackness that surrounded her, all Lily knew was sound and movement. The rustling of Strangford's uniform, the scrape of the table legs against the floor. A soft push of air against her face like a breath and then the resounding crack of the table swinging into the bricks that blocked the far end of the crypt.

The scent of fresh dust joined the reek of smoldering straw and bone.

Something scratched at the door behind her, claws scraping against steel.

"Again," Strangford urged.

The table hit the wall once more, this time with a rougher crack and the sound of small pieces of mortar pinging against the ground.

"Let me help," she said.

She felt her way through the darkness until her hands met the flat steel surface.

"On three," Kazi barked. "One ... two ..."

Lily ran against the table, shoving at it as the two men made their third swing.

Bricks crumbled, a faint light spilling into the room, illuminating the gray profiles of Strangford and Kazi. Air flooded through, damp and fresh.

Strangford shoved at the suspended bricks, widening the gap. He kicked out a few swift blows with his tàijí.

Behind them, the door thudded, one of the hinges twisting with a truncated squeal.

Kazi grabbed her sleeve, shoving her past him through the narrow space between the table and the wall.

"Go—get out.!"

She scrambled through the opening, half falling into the soft gloom of the underchapel. Strangford followed her, Kazi lingering with his pistol aimed at the door. Lily could just see the gleam of the wood of her walking stick, still jammed against the handle.

"Move, Kazi," Strangford rasped. "He's taking the door apart."

The inspector ducked nimbly into the chapel even as another scream of wrenching metal sounded behind him.

They ran.

Lily burst into the storeroom. Through the thick wall, the sound of the other soldiers at the door to the lab was only a muffled rumble.

With his longer stride, Kazi took the lead. He arrowed for the cobweb-covered door leading to the outside and slammed back the bolt, wrenching it open.

Daylight spilled in, blinding in its intensity. A single soldier guarded the steps to this rarely-used entrance. He was little more than a black shadow in Lily's overwhelmed vision.

Kazi lifted his pistol, but before he could fire, Strangford stepped into the opening. The young man blinked in confusion at the sight of his uniform.

"Deine Gewehr, Gefreiter," Strangford ordered.

The soldier handed Strangford his rifle.

"Danke. Entschuldige uns," Strangford said, stepping neatly past the boy.

Kazi, just behind him, grabbed the disarmed soldier by the front of his jacket and hauled him inside, throwing him to the ground.

Lily ran past him, and Kazi yanked the ancient door shut behind them.

She nearly tripped down the stairs as her eyes struggled to adjust to the glare. Though she could hear voices nearby, this section of the yard between the castle and the looming walls was miraculously empty of anything but pigeons. The birds fluttered up in alarm at their appearance, whirling overhead before darting away in a tidy line.

Muffled shouts began to sound from beyond the door.

Kazi leapt down beside her. Strangford's hand found her elbow, propelling her into a dash.

A whistle sounded from above. Lily looked up to see Sam framed in the window of one of the guardhouses that dotted the outer wall.

The pigeons darted away from him, startled by the sudden noise.

Lily pivoted, shoes grinding against the dirt as she sprinted for the scaffolding that climbed the wall. She scrambled up the wooden ladders of it, her feet slipping against the boards.

Sam caught her at the top, half tossing her into the guardhouse, Kazi and Strangford at her heels.

"I take it we're blown," he said.

"Rather," Kazi replied, moving to press himself to the wall beside the window and quickly reloading his pistol as he studied the courtyard.

Boots pounded across the pavement below, accompanied by a chorus of shouted orders.

The guardhouse was small, no more than six feet long, perched on top of the wall. The castle loomed in front of them.

A row of black birds was just visible on the distant line of its roofless upper hall. Lily recognized their thick profiles.

They were ravens.

A door slammed open. Vogel's voice joined the others ringing off the stones. It sounded closer than Lily would have liked.

Another window in the guardhouse faced the forest. Lily pressed herself to it, looking out. Below her lay the immense length of the wall and sheer face of gray stone. She was looking down at the tops of the trees.

"The rope won't reach," Sam said.

"Have you another suggestion?" Kazi snapped.

"Matter of fact," he drawled in reply. "This way. Stay low. We see anyone on the ramparts, use that iron of yours."

"They'll hear the shot."

"It's yours or theirs—unless you've a knack for throwing daggers you failed to mention."

Sam slipped out of the guardhouse, crouching down to keep his head below the parapet that blocked sight of them from the ground.

Black wings rose from the roof of the castle. They swept down over the wall.

Kazi followed after Sam, but when Lily glanced back, Strangford still leaned against the guardhouse, using his stolen rifle almost like a crutch. His free hand clutched at the front of the German jacket as though he were trying to tear it from his back—not that it would help him, still clad in the rest of the dead man's uniform. His face was pale, his breath uneven.

"Anthony." she whispered urgently.

He released the jacket, collecting himself with an obvious force of will.

"I'm alright," he cut back sharply.

"Go first. Don't argue with me," she continued before he could protest. "It's that, or I'll keep looking back for you."

His mouth thinned unhappily in response, but he obeyed her, following the others.

Sam waited, crouched halfway along the wall, waving Strangford past.

Lily started toward him but was drawn up by the sound of a harsh croak. She startled, turning back to see one of the ravens sitting in the frame of the window.

It ruffled its dark feathers, cawing again. Then it was gone.

She shook off the chill of it and hurried to where Sam waited, half crawling to stay below the low barrier of the parapet.

"Come on," she urged as she reached him.

He didn't move, his fingers clenched against the stone.

"What's wrong?" she demanded in a whisper.

"New mark," he rasped, tight with tension.

"Mark?"

"The birds," he hissed, glaring at her. "They've marked someone."

Understanding dawned with cold horror, ripe with the memory of the dread and guilt in Sam's voice during his confession on the road to Luxembourg.

"Here?" she protested. "Right now?"

"If I could plausibly come back, they might show some patience. But they bloody well know that's not an option—so yes. Now."

Strangford and Kazi had reached the next structure on the wall, the upper floor of a weathered outbuilding that clung to the ramparts like a barnacle. Kazi looked back at them, his face lined with frustrated impatience.

"We are running for our lives," she pointed out darkly.

Sam met her gaze without flinching. Something in him looked both resigned and dangerous.

"They don't care, but don't mind it. They'll make sure I get my shot. That's how it works."

His words were bitter.

German voices echoed up as the search for them continued. A door was kicked in somewhere below, alarming another cluster of pigeons.

"Lily, I can't ... " he started, his expression bleak. He caught himself and pressed on. "If I don't do it, they'll take someone else. One of you. We're running for it. It'd be easy for them. Plenty of ways your luck could turn. Your husband's. My sister's."

Lily felt the horrible plausibility of it. Strangford was already wrung thin by the effort of wearing his stolen uniform. She thought of Kazi with his noisy, beautiful children waiting for him at home. Of Zhao Min and everyone who depended upon her ... of the life she carried in her own body, and knew what her answer must be.

"Sam, you can't bargain for us. Not at that price."

His eyes narrowed, going hard.

"It ain't your choice," he retorted, then scrambled away from her, hurrying along the wall.

Lily scurried after him into the next structure.

Strangford had slung the rifle over his shoulder. Lily could still see the ragged edges of his composure in the tight lines around his eye.

Kazi peered out another window.

"There's no sign of that ... thing."

"Let's be grateful for that," Strangford said, breath short.

Lily thought of Bülling's blackened hand reaching up from behind the table. She suppressed a shudder.

Sam moved to a square of wood in the floor and yanked it open, revealing a hole descending into the gloom. He slid into it, catching hold of a ladder and nimbly descending.

Lily followed, the ladder bringing her into a dim chamber that smelled of oil and dust. She heard Sam's boots hit the ground.

"Tàipíng," he called out lowly.

The word was clearly a code. At the sound of it, Zhao Min stepped from the shadows, a thin fall of light glinting off the exposed blade of her razor. She flicked her wrist, snapping the weapon closed. It disappeared into the pocket of her borrowed trousers as Kazi reached the bottom of the ladder.

Lily's eyes adjusted to the gloom. A decaying carriage sagged in a corner, the wheels collapsed, axle broken. A sliding bay door, clearly half-rotted, covered an entrance that must lead out into the courtyard. Light stabbed through the gaps in the warped boards.

Before the door, a long object sat covered in a new waxed canvas tarpaulin.

Strangford joined her. Lily wished she could communicate what Sam had revealed on the wall, but she didn't want to add to the burden he was already carrying.

Sam yanked away the canvas, revealing a gleaming yellow and blue automobile.

"Audi Type B. I'm guessing it's the commanding officer's toy."

Sam's tones were clipped. It felt wrong. Even under dire circumstances, he should have been delighted by the prospect of getting his hands on such a vehicle.

He reached over the door and started winding a crank.

"We'll be totally exposed in that." Kazi pointed at the roofless vehicle.

"And fast." Sam switched to pumping one of the handles. "Get in the back and cover our rear. Lily, in here."

He slapped a hand against the driver's side.

"What?" Lily protested.

"Get in. You're driving."

"But I barely know how," she protested.

"Would you rather shoot?" he snapped back.

He pulled his service revolver from a holster under his coat. Lily had nearly forgotten he still had it.

The terrible conundrum of it wrenched inside of her. Sam should be *driving*, not looking for someone he was supposed to murder.

And if he didn't, one of them would very likely die.

The rifle Strangford had stolen hung limp at his side. He was in no condition to use it.

Lily couldn't solve this. There was no time. The truth of it choked her.

Sam swung himself easily into the passenger seat, leaving Strangford to find a place with Kazi and Zhao Min in the rear. He reached under the dash, where Lily could see a panel had already been unscrewed, and connected a pair of wires.

"Flip the ignition switch," he ordered.

Someone called in German from just outside the building. A door slammed nearby.

"Get in and hit the switch, Lily." Sam pressed thinly.

She climbed in.

The engine purred to life at her touch, the rumble echoing off the walls of the old carriage house.

"What about the door?" she protested, knowing the sound would be clearly audible from outside, serving as a beacon to alert the searchers to their location.

Beside her, Sam had taken his position, crouching in the seat as though it were a gunner's cockpit, increasing his turning radius.

"Go through it," he replied coldly—and then they were out of time.

Shouts rose outside. Lily slammed the accelerator and the Audi leapt to her command, tires screeching as they gripped the stones and hurled her forward.

She closed her eyes and ducked as they hit the boards, the rotted wood exploding into splinters at the impact.

The Audi burst into the courtyard in front of the shocked faces of six German soldiers.

Lily hauled the wheel, screaming them into a turn to avoid colliding with the solid wall of the castle. The Audi see-sawed dangerously before regaining traction.

Kazi snapped off a quick burst of rounds. The soldiers scrambled for cover, three of them diving behind Zhao Min's borrowed carriage. The old horses reared with panic at the sound of the shots, then bolted, the vehicle swaying dangerously.

As she pressed the accelerator, Lily heard a wrench of splintering wood and an equine scream.

She wondered how many bullets Kazi had left.

The perfectly tuned engine purred at her touch. She pulled them into a turn, the ancient stones of the walls blurring as they passed. The gate came into view. The wooden barricade was lowered but looked as flimsy as a toothpick in the face of the Audi's power.

Above the gates, the Germans in the machine gun nest were frantically bringing their weapon about to face an unanticipated enemy from within.

Sam raised his pistol. He took aim, his finger on the trigger—and then stiffened.

Without explanation, he twisted, abandoning the target of the machine gun crew. He swung his weapon up and right to where a young private was just emerging from the door at the top of the castle stairs.

The soldier's eyes widened in surprise. His hands were empty, his firearm still slung over his shoulder.

Time held its breath. Lily could see the boy with perfect clarity—sandy blond hair, a nose that had once suffered a break, hollow cheeks under frightened eyes.

He couldn't have been more than nineteen. They would be past him before he could scramble for his gun.

She felt it like a pulse of her onmyōdō—the sense of something vast and ancient brushing over the world.

"No!" Lily screamed, her hands trapped on the wheel of the automobile.

The folds of his great black coat falling into place around him, Sam pulled the trigger.

The boy's head snapped back. He crumpled to the landing, landing in a heap.

Then they were past him, racing towards the gate where she could see the ancient iron portcullis beginning to descend … and a machine gun barrel coming around to point at their heads.

Kazi snatched up Strangford's rifle. He had risen to a crouch, bracing himself with a knee to the back of Lily's seat.

She heard his breath—could almost feel him draw his focus. He snapped out three quick shots.

The first took a man in the head. The second hit a shoulder.

The third struck the magazine of the gun, wrenching it askew.

At the gate stood the young private who had checked them in. Instead of a clipboard, he held a Mauser, the barrel aimed directly at Sam.

A wind breathed over her, soft as the beat of a black wing.

The front wheel of the Audi hit a pothole, sending the automobile jolting.

The gun cracked, followed by a tinny ping.

A plume of dust rose to her right as the bullet, deflected off the headlamp, embedded itself harmlessly in the walls of the castle.

Sam whirled, bringing his handgun to bear and putting a bullet into the shoulder of the private, who stumbled aside, dropping his weapon.

Iron bars descended, even and relentless, narrowing the window for their exit.

Lily slammed down the accelerator.

She gripped the wheel and turned her face as they flew into the passage through the walls.

There was a scream of metal, a scrape—a sharp jolt of impact. Then the wooden gate was splintering across her fender, and they were through.

Lily raised her head. The windshield was cracked through the middle, the top corner of the frame wrenched where one of the points of the portcullis had caught it. Pieces of glass from where part of it had broken away peppered her skirt.

She didn't touch them. She yanked the wheel around a hairpin turn of the road, aware of other engines echoing off the walls of Vianden—then the portcullis came to rest with a clang.

A smattering of gunshots rattled at them from the far side of the trees as Lily flew around another switchback of the road—and they were gone.

TWENTY-ONE

$\mathcal{V}$IANDEN FELL QUICKLY BEHIND. The Audi glided along the winding forest road, engine humming powerfully. Wind rushed against Lily's ears, the world blurring past the cracked glass of the windshield. Glittering shards from the chipped corner still rested on the wool of her skirt.

Strangford yanked at the buttons of his uniform coat, hard enough that one of them popped free, pinging to the floor. He shrugged the garment off, moving awkwardly and a little desperately in the close confines of the rear seat. He shoved it down between his boots and rested like that for a moment, his hands in his hair, elbows on his knees as though suffering from motion sickness.

Removing the jacket was a symbolic protest. Though Strangford's shirt was his own, the trousers and boots belonged to the uniform.

Lily realized there was nothing else for him to wear. They had left everything else they possessed back at the inn. There was no returning for it. How long would it be before they could safely acquire an alternative?

"One of you ought to change clothes with him," Zhao Min stated. She shifted her penetrating gaze to the police inspector beside her. "You are the nearer fit."

At Kazi's flash of discomfort, the dilemma became clear to Lily. Lending Strangford an article of clothing was, in effect, extending him an invitation to discover all your secrets.

"I'm not sure that's ..." Kazi began awkwardly.

315

"He can have mine," Sam cut in.

He was slumped down in the passenger seat beside her, gazing blankly at the passing trees. They were the first words he had spoken since they escaped Vianden.

In her mind, Lily could see the angle of the German soldier's head as it snapped back with the force of Sam's bullet.

"I can manage," Strangford slowly replied, the words rasping in his throat.

Sam rolled his eyes.

"You don't look like you're bloody managing." He crossed his arms, still slouched. "You'll have already had the worst of my dirt from her already anyway."

He jerked his head toward Lily. It felt like an accusation of betrayal, for all that there was little she could have done to prevent it.

Strangford looked down at his hands, and Lily knew he was feeling that pang of unavoidable shame as well.

"Turn here," Zhao Min ordered after a little while.

The opening in the trees was another unpaved road half covered in grass, obviously rarely used. Lily slowed the Audi to navigate the narrow line of it, weaving them through the forest. Woodcocks startled from the brush, fluttering with plump brown alarm. The car bounced over the uneven ground until Lily brought it to a halt.

She examined the dashboard, finding the switch to kill the engine. Silence descended around them, gradually resolving itself into the rustle of leaves and the gentle chirp of insects.

They climbed out of the car, Lily feeling as though she were moving through the fog of a dream. The glass fell from her skirt, spilling to the dry leaves around her boots, her hands trembling as she shook the last pieces clear.

She hurried over to Strangford. He held himself like a man twice his age, every motion seeming to take more effort than it should.

A crash resounded from back at the car. Lily whirled to see Sam standing beside the Audi as great shards of glass slid across the hood to fall to the ground. He held the stolen rifle in his hands, the butt directed at the now obliterated windscreen.

"Ain't safe to drive with." He jerked his head to Strangford. "Let's get on with it, then."

He tossed the gun into the seat and stalked into the woods.

Strangford squeezed Lily's hand, his eyes darkened with tired concern, and then followed him. The pair of them slipped from view behind the vibrant green.

"You should find a place to hide for a few days," Zhao Min said. "Not back in the city. Your presence would put others at risk there. In a week, your descriptions will have faded in the memory of those watching the borders, and you may be able to find smugglers to get you into neutral territory. I should caution you that the process is both expensive and potentially fatal."

"We can't wait that long," Kazi said.

He circled the Audi, casually opening up anything that could be opened—the toolbox bolted to the running board, a storage compartment behind a seat back. He examined the glove box in the dashboard and took out the slender metal tube of a cigar case. After contemplating it for a moment, he slipped it into his jacket pocket.

It surprised Lily. She had not thought that Kazi smoked.

"You can't outrun a telegram," Zhao Min countered. "They will be waiting for you."

"The information we possess must be delivered to London as quickly as possible," Kazi replied.

Strangford returned to the clearing. He was still in his shirtsleeves but had on Sam's trousers. Lily knew they must be an inch or two too long for him, but he had tucked them into the tall German boots. It had the added effect of preventing Strangford from coming into contact with the leather and whatever impressions it still carried.

He had lost some of that desperate tension, but there was another weight to him now, one that Lily knew lay in Sam's dark memories. There would have been only so much of that terrible history Strangford would have drawn from Lily.

He would know more now—likely including much that Sam had not chosen to share with her.

Sam wore the German trousers. The cuffs hung at his ankles. He sat down on the wheel cover of the Audi and pulled out his knife, setting to work picking out the stitches Mila had put into the uniform when she altered it for Strangford.

He raised his eyes to Lily. His glare felt like an accusation.

"Surely a few days wouldn't make that much difference," Lily protested.

"It would," Kazi bluntly insisted.

"Then you must cross on your own. It is fifty miles to the border with the Netherlands, but you cannot approach the checkpoints—not even if you push him back into that uniform," Zhao Min added with a nod at Strangford. "Your descriptions will have been circulated by the time you arrive. You will have to attempt the fence."

"What—the Wire of Death?" Sam exclaimed. "Are you mad? It's 2,000 bloody volts, manned day and night by patrols that'll bore holes in anyone they see."

"How much fuel have you?" Zhao Min asked.

Sam rubbed his face, controlling his exasperation.

"Tank's more or less full."

Zhao Min's mouth twisted.

"Of course. There is no petrol shortage for the officers of Abteilung IIIb." There was an edge of steel in her words. "You will cross northwest of Lommel. The area there is forested. Sound will not carry so far, and the patrols will have a more limited field of vision. You must abandon the car before you come within earshot of the border—if the Germans hear it, they will be hunting for you."

"That doesn't get us through the fence," Sam pointed out.

Zhao Min fixed him with a bland look.

"Come now, Dìdi. Surely you are clever enough to think of a way around that."

Sam opened his mouth to snap back a reply—then stopped as though the word were a spell.

Dìdi.

Lily could feel the significance of it, the easy intimacy with which it had been delivered as Zhao Min forgot, for a moment, to resent him.

Whatever it signified, Sam carefully chose not to bring attention to it. He turned his attention to the Audi, scratching his ear thoughtfully.

"We'd need a wrench ... " he muttered, moving to the toolbox. "And an iron."

"We had best exchange wardrobe as well, Lady Strangford." Zhao

Min rose. "I suspect you will require your trousers."

~

They made the swap in a beech grove, returning to the clearing a few minutes later to find Sam underneath the Audi, his black coat thrown casually over the rear seats.

Kazi was pacing restlessly.

Strangford leaned against the thick gray trunk of a linden tree. Lily joined him there. He looked exhausted.

"Would you mind terribly if I ..." he began.

"Of course not," Lily replied, extending her hand.

Strangford slipped off his glove and clasped her palm. His breath came out in a shudder of relief at the contact. Lily brushed her fingers along his face, wishing she could do more.

"You aren't coming with us," he said.

It took Lily a moment to realize he was speaking to Zhao Min.

"I am not," she confirmed.

"What?" Sam exclaimed, his attention diverted from the automobile.

"Her responsibilities are in Luxembourg," Lily answered, immediately understanding.

Lily thought back to the house on Rue Sainte-Zithe, to the uncanny discomfort of Inês's mind pushing her away.

It could be a simple coincidence that Zhao Min had chosen to take in a child with powers akin to those of her estranged brother— of the circle that had once haunted an unassuming house on Bedford Square. The refuges Zhao Min built would never be stuffed with Hindu esoterica and the memoirs of dead Irish saints, but then Zhao Min had other things to teach.

How to hide in plain sight. How to stay alive.

The thought made the ground seem to shift beneath Lily's feet, and for a moment, she felt herself drift somewhere else.

A hallway where women laugh conspiratorially. Children dashing through elegant rooms, chased by the stern caution of a lecture.

Fires sparking without matches. Flowers blooming out of season.

The knowledge slipped from beneath her, landing Lily roughly back in her skin in the dappled quiet of a Luxembourgian forest where Sam knelt beside the gleaming yellow motorcar, and Kazi restlessly paced through the dry leaves that covered the ground.

Zhao Min watched her with narrowed eyes, her mouth a firm and impenetrable line.

"Lady Strangford is correct," Zhao Min finally said. "My work will not be complete here until the war is over."

"You might be dead by then," Sam snapped.

"That is my risk to take."

"Of all the bloody, stupid—"

"We should thank you," Strangford cut in smoothly. "For everything you have done for us."

Lily half expected a sharp warning not to expect too much of it, but after the briefest pause, Zhao Min merely nodded, the gesture like a queen accepting tribute from a respected subject.

"Do you need funds?" Strangford continued, managing a tired smile. "Box of matches? Bit of pocket lint? I'm afraid we haven't much else to offer you."

Zhao Min almost smiled.

"I am capable of supplying myself with what I require."

"That I do not doubt," Kazi noted dryly.

Zhao Min didn't answer, instead eyeing the inspector thoughtfully.

"What?" he demanded, noting her attention.

She shook her head.

"Nothing. I was merely considering doing something foolish."

"You know something," Strangford declared.

Zhao Min's look was sharp enough to cut, but a moment later, the corner of her mouth curved into the semblance of a smile.

"One might almost think we had exchanged some intimacy, my lord." Her gaze took in the three of them. "I have a piece of intelligence you may deliver to your masters alongside what you collected in Vianden."

"What sort of intelligence," Kazi demanded.

"The train journey to Lens is a round trip," Zhao Min replied.

"A round trip?" Lily echoed. "What do you mean?"

Beside her, Strangford had gone very still.

"The agents watching the train networks will have reported seeing carloads of German soldiers being unloaded at Lens over the last week. But they will almost certainly have failed to notice that those same soldiers are then reloaded onto the trains after nightfall and transported back to Lille."

"But why would they do that?"

"So that it would appear that they are sending reinforcements to Lens," Strangford replied, his eyes on Zhao Min. "When in fact, they are massing their forces for an attack somewhere else."

"What about La Basse?" Kazi said urgently. "Hollebeke? Feuchy, west of Arras? Our networks have reported troops being delivered across a fifty-mile swath of the front."

"They could be marching them all at night." Sam's voice cut in from the Audi, where he snapped shut the toolbox. "They'd move slower, but they wouldn't be visible to the observation flights."

"March them at night where?" Lily demanded, feeling a flicker of fear in her chest.

Strangford released her hand.

"Bailleul," he replied.

The words came back to her, falling from the lips of the cheerful German unteroffizier who would later turn into a nightmare.

Wir sehen uns am Mittwoch. Bei Bailleul.

"Mittwoch," Lily whispered.

"See you there on Wednesday." Strangford translated, then turned to the others. "One of the Wulfstruppen said it to me back at Vianden."

"Bailleul is eighteen miles from Lille," Kazi noted. "If the troops were being returned to the junction at Lille from Lens and the other stations, they could make the march in a night. And it is only a mile and a half from Bailleul to the front."

Lily thought of how the bright young officer had sprouted teeth and claws, rising even after his skin had been crisped to black. The monstrous impact of his body against the door of the crypt.

How he kept coming with impossible strength after injuries that would have left any ordinary man writhing on the ground with pain and shock.

Were more of those monsters to throw themselves at the depleted British ranks holding the front lines . . . Lily could all too easily imagine the devastation. It would be even worse if the place where they

321

struck was already thinned out as any available reinforcements were sent to the areas where the German troops were reportedly being transported.

Were the front line to break with a massed German force on hand to exploit the opening, the British and French armies could be riven apart. The Germans could roll over the exhausted French forces, easily taking Paris. Or they might drive the British back into the cold waters of the channel, where they would wait until France had fallen and the Kaiser turned his imperial eye on another target.

"What part of the front faces Bailleul?" Lily demanded, her voice hoarse.

"Mont Noir," Kazi grimly replied.

The French word sent a chill down her back. It sounded empty, like a void filled only with fear.

"How many of them are coming?" Kazi demanded.

"Perhaps twenty." Strangford said. "But it's only an impression. I can't say for certain."

"Twenty." Sam cut in, disbelieving. "You lot are worked up about a score of men?"

"They aren't men," Strangford returned. "Not anymore."

"And I estimate there are two full divisions of the Fourth Army at their backs," Zhao Min added.

Kazi's face drained.

"That is forty thousand men." He loomed over the slender figure of Zhao Min. "How do you know this? I need more than your word to bring this to headquarters."

Zhao Min's dark eyes flashed with fire.

"I will not compromise my informants."

"This could mean the war," Kazi shouted back.

"Inspector," Strangford forcibly cut in.

Kazi and Zhao Min faced each other in a prelude to their own battle, the tension stretched like a wire—then Kazi turned and stalked back to the Audi. He pulled back his boot and issued a swift kick to the tire.

"Oy. We're going to need that," Sam reprimanded, shrugging back into his coat.

"I cannot imagine it is terribly offended," Strangford offered tiredly, leaning back against one of the trees.

"I think I can get us across the wire, so long as one of you lot can carry a tire for a mile or so," Sam announced.

"And what would you be carrying?" Kazi asked crossly.

"The other bloody tire," Sam retorted.

"We require two of them?"

Strangford peeled himself from the tree, offering Zhao Min an elegant bow.

"Miss Wu. Your assistance in this matter is greatly appreciated."

"Yes. Quite," Kazi added, his voice clipped with lingering irritation.

He slammed his way into the Audi, then leaned back in the passenger seat with his eyes closed, still rigid with tension.

Lily found herself studying the other woman—the quiet steel of her poise containing an immeasurable ferocity. For a moment, it almost seemed as though she could sense one of the glittering threads Evangeline Ash wove through her fate-inspired art, a slender arc that bound her and Zhao Min together.

Who better to break the world than two women returned from the dead?

"When this is over . . . I should like to know where you find your-self." Lily finished, stumbling over the words.

Zhao Min offered her a careful nod.

"I shall take that into consideration."

With nothing left to say, Lily joined Strangford and Kazi by the automobile.

Sam stared at his sister.

For a moment, the entire forest seemed to go still, even the birds quieting in the trees.

Zhao Min offered an elegant, distant nod.

"Gàocí, Wu Xiang," she said.

At her formal words, Sam's face twisted with a mix of longing and hurt. He stalked toward the car—then stopped, turning back.

"Zài jiàn, Jiějie."

The more intimate phrase was fierce, with the feeling of a declaration—a demand Sam would not compromise.

Zài jiàn. See you later.

323

There was just a flicker of reaction on Zhao Min's face, a breath of vulnerability before it slid back into self-control.

Sam did not wait for an answer. He climbed into the driver's seat, slammed the door, and started the engine. The Audi roared back to life. His arm slung over the seat, Sam lurched them in reverse down the bumpy, overgrown road.

Looking ahead over his shoulder, Lily saw Zhao Min standing in the softly waving grass, her slender gray figure gazing at them as it receded into the distance.

TWENTY-TWO

Saturday, April 27
Night

$\mathcal{L}$ILY WONDERED HOW MANY men they had left dead at Vianden. Kazi had felled at least one of them with the bullet that struck the skull of the machine gunner. She knew he had hit at least two others, and Sam had put a round into the shoulder of the guard blocking their way through the gate.

And there was the boy on the steps, of course.

It felt so meaningless. They had passed a dozen others like him, men too surprised by their unexpected and bizarre passage to think to lift their guns. Why had he been the one chosen to die? Something in it reminded her of the impersonal forces of fate in the mural at The Refuge . . . forces she had never been particularly comfortable with.

She could still hear the crack. See the angle of his body as he fell.

Sam drove the Audi in silence, his jaw set, hands firm on the wheel. If all he had told her was true, his likelihood of dying in this war was far lower than the rest of them.

And what about when there wasn't a war anymore? What would happen to Sam when there weren't battles to conceal the deaths he was compelled to bring about?

The road twisted through richly forested valleys and a sign pointing east that read *Deutschland*. They crossed the border into Belgium a couple hours later, the remote transition between the two occupied territories marked only with a hand-painted wooden sign.

Sie verlassen jetzt Luxemburg. Bienvenue à Belgique.

Someone had painted a rude remark over it directed at the Germans.

In Belgium, the land slid from forest into fertile farmland, the signs of occupation more visible. Fields that should have been plowed by now were still overgrown. They passed the burned-out shell of a house, an abandoned tangle of rusted wire.

Sam avoided the villages, keeping to roads that were sometimes little more than dirt tracks as the afternoon decayed into the orange glare of evening.

It was past dusk when he killed the headlamps and turned the motorcar off the road, bouncing them slowly past a broken gate and along a track through the fields.

Kazi woke, head snapping up as he came to attention. Sam killed the engine. The silence that settled in after the familiar rumble of the Audi had presence, remaining heavy even once the chirp of crickets and the tick of the engine cooling asserted themselves.

"Near out of petrol anyway." Sam said, climbing out.

Lily gazed at the landscape around them as Sam retrieved a jack from the toolbox.The dusk-shrouded farmland was edged with a black line of trees. The air tasted softly of spring. Tiny pinpricks of golden light in the distance marked a scatter of homes. There was no moon, only a blanket of stars rapidly emerging from the purpling sky overhead.

Beyond the fields lay the border with the Netherlands and neutral territory—the way home.

The last week felt like a dream. Had the nightmare of Vianden really taken place just that morning? And the surreal descent into the glacier at the Stelvio Pass only a few days earlier?

It felt like a lifetime, but they had accomplished what they had come for and more. She thought of the flames devouring Kirchweger's lab. His prima materia, his serum, his notes—it would all be ash now. Lily was grateful for the destruction. The vision of the hand of that charming unteroffizier rising from the flames still haunted her, sparking a primitive and terrible fear.

But they had ended it. Lily sought to feel reassured by that as the wind whispered across the blades of grass.

She couldn't. Not yet.

A tire, stripped from its wheel, hit the ground in front of her.

"Inspector," Sam called.

The Audi bounced down roughly as he collapsed the jack and moved to the other side.

Kazi sighed, then carefully unknotted his necktie and loosened the top button of his shirt. He threaded the strip of cloth through the tire and slung it over his shoulder.

The Audi dropped to the ground again. Sam kicked another loosed tire. The black ring of it bounced across the grass before flopping onto its side.

"Let's move along, then," he declared.

They trudged across the fields, pushing through barriers of tangled weeds and shrubs before entering a low, swampy woodland. The ground was soft and spring-wet, crisscrossed by narrow canals and standing pools of water between stands of oak and alder. Night birds chirped in the branches overhead, mingling with the croaking of frogs.

The shining eyes of a family of opossums startled out of the darkness. They looked at Sam and then scurried away.

Not long after that, the forest halted.

The line of it was abrupt, the dark shadows of the trees giving way in a moment to a twenty-yard sprawl of hacked stumps and ragged grass ending at the unnatural line of an eight-foot wire fence.

Kazi raised a hand, motioning them silently to a stop. Sam had already crouched behind one of the last of the trees, eyeing the fence carefully.

The stars were thick and bright across the cobalt of the sky, illuminating the paler line of a path worn into the dirt on the far side of the wires. Lily knew it must be the way the German patrols took on their rounds. The fence lay just within their side of the border, and the Dutch had no need to patrol it since it did a fair job of killing anyone who might otherwise try to get through.

The wires were spaced a mere foot apart as they climbed the posts. She could hear the low hum of machinery from a little hut several yards down the line, its windows glowing with warm lantern light. There was no cover as far as she could see, the forest hacked mercilessly back to provide a clear line of sight for the patrols.

A wooden sign painted with white letters was nailed to a post nearby.

Achtung

Hochspannung-Lebensgefahr

Lily did not know much German but could recognize the word for danger.

"How strong is the current?" she asked, her voice a bare whisper.

"Two thousand volts," Kazi replied flatly.

It was more than enough to kill them … if they weren't shot before they could reach it.

"I am beginning to suspect why we have brought the tires," Kazi noted under his breath. "And I cannot say I am pleased with the idea."

"Got a better one, then?" Sam's low whisper still managed to carry a hefty East End disdain.

"No," Kazi admitted flatly.

The fence loomed ahead of them like a scar in the star-shadowed landscape.

"They double the patrols at night," Sam noted softly.

Even as he spoke, Lily could see confirmation of it. The dark-clad form of a German soldier walked the line, his rifle at his back. The patrols here would likely be bored, well settled into a dull routine, but they could not rely on that to get them very far.

"The ground could also be mined," Sam continued.

"Mined?" Kazi had the presence of mind to keep his voice low even as he objected.

"Could be," Sam emphasized. "No way to know from looking whether they've done this stretch or not."

"I'll test the way." Strangford announced.

Lily bit back a protest, knowing it would be far louder than it ought to.

"Think I might be better suited to that than you, your lordship," Sam said. "Being more accustomed to sneaking about."

Strangford looked at him steadily through the darkness.

"But would your path be safe for the rest of us?" he asked gently.

Sam paled.

Strangford was right. If Sam made it across, there'd be no way to know whether he'd found a safe way or whether some darker influence had caused the mines to fail to trigger.

"I'll go," Kazi offered.

"You've three children at home who depend on you."

Strangford's justifications were relentless. Lily's frustration rose to a peak.

"Blast the whole lot of you," she seethed and shot forward.

She moved quickly, knowing all three of them would try to catch her if they had the chance. She scurried from the cover of the wood, keeping low until she was past the point where they could reach her.

Crouching down in the grass, she paused, staring at the line of the fence. The guard was visible fifty yards to the south, the switching station half that distance to the north. There could well be another man inside.

Drawing in a breath, Lily sought the same power that steered her through a fight, setting it a different challenge.

Move me.

The answer pulsed inside of her. Lily felt it like the subtle pressure of a partner in a dance, signaling when to spin.

Go.

She crawled forward, propelling herself across the ground, her toes scrabbling for purchase. The damp of the evening dew soaked into her shirt. The impulse pushed her to move as quickly as she could without raising a racket. The rustle of her clothes against the earth still felt like a roar in her ears.

She was just over halfway to the fence, hurrying through a sparser place in the grass, when she wondered whether it would simply be a straight, well-timed crawl. Were there no mines here at all?

The order blazed across her mind like an illuminated sign.

Left.

It was more than a direction. It was an imperative. Lily shoved off with her hands, throwing herself to the side. She rolled over once and was then arrested by another blazing impulse, a screaming urge to *stop.*

She thrust a palm against the earth halfway through a roll, tiny stones scraping her skin as she skidded to a halt on her back.

Every instinct in her body urged her not to move a hair to either side—only straight ahead.

Feeling half-mad, Lily dug the heels of her boots into the earth and pushed herself—slowly, gingerly—across the ground, her jacket pulling at her shoulders as it snagged against tiny stones.

Freeze.

Lily stilled, staring up at the thickly starred sky visible through the blades of grass that furred the periphery of her vision. Somewhere in the distance, a train whistle blew, a haunting lilt of sound that carried through the stillness of the night.

Her pulse throbbed, the pace frantic despite the quiet that surrounded her.

Boots crunched softly on dry earth. Lily caught a whiff of cigarette smoke. Without daring to tilt her head to confirm it, she knew the German guard was passing no more than six yards from her skull, returning to the narrow rectangle of the switching house.

He passed. There was a murmur of voices from the north, followed by a bark of laughter.

Fear had broken the thread of her focus. Lily forced herself to steady, reaching for it again.

Right path, she begged. *Right path.*

The response came in a gentle pull to her left.

Lily rolled. On her stomach once more, she worked her way forward. She wanted to go slowly, conscious of how close the guards must still be, but the impulse propelled her faster, sparking with urgency.

She came within two yards of the fence and tucked herself behind a stump, waiting.

In the stillness, she could hear the scrapes and soft rustling signals that told her the others were following, using the bent grass and disturbed earth of her passage to deduce her path.

As she heard them draw nearer, footsteps crunched outside the switching house. Lily tried to make herself smaller.

On the far side of the Wire of Death, the guard continued past, his pace easy.

Someone slid down beside her, pressing close to share her cover. It was Sam, clutching a tire to his chest.

"The Peeler knows what you are."

His whisper sounded like an accusation.

"Do you think I told him? No—don't answer that. What now?"

Sam rolled to his side, watching the progress of the guard with careful eyes.

"I should kill him."

"Are you mad?" Lily fought to keep her voice low.

He shifted his gaze to her as he lay beside her in the gloom.

"You know I can."

"That doesn't make it right," she hissed.

"He's the enemy." Sam countered through his teeth. "I could do it with a knife before he makes a sound, and the rest of you would be clear to move through."

"Or he'll scream," Lily returned, glaring back at him. "And you'll live while the rest of us are shot."

His jaw tightened, eyes flashing with anger and hurt, but when he spoke, his voice was steady.

"One of these days, you'll learn you can't always avoid a fight."

The words burned. Lily had no answer for them.

Strangford slumped against another stump to her left, Kazi behind him.

They could not linger for long.

The guard was the problem. She did not doubt that with his cursed luck, Sam could kill him, but he had enough blood on his hands already. Kazi still had a shot or two in his pistol, but the sound would be unmistakable and bring reinforcements running. Strangford had his tàijí, but he'd never get close enough to use it.

Lily had something better. She could almost feel the anticipation of it hiss through her veins—the movements of her walking stick that would thrust the guard against the current of the fence, allowing what he guarded to destroy him in turn.

But she had no stick. She had lost it at Vianden, and the thought of watching a man fry turned her stomach.

There had to be another way.

"What else is here?" she asked in a whisper.

Sam flashed her a look but did not mistake her meaning.

"Near enough to be of use? Nothing but mice."

Mice, Lily thought . . . little brown field mice.

The idea began to pull together inside her mind.

"How many of them?"

Sam rolled his eyes, clutching the tire against the black wool of his coat.

"Where there's one, there's dozens."

Seeing the look on her face, his expression shifted to one of cautious interest.

"What've you got in mind?"

Lily told him.

~

All told, it took a little less than a quarter-hour. Through most of it, Lily simply lay still beside Sam behind the stump as tiny feet skittered across her coat, small brown bodies pausing to sniff at her hands or her chin before scurrying off.

"They're ready." he said at last.

"Do it."

Nothing changed. The quiet monotony of the night continued to hum around them in the croak of a frog and the soft buzz of the wires. Lily could hear the shuffle of the guard's boots on the far side of the fence as he kept his dull watch, lighting another cigarette.

She took a chance, crawling forward to peer around the side of the stump, keeping her head down in the grass. She could see the guard through the blades, the cigarette glowing in his lips, rifle silhouetted against his back . . . and a strange flicker of movement by his boots.

A darting brown form scurried past him. Then another—a third.

The guard didn't see it, gazing blankly at the wood line.

"He isn't looking down," Lily hissed.

"I have it," Sam replied steadily.

He grew quieter beside her. She could almost feel his focus drawing inward and knew he must be doing something like what he had done for her in the ruined barn back in Luxembourg. The merest whisper of mind to mind, the gentle tug of a suggestion.

The guard stilled mid-puff, an air of distraction coming over him.

He scratched his head, then looked down . . . and saw the stream of mice hurrying past his boots.

He jumped back, the rifle swinging into his hands.

The mice kept coming, one small brown body followed by another, all racing past him in the same direction.

The rifle lowered. The cigarette fell from his mouth, forgotten as he stared at the rodents.

He darted a quick glance back at the switching house. Then, as Lily had prayed he would, he set off after the mice.

"Chop-chop," Sam ordered, rolling out from behind the stump.

He darted forward, swinging the tire off of his shoulder. He shoved it beneath the fence and made an urgent gesture.

Kazi joined him, Lily and Strangford following.

Sam grabbed the second tire. He set it down on the near side of the fence, then climbed on top of it, his boots balanced on the rubber circle.

He reached forward.

Kazi grabbed his arm.

"Are you sure about this?"

"It's bloody science, mate," Sam returned.

Shaking him loose, he grabbed the wire.

Nothing happened. There was no jolt of terrible damage, no instant death. Sam pushed the wires apart with his hands and ducked through, carefully setting his feet down on the other tire. He completely extracted himself from the fence, leaning back with his arms wide, before hopping backward onto the ground.

"Don't leave the rubber until you're full clear of the wires," he cautioned, stepping back to make way for the rest of them.

"I know it is science," Kazi sighed as he stepped onto the first tire. "And yet it feels like lunacy."

~

They climbed through without incident, the insulation of the tires preventing them from grounding out while in contact with the deadly current of the fence. Lily felt only an odd tingle in her hands and back as she brushed through it, aware the whole time that she was holding on to something that could easily have killed her.

333

It took less than two minutes for all four of them to cross and dash across the field into the cover of another tree line—Dutch trees, Lily realized. Neutral trees.

They slept in a field two miles northeast of the border. Strangford cradled her. With her head on the warmth of his chest, sheer exhaustion pulled Lily under in a matter of moments. She was aware of nothing until she felt his hand on her cheek and opened her eyes to the light of a clear, early dawn.

"Time to go," he said gently.

They reached Eindhoven by midday. Kazi arrowed straight to a telegram office to send another coded missive to his superiors. The Dutch passers-by regarded Lily, Sam, and Strangford with either wariness or pity, making her awkwardly aware of how ragged they were.

Eindhoven was orderly and trim. It was also close to home. Kazi's telegram should see some form of transportation back to England arranged for them. It felt almost surreal that she could soon be returning to the life she had known—donning her WRNS uniform and heading out on her courier runs. Sleeping beside Strangford with Cat lumped on their toes and Mrs. Jutson clattering in the kitchen downstairs.

Would what they had accomplished make a difference? Lily knew it must, and yet a thread of uneasiness remained. She set it aside. They had more than done their part. They had earned the right to go home.

As they waited for Kazi on a bench outside an elegant church, an older woman approached and pressed a paper-wrapped bundle in Lily's hands.

"Hier. Voor jou," she urged.

Lily opened the paper to find hearty pancakes stuffed with cheese and greens. Her stomach made an audible response to the gift.

"T-Thank you," she stammered in English.

The woman smiled, patting Lily's dirt-streaked cheek.

"Welkom in Nederland," she said, then continued on her way.

~

Kazi returned an hour later. Somehow even the crawl through the

Wire of Death had not disheveled him much.

"A Dutch ship will transport us, departing out of Vlissengen this evening," he announced. "We'll make our way along the coast of France to Dunkirk."

"Dunkirk," Lily echoed in response, shocked to her feet. "What about Dover?"

Sam had been slouched on the other end of the bench, his head back in a near doze. At Kazi's words, he slowly straightened beside her. Lily could feel his attention sharpen on the inspector.

"Dover will come after we have been debriefed in Dunkirk," Kazi replied.

"Debriefed?" Sam echoed carefully.

"Army Intel would like the information we carry immediately without waiting for it to be couriered through the London office. A representative will meet us in France. It shouldn't take more than a day or so, and you'll be on your way again."

Lily looked at Strangford, unsure how to respond. What Kazi had said was perfectly reasonable. She still hated it.

Strangford squeezed her hand with his gloved fingers.

"We shall be glad to offer whatever assistance we can, of course," he replied neutrally.

Kazi's short nod looked a little bit guilty. He knew they had already given him far more than they had agreed to.

"What about Sam?" Lily demanded.

"He was shot down behind enemy lines and has been actively trying to return to his unit," Kazi replied. "I expect they'll be quite happy to see him."

"Didn't exactly clear my flight plan before I took off." Sam pointed out.

"Even if they go through with a court martial for that—which I think very unlikely—you'd get a slap on the wrist at most. Being returned to your post by Army Intelligence is only going to help confirm your story."

Kazi's explanation was perfectly logical.

Sam stayed quiet.

Dunkirk. It was far from ideal, another delay before they could be finished with all of this, but it would only cause more trouble were they to try to avoid it—if they even could.

"There is a train leaving in twenty minutes." Kazi glanced at his watch. "Shall we?"

~

Their transport in Vlissengen was a fifty-foot ketch. The sailboat was verging on antique but lovingly kept up. It was captained by a taciturn Dutchman, Meener Stoepker. He quickly oriented them to the craft. The cockpit was enclosed, the interior of it all polished hardwood. There was a small cabin below decks, reached by way of a galley and a bunk room with four beds bolted to the walls.

Lily and Strangford were granted the cabin. Still exhausted from the night before, she collapsed onto the bed inside of it, immediately lulled by the soft rocking of the boat. She was only vaguely aware of Strangford tugging off her boots before he dropped down on top of the blankets beside her in his shirtsleeves and trousers, his feet bare.

"Stoepker dreams of a woman," he noted wearily.

Lily sighed.

"You really oughtn't read his blankets."

"Too tired not to," Strangford mumbled in reply. "Too tired to make proper use of you and this bed, either."

"You are in need of a bath."

"Assuredly." he agreed, yawning.

"In England," Lily promised him.

"In England," he agreed, eyes drifting shut.

~

She woke the next morning with a jolt, startled by the unfamiliar motion of the mattress beneath her as it rolled along with the rest of her world. The hull creaked mildly, water lapping at the boards.

Strangford breathed easily beside her, still sprawled across the blankets in his clothes. He looked younger in his sleep, some of the exhaustion and worry falling away from him.

Through the porthole, Lily could see that the sky was beginning to lighten behind them. She slipped out of the cabin. Sam was still snoring in one of the bunks. She made her way past him to the ladder.

The salt air rose to greet her as she climbed. Stoepker acknowledged her with a nod and pointed a finger at a paraffin stove on the deck.

"Thee," he said and returned to his watch.

She poured herself a cup, the tea a little smoky in flavor. There was nothing to add to it, so she took it black.

Kazi was at the prow, looking out over the dark waters to the west. Behind them, the sun was just breaking the horizon, the light warming the line of the shore they followed.

"Where are we?" she asked.

"Past De Panne," Kazi replied. "This will be France soon, if it isn't already."

"But we are beyond the front line."

"We are," he confirmed.

The motion of the boat was more pronounced at its fore, the bow rising and falling steadily across the swells. A breeze tugged at her hair. The silence that fell between them was unexpectedly easy, reminding Lily of just how much had changed.

"What will you tell them?" she asked at last.

Kazi didn't pretend to misunderstand her.

"What they need to know, and no more."

The boat creaked, rising with another gentle wave as the sky shifted in hue behind them, orange joining the peach of early dawn.

"I'm sorry." she said after another moment. "I shouldn't have had to ask that."

He looked down at her.

"You have had every reason for caution."

Lily lowered her head, watching the water slip past her.

"For what it is worth, I don't feel the need for it any longer."

He shifted uncomfortably beside her.

"Yes. Well."

He cleared his throat, adjusting his grip on the rail. There was something endearing in his awkwardness.

"Have you completed it, then? Your mission?"

For just a moment, it seemed he flinched at her words—but perhaps she had imagined it.

"I have," he replied shortly.

~

Lily excused herself a few moments later, the aggravated motion of the bow setting off her regular morning nausea. She made her way to the stern, the bulk of the cockpit blocking her view of Kazi and their captain. She could barely hear the low murmur of their voices over the soft splashing of the water. Sitting down on the deck, she turned her gaze to the east. In the growing light, she could just make out the sleek brown heads of a herd of seals dancing along in their wake. If they had mistaken the ketch for a fishing boat, they would be disappointed.

The boards beneath her vibrated. A moment later, Sam plopped down beside her.

"I thought you were sleeping," Lily said, turning to look at him.

His rebellious beard had been growing in well, nicely shadowing his jaw and chin. It made him look older.

He was holding a bundle wrapped in oilcloth and tied with rope.

"I'm cutting out," he said.

Lily startled at his words.

"Why."

"Don't much feel like leaving myself to gentle ministrations of Army Intel," he replied. "They'll treat your lot well enough, but I'm not some toff officer. Won't do me any favors if they get curious and decide to poke into my background. Still says 'British Subject' on my papers, and we all know that's a gag. I'd rather not get bagged for enlisting under false pretenses."

"Oh, Sam," Lily exclaimed, softly mortified. "This is my fault. I should never have dragged you into this."

He glanced over at her, mouth twisting into the ghost of his usual smile.

"You wouldn't have made it off the ground without me."

"No," Lily agreed. "I wouldn't have."

Sam shrugged awkwardly.

"Well—what else would I do? We're friends, ain't we?"

"I think perhaps we are rather more than that," she replied, the words catching a bit in her throat.

"Don't you start," Sam warned.

Lily straightened, fixing him with a glare.

"I'm not the one threatening to jump off the boat."

"I'm not heading for Ochey yet. I'll hang about Dunkirk for the night, set you a way to find me if you need to—if you aren't happily passed out in some posh Army digs by then."

"I won't leave without finding you," Lily asserted. "Not if I can possibly help it. But what about Kazi? I'm not sure I can convince him to leave you out of his story."

Sam laughed softly.

"Let him. They go looking for a Wu, they ain't going to find one, are they? Just Sergeant Wood here, sir," he said, snapping into a perfect Tommy accent. "Your inspector never knew my station. I might've flown you in from anywhere. Let him talk."

"It's still a risk," Lily pointed out.

"It's all risks," Sam returned. "Look—I've a few resources to port for the moment. I'd best get on."

She didn't want to let him go, grasping for an extra moment before she had to say goodbye.

"You know they'll make you shave that beard as soon as you get back to base."

"I was mostly doing it to rile up Jiějie. Won't mind having my own face back. Now do us a solid and distract the Dutchman and the Peeler for a spell, would you?"

When Lily returned to the bow, she managed to spill the tea. In the ensuing fuss, no one noticed the addition of another sleek black head cutting through the water alongside the seals.

TWENTY-THREE

Monday, April 29
Morning
Approaching Dunkirk, France

$\mathcal{D}$UNKIRK WAS A MASS of gray ships framing dawn-gilded buildings punctuated by the towering lines of the cranes at the port. Someone waited for them on the docks, the lines of a British Army officer's uniform gradually resolving into something more familiar.

"It would seem our old friend Captain Hume will be receiving us," Strangford said, joining Lily at the rail.

Lily supposed it should not have been a surprise. Why wouldn't the intelligence officer from Paris be meeting them? Kazi had said he ran the entirety of Army Intelligence's French operation.

Stoepker brought the sailboat neatly into its berth, navigating with expertise clearly garnered over decades. A harbor worker caught the rope he tossed and tied them off.

Kazi moved past them to hop nimbly onto the dock before the boat had entirely stopped moving, extending a hand.

"Captain."

"Inspector," Hume replied.

Lily found herself paying close attention to the dynamic between the two men. It was entirely professional. There was no warmth of friendship here—perhaps even a hint of cautious skepticism. They did, after all, work for different bureaus. Though England's various intelligence departments were required to engage in a certain degree of cooperation, they weren't known for liking it.

"Lord and Lady Strangford. How nice that we can do away with pretenses."

Hume's welcome had a disapproving chill to it. Lily doubted the intelligence officer appreciated being played when they first encountered him back in Paris.

"Our apologies for that," Strangford replied. "We thought it best to keep our involvement in the matter quiet as I was aiding the inspector . . . outside of the usual channels. It seemed more expeditious than involving NID."

"Yes. Well. So long as we are agreed on candor moving forward?"

Lily flashed the captain a pale smile as she accepted Strangford's hand and stepped onto the dock. There was something deeply satisfying about feeling her boots strike French territory.

Stoepker climbed out of the hold, calling over to Hume in Dutch.

"Was there another with you?" Hume asked.

Kazi looked around with a frown. His gaze stopped on Lily. Reading her expression, the frown deepened into a momentary grimace.

"I'll explain later," he said.

Lily didn't worry about Sam quietly finding his way to Dunkirk. Out of his RAF uniform and obviously of East Asian descent, he wouldn't be pegged for a rogue soldier but would most likely be assumed a member of one of the groups of Chinese laborers that peppered the coast of France. Thousands of his countrymen were stationed here in corps that dotted the countryside, digging trenches, repairing railways, and completing other work critical to the war effort.

Lily knew he would find a way to keep track of them. It made her give the seagull perched on the piling nearby an extra look.

She immediately dismissed the idea. There was no way seagulls were that cooperative.

"I see," Hume replied curtly. "Right, then. This way, please."

Lily wondered where he would be taking them. She hoped it was somewhere with a tub and a proper bed. Exhaustion still dragged at her.

Hume led them down the docks and into the town, stopping at a palatial building that faced the road along the harbor. Grand archways accented with white brick dominated the facade, giving the place the feel of a cross between a castle and a seaside arcade. At the west end of it stood an octagonal tower crowned with an enormous lantern.

Beside the fortress stood a row of tents where newly-arrived soldiers were bunking before transfer to the front. The place crawled with khaki uniforms.

Two of the building's three doorways were boarded up. A pair of Army guards stood by the other. They saluted Hume as he approached and opened the way for them.

"They call the lighthouse the Tour du Leughenaer. It's Old Dutch for 'liar,' if I'm not mistaken," he said as they passed inside. "Rather appropriate spot for Intelligence to hang about, isn't it?"

They pushed into the fortress. The rooms were large, walled with bricks painted a hasty white. The first housed a desk of telegraph equipment and a pair of typewriters. A woman sat at one. She looked at them with wide eyes as they moved past.

In the next chamber, a trio of men ate breakfast around a table. Lily could see by their uniforms that all were officers. They snapped to attention as Hume entered and the captain waved for them to be at ease.

The last room was clearly being used for storage. Boxes of telegraph equipment were stacked to one side next to crates labeled *Tinned Pork*.

Lily found herself rather certain they did not contain cans.

A pile of older junk occupied the opposite corner. There was a stack of antique furniture and a jumble of medieval weapons. Strangford fingered the blade of an ax with his gloved hand.

"Surely the Army isn't running that short of supplies," he quipped.

"The local historical commission was planning to convert the tower into a museum," Hume replied.

Lily's gaze stopped at the now familiar profile of a medieval halberd. The long staff was topped by a pike and the blade of a slender ax head. It appeared to be in better shape than the one Strangford was playing with. Perhaps it was a replica.

The blade looked sharp. It loomed in her vision until she felt as though she were falling into it, her heart beating with the rhythm of her onmyōdō.

She snapped back to herself, realizing the men were still talking.

"We will need each of you to go through a complete debriefing, of course. We will undertake it as promptly as possible. I am sure you are eager to return home." He turned to Kazi, extending his hand. "The courier is ready to depart to Porton Down."

Porton Down.

Lily knew the name. She could recall the sound of it on Zhao Min's lips. It was the secure location where the British Army conducted its own war-related scientific research.

Why would they need a courier to Porton Down?

The answer crept over her—the only possible explanation.

No. He couldn't possibly …

Kazi glanced over at her, and Lily saw the flash of emotion in his expression. It looked almost like an apology. Then he reached into his coat pocket and pulled out a slender tin cigar case.

It was the case he had taken from the glove box of the Audi after they had escaped from Vianden—from the lab where the Wulfstruppen had been made.

Hume took it. Unscrewing the top, he slid out a slender wax-stopped tube Lily had last seen sitting in a safe in Kirchweger's lab.

It was a sample of the Wulfstruppen serum. The serum she thought she had destroyed.

Kazi had taken it. He had taken it with him, concealing it from all of them.

"So this is what took down the Alpini," Hume said, eyeing the vial thoughtfully. "Some kind of biological agent?"

"Yes," Kazi replied thinly. "But not the sort you are thinking of."

The sense of betrayal choked her, making it hard to breathe.

"How could you?" she bit out.

"I was ordered to retrieve the technology if at all possible," Kazi replied. "It was my duty."

He sounded sorry.

"*Your duty*," Lily hissed.

Fury whirled up in her. It tasted of violence. Lily let it come, torn between two bitter impulses.

Destroy the vial. Destroy the man.

Her power bloomed like smoke, hissing into her limbs—and then abruptly snagged.

Strangford's arm was around her waist, holding her back.

Lily looked into the barrel of Captain Hume's sidearm.

"I see," he said calmly. "Caffrey."

The door opened, one of the officers from the break room coming in. At the sight of his commander holding a gun, his eyes widened.

"I am afraid Lord and Lady Strangford must be temporarily detained," Hume announced. "Please see that they are secured in the tower—comfortably."

Caffrey called to his colleagues.

In a moment, they would be surrounded.

The solution unfolded in her mind, painted a bloody red. Her limbs itched with anticipation.

"Patience," Strangford breathed against her ear, his eyes on the others.

Impulse battled constraint. Lily gritted her teeth, willing it into submission. Strangford was the military man and spy. This was his world, not hers. She had to trust him.

The men in front of her wore the uniforms of her own country. She could picture the blood on them inside her mind.

She turned the full force of her glare on Hume.

"You have no idea what you are holding in your hand."

"Remedying that is precisely the point of this exercise," he replied. "Gentlemen?"

"This way, please," Caffrey said, motioning them on.

Only one of his two colleagues was armed. She could kill them all before they knew what was happening.

"Come along, Lily." Strangford quietly urged.

She went.

~

The chamber at the top of the lighthouse looked out over the entirety of Dunkirk, from the sprawling tent city to the south to the uneasy waters of the channel. The lean gray lines of Navy ships filled the harbor, accented by the long, thin needle of the mole, the narrow stone breakwater that extended half a mile out into Dunkirk's harbor.

The room was round and empty, accessed through a set of stairs that rose up through a hatch in the floor. A ladder led to a trap door in the ceiling, presumably to the light itself.

As prisons went, it was an effective one. Though the windows were unbarred, only a madman would attempt the descent, and the stairs could easily be watched by a single guard.

A pair of soldiers carried up two Army-issue cots and a bundle of blankets, then returned with lunch rations and a change of clothes. Somehow they had found a Navy officer's uniform for Strangford. Lily was provided with a plain but serviceable dress. It was a couple of inches too short.

The men were awkwardly polite, as if not entirely sure whether to treat them as prisoners or guests.

"Anything else I can get for you, my lord?" one of them asked.

"A bit of warm water and a flannel, if it isn't too much trouble," Strangford said.

"Of course, sir," the man replied.

He seemed on the verge of offering Strangford a salute, then caught himself, hurrying out.

"How long can they hold us here?" Lily demanded once he was gone.

"As long as they like," Strangford replied, sitting down on one of the cots.

"You are an officer with the Naval Intelligence Division," she snapped.

He raised his head. He looked tired.

"NID won't know that I'm here. Hume wouldn't be such a fool as to inform them before he's had whatever he needs out of us."

She wrapped her arms around herself, chilled.

"And what does he need from us?"

"Everything we know about the Wulfstruppen serum. And likely an assurance we won't share the information with anyone Hume doesn't think should have it... which will most likely be everyone but Hume and his higher-ups. There will be legal puzzles to figure out, like how to ensure I won't face charges for withholding the information from my own superiors."

He made it sound terribly mundane, the sort of wrangling between intelligence agencies that happened every week.

"What will they do with it?" she demanded.

"At the very least, they will want to determine what it does. Whether it can be neutralized. How they might defend themselves against it."

"Would they use it?"

Strangford's face was drawn, his eye shadowed.

"I don't know, Lily. As I understand it, the policy at Porton Down is only to match or defend, not escalate. But as the Germans have already created a field unit, they may feel justified in doing the same."

Her desperation felt out of place, fueled by something other than logic.

"We can't let them do that."

Strangford rose. He slipped his arms around her waist, pulling her closer.

"Let's tackle one insurmountable obstacle at a time," he said.

The laugh choked out of her, half strangled by the turmoil roiling inside her chest. She clutched his lapels, her hands clenching into fists.

"I could have taken them."

She felt his lips press against her hair.

"They are not our enemy, Lily."

She raised her head.

"Are you certain of that?"

He sighed, releasing her.

"I would rather at least we had a better notion of exactly where the cards lay before you set about—"

He caught himself, stopping. Lily felt ill.

"Slaughtering our own people?" she filled in.

"That isn't what I meant."

She went to the window, pressing her hands against the rough stone as she looked out over the long arm of the mole, black against the paler water of the harbor. She wished she could open the glass. She wanted air.

"But it's what I do."

He turned her face to him, black-gloved fingers gentle against her skin as he forced her to meet his gaze.

"And I violate souls."

The words were bitter, writhing with an old shame. He pressed his forehead to hers. His words had the weight of a benediction.

"We are more than that. You know that we are."

She nodded, unable to speak.

"What about Kazi?" she finally demanded.

He straightened, turning his own gaze to the harbor.

"Kazi is trying to find his way through this, just as we are. Duty is important to him, and it was his duty to both learn of any weapon the Germans had used at the Stelvio Pass and to acquire it if possible."

"But he saw," Lily protested. "He was there. He knows what it … How could he possibly …"

She trailed off, unable to voice the rest.

"You should have read him. If we hadn't been so stupid as to trust him …"

His hands fell from her. She felt the sharp bite of her own words and regretted them, but there was nothing else to say.

She pushed away from the window—away from Strangford.

"I'm tired. I'm going to lie down for a while."

~

Lily woke with a jolt and sat up, rubbing her eyes. She stumbled to the window, needing to reorient herself. Dunkirk Harbor greeted her, clouds shifting in the sky above it.

The thin black barrier that arrowed out into the harbor was covered with packed rows of khaki uniforms. The sight rang through her with a sense of strange anxiety.

"Why are all those men on the mole?" she asked blearily.

"What's that?" Strangford replied, sitting up.

He had put on the uniform, his too-short hair lightly mussed with sleep.

Lily blinked. The long needle of the barrier was bare, nothing but a narrow line of stone.

"Nothing," she said, shaking her head as Strangford came over, frowning at her with quiet concern.

She reached out, rubbing her fingers against the blue wool that covered his chest.

"Is it …?"

"Nobody died in it, if that's what you're asking. Though the local bursar is skimming cigarette rations. It's tolerable," he assured her.

Lily had not put on the dress they had brought for her. Somehow wearing it would have felt like another form of confinement. She felt safer in her trousers, for all that they were filthy.

Someone knocked against the hatch in the stairwell, the closest thing they had to a door.

"Come up," Strangford said.

The hatch swung back and Kazi came inside.

Lily fought the urge to stride over and shove him back through it again.

"Have you everything you need?" he asked.

"Besides our liberty." Lily snapped back.

The anger she had expected. The hurt she felt at the sight of his face was a less welcome surprise.

I trusted you. I thought we had become friends.

"So. How long exactly were you lying to us?" she said instead.

"I didn't lie to you," he returned carefully, closing the hatch behind him.

"Failing to mention that you intended to steal that hellish stuff and hand it over to men who will not hesitate to use it for themselves is a lie, Inspector," she seethed.

To her surprise, the blow hit.

Kazi sat down on Strangford's cot. He looked exhausted.

"We thought it was a new form of light artillery or perhaps a type of animal conditioning program. I was under strict orders to maintain total confidentiality. Which I broke," he added, looking up pointedly.

"Are you looking for a thank you?"

Her sarcasm was a whip—one that recoiled. She turned back to the window, not wanting him to see her face.

The feeling that the serum should have been destroyed was visceral, rising from a place much deeper than logic. Every cell of her body screamed that it was true. It should have vanished in Vianden, burned there with the rest of it.

Those monsters of history—the berserkers in Cairncross's books, even Cairncross himself—had been chosen by the impenetrable directives of fate. That such terrible power for violence could be bestowed at will by mere mortals—by the self-important men who rose to authority—terrified her in a way she found hard to articulate.

Kazi had made that fear real.

"Did you tell them about Mont Noir?" Strangford asked.

"Yes," Kazi replied.

She could hear the rest of it in the thread of tension in his voice.

"They didn't believe you," she said, turning back to face him.

He rubbed a hand over his face. Shadows hollowed his eyes. He had not changed his clothes yet, either.

"Multiple intelligence sources are confirming troop transports from Ypres to Lens. The British Army will not alter its strategy based on a single contradictory report. Not even from Moonshadow."

His use of the Secret Service Bureau codename for her father's mysterious source clicked something into place.

"You didn't tell them who she is," she stated.

"I gave my word," Kazi replied deliberately.

"And we all know what that is worth," Lily snapped back.

Strangford leaned against the wall, his arms crossed.

"They aren't allocating reinforcements," he said.

"No," Kazi confirmed flatly. "They are not."

Her anger at the man faded, blown away by the shock.

"But they must. Surely they understand what they are facing. Tell me that you told them—"

"I told them," Kazi cut in, his own anger flashing in his gold-flecked eyes. "I told them exactly what they are up against. Not just Hume. An attaché from Haig's office was there, and they sent a coded wire back to GHQ and to my superiors in London. Army Intelligence is to conduct a second review of the train-watching reports for any previously overlooked evidence in support of Moonshadow's intelligence, but no change in strategy is to be undertaken at this time."

"They will not take the word of a single third-party intelligence source against the reports of their entire network," Strangford filled in quietly. "Not even one who has proved her value over and over again."

"They will not." Kazi looked up at them. "I tried to communicate the urgency of the situation. They accept that the German serum is capable of increasing strength and pain resistance. They have been working on drugs with an aim towards such an effect themselves, but they cannot really conceive …"

He trailed off. He knew that in Lily and Strangford, he was looking at two other things the British Army would find difficult to comprehend.

"They will not act on it until something of it all has been independently confirmed," he finished.

Strangford pushed away from the wall.

"To doubt their sources is to doubt their own capability as handlers," he said. "And men do not rise to the upper echelons of command by doubting themselves."

"Nor are there any reserves to deploy." Kazi added. "To reinforce the line at Mont Noir, they would have to remove men from somewhere else. No matter what we do, we leave ourselves vulnerable."

"And so, of course, they choose caution," Strangford concluded grimly.

"But they are wrong," Lily burst out, her hands clenched.

"They are," Kazi agreed.

The bleakness in his expression caught her off guard. It felt final. They had risked everything to bring the truth about the Wulfstruppen back. It had been passed to the highest levels of command … and it didn't matter.

Because it was magic. Because it came from a player in their game that they did not control. Because it contradicted their own self-images as men of competence and power.

Twenty Wulfstruppen would slam into an overextended piece of the front manned by exhausted men who had been harried by German advances for a month. They would tear the British line apart, and the massed force of the German reinforcements would pour through it.

Britain would be cut off from her allies in France. The Germans would hold them apart and pick them off, one after the other, until there was nothing left.

"I will keep trying to make them understand the urgency." Kazi concluded, rising.

Lily was surprised to realize that she believed him ... not that it made up for what he had done.

"It won't end at Mont Noir. Thanks to you."

Kazi stiffened.

"We are not the aggressors. We are defending ourselves against a technology that they have created."

"Do you honestly believe that is where it will end? With defense?"

"Yes!" Kazi shouted back. "Because that is the difference between us and them. We didn't invade Belgium. We didn't create chlorine gas and unleash it on a bunch of unsuspecting boys so that they could die like gasping fish."

Lily thought of Joseph Hartwell as she faced him across the peak of a snow-covered rooftop. Of Lord Bexley. Of the men who had turned Zhao Min into what she now was.

"I think, Inspector, that I have had a different experience of the honor of Britain's finest than you have."

"It is also conceivable that the Germans could replicate the serum again from the blood of those already transformed by it," Strangford noted. "I cannot say for certain. I am not a scientist. But this curse might be well past containment."

Lily thought of what that could mean. Armies of monsters unleashed upon each other and everything that stood between. The driving need for more, until control was lost. Until there was nothing else left.

Images from her visions flashed across her mind, making the horror real.

Her rage spluttered, strangled by a growing sense of helplessness.

"When you are debriefed, you should attribute any intelligence that might otherwise be ... difficult to explain to Moonshadow," Kazi ordered.

"You're talking about us," Lily clarified flatly. "Strangford and I. What we can do."

"Yes," Kazi returned, unflinching. "It is well known that Moonshadow's continued work for the Allies depends upon the

352

security of her anonymity. Hume will know that he cannot push you too hard on any matters relating to that source. However much his superiors might be unwilling to take her intelligence at face value when it comes to recent troop movements, they will not want to risk losing the source altogether."

"What about Sam?" Strangford asked.

"He was declared missing in action. I have explained his involvement. RAF headquarters has been wired. He should rejoin his unit at the earliest possible opportunity."

"I shall be sure to tell him that as soon as I am no longer being held prisoner," Lily retorted.

Kazi's shoulders dropped.

"I'm sorry."

It sounded like he meant it.

"I have assured Captain Hume your discretion can be relied upon. Lord Strangford's record clearly speaks to it, but he is determined to act on the side of caution until he can assess you both himself."

"And when will that be?" Strangford asked.

"Tomorrow. He has been called away on urgent business for the rest of the day."

"Seeing that his prize is safely on its way to Porton Down?" Lily snarled.

"More than likely." Kazi replied, meeting her gaze. "Is there anything else you need?"

"Not from you." Lily's words were edged with ice.

There was a brief hesitation before Kazi nodded.

"Then I will check on you again in the morning." He reached for the hatch in the floor.

The words spilled out of her, propelled by the maelstrom raging inside—by hurt and anger and fear.

"You have made a grave mistake, but I cannot wish you will ever realize it. It will be that much worse for all of us should the rotten potential of this come to pass."

Her words echoed off the ancient stones of the tower. Then Kazi was gone.

Lily paced the room. The sun had lowered in the west, slipping under the cover of the clouds and limning the ships that lined the harbor with a hint of crimson.

"What now?" she asked dully.

She could hear Strangford sigh behind her.

"Hume deserting us here is likely intentional. He knows I am a peer and an intelligence officer in my own right. He will expect that, given a bit of time to cool down, I will take the reasonable point of view."

"And what is the reasonable point of view?" Lily demanded, unable to keep the snide note from her voice.

"Reasonable as he perceives it," Strangford patiently corrected her.

"Leave off about Porton Down, agree to keep what we know confidential, and go back to our regular duties in service to the crown," Lily filled in for him.

He nodded.

The notion filled her with panic. It felt like the room was turning grayer around her.

"Is that what you think we should do?"

"It would be the safest course of action."

She looked at him warily.

"That's not what I asked you."

"I don't know, Lily." he admitted, leaning against the wall and looking up at the ceiling as though it might offer an answer.

She turned back to the harbor.

"Those men are back on the mole again."

The words fell automatically from her lips. She felt distant, halfway to somewhere else. The close-packed bodies covered the astonishing length of the breakwater. They were still as ghosts waiting for a call to eternity.

"They aren't there, Lily." Strangford said carefully from beside her. "Not yet."

She blinked. The men vanished. The sense of urgency remained. Lily searched for the cause of it.

"This doesn't feel right."

"What doesn't?" Strangford asked.

"Just … waiting here like this."

He watched her thoughtfully.

"If we stay here until Hume comes back, answer his questions—
even admit your disapproval of any British investigation of the serum
but assure him that we are content to let our part in this be done—
then we will be sent home. Any record of our service that exists will
almost certainly note that it was executed honorably. We will be done
with this, all of it."

She could almost smell the peat fires at Allerhope, hear the wind
whipping outside the glass as the voices of those she loved murmured
nearby.

The scent of pine. Strangford's hair under her fingers.

The words rang oddly against her ears. *Done with this.*

"Or we could continue to press the case in London if that was
what we felt we must do," he continued.

"Wednesday." Lily said. It sounded like a curse. "That's when they
are coming. The day after tomorrow. By the time we got to London, it
would be too late to do anything about it. If we stay here, we're letting
Hume decide everything that matters." She raised her eyes to his face,
feeling bleak. "Is that right?"

Strangford brushed his gloved thumb across her cheek. His smile
was tired and sad.

"I don't know the answer to that."

Lily's throat felt dry. She forced out the words, knowing that holding them back would only taste of regret.

"I think we need to go."

Strangford's hand dropped.

"We could likely manage it," he said. "This place clearly isn't typically used to house prisoners. They won't have the routines for it, the
protocols. But it would take a fight, and it would almost certainly
look like treason. I am not sure it would not *be* treason. And there
would be other risks."

She did not have to guess at what he meant. Her hand slipped to
her abdomen.

Returning to England seemed like the obvious way to protect
both Strangford and the life that was growing inside of her . . . if she
assumed that the threats on the continent could never make their
way across the channel.

Lily knew that wasn't true. The flashes of vision that had been whispering to her these last weeks spoke to it in a way she could not deny. No matter how much she wanted to.

England wasn't safe, not for any of them. If the future rolled forward unimpeded, any haven they found there could only be temporary, a sliver of borrowed time.

"If we do it, what then?" she pressed.

"We find Sam. Go after the serum, or to your father. Churchill. The king himself, if that's what it takes to find someone who will listen. We'll find a way, Lily."

She tried to let his words reassure her, but the notion of what they were contemplating still made her queasy.

"But how would we get out?" she demanded a bit desperately.

"The stairs, I presume," he replied. "It is rather less abrupt than the window."

She laughed. It hurt and felt dangerously close to crying.

"Alright, then," she said. "The stairs."

TWENTY-FOUR

$\mathscr{I}$T DID NOT REQUIRE Lily's power to determine the right moment to move. Strangford managed it with his ear pressed to the wooden panel in the floor.

"Cigarette smoke," he whispered up to her. "Means at least one hand is occupied."

Lily nodded, readying herself. Her own hands felt awkwardly empty.

Strangford tossed open the hatch and started down, straight-backed in his Navy uniform as though he belonged there.

"Oy." the guard protested, fumbling with his smoke and reaching for the rifle slung over his shoulder. "You're not supposed to—"

The rest of his protest was cut short by Strangford's blow to his chest.

He dropped to his knees, gasping. Strangford twisted him into a hold, slipping the rifle clear and tossing it to Lily, who leveled it at the guard.

"Best keep quiet," Strangford assured him. "And sorry about the braces."

"What about my braces?" the man demanded.

He was answered when Strangford plucked the trench knife from the man's belt, flipped up the back of his coat, and neatly sliced through the suspenders holding up his trousers.

"Your hands, please," he ordered courteously.

With a dejected glance at Lily and the rifle, the soldier complied.

Strangford picked up his Navy officer's cap from where it had fallen on the steps and set it neatly back on his head.

They left the man gagged and tied on the landing. A glance around the corner at the bottom of the stairs revealed the storage room to be empty.

Lily could hear a laugh from the officer's lounge on the far side. Strangford pressed himself beside the door and carefully cracked it open, peering through. He flashed a signal back to Lily with his gloved hand.

Three.

Lily was still holding the rifle, but if she shot it, the sound would certainly be audible to anyone outside. It could very well raise an alarm at the tent next door where an entire division of soldiers was gathered. The gun was essentially useless, and it would take only one reasonably clever fellow on the other side to realize that and call any bluff they tried to make with it.

Strangford was a capable fighter when unarmed, but not skilled enough to overcome those odds—especially when any one of the men inside the room could have a service pistol with him.

If they were to stand a chance, Lily needed a weapon she could actually use.

The tumble of museum pieces in the corner tugged at her.

She walked over to them. Her hand settled on the haft of the halberd, drawn there by a whispering impulse. Setting down the rifle, she explored the balance of the weapon in her hand. The weight was strange, and yet something in the texture was familiar. The wood was worn smooth by age, but solid. There was no way it could be in such condition if it were centuries old. It had to be a replica, but it had clearly been made by someone with an eye to authenticity.

She ran a finger across the blade, feeling the edge catch against the ridges of her skin.

It was sharp. She gave the weapon an experimental swing.

Something inside of her sang in response, a sense of rightness crashing over her like cymbals in an orchestra. The feeling of it sparked a familiar hunger, her power sliding across her skin like smoke.

Strangford's gaze moved from the weapon to the look that must have blazed from her eyes. His brow furrowed with worry, and Lily's rush crashed against an abrupt and chilling guilt.

She forced a deep and unsteady breath. She just had to let that fluid and violent foresight in enough to disable the threat—and no more. It was a simple matter of balance.

She could do this.

Strangford waited for her to approach, his hand on the door. At her nod, he pushed it open.

Two lieutenants and a captain were gathered around the table. They looked up in surprise as Strangford stepped inside, one of them holding a cup of tea halfway to his lips.

"Hold on, you're supposed to be upstairs," the captain protested.

Strangford raised his hands, smiling as he took a step to the side, moving further into the room. The move revealed Lily on the threshold, the medieval weapon in her grip. A ginger-haired lieutenant at the table frowned at the sight of it, surprised by the incongruous appearance of the antique.

"Any chance you'd be willing to overlook that?" Strangford asked.

"Michaels, O'Donnell!" the captain barked.

The two lieutenants rose from their chairs, quickly enough that one of the wooden seats tumbled to the floor.

Strangford darted to the one nearest him, a dark-haired officer with a prominent nose. With a twist of his hand and a well-placed foot, he tripped the man into the wall.

Lily looked to the ginger-haired lieutenant.

Just enough to win, she told herself.

Win, her power echoed darkly from within her. *Win*.

The man was about to grab for her.

She moved with the shaft end of the halberd, intentionally keeping the blade away as she twisted the wood to deflect his grip.

Her opponent reached for the trench knife at his belt.

Fire raced down her arms, turning her blood to steam as the power flared to sharper life.

When the halberd moved again, it felt like grace—anticipating, ready. A sharp swipe knocked the blade from his hand. The backswing took him across the cheek. The impact made a sound like a cricket bat.

Behind her, the captain stumbled to his feet. He was tall, his face distinguished by a thick gray mustache. Unlike his comrades, he was wearing his sidearm ... and he was about to reach for it.

Lily's world narrowed, time slowing to a crawl as the threat that lived inside of her bloomed.

Win.

The right path blazed before her, shining like a ribbon of gold.

Lily snapped the haft of her weapon into a green glass bottle on the table. It exploded towards the captain, who raised his hands to cover his face, screaming a curse.

There was no need to pause, to think of what came next. She simply knew.

Lily whipped the halberd around again at the ginger lieutenant, snapping it against his knee. He screamed as it buckled, dropping him to the ground.

She flipped the table with a powerful kick of her motorcycle boot as the captain pulled a shard of glass from his cheek with a shaking hand. The other fumbled with the clasp of the holster on his belt.

He should have ignored the glass and used both hands. The mistake broadened her way, making it easy.

She whipped the blunt end of the halberd at his temple, the blow swift enough to stun him. The weapon flipped in her grasp, a movement that felt as natural as breathing. She pressed the pike against his throat.

The blade dented the soft flesh above his Adam's apple. He went still, a line of blood curving down the side of his face. More glass protruded from his sleeve where he had used it to protect his eyes.

What came next flowed over her, rich and warm. The blade was an extension of her being, the foresight a razor that amputated any possible defense as lives gave way to her like wheat to a reaper's blade.

The thrust. The soft resistance of boneless flesh. The blood pouring onto her hands, spilling across the front of his uniform.

British khaki. British blood.

Strangford was there, the confiscated sidearm in his hand. The other held her arm. He was speaking to her. How long had he been speaking?

"Enough, Lily. That's enough."

Someone was pounding on the door to the storage room. It had to be the dark-haired lieutenant, whom Strangford must have forced from the room. A chair was braced against the knob, holding him out for a little while.

His ginger companion—whom Lily could now see could not be more than twenty—clutched at his leg, which was bent at the knee at an unnatural angle. He was sobbing quietly. His skin was split where the staff had met his cheek.

Her arms ached to press her blade home. She wrested back the urge with force.

Her mind burned with the image of the Wulfstruppen unteroffizier. With the knowledge of what was coming for Mont Noir.

"You have no idea what you are up against," she choked out.

"You're a monster," the captain spat back.

Blood splattered the wall. Someone was crying behind her.

Strangford watched her, his expression pleading and edged with fear.

She stumbled back, fighting the need to vomit.

"Your bootlaces, please," Strangford ordered, shifting his attention to the captain with a cold and controlled authority.

The man's eyes moved from Strangford's pistol to the halberd Lily still held in her hands. She wondered if he could see they were shaking.

There was soup on the floor, mingling with the foam of the shattered bottle of beer.

Something inside of her threatened to unravel.

"Come along, Lily." Strangford urged her.

He had tied the captain. The other lieutenant was still pounding on the far door.

She led him lead her out.

The telegraph room was empty, the woman they had seen there earlier departed for the day. Strangford shut the door to the officer's lounge, muffling the sound of the sobs from the man whose leg Lily had broken.

"We'll try this straight." He kept his voice low, speaking quickly. "The men at the doors will be there to keep people out, not the other way around. We just have to hope Hume didn't think to tell them to watch for us, and I doubt he would have anticipated ... "

"Me," Lily filled in when his words trailed off.

Strangford looked at the halberd.

The sense of possessiveness that rose in her was a force. Her hand tightened on the haft hard enough to show the whites of her knuckles.

"*No*," she said.

The word felt like a threat.

A red scarf hung from a coat rack by the desk. Strangford tugged it free and offered it to her.

"Put this on."

"Why." she managed, her voice thin as a thread.

"To cover the blood," he replied.

She took it, swinging it around her neck with a shaking hand, letting the ends fall down across her shirt.

"Just . . . keep it low," Strangford ordered, eye flashing to the weapon she clutched like a lifeline.

He opened the door.

They stepped out into the evening, the sun streaking the low clouds with splashes of pink and gold. A small flock of sparrows scattered from under their boots. A few of the birds swooped off over the town, quick black shadows fluttering against the sunset-streaked sky.

The two guards outside looked at them, backs straight.

"As you were, gentlemen," Strangford said, straightening his cap and quickly pulling the door shut behind him.

Lily held her breath. The tent to her left hummed with the cheerful noise of a full battalion of soldiers cracking jokes and eating supper. They were paying no attention to what was happening at the building beside them.

That would likely change if were Lily to stab someone.

The guard to her left glanced at the insignia on Strangford's borrowed uniform.

"Sir," he said, giving him a brief nod.

With his hand on her elbow, Strangford steered her away.

A few privates from the battalion were clustered by a lamppost, trading rations. One of them elbowed another, nodding to Lily's halberd as she passed. She heard a snigger.

"Don't look back," Strangford warned under his breath.

She should have left the weapon behind. It would only make them more conspicuous.

She couldn't bear to. The need for it was primitive, laced through with something deeper.

Strangford guided her around a corner and the smell of cigarettes and stew faded.

"Where are we going?" she demanded.

"I don't know," he replied, his voice thin with tension.

Lily's heart sank as she wondered how much of it was her fault.

"We have to find cover," he added, glancing around.

A few more birds flew overhead—sparrows, Lily realized. They swept down to land in the street, far closer to Lily's boots than she would have expected.

One of them hopped nearer, chirping. Black eyes looked up at her curiously.

A suspicion slowly began to dawn.

She took a step forward. The bird hopped back but did not fly. It ruffled its feathers, tweeting again.

"We need to follow them."

As though sensing the change in Lily's tone, the cluster of sparrows rose again, fluttering to the corner. They stopped, perching there and waiting.

Lily moved after them, Strangford falling into step behind her.

Raised voices echoed to her softly from somewhere in the distance, and she knew that the injured officers in the lounge must have broken out. A search would soon be raised for them. Thankfully, there weren't many people out on the quiet, narrow way they walked.

They followed the sparrows through a maze of streets until they reached the glittering waters of a canal. The birds swept into one of the houses that lined it. Once fine, it had been struck by a bomb at some point in the past. It was empty, windows broken, the roof nothing but struts exposed to the sky.

Inside, wallpaper peeled from the plaster, some of it scorched with the mark of an old fire. Broken glass crunched under Lily's boots.

They found Sam in what had once been a dining room, sitting on top of a scarred, stained table shoved up against one of the walls. He wore his black overcoat and appeared to have generally dried off from his swim to shore.

He had acquired a fresh pack of cigarettes somewhere. He smoked one as the sparrows hopped into place around him, one of them perching on his knee. In the gloom, the shadow of his beard gave him a rough, dangerous air.

"You took your time about it," he said in greeting.

His quick, assessing gaze stopped on Lily's halberd.

"That's new."

Lily brought it closer, clinging to it. The movement raised the blade into the remaining light spilling through the windows.

"You did it again, didn't you?" Sam said.

She let the wall take her weight, not quite trusting to her knees anymore, as the despair washed over her.

"I could have killed them. I could have killed every one of them. I wanted to." The words spilled out of her as she slid to the ground, then raised her eyes to where Strangford stood. "How can you stand to touch me?"

Behind Strangford's shoulder, Sam's face fell, his mask dropping away. The sympathy in his eyes made her ache.

Strangford knelt. He raised a gloved hand to her face, the familiar texture of the leather caressing her cheek.

"You are the one thing in this world that will always be safe to me."

The words were a brand. Lily felt them burn against her skin, claiming her. She broke against it, all that she had been holding back spilling loose—the fear, the self-loathing, the guilt.

He caught her, his arms slipping around her back as he pulled her against him.

"I could have killed them," she moaned again, her face against his shoulder.

"But you didn't," he replied, the rumble of his voice tangible where her hand met his chest.

The question fell out of her—the one she had been too terrified to ask.

"Am I one of them?" she demanded. "Am I a . . . a monster, like that thing at Vianden ..."

"No."

"How can you know that?"

There was a shadow in his gaze, one that spoke of pain and fear.

"You don't feel like they do."

She closed her eyes, understanding too well how he had come by that knowledge.

"Then what am I?"

It was Sam who answered from where he leaned against the ruined wall, his black coat a deeper patch of gloom.

"You can fight. And you can see the future. What you are is dangerous."

"What if part of me wants it?" she challenged.

"Why shouldn't you?" he shot back. "Ain't nothing noble in being helpless."

"And is it worth it?" she seethed, the darkness flaring up in her at his challenge. "All the death it takes to survive?"

Sam flinched.

They were forced to silence as an automobile drove slowly past, the headlamps briefly illuminating the mildew that stained the walls.

Lily knew better than to try to take it back. She closed her eyes. Like the shattered shell of a building that surrounded them, the war hollowed everything out, leaving rubble behind. It was turning all of them into monsters.

"Where's your inspector?" Sam asked.

"With his handlers, I suspect," Lily replied. "Most likely telling them everything he knows about the berserker serum he smuggled back with him."

"What?"

Sam's voice was flat with shock.

"Inspector Kazi was less than forthcoming about the full extent of his mission," Strangford said.

His words from the starlit garden at Vianden drifted back to her. *Please, Lady Strangford. I am not a threat to you.*

She had believed him. No—more than that. She had known he meant it. How could something be both true and a lie at the same time?

Sam was a lean wing of shadow against the gloom of the ruin.

"How bad could that get?" he demanded.

365

In another gathering, it would be an invitation for speculation. Here, with Lily, it was something else.

"Do you really want to know?" she asked.

"I think perhaps we need to," Strangford said. "If we're going to decide where we go from here."

Rebellion surged in her.

"We should go back to England. All of us. Hide away someplace quiet. Somewhere safe."

"And if we do?" Strangford prompted.

Lily didn't want to answer, but something in her responded to the question as though compelled by it. Knowledge welled up, spilling forth so effortlessly that Lily knew it had all the weight of plausibility behind it.

A humble door flying open to khaki uniforms. The sound of her father's voice shouting in a gray stone hallway.

Sam standing before a blood-spattered wall, gazing dark defiance at a line of rifle barrels.

A cacophony of black beaks. Of wings.

The gray hulls of battleships lurking along British sand. The snap of a foreign flag in the wind.

Things spun further. Faster.

People huddle in dank rooms from the rumble of heavy engines, of boots striking pavement.

After nightfall, something darker. Faster. Beasts tear through alleys, clashing in sprays of blood.

Smoking piles of the dead. Cities crumbling. Flags nothing more than tatters.

And finally the forest, stinking of rotting meat. The trees that go on forever.

The monsters that hunt in them.

Lily doubled over, only the strength of Strangford's arm keeping her from the ground. Her throat was scraped raw by bile.

"That bad," Sam noted thinly.

He handed her a canteen, undoubtedly stolen. She washed out her mouth, then took a sip. Her heart finally slowed so that she no longer felt as though it were about to jump out of her chest.

"So we must go after it," Strangford determined grimly.

"No," Lily said, the response flaring up in her.

Only once she had voiced it did she sense what had driven it—the familiar, uncomfortable hum of the onmyōdō.

Lily took a breath, forcing herself to face it. She had seen what was coming, the future that was all but paved before them unless something changed it.

If they wanted to stop it, they needed to know what lever must be pressed—what moment in the present carried the potential for a different outcome, if only someone could flip the switch.

Lily could find it.

The image of Evangeline Ash's mural rose into her mind—the portrait that Lily had rejected with every fiber of her being. The woman of flames, daughter of a wounded king, who held the key to unlock the myriad doors of the future.

If she had been made at all—if she were not a mere accident—then it was for precisely this.

But what would it cost her?

The onmyōdō was concerned with something larger than her own well-being or that of the people she loved. Every time it had spoken to her before, it had done so to move events on a massive scale.

She could still hear the howls of the future echoing inside her mind.

"I can see it." She lifted her eyes to her lover, then her friend, as the fear swelled up inside of her. "Should I see it?"

Strangford held her hand.

"You are the only one who can answer that."

Lily pushed up from the floor, the accumulated debris of years of neglect crunching under her boots. She moved past both Strangford and Sam, walking through the broken wall of the house into a small, overgrown patio.

Grass slipped up through the cracked stones. Buildings rose around her, their stones salt-worn with a century of ocean wind. Shutters and blackout curtains were pulled tight against the encroaching night with its threat of raids. It was as private as a tomb.

She sat down in the center of it. A breeze rustled the ivy that covered the wall. The cracked-open side of the bombed house felt like the Gothic arch of a cathedral and was just as quiet.

A few of Sam's sparrows settled around her, heads cocked with curiosity. Lily ignored them, turning her focus inward. She steeled herself against what reopening the door to the future would entail— and plunged into it.

A spray of blood against stone. The rusted corpse of a tank. A scream of animal fear.

She sharpens her will, wielding it like a blade.

Find a way out. Show me how to stop it.

Possibility spills out from where she sits—myriad paths. Myriad outcomes. She can sense the ones with the weight of probability behind them, the implacable momentum of the present like a stone against her chest.

She pushes against it, honing into her will. The future thrusts back.

Blade. Fire. Conquest.

Ruin. Blood. Decay.

The doors spin past her, all opening into the same horror. Lily resists, pressing more of her substance into a single, needle-focused thought.

Show me how to stop it.

Possibility shudders. Something sparks in the periphery of her awareness—whipping threads of golden light bleeding through the violence.

A scent of brine. The soft rush of endless waves. A black croak against a twilight sky . . . and then she is through it, spilling into somewhere else.

Her boots sink ankle-deep in mud. A roar like a rising tide resolves itself into the voices of a hundred men screaming their determination as they charge.

The sleek, silver glide of a blade.

A passing veil of midnight feathers. Blood sticky on her hands.

Something that is not thunder cracks across the sky as the ground quakes beneath her feet.

Then comes the dark.

The stones of the overgrown patio were cool beneath her cheek. Lily pressed herself up from them to see Strangford crouched in front of her, waiting.

Sam had hopped onto a jagged edge of the broken wall. He perched there with his hands stuffed into the pockets of his coat.

The answer she had sought fell from her lips, softly vibrating with certainty.

"We need to go to Mont Noir."

Reality crashed in.

Horror stole her voice at the implication. She snapped her eyes to Strangford, understanding what she had just done. Where she was taking them.

The front. The war.

The moment when she risked losing him forever.

He knew it. The truth of that was etched into the lines of his face. He turned to Sam.

"You don't have to do this," he said.

"He does," Lily countered, the words snapping out before thought.

They sparked another well of horror. She looked up at Sam, shattered by the knowing even as the rest of it forced its way out of her.

"We need him."

Sam didn't reply, sliding from his perch to drop to the ground. His eyes were dark.

She whirled back to Strangford. Every part of her wanted him to tell she was wrong. Of course they weren't going to the front—to the very place on the line where a platoon of monsters was set to attack, creatures that had already slaughtered every man on the Stelvio Pass.

Strangford smiled sadly.

"I suppose it's not worth asking whether there's still a way for us to save the world if we go to Brighton instead."

Lily covered her mouth to stop a laugh from coming out. She was too afraid it would twist into a sob and that she wouldn't be able to stop.

"And at Mont Noir, what exactly are we supposed to do?" Sam cut in.

Lily climbed to her feet, Strangford steadying her. She clung to his arm, reeling from the possibility—the terrible likelihood—that she was about to lose him. She faced Sam, refusing to flinch even as what she was saying made her want to scream.

"Kill them," she replied, the words rasping from her throat like something forced through sandpaper. "Kill them all."

The garden was silent save for the breeze rustling the leaves of the ivy. Lily wanted to be wrong. She wanted to scream that of course it could not be the right path. There had to be another way. Or perhaps the future they sought to escape was less terrible than she feared.

All of which she knew was a lie.

"No," she said, stumbling back. "No no no ..."

Her hands were clenched, shaking. The rage was a tumult, crashing against the onmyōdō—against whatever forces in the universe had brought her to this.

The man she loved. Her best friend. The life that glowed silently inside of her.

She was marching all of it into Hell.

"Lily ..." Strangford began, reaching for her.

She raised her hands, warding him off. She could not bear for him to touch her—not now, not as the fury roiled inside of her, threatening to pull her part.

He stopped, even though his face nakedly showed how badly he wanted to go to her.

Sam watched from the shadows, his expression one of grim understanding.

Lily pressed her palms to her eyes as though the pressure could drive away what she had seen—what she knew.

"I didn't *ask for this.*"

The words were more than mere sound. They were bone-deep, soaked through with all of it—all the pain. All the suffering. All the helplessness in the face of foreseen horror. Discovering belonging only to have it torn away. The further curse of her onmyōdō and all the power it promised crushing her with a yet deeper burden.

She had the power to change the future—and to discover the sacrifice it required of her.

The courtyard was silent, the two men watching her through the gloom.

"I hate it." The confession spilled from her with all the force of the truth. "I hate it so much ..."

Her knees were giving way before she realized it, but Strangford was already there. His gloved hands slipped under her arms, taking her weight and softening their mutual collapse to the ground. She fell against him as he lowered to his knees, holding her to his chest, the familiar smell of him present even through the borrowed uniform.

Worn black leather softly brushed the hair from her cheek, a feeling utterly and irreplaceably Strangford.

She could not lose this. And to face those men turned monsters—not just one of them but a score, with the fate of the war and so much of what was most precious to her in the world hanging in the balance...

Simply to survive it would require every fragment of that most terrible facet of her khárisma, the mark of violence she carried in her soul. She would have to give herself over to it completely.

What would be left of her in the end if she let that in? What would it mean she had become?

What else would it cost her?

She twisted her fingers in the dark blue wool of his uniform, the desperation threatening to choke her.

"I can't lose you," she pleaded.

Sam's voice cracked through the silence.

"Maybe you won't."

The words were cold.

Strangford's hands went still against her skin. Lily pulled her cheek from his shoulder, looking over to where Sam stood, his face a pale oval against the charcoal-shadowed landscape of the courtyard.

"What he's got. It's worth a life—for a day. Longer than that, and there'd be a price." His eyes flashed at them like dark stars. "One you'd not like to pay."

He turned, walking into the black mouth of the ruined house, leaving behind only the chill that crept into her skin through the stones.

"He's talking about the ravens," Strangford said slowly, still holding her.

Lily felt each beat of her heart like a slow, distant drum. She remembered that terrible day at the Ludgate Viaduct when Strangford took the cold metal threat of the mortar from her hand and claimed it for himself. The sight of his crumpled form bleeding onto the stones as lazy black wings circled overhead.

There's some consider that a sacrifice.

She carefully extricated herself from the gentle prison of his embrace, putting a distance between them that she would need if she was to keep from going mad during this conversation.

"He told me you have a boon," she replied, each word like something sculpted out of stone. "After Blackfriars."

She did not need to remind him of the moment. The dark patch on his scarred face was sign enough of what it had cost him.

Strangford rose, moving with the same subtle grace that underlay everything he did. He stepped away from her, looking down.

"I knew there was something. Something...complicated."

The tenor of his voice was a low bell that brushed against her skin. Lily put her arms around herself and shivered.

"Something you did not wish to talk about," he finished.

"It means you can live," she said.

Sam's reminder should have been a relief. Lily ought to have felt something like hope. Instead, she was consumed by a bone-deep dread.

She could see Sam's chest again in her mind, his golden skin peppered with the indelible marks of so many near-misses . . . so much terribly purchased luck.

Lily pushed herself to her feet as well, feeling the wind dance with the loosened tendrils of her hair.

"It's only for a day. You must wait until we're there to use it."

She forced her voice to sound reasonable, certain. What she really felt was something like a scream that continued to go on inside of her, constantly finding more horror to fuel it.

Strangford's gloved hands tensed at his sides.

"Lily ..."

She was afraid to have the rest of this conversation. It could only lead to a place she couldn't bear to face—not now. Not if they were going to go through with this.

And they had to go through with this.

"Come on," she cut in briskly before he could say anything more. "Let's fetch Sam. We'll need transportation."

She did not give him time to protest. There was nothing he could do but follow her.

TWENTY-FIVE

Ten o'clock that night
Outside Dunkirk

$\mathcal{S}$AM LED THEM TO A cavalry depot. It was hastily constructed out of the remnants of an old football pitch, likely rigged up after more permanent accommodations were overrun by the German advance. The old goal net hung in ragged tatters. The grass was overgrown in places and peppered with weeds. The adjacent building, formerly the club headquarters, had been abandoned for years and only haphazardly rehabilitated.

It was easy enough to pick their way through the darkness and up to the wire-fenced paddock. At a few whispers and strokes from Sam, the horses turned into willing accomplices in their own theft.

They led the beasts out into the countryside, a safe distance from any Army outpost, before mounting. The animals were bridled but otherwise bare. Tack had been easy enough for Sam to steal, but saddles would have been too great a risk.

There should have been a bit of joy in it for Strangford. He had been born to horses at Allerhope and rarely had the opportunity to ride any longer.

Instead, he looked solemn and heavy.

Lily felt certain she was the reason. She wanted to take it back, but it would be a lie. All three of them were critical, somehow, to this imminent point of balance between possible futures. Nor would this be a simple pivot to shift. It was not the light impulse of a relocated vase that awaited them.

Changing this one would be hard.

She reminded herself forcibly that both Sam and Strangford would be protected, so long as he called on his own bargain with the birds and whatever force they represented—that dark and uncanny arbitration of life and death, of luck and ill chance.

She could almost feel the whisper of it breathing down her neck.

As for that other life …

The notion of it threatened a blind and bottomless panic. There was no way to separate the child's fate from her own.

Her horse startled, dancing back a step. Suddenly Strangford was there, working a magic on the animal born not of preternatural skill but of practice and experience. The brown mare calmed with a final toss of her head, snorting into his palm. Strangford gently took hold of the reins and dropped to a knee, turning his thigh into a step. He offered Lily his free hand.

"You're riding bareback," he instructed her patiently. "It will be different from what you're used to. You'll want to hold her with your thighs and calves, but don't—she'll take it as a sign to run. Just find your balance."

Lily nodded, firmly setting aside her nerves. Both Sam and Strangford had told her horses were good at picking up on fear.

She stepped onto Strangford's leg and swung onto the mare. She fought back another burst of unease as the animal shifted beneath her, the feeling so different beneath her thighs than riding in a saddle.

The halberd rested across her lap. Lily had hesitated before plucking it from the interior of the ruined house. The weapon had already caused more damage than she liked to think of. It was brutal, but she needed something to fight with, and the halberd felt somehow . . . familiar. Perhaps the dynamics of wielding it were near enough to those of her walking stick.

Strangford handed her the reins. Lily waited as he and Sam mounted, then they set off through the darkness, the road ahead illuminated only by a thin sliver of the moon.

~

They stopped for the night in an abandoned house outside Bergues. There were many like it in the area. The families had fled, either recently in the face of the advance or years before. It had been broken into, whatever was left behind rifled or smashed for the seeming pleasure of it, but at least the roof was intact. It had been so long since Lily had enjoyed a decent bed, she had grown accustomed to sleeping on the floor.

The next morning, she left the halberd with Strangford and ventured into Bergues with Sam, borrowing his hat to cover her hair as he donned his tinted glasses.

Well-built houses lined the streets, many of them wrecked, their roofs exposed like jagged scars. The town had clearly been a target for repeated bombardment. With their tidy gables and neat back gardens, those houses that remained occupied sat cheek-by-jowl with the ruins.

She found the telephone office and named the destination for her call. The woman clerking the desk raised her eyebrow but picked up her handset and chatted to the operator in rapid French.

It took a few minutes, but finally, the clerk pointed Lily to the booth in the corner.

She picked up the receiver and set it to her ear.

"What's that? Someone there, then?"

A familiar voice crackled through the line, chopped by the intermittent static of a bad connection.

"George?" Lily asked.

"What—that you, Sis?" The line crackled. "... alright then?"

"George, listen." She plunged in, knowing that at any moment the call could fail, praying he could hear her. "I don't know if there's anything to be done about it, but there's to be an attack tomorrow morning. At Mont Noir, near Kemmelberg. I can't ... tell you how I know."

She was conscious of the clerk behind her and of whomever else might be listening on the line somewhere along the miles of connections that had gotten her through to her brother.

"And I know it goes against what ... other sources must be saying, but ... it's real. And it's going to be bad. Please, George."

She was embarrassed to realize her voice was breaking. Sam

377

glanced over at her from where he stood by a rack of magazines.

The line was all static, popping and hissing. She wondered if anything she had said was getting through.

It had been a hope thrown into darkness anyway. She should not be shocked if it failed.

The line crackled.

"Can't ... not sure I ..."

Despair threatened to rise up. She swallowed it, forcing herself to stay calm. Screaming into the handset would do nothing to improve the connection.

"I don't know if you can hear me—if there's anything you can do—I just ..." She swallowed, her voice cracking. "I need help."

There was a sound like a train rushing by, then the thinnest sliver of a voice, tinny and distant.

"... never underestimate ... schedules ..."

With a click, Lily was left with nothing but the soft hiss of silence.

She kept the receiver to her ear, begging for the connection to restore itself. Finally, a voice cut in from the desk.

"Désolée, madame."

Lily set the receiver back on its hook and stepped back. She had done what she could. There was nothing now but to trust the rest to fate.

~

Lorries began to rattle past them around dinnertime. Those going south and east were loaded with crates of food, bullets, medical equipment, and artillery shells. Those returning were empty or carried wounded men.

Despatch riders zipped by on their motorcycles, making Lily yearn for her Triumph. The road itself grew wider and more rutted, choked with mud in places. Planks roughly hewn from new-felled trees had been thrown down over the worst patches, but they still passed a lorry stranded in the muck, the driver and a passing cadre of French soldiers in sky-blue uniforms shoving at its bumper.

It signaled they were nearing their destination, and then abruptly, the front unfolded before them.

The green fields and tree-lined lane gave way to a sprawl of mud and tents, cut through with long rents in the earth like the claws of a great cat had torn at it from the sky.

Muddy, rutted tracks sprawled in every direction. Lorries competed with horse-drawn wagons for passage, woven through by ambulances with their distinctive crosses. Clusters of men lingered around cookfires, stirring enormous kettles of stew and tea. A handful of officers sipped from tin mugs, smoking cigarettes around a folding camp table behind a lorry.

A sprawling cemetery sprouted jagged wooden crosses. The names painted on their surfaces were already weathered from the winters that had passed since this land was last wrested from one side to the other, leaving behind a harvest of tortured ground and the dead.

Mont Noir rose on the far side of it. It was more hill than mountain, sloping up gently from a landscape that had once been farmland. A bit of woodland still crowned the higher reaches, mostly pines, their needles dark against the hazy gray of the sky.

The front line itself would lie just beyond it.

Beside her, Strangford was straight-backed in his uniform, his seat on the horse natural even as her own legs ached. She could almost hear the blood-soaked ground calling for him as though eagerly anticipating closing its jaws around the body of the man she loved.

It would not be that way, she reminded herself. He would use the boon . . . and ravens were never far from a battlefield.

The sight of the three of them on horseback drew a few surprised looks from those who could muster the energy for interest. The soldiers they passed were all ragged. This sector of the line had been harried for a solid month. Many of those here would have been at the nearby city of Bailleul two weeks before when it fell. There would have been no rest since then. There was no one left to relieve them.

As they drew nearer to the hill, the tents fell back, giving away to a pitted landscape of dugouts and trenches that housed the forward encampments.

Many of the excavations were only sketchily fortified. The well-dug and reinforced network of the old front line where the men had crouched through months of the winter now lay beyond German-occupied Bailleul. Efforts had clearly been made to establish a new fallback line, but both supplies and time had been limited.

A force of Chinese laborers was at work digging as they passed. They wore their own uniforms, their faces sun-darkened and muddy from a day's work. They called to each other across the road, their language carrying notes of both tired banter and organized routine.

One of them spotted Sam.

"Xiānsheng! Yǒu xiāngyān ma?" he shouted up.

Sam frowned, then reached into his black coat. He pulled out his half pack of cigarettes and tossed it down to the man who had called to him.

"Xièxiè!" the laborer called with a bob of respect and a grin.

A few of his colleagues turned to him, cheerfully demanding he spread the wealth.

Beyond them, a corps of Army sappers staked out a section of ground with surveying equipment. A cluster of men shoved a massive gun over the road, a few horses pulling from the front. Others threw planks under the great iron wheels as a unit commander and a sergeant from the Engineers shouted orders.

Other great iron beasts of the artillery dotted the sprawling length of the landscape.

They passed a large paddock that held only a single horse, a make-shift mail sorting station . . . and then the road ended in a sprawl of barbed wire at the base of Mont Noir.

The hill loomed larger now that they were close to it. Packed earth expanded into a yard that hugged the slope. Supplies were mounded in piles, a couple of lorries struggling through a three-point turn to reverse course between clusters of irritated horses. A despatch rider astride his motorbike argued with a rifle-bearing sentry. Everything smelled of exhaust and sweat.

Above them on the hill, the black pines trembled in a breeze Lily couldn't feel.

"What's your business?" another sentry demanded, coming up to them as they dismounted.

He frowned at the sight of Sam's tinted glasses. His glance at Lily turned from curious to suspicious as he noted her halberd.

Lily found herself staring at the fellow's shins.

The sliver of pale skin was just visible as he stepped forward.

Under the familiar khaki of a British Army private's jacket, the man wore thick folds of rich blue and green plaid, the fabric falling just shy of where his puttees wrapped up the length of his calves. She realized with a start that this part of the line must be held by one of the Scottish units still granted the historical privilege of wearing kilts into battle.

"I need to speak to the forward CO," Strangford replied.

The kilted sentry's eyes flicked from Strangford's eyepatch to the insignia on his uniform as he measured whether he looked worth the potential bother to his commanding officer.

"Don't see much of that blue around here," the private noted.

"That's bloody 'sir' to you, Steve," Sam snapped from the rear, pulling off his lenses. "Or do you not know brass when it's staring you in the face?"

The sentry straightened at Sam's authoritative tone. Of course, Sam himself was a sergeant, and as a pilot was used to having authority over his entire crew, even the men who technically outranked him.

"Yes, sir. Sorry, sir," the private said, snapping off a salute and straightening up.

"Now, are you going to let him through, or would you like to explain to your CO why you're holding up his comms?" Sam pressed.

"No, sir. I mean—down the Queen's Avenue. Pass the chapel, right at Susie, left down the Mile. Command dugout's in the old farm."

"Thank you, private," Strangford calmly replied. "If you could have someone see to our horses?"

The soldier watched Sam pass with something like awe, as though trying to solve the puzzle of a Chinese fellow in a toff's coat spouting East End English and clearly accustomed to command.

They passed around the barbed wire barrier. A set of muddy stairs led down into the trench.

It was like a portal to another world. The walls of reality narrowed, sliding up to either side as Lily descended until there was nothing but the earth held back with woven wooden branches or rough planks that still smelled of fresh pitch. They rose over Lily's head so that the Mont and the fields around it vanished. There was only the channel in the earth and all that inhabited it.

Men plodded ahead of them, others squeezing by in the opposite direction, boots tromping on the boards underfoot, half of which were rapidly sinking into the mud. Clusters of kilted soldiers tucked themselves into dugouts or corners, smoking cigarettes under mud-darkened faces pinched with exhaustion. Some of them laughed with determined cheer. Others lurked quietly with something more haunted in their expressions. Occasionally they passed gatherings of pale blue uniforms, sporting beards in addition to their mustaches, and chatting in French. The two armies met and intermingled here, more so since the line had been scrambled by retreat.

All of them had already seen a great deal of death.

The Queen's Avenue was a supply trench that wended around the slope of the hill before emerging on the far side of Mont Noir. The angle of their descent briefly offered Lily a startling view of the front line and what lay beyond.

The ground was a moonscape of shell holes. The trenches them-selves were zigzagging wounds in the earth. Between them, the land was scoured bare of everything but stumps, some of them freshly cut, others obviously older. They were remnants of the forest that had stood here before the war swept back and forth across this stretch of land, razing some swathes of it while leaving others intact in an act of seemingly random grace.

Lily tried to imagine what this place must have looked like a few years before. It would have been a landscape of old and quiet beauty. The thought filled her with a surprising sense of grief.

The forward trench cut right through the slaughtered trees. Beyond it lay a hundred yards of emptiness. Nothing grew there, not so much as a patch of grass. Lines of barbed wire framed it, blasted away by artillery in places and then hastily repaired.

From her vantage on the slope, she could make out dark, tattered dots here and there on the stripped and battered ground—bodies of the dead which neither side had been able to collect.

The air carried a faint note of rot between the aromas of raw-cut wood and latrines.

A jagged black line was just visible through the haze of drifting smoke and fog on the far side of it all, the wire and fortifications that marked the German side of the front.

It was a picture from a nightmare, a hell that she had dreaded encountering for four years, ever since the cold February night when she had watched Strangford die in it.

"Let's keep going," Strangford said, his hand on her arm.

A hand-painted sign nailed to the planks holding up the wall marked their turning. They followed it, pushing to the side to allow a line of kitchen orderlies through, their packs now empty. The mud rose in places, coming high enough that it sucked at her boots. Lily could feel the cold damp of it at the bottom of her trousers.

Another turn ran them into an obstacle, the way forward blocked by a group of men working on widening the passage. Two stood by watching while a third sawed at a thick root protruding from the earth. Lily looked for the tree it was once attached to and realized there was nothing left of it but a shard of an old stump, just visible overhead.

"Hello, then," one of the younger soldiers greeted them cheerfully. "Who are you lot?"

"He's got a message for your CO," Sam replied with a jerk of his head towards Strangford.

"The captain's in the dugout," an older soldier answered, still hauling at the saw.

"I'll show ye there," the younger one quickly offered, leaping to his feet and flicking out his cigarette. "Sergeant?"

He had clearly decided that the three of them looked more interesting than waiting around in the mud.

"Aye, go on," the older one returned crossly.

Their guide had ruddy brown hair and a thin excuse for a mustache. He was young enough that trying to grow one at all was an act of hubris. A smattering of freckles across his nose complimented his bright greenish-hazel eyes.

"What unit are you with, private?" Strangford asked as the soldier led them down the trench.

"Eighth of the Royal Highlanders." The lad flashed a proud grin. "Coming through!"

A pair of French soldiers pressed against the side of the trench as they trudged around a sharp turn, the way narrow enough that Lily had to turn her shoulders to squeeze past.

"You're Black Watch?" Sam cut in.

"What—did you not know you were mingling with The Ladies from Hell?" the private replied cheerfully.

The nickname rang a bell. Lily vaguely recalled having heard of the regiment—some story about going over the top at Passchendaele to the call of the bagpipes.

Passchendaele had been a slaughter.

She looked up at the high tower of a concrete pillbox. It sat at ground level just ahead of them, reinforced with a barrier of sand-bags. Behind it hung a ragged camouflage net, clearly an effort to make the trench below a less attractive target to any passing German bombers.

"Mary Pickford's Left Teet!" their guide called out as they approached.

"That's not the bloody password, Wallace," snapped the reply from around the next bend.

The private sauntered around the corner, leading them to a slightly wider section of trench, the whole of it shadowed by the netting. Through the holes, Lily could just make out the oiled length of a machine gun hiding inside the pillbox.

"You knew it was me, anyway." Wallace asserted.

"I should put a bullet in your arse," the other sentry complained, setting the butt of his rifle back onto the ground.

His pale eyebrows rose at the sight of Lily and the others.

"What's she got a bloody ax for?" he blurted.

"These ones are for The Flash," Wallace retorted authoritatively. "The old man downstairs?"

"Not precisely."

The reply came in the Scots equivalent of a distinguished public school accent from a man of perhaps thirty. He wore a cleaner kilt and jacket, emerging from a dark doorway in the wall of the trench. He was shorter than Strangford, with a lean athletic build and a shock of black hair.

There was a bloody scar on his knee, an older one marking the skin below his ear. He was an officer, clearly a seasoned one who did not hide behind his men.

"You can't bring that in here," the sentry insisted, still eyeing Lily's weapon.

"It's a bloody antique," Sam protested.

The dark-haired officer raised an eyebrow.

"It's alright, Ferguson," he said, nodding for the sentry to stand down.

"You're in command here?" Strangford asked.

"Captain Fletcher Ambarsan," the officer confirmed.

"Hold on, then," Sam interrupted. "You aren't *Flash* Ambarsan. Glasgow Celtic? 1911 finals?"

"The same, boyo!" Wallace shouted from behind him.

"Mate, you are bloody brilliant!" Sam exclaimed, then caught himself. "Uh—sir, I mean."

Lily knew that many professional footballers had given up the game to serve. She still hadn't expected to find one at the front lines.

Captain Ambarsan accepted Sam's praise with a quick twist of his lip, his eyes returning to Strangford—and then Lily behind him.

"Why don't you all join me below for a chat?" Ambarsan said. "Not you, Wallace."

The private spun neatly on his heel, turning from following them to stroll back toward the sentry.

"And leave Ferguson to his duties!" the captain warned before leading them down a set of stairs.

The underground room had walls of neatly laid fieldstone that had clearly been there for years. It looked like a farmhouse cellar. Lily realized with a start that must be exactly what it was.

It begged the question of what had happened to the farmhouse.

Pale afternoon light drifted down from the stairs, augmented by a pair of paraffin lamps. The space still felt shadowy and cave-like.

"Could we have the room, Sergeant Beveridge?" Ambarsan asked.

An older, thickset man in a uniform and kilt raised his head from a folding table covered with maps, looking at the newcomers with surprise. He had a ruddy face marked by a thick silver mustache.

"Aye, captain," he replied. "I'll leave you to it."

Ambarsan waited until the sergeant had gone upstairs before turning to the three of them.

"Now, if we might get the rest of the introductions out the way." he prompted.

Strangford stepped forward.

385

"Lord Strangford." He gestured to Lily. "My wife, Lady Strangford, and Sergeant Sam Wu of the RAF."

Ambarsan's eyebrow rose just a touch at the title.

"You're from the Admiralty." he asked.

"Naval Intelligence," Strangford replied, then caught himself. "More or less."

"And what brings you to Mont Noir?"

"We have come to inform you that your sector of the line will be attacked tomorrow," Strangford said.

Ambarsan's expression grew serious.

"Forgive me for asking, but why isn't this coming through the usual channels?"

"Because the usual channels don't believe it's going to happen," Strangford bluntly replied.

Lily watched the captain, aware of how much depended upon his reaction to this. Ambarsan's dark eyes were thoughtful.

"And why do you believe differently."

"I was told as much by a German unteroffizier in Luxembourg four days ago."

Lily fought to conceal her surprise at Strangford's quick admission. She had to trust that he knew what he was doing. Of all of them, he was the most skilled at reading a stranger.

"Told? In Luxembourg?" Ambarsan echoed.

"To be fair, the poor fellow was quite convinced I was a German at the time," Strangford admitted wryly.

"Are you good at that, then? Convincing people you're a German."

"He speaks Kraut if that's what you're asking," Sam offered.

Ambarsan paced the room. There was a coiled, careful energy about him, something that told her he would not be over-quick to reach his conclusions.

"Where are your family lands, your lordship?"

"Northumberland," Strangford said. "Southwest of Morpeth."

"Follow football?"

The question seemed bizarre.

"I will admit it is . . . generally peripheral to my interests," Strangford said.

"You'd be for Newcastle, though, wouldn't you?" Ambarsan

carefully pressed. "Must have been quite the disappointment when your club lost the title in '10."

"Naw, that was '09," Sam cut in. "Aston Villa took it in '10. Last-minute score by the Wellington Whirlwind, that was. Harry Hampton. Man's a legend."

Ambarsan blinked at Sam.

"Well. You're certainly English at any rate. Have you known his lordship long?"

"What, him?" Sam returned, scratching his ear. "Since I were a nipper."

"Thank you, Sam, for confirming that Anthony is not, in fact, a German spy." Lily said, thinly concealing her rising frustration.

They had known this could not be easy. Ambarsan was not being unreasonable. Lily knew she needed to have patience for whatever time it took to convince him, but that was also precisely what they lacked—time.

"So why doesn't GHQ credit your story." Ambarsan demanded.

"Army Intelligence is . . . skeptical of information that contradicts the apparent accuracy of their own networks," Strangford carefully explained.

Ambarsan let out a bark of laughter, leaning back against the table.

"Now that, I do not doubt in the least. I've had little reason over the last month of being chased from Flanders to France to much credit the quality of Army Intel. They've told us the Germans are everywhere—which they bloody are—but nothing about which sector should expect the next attack. Reinforcements have been spread willy-nilly across the line, and we're all down men."

His last two words emerged with a deeper note of bitterness. Lily could hear perfectly well what lay beneath them.

Down men.

She thought of the ragged black shapes that peppered no man's land. The ambulances still carting casualties to the hospital tents.

The captain, the boy in the dugout above, the men they had passed in the supply trench—those were the survivors. They would all have seen friends and colleagues torn apart over the last month.

Strangford had just told them they were facing more. More loss.

More death—and they still did not really know the half of what waited for them with the dawn.

"May I take that to mean that there are no reinforcements coming?" Ambarsan pressed.

"That had best not be relied upon," Strangford quietly returned.

The captain took a moment to absorb it.

"Well," he finally said.

There was the weight of a world in that syllable.

"You say the attack is to come tomorrow," he continued, straightening.

"It will," Strangford confirmed.

"If it follows type, they'll spend the early hours of the morning pounding us with artillery before they send in the stormtroopers at dawn," Ambarsan said.

Lily and Strangford exchanged a look.

"This attack will be something less than entirely conventional," Strangford carefully explained.

Ambarsan's eyes narrowed.

"What have you not told me?" he demanded.

"Think I'll just go find myself some gaspers." Sam backed up a few steps, then made his exit.

"You may find this part more . . . difficult to credit," Strangford quietly warned.

"It'll not get any easier with waiting," Ambarsan retorted.

TWENTY-SIX

$\mathcal{T}$HEY TOLD AMBARSAN a slantwise version of the truth—that the stormtroopers who would be attacking his sector were a new elite unit that had been medically enhanced for exceptional strength and pain resistance. It felt inadequate, but to inform the urbane captain of what was really coming for him would risk his discrediting their story entirely.

As it was, Lily wasn't entirely sure that Ambarsan believed Strangford's insistence that a single unit posed a dire threat to his entire company, but Ambarsan had not survived so long in the war through lack of prudence. When he ordered the old sergeant, Beveridge, back into the dugout and started talking about a great quantity of black powder, Lily had felt something like relief.

As Strangford debated with the two men over a table covered in maps, Lily slipped from the room, her presence forgotten. She found herself a perch behind the ruin of another pillbox, this one blasted into a single remaining wall by some long-ago shell strike. It was enough to protect her from any stray German snipers, and the relatively high ground afforded her a view of the better part of this section of the Allied front.

The air was warm, and every now and then carried with it the scent of some spring bloom like a thread of fairyland wending its way through the haze of smoke and close-packed men. She was impressed by the hive-like organization of the network of rents in the earth. However rough the fortifications appeared with their sinking floorboards, cold food, and stench, it was clear that each piece of this great human machine knew its role and executed it with diligence.

Lily heard Sergeant Beveridge's thick brogue as he emerged from the dugout to shout orders, sparking a renewed flurry of hammering and shoveling. The furious preparation was all happening in the trenches, but snippets of overheard conversation indicated the bulk of the sergeant's black powder project would be constructed beyond the sandbag barrier after night fell, a few yards out into the no man's land that ran between the British and German lines.

She hoped it would make a difference.

The halberd rested across her knees. The Black Watch soldiers who passed her perch flashed it a salute, apparently having appointed both Lily and her weapon as some sort of mascot. One of them whistled and tossed her a wide-brimmed steel helmet.

"Keep yer noggin free of holes, lass," he called.

Lily set the helmet over her tangled hair. She could feel the weight of it in her shoulders and leaned her head back against the wall to relieve it.

The blood-splattered snow of the Stelvio Pass flashed across her memory.

It had been madness to come here.

Even as she thought it, she caught sight of Private Wallace's freckled face as he laughed with one of his comrades and knew they could not have abandoned these men to what awaited them. Lily didn't know what difference she, Sam, and Strangford could possibly make, but perhaps the warning they provided would save a few lives.

Exhaustion tugged at her. They had ridden through the night, and her sleep in the tower during her day of imprisonment had been far from restful.

Strangford's dark blue figure was easy to follow as he moved through the trenches, standing out in stark contrast to the khaki and kilts of the Scots and the paler blue of the French uniforms. She watched as he spoke with the French commander who held the neighboring sector of the line, whom she had briefly met back in the dugout. Capitaine Tremblay was taller than Captain Ambarsan, stick-thin and sun-weathered with warm brown eyes.

At least Strangford would be doing his share of the fighting from within the trenches. His lack of peripheral vision made him more vulnerable on open ground, particularly when bullets were flying. It was Strangford's brain they needed more than his tàijí.

She had few illusions of how well those talents would stand him against the fury of a berserker.

~

Lily did not realize she had fallen asleep until a shadow fell across her body, blocking the warmth of the April sun that managed to break through the haze.

"Eat."

Sam loomed over her in his black coat, a tin bowl in his hand. He did not bother to tuck himself behind the wall of the pillbox, indifferent to the threats that had the rest of the men crouching below the mud, steel helmets crowning their skulls.

"It's edible ... more or less," he pressed, pushing the bowl at her.

Lily took it. It was stew and smelled less awful than she might have expected, even if it was cold.

She started eating as Sam took a draw on a cigarette. He must have convinced one of the other soldiers to share their tobacco ration with him.

Either that or he'd stolen it.

"Ready for your part in all this?" he said, exhaling a plume of smoke.

"Are you?" she shot back.

The halberd was still resting across her knees.

Sam frowned out over no man's land.

"You should sit down," she noted quietly. "Or someone might wonder why you're not afraid."

Sam stiffened, then joined her in the shelter of the pillbox, extending his legs lazily out before him.

"They'll know we ain't like the rest of them soon enough," he countered crossly, looking out across the trenches.

The truth of it sent a chill down her spine.

"No need to rush to it," she replied, eating more of her stew.

Sam reached over his shoulders and pulled out a pair of blades. The sight stopped Lily's spoon halfway to her mouth. They were steel, extending roughly eighteen inches in length. He held one in each hand. Lily realized that a pair of leather scabbards were on his back, the straps crossing his shoulders.

The hilts looked odd to her—and then abruptly familiar.

"Are those bayonets?"

"French type," Sam confirmed. "Bit shorter than the Tommy sort. They feel like bloody big knives rather than some banging sword. The Poilu who chased 'em up for me had a whetstone on him. They're sharp enough to slice a bit of bacon."

Lily felt a bit ill looking at them.

"Wouldn't you rather a rifle?"

Sam's eyes looked dark.

"You said pain don't stop 'em. Only something that makes it so a body plain can't work any longer. It's easier to know what you're hitting with a blade in your hand than a rifle in the dark."

The horror of it was like a shadow passing over the trenches.

"You can't wield a blade from a distance," Lily pointed out thinly.

"You don't say."

She closed her eyes.

"They're fast, Sam. Very fast."

Sam's mouth formed a thin, tense line. He shoved the blades back into his scabbards.

"Don't suppose that matters much for me." He rose to his feet in a graceful fall of black wool and turned turned his face west, a rogue beam of afternoon light limning his sharp profile.

"He done his business with the birds yet?" he asked.

Lily followed the line of his sight to Strangford's distinctive blue figure following the path that curved around the hill.

"Thanks for supper," she said, rising and handing Sam her bowl.

Hefting the halberd in her hand, she set off after her husband.

~

She found him in the orchard.

It lay to the southwest of Mont Noir, nestled in a green and sheltered hollow. The gnarled trunks of the trees revealed their age, while odd branches sprouting from their otherwise leveled crowns signaled at least a season or two of neglect. They were apples in full bloom, branches heavy with delicate white petals edged with the palest pink.

The place seemed impossible, a fragment of another world slipping through into the one where war had scoured the land into a churn of mud and wire. It felt old, suffused with the quiet of growing things.

Under the delicate fragrance of the blossoms, Lily could still smell death.

Strangford's uniform stood in dark contrast to the bright green grass and pale flowers. His gloves were off, his fingers brushing softly over the branches. Lily knew why he must have come—to soak up some tangible bit of peace before returning to the overwhelming cacophony of the trenches, with all the danger and fear that awaited them.

Strangford would feel all of it so much more forcefully than the rest of them, gifted as he was with his exquisite sensitivity.

Something rustled from the branches of one of the trees as she approached, a flash of dark movement fluttering in the corner of her vision, gone before she could fully register it.

The wood of the halberd felt rough, the weight of it heavy in her hands.

"It's time to call in your favor." she announced, pulling off her helmet and dropping it to the grass.

A breeze danced through the gray trunks, lifting the tendrils of her hair. As Strangford turned, it loosed a fall of white petals from the trees. It was like warm and fragrant snow falling slowly towards the verdant ground.

He looked worn, the lines of his face etched deeper, and yet something in him was as calm as Lily had ever seen.

"I already have."

A subtle note in his words flashed a warning. She thought back to that flutter of heavy black wings—the conclusion of a meeting she must have just missed.

A meeting Strangford had sought without her.

"No."

The syllable fell from her lips, woven through with a dread that smelled bitterly of foresight.

"I gave it to you, Lily."

The world blurred. A wind was howling at her ears, tearing at her skin.

It could not be happening. It could not be real.

"*No,*" she cried again, the word a croak—a terrible rasp.

The halberd fell from her fingers to be embraced by the grass at her feet. The petals drifted down around them.

"It will protect you. And him." He nodded at her abdomen with a sad twist of a smile. "Or her."

"I can protect myself."

The words shook. Lily was shaking, her muscles rigid with shock and fear.

Strangford's smile fell.

"No," he replied quietly. "I am not sure you could. Not this time."

The peace of the orchard roared at her like an assault. She couldn't take it, her senses threatening to crack.

"How could you?" she gasped.

Strangford stepped forward, reaching for her.

"It was the only choice I could make."

His words were solemn as a vow. Lily shoved him back.

"No," she growled, rage rising up like a lifeline. "How dare you? How *dare* you claim more right to die than I have?"

"Because it is true. And you know it."

Lily's hands clenched against her stomach. For a breath, her rage turned inward, flailing against the life she carried inside of her— against the accident of fate that had made her survival worth more than that of the man who was her family. Her love.

Her anger shattered against what it found there, fading into the terrible beginnings of despair.

"Then run," she declared, the urge leaving her breathless. "Get out of here."

"You know I can't do that."

"But you'll live if you go!"

Soft leaves rustled overhead, the perfume of apple blossoms singing through the air as the pain of it choked her.

"You brought us here for a reason."

"Damn the reason!" Lily burst out, her nails digging into the skin of her palms deep enough to mark her. "Damn this bloody power.

Ash's Tao. His Parliament of Stars. *I want nothing of it!*"

The words burst from her like a curse, burning with the pain of decades—with all the weight of this awful gift. With everything it demanded of her.

"You ask me to have faith in something I never asked for. Something that has taken everything from me. That has threatened you for *four years.*"

"Lily." he began, his gaze warm with sympathy.

"No," she cut back. "Don't say you understand. If you understood, you could not have possibly …"

There was no breath for the rest of it. It was done. There was no pivot that could change the past.

A welling grief stole her voice, leaving her with nothing but sobs that threatened to choke her if she did not let them out.

When he came to her then, she grasped him, clinging to the wool of his coat as the war on the horizon waited to devour him.

The grass at her feet was dusted with flower petals.

~

Dusk was falling as they returned. The black pines that crowned the hill above were frosted with the last rays of sun that drifted down behind no man's land, the light diffused by the gray pall that hung over the battlefield. It had thickened over the last hour, the air taking on a damp edge that promised rain.

Sergeant Beveridge's gruff voice boomed out to Strangford as they approached. Strangford flashed Lily a helpless glance.

She didn't want to let him go. She wanted to cling to him as though her fear of losing him might hold him to life in spite of all the weight of chance that said otherwise.

"Go on," she ordered dully instead.

He didn't argue. He leaned in and kissed her forehead, his hand warm against the back of her neck.

"I'll find you after," he promised softly, then slipped back into the trenches.

As soon as he had gone, she thought of all that she should have said to him instead. Of course he had given his boon to her and their unborn child. It was the only honorable course of action, and

Strangford had always been honorable.

She could at least have seen that her last moments with him were spent in love and compassion instead of helpless rage.

She wanted to call him back, but Beveridge had already reached him, leading him to the forward trench to discuss the trap they would start rigging in no man's land as soon as the last of the light faded away.

It was too late.

She put her hand to her stomach and tried not to feel sick.

"You should be heading on, my lady."

Lily glanced back to see the young private, Wallace, coming down the path. Reaching her, he plopped down onto a stump, his kilt falling back to reveal his dirty knees. His bayonet flashed at his hip, a pair of grenades knocking like chestnuts at his belt.

"You'll not want to be anywhere near here when the shelling starts," he cautioned, uncharacteristically grim. "It's not a fit thing for a woman."

They had been stretching Ambarsan's credulity enough with their talk of a new breed of German super-soldiers. By silent consensus, they had deemed it prudent not to inform the captain that Lily would be joining the charge against the enemy.

"I'll take the appropriate precautions," Lily lied.

The mist around them darkened as the sun fell behind the clouds dulling the western horizon.

"It's going to be a bad one."

Lily startled as Wallace's words broke the silence that had descended between them. His face was unlined beneath the smears of mud and his light smattering of freckles.

"It's not just nerves talking. I've dreams. They're always the same. I see a great black hound on the strand by Kincardine, and I know it's ill news. Had one of them the night before last."

He scraped his boot against the dry earth.

"Sounds tapped. I know."

The wind rustled the black needles on the low summit behind them.

"You'd be surprised what I find tapped," Lily replied.

She leaned against the staff of her halberd, looking grimly past the tangled razor wire to the dark, silent line of the German trenches.

"I wish I could tell you to get on yourself." she said.

"Oh, not me," Wallace protested quickly, rising from the stump. "I've my duty. And at any rate, that old black hound hasn't caught me yet."

He flashed his teeth in a show of deliberate charm, then headed back down the curving path to the mud-soaked, stinking maze of the front.

Lily followed after him a few minutes later, threading her way back into the narrow warren of plank-lined tunnels, stepping aside to make way for the men who hurried back and forth carrying spools of wire or wooden crates labeled with the calibers of different bullets.

She ducked back from a sapper carrying four stone's weight of cable then rounded a bend in the trench to find herself looking at the back of a man in a gray coat and fedora—a man whose bearing was unmistakable even in the lowering gloom of the evening.

Her grip on the halberd shifted, transforming it from a walking staff to a weapon. The blade caught a fragment of light from a nearby paraffin lantern, glinting white. Violence whispered through her arms, merging them with the wood and steel. The low song of it began to hum through the back of her mind.

"Stop right there," she ordered.

Inspector Tariq Kazi turned to face her.

"Lady Strangford," he said carefully.

He showed no sign of being intimidated by being menaced with a halberd.

"Where are the rest of them?" Lily deliberately demanded.

"The rest of whom?"

"Your handlers," she snapped.

"Not here, as I imagine you can see for yourself."

She shifted the angle of the weapon. The move felt like instinct, better positioning the curved blade of the ax to slice through the inspector's throat.

"When are they coming?"

"They aren't," Kazi replied flatly, a flash of unnamable emotion showing in his eyes.

Something in his tone penetrated the crimson haze clouding her mind. Lily stared at him in surprise from across the shadows of the trench.

"Then why are you here?"

His shoulders were rigid, his face like stone.

"Because *no one is coming,*" he replied.

Kazi set his fist against the woven branches that held back the earth of the wall.

"I went to Montreuil. Over Hume's head—over that of my superiors. I tried to make them understand the urgency . . . Wallah, the necessity of reinforcing this sector of the line—"

His words failed, catching against some deep-rooted feeling.

"Did you expect the entirety of the British Army would move to your will?"

"It's not will," Kazi snapped with a hiss of temper. "It's truth."

Lily had no answer for that. She waited, holding her halberd.

"You didn't help matters by nearly slaughtering three of our own officers," he noted thinly.

"I quite deliberately refrained from slaughtering them," Lily returned.

Her voice was more steady than it had a right to be. She adjusted her grip on the staff, her hand damp with sweat.

"Are they alright?" she demanded, unable to suppress the question.

"A dislocated knee. A broken jaw. Multiple lacerations. But they should fully recover if that is what you are asking."

Someone called from around the corner. Lily and Kazi were forced to step closer together as a line of kilt-clad soldiers jogged past, their boots squelching the planks deeper into the mud.

Kazi's own shoes were already splattered with it, though the rest of him looked immaculate as usual. It was uncanny to see him near so much filth.

"I knew I would find you here," he said after they had passed.

Lily glanced up at him sharply. His elegant face was drawn. Exhaustion and defeat darkened his eyes.

"You might have gone anywhere else. You do realize that, don't you?" he pressed tiredly. "That any rational person would have hopped onto the next boat for England or America. That coming to the one place where it's all going to fall apart is the definition of madness."

"You're here too," Lily pointed out.

He rubbed a hand over his face. It left a streak of mud on his cheek.

"The British and French lines are mingled here. It makes this sector exceptionally vulnerable. If the Germans are able to break the line here with enough reinforcements at their backs to press on to Hazebrouck, we will be entirely severed from the French. They will not fail to exploit the obvious strategy of rolling our forces back to the—"

At last, she understood. He had not come to play the arm of the law, but from the same desperate instinct that had driven all of them to this terrible place.

She set her hand on his sleeve. He stopped, the rattling flow of logic cut off by her touch. Her feelings warred inside of her, betrayal and rage fizzling against a helpless irritation. A begrudging respect.

"Thank you," she said at last.

He nodded shortly, not trusting to words.

She pulled her hand back.

"But you should not have given them the serum."

His mouth firmed, turning stubborn.

"I had my duty."

"When this is over—if we survive—you can tell me whether your duty was worth it."

She didn't wait for an answer, slipping into the maze that wound towards the front.

It was time to take up the watch.

~

It had grown cold.

Around her in the trenches, men slept in shifts. She could feel the thread of doubt in them as they maintained the watch. Would this promised attack even happen?

Lily felt no doubt. Something was coming for them. She could feel it hanging in the air like the beat before a symphony.

She sat in the wider area above the command dugout under the cover of the camouflage netting. It was quiet and dark, the air damp and raw. The lanterns had been shaded to minimize exposure to any planes that might fly overhead. There were no fires. To stay warm, the men simply layered on more clothes or huddled together in corners.

Voices murmured in the shadows, trading low jokes or whispering a prayer.

Sam dozed beside her, snoring lightly, his long legs sprawled out in front of him.

Strangford climbed from the dugout. His uniform was stained with mud, two days of beard shadowing his jaw.

They hadn't spoken since that terrible moment in the orchard. With the knowledge that the night was wearing away chilling her bones, she found she lacked the energy for anger. When he sat down beside her, she leaned into him, resting her head on his shoulder and letting him slip his arm around her back.

She didn't have to speak. She knew he could feel her through the place where his cheek rested against her hair.

"I keep asking myself whether it could have been different," she said, offering the words into the darkness of the trench. "Whether there was something else we might have done—some other choice or accident—or whether it was always going to be this way. Whether it was …"

"Fated?" he filled in.

He pulled back a bit, turning her face to his with a slide of his fingers. The night lent a deeper shadow to his missing eye, his too-short hair. He ran his gloved thumb gently along the line of her cheek.

"I wonder, Lily, whether 'fate' really means what you think it does."

She straightened, frowning.

"What do you mean?"

"You are … hostile to it. Because you fear what it might take from you." His eye was warm and terribly sad as he touched her. "But all of this was only ever borrowed. You might be able to change the future, but you could never change that. This isn't some terrible price you had to pay to do great things, Lily. Losing what you love is just … living."

Lily's world quietly shattered.

He was right—of course he was right. She knew it better than anyone. In a way, it was what all of them had been trying to tell her for so long—Estelle with her affectionate dead, Robert Ash with his polished wisdom, and Sam with his bitter common sense.

Lily had been raging for years at all that fate—the Tao, her path— had demanded she risk. At everything it had taken from her ... but it had never really been about the cost.

All of this was only ever borrowed.

She entwined her hand with his, her muddy and calloused fingers mingling with the familiar texture of his leather.

"I want you for longer than this," she said.

It felt like a prayer, one roughened by the force of her need.

His gloved fingers held her in return. He leaned in, pressing his forehead to her own.

"Then find a way." he said fiercely, tightening his grip on her. "If anyone can do it, it's you."

She threw her arms around his neck. He held her, his arms strong, clinging to her with equal need. She felt the rough texture of his cheek. The scent of mud and sweat mingled with the cedar and woodsmoke of Strangford.

All of which she knew in her bones could be gone by the time the sun rose.

"I promise to do whatever I can to assist with the endeavor," he added dryly.

The laugh fell out of her in response, and for the first time in days, it tasted of something other than anger and despair—something she wasn't quite sure how to name.

The change that came next was as subtle as a brush against the hairs on the back of her neck, but Lily knew what it signified in a way that flooded her core. She slid from Strangford's embrace, catching up her halberd as she came to her feet, her gaze drawn to the west—a hundred yards across the night-black field of barbed wire and the dead to where the German Army waited.

"They're coming," she voiced, feeling the uncanny harmony of both foresight and onmyōdō dancing through her veins.

Strangford rose beside her.

401

At their feet, Sam woke, popping easily to alertness. He hopped upright, running a quick hand through his disheveled hair and straightening his coat.

He glanced over, quickly assessing Strangford, Lily, and the halberd she gripped in her hand.

"Time to cry havoc, I see," he said.

TWENTY-SEVEN

Thursday, May 2
Four-thirty in the morning

*T*HE CALL TO ARMS was a whisper. It passed down the trenches from man to man, sometimes in a word, sometimes a mere tap or gesture, rousing them from sleep. The darkness was suffused with the soft click of rifle bolts, the slide of mounting bayonets. The harder men smeared mud across their faces to darken them. The younger followed suit, quickly intuiting the reason for it.

Rows of wide-brimmed steel helmets lined the wall of the forward trench, men seeking places to stand or crouch with their guns held ready. In the surviving pillboxes or behind makeshift barriers, the machine guns aimed their deadly potential out into the void.

Lily waited in the midst of it.

Kazi sat on an empty ammunition crate next to a near-shuttered lantern, neatly siding rounds into the clip of his Webley. He checked it, then snapped it closed and slid it into his shoulder holster. A second Webley materialized from beside him. He slotted in three more bullets, making the same practiced assessment, and tucked it into another holster at his belt.

Beside her, Sam's eyes widened as Kazi took out a third pistol.

"How many of those have you got?" he demanded.

"Four," the inspector calmly replied, notching in a few more rounds.

"Where did you get four bloody guns from?" Sam exclaimed.

"The company quartermaster has more firearms than men at the moment," Kazi returned. "And it is faster to pull another gun than to reload."

"Is that one a Mauser?"

Sam's tone shifted to one of irresistible curiosity as he went over for a better look at the German handgun.

The wind that blew from no man's land was cold, whispering of death.

"Are you sure they've been spotted?" Ambarsan asked as he and Strangford approached. "There's usually rather a lot of artillery before any attempted incursion unless they're simply raiding for captives to interrogate. The Krauts like to soften us up with a few hundred tons of cordite before they waste any of their men."

Lily thought of Bormio, sleeping quietly as the Stelvio Pass was silently ravaged.

"Not this time," Strangford grimly replied.

He was thinking of it too. He would still be able to taste the fear of the men who died there.

Ambarsan's skepticism continued to grow.

"Look, my lord—I don't want to sound . . . unappreciative, but—"

"I know you don't credit everything I have told you," Strangford calmly cut in. "You have made what preparations you have out of simple pragmatism. A German attack must come at some point, and it is better to act as though even an unlikely warning were true than to be caught unaware. Nor have I told you all that I could. You'd have dismissed me as a madman if I had. You will see things tonight that you would not have thought possible outside the realm of dreams. I am sorry that this burden has fallen to you, captain, but it is upon us whether or not you choose to recognize it."

"He's telling you the truth," Kazi said.

He had finished loading his Mauser. Having run out of holsters, he simply kept it in his hand.

"Who are you?" Ambarsan demanded.

"Tariq Kazi. Foreign Section—MI1c."

"And what the devil are you here for?"

"To shoot things, I suppose," Kazi sighed.

Dark air brushed the back of Lily's neck, blown across the empty space that lay beyond the sandbags and the wire. A cold, animal fear electrified her skin.

"It's happening," she announced.

Sam turned his narrow gaze into the night, the breeze ruffling the raven-black feathers of his hair.

Ambarsan's mouth thinned. Strangford's speech had inflamed his doubts. In another moment, he would label the whole lot of them lunatics and order his company to stand down.

The first cry broke the silence.

It was singular, guttural, torn from a throat that did not sound entirely human. It echoed from the impenetrable shadows to the east.

In the trench, the close-packed bodies shifted as men up and down the line responded by instinct. Rifles cocked, boots grinding for traction against the packed earth as eyes moved to the gaps between the sandbags.

Strangford turned to Ambarsan urgently.

"Remember what I told you. Let them reach the trench, and it will be a slaughter. You must stop them before the wire. Send the men over the top if you can. They will only fight in close quarters—they carry swords, not guns—"

"What?" Ambarsan broke in, shocked.

Another scream sounded through the night—a third, a fourth . . . then a chorus of nightmarish howls from out of the age of monsters.

"Fire the line," Lily ordered, her bones humming with the necessity—the rightness—as her muscles coiled in readiness. "*Now.*"

Ambarsan hesitated.

Kazi swept to his feet, taking hold of the front of his lapel.

"She bloody knows, damn you," he seethed.

The captain swung between disbelief and horror, then pivoted, shouting the order down the trench.

There was a breath, a click—and the world in front of Lily blazed into fire.

Forty yards out, Beveridge's trap lit up a quarter mile of the line with a snap of burning air, turning small rubble into a storm of deadly projectiles. Ten black shadows were illuminated by it, caught in the quick-swirling blaze.

The screams changed in tenor, shifting from violent anticipation to shock and rage.

The shadows, now torches, staggered forward . . . and once more began to run.

Ambarsan's face paled in the firelight beside her.

"My God, they're still coming."

"They haven't burned enough yet," Lily returned grimly.

Her hand gripped the rough wood of the halberd. Her calves flexed, boot poised against the step of the ladder. She glanced back at Strangford, his scarred face illuminated by the dancing light.

"Go," he said.

Foresight sparked through her, violence hissing in her blood.

Lily launched herself over the top.

The battle cry rose behind her with a vibration she could feel, punctuated by the rattle of steel and iron as boots ground against the mud. Firelight flashed off Sam's blades as he ran in her periphery, his coat merging with the shadows.

The awareness that she was leading a charge fell away as everything inside of her focused on the demons running towards her encased in flame.

Their burning clothes and flesh turned the Wulfstruppen into illuminated targets. A machine gun rattled. One to her left took a hail of bullets, the force of the impact jerking his chest and shoulders. He took a staggering step forward once the gun fell silent, the light glinting off the sword in his hand, and fell.

Then his comrades were upon them.

Metal flashed, moving at impossible speed. Grotesque forms slammed into the frail and slender defenders of the Allied line. Men fell like cut grass, screaming through severed limbs, blood thickening the ground.

Lily forced it from her mind. There was space only for the years of training woven into the strength and agility of her body, and the familiar instinct that rose from inside of her with fierce, deadly joy.

Lily rode it like the crest of a wave as she charged toward the enemy.

Her target presented itself in the blazing form of a German

berserker. One arm was blown away, the other raising his sword as his mouth opened in an inhuman scream.

The path ribboned out before her, spilling forward like water over stone.

Duck. Twist.

The halberd flowed as she swung the ax from behind, slamming the razor-edged blade into the base of the monster's skull.

Nerves severed. The berserker's body dropped. His arms and legs went still.

A pale blue eye framed in blistered flesh rolled up to where she stood, elongated teeth opening as though still trying for a bite. The nightmare of it threatened to paralyze her.

Move, move, move ...

Lily brought the ax down again, this time through the thick bone of the skull.

Small fires burned across the battlefield, consuming the bits of scrubby grass by Beveridge's trap, the charred remains of a few tree stumps. The orange light glazed the bodies of the dead. In the few moments it had taken her to kill the man at her feet, there were already so many fallen, both British khaki and French blue darkened with spilled blood.

Another nightmare of cracked and blackened skin screamed towards her through the smoke.

She met his blade with the ax, ready for the blow. It still jarred the bones of her arms, sending an electric pain through her joints. Her knees collapsed under the force of it, bringing her to the ground.

The sword slipped closer as her muscles screamed.

A bullet struck his shoulder, weakening his arm.

Lily lurched away, scrabbling against the mud.

A hand clenched around her arm, tossing her through the air like a rag doll.

She hit the obstacle of a tree stump, the impact pushing the breath from her chest.

The monster pounded towards her, sword raised, mouth red, ready for the kill.

Right path, she willed, pushing herself deeper as she scrambled for purchase against the wet ground, clasping desperately to her halberd.

Right path.

Lily felt it, thin and gold, quick-moving as a snake, and threw herself into it with all the desperation of the damned.

A grenade flashed, cracking white against the darkness. She bolted, the direction pulling at her like a hooked line as some small animal part of her mind screamed that he would catch up to her— cut her down. He was simply faster than she was. *He was too fast.*

Here.

The knowing blazed at her. Lily pivoted, slamming the base of the halberd into the earth and angling the pike, bracing it with her body.

The sprinting bulk of the berserker slammed into it.

The halberd drove into his chest, the force of his speed embedding it halfway through the ax as the base of the weapon sunk further into the ground, Lily's boots sliding a few inches across the churned-up earth.

Now.

Deliberately, without hesitation, she fell.

Lily hit the mud on her back with a skull-jarring impact, looking up at the blade of the monster's sword as it swung towards her face— and then jerked, caught in a hail of machine gun fire.

His body danced against the skewer of the halberd.

When the burst of shots abruptly halted, he was still.

She pushed herself to her feet. Setting her shoulder against the dead man's bloodied flesh, she shoved. The berserker toppled sideways. Grasping the haft of the halberd, she wrenched it free.

Back at the line, Kazi crouched in the cover of the broken pillbox, unloading his Mauser into the charred face of a nightmare. He kept firing even as the gun emptied. The smoking form of the berserker collapsed.

The firelight danced off a field of corpses. Her arms ached. Her ribs were bruised.

Behind her, a second line of Wulfstruppen slammed through the remnants of the blaze.

They were virtually untouched by it, moving with a fluid and impossible speed. One of them reached a stray Black Watch private. With a whip of his sword, he embedded the blade halfway through the soldier's torso.

The berserker yanked it free. Another blow took off the man's head.

They were already past her, around her. She heard the sound of tearing flesh in the darkness, choked screams of agony followed by a roar of victory.

Someone threw a flare. The red light bloomed from a shell hole to her right, casting a hellish illumination over no man's land.

A berserker was tangled in the barbed wire that marked the last defense before the trench. His body jerked with the impact of gunfire even as two more leapt, impossibly, over the barrier, falling into the vulnerable underbelly of the line.

Six yards to her left, something that had once been human yanked its sword out of the back of a fallen French sergeant, then charged for a boy with a twisted leg who pulled himself desperately towards the sandbags.

Move, Lily thought numbly, the impulse muffled as though by distance. *Help him.*

The impulse focused, sharpened by the glitter-bright lens of the onmyōdō.

MOVE.

Lily ran. Her boots tore at the earth as she sprinted, calculating a quick and desperate trajectory. With a final push of speed, she slid between the monster and the boy, adding her momentum to the force of the blow she slammed into the berserker's sword arm.

Flesh severed, the limb hanging from a cord of sinew as the sword thumped to the ground.

Her enemy turned, wearing the shredded remnants of a German officer's uniform. He screamed with rage as his surviving hand grasped at her throat.

Possibility narrowed, the path that did not lead to death thinning like a thread.

It blinked out of view as her windpipe closed.

In the space of a single heartbeat, Lily was exquisitely aware that the nightmare before her had the strength to simply rip out her throat.

The silence was broken by a sound like a splitting melon. The hand on her throat convulsed and then fell limp.

The rest of the German followed, collapsing to her feet.

Sam stood at his back.

The white shirt under his black coat was splattered with crimson and rent through by four long, jagged lines. Lily could see that the damage went through to the flesh beneath. It looked like something done by claws.

Sam bent down. With a jerk, he yanked the blade of one of his bayonets from the back of the dead man's head.

Lily's gaze shifted to the boy she had charged in to save. Blank eyes stared up from the ground above a ripped-open chest. Freckles mingled with the blood. She recognized Private Wallace.

Her boot slipped against the ground. She looked down to see a spill of pink intestines.

Not mine, she thought desperately. *They're not mine. Not mine.*

Horror leached the strength from her arms.

"So he gave it to you, then."

She lifted her head numbly at the sound of Sam's voice. His eyes were dark save for the orange glint of reflected firelight.

"Gave it?" Lily asked, her chest hollow as a cave.

"The boon."

Screams resounded from the trenches behind her, punctuated by a smattering of desperate gunfire. In the red haze beyond Sam's shoulder, a French soldier raised his bayonet only to lose his arms to the sweep of a sword.

Terror dizzied her, the hellish orchestra of the battle crashing against her ears. She did not realize she was falling until Sam caught her.

Lily clung to his coat, willing her knees to cooperate. His familiar scent was tainted by smoke and blood.

A hand gripped her chin, forcing up her face. Sam's eyes were inches from her own, black with intent.

"We're losing," he barked, the words whip-sharp. "*Bloody use it.*"

Then he was gone, the wool of his coat burning her palms as another berserker slammed into him, driving him across the ground.

Her mind rang with terror. A fresh flood of desperate adrenaline tightened her joints.

She wanted to run to Sam. She could vividly, painfully visualize

Strangford being slaughtered back in the trenches. The fear-driven image of it was sharp and clear in her mind.

It made her want to scream . . . even as a stranger thought crept into her awareness.

How had Sam known?

The answer bloomed like a night-dark rose.

Because that's why he had been there.

Lily gazed down at Private Wallace—the red wounds in his chest, the shallow emptiness of his eyes.

Something new rose within her. It spilled up from beneath her fear, pushing out to her skin. It was hot, red, and tasted of flesh.

She thought of the beast that killed him, and her body warmed with the hunger of a predator.

Muscle shifted, her limbs turning supple. Somewhere in the periphery of her mind, a forest breeze ruffled against bright silver fur.

Through it all wound the future, weaving itself into tendon and bone—clear, sharp, and dangerous.

The force that raced through her blood knew it was the most dangerous thing on this tortured piece of earth . . . and the gods of death had bound themselves to look away.

She held the blood-slick staff of her halberd, felt its perfect balance. An iron taste filled back of her mouth. Knowing burned in her like a cleansing fire.

Lily did not go to Sam. He did not need her.

Tearing her gaze from the dead eyes of Private Wallace, she darted after the nearest thing to kill.

~

The rest of it graciously blurred into obscurity. There was a resistance of flesh against the head of her ax. The uniquely jarring impact of steel on bone. She was aware of a scream, scraping her throat raw. It tore out of her as her blade found another mark, slipping past the attack that should have maimed her to find its target with surgical accuracy.

There was no fear. No hesitation. The knowledge of what was next and what could be glimmered through her, spilling into a perfect

411

understanding of the right and deadly path. Lily wove through it like a dance, a perfectly choreographed routine of violence.

The influence of the birds sparked through it all. A blow that should have killed her slipped to the left. A wrong step, a stray bullet, a grasping root neatly conspired to save her.

The path to the future broadened, liberated from her own vulnerability. She seized it, wading in with terrible grace.

Somewhere in that welter of blood and death, she laughed, overwhelmed by the sheer joy of her own inhuman power.

The sound burned into her memory, sharp and inescapable.

As another serum-twisted body collapsed at her feet, the spell broke. The bloodlust, the power, the knowing—they slipped away like a dream, leaving only Lily behind.

She was hollowed out, her muscles trembling with a mad excess of exertion.

The tarnished blade of her halberd thudded to the ground, and she realized that her hands were wet. She looked down at what covered them.

Stumbling to her knees, half-braced by her crimson weapon, Lily vomited across the churned-up earth.

The sky had grayed with the soft light of rising dawn, revealing the landscape around her. No man's land was a charnel house. Between the shattered stumps of what was once the forest, corpses littered the ground, dismembered and bullet-riddled. Too many of them wore kilts or the soft sky blue of their allies.

Scattered amid thicker piles of the dead were the berserkers. One of them lay at Lily's feet, its face half cleaved away above a torso and an arm, the rest lost to a hit from a perfectly timed grenade.

The sounds of the battle had shifted, taking on a different tenor. It was this more than anything else that told her the attack was over.

A few yards away, three men worked to extract a groaning corporal from the barbed wire onto which he had been thrown. As though sensing her attention, one of them turned to look at her. It was Kazi, his warm skin drawn pale, eyes grim and shadowed.

The man pinned to the barbs gasped, and Kazi pulled his attention from Lily, carefully removing the corporal's arm from the wire as a young private with blood-soaked hair held it open. The corporal, finally loosened, fell to the ground with a cry of pain.

Lily pushed herself to her feet. She needed the aid of the staff of her weapon to do it. She trudged toward the Allied front line, passing through a swath of razor wire that had been torn apart as though a tank had driven through it.

At the edge of the trench, she looked down to see a trio of kilted Black Watch privates stab their bayonets into the fallen, twitching corpse of another battle-warped German. The mud beneath their boots was red.

A medic rushed to treat a boy whose leg had been severed at the knee.

The Wulfstruppen were dead. The growing light revealed what it had cost them.

The battlefield was covered in corpses. The men she had heard joking or praying during the night—sons, brothers, husbands—were gone. Those she could see left standing were only a fragment of what had been here when the sun went down.

The sky overhead was thick and gray. Through the haze of smoke and blood, Lily could smell rain. A few fat drops of it pinged against her skin, raw with spring chill.

"How long have we got before the rest of them?"

Sam stood behind her. He was soaked in blood. Another cut marred his cheek, complimenting the rents in his chest. Two bullet holes let gleams of light through the flap of his coat. He still held his twin bayonets. They were sticky with gore.

He nodded darkly toward the German front line, lost in the gray haze.

The thought leadened her arms. The Wulfstruppen had only ever been the first wave. There was a German army on the other side of the smoke, waiting to spill across the field of dead and break them.

The rain thickened into a regular patter. The ravaged ground opened for it, rapidly softening into mud.

"I ..." she began.

Words failed her. Her fingers clenched the halberd reflexively. It was sticky. She fought back a wave of nausea and shook her head.

"I need to find Strangford," she finished.

Turning away, she stepped between a pair of blasted stumps and

413

hopped down into the trench.

Mud squelched under her boots as the drops turned to a steady drizzle, the damp seeping in through her coat. She moved aside for a pair of privates rushing past with a crate of machine gun ammunition. It put her closer to a trio of corpses. Someone had piled them on top of each other to make room for others to get by.

She found Sergeant Beveridge around a corner, his breath shallow as the company physician worked to carefully pull a piece of metal from within the gray hair on his chest. Another soldier held his uniform jacket over them like a makeshift awning.

Ambarsan shouted behind her. She looked back to see him limping, a plank under his arm serving as a makeshift crutch. The rain had plastered his black hair to his skull. He had tied his own shirt around a wound in his thigh, his coat hanging open over his undershirt.

"Galloway—follow that line until you find where it's broken. We need to get word to the major *now*. Wallace! Where's Wallace?"

The rain reached her skin, the clinging cold of it like a shroud.

There were too few of them. The line had held, but the Wulfstruppen had taken their toll in flesh. For what was left to hold against two divisions of fresh, unbloodied troops, it would take a miracle.

Lily was out of miracles.

She turned away from the captain and saw Strangford standing at the other end of the trench.

The arm of his uniform jacket was torn. He had lost his eyepatch somewhere, his face splattered with mud, hair messed. He held a calvary sword, and there was a splash of blood across his chest, the line of it blurred by the downpour.

It was not his own.

Relief washed over her. He was intact. Alive. She saw the same feeling echoed in his expression as he looked at her, his eyes closing in something like a prayer.

The low clamor of men and equipment in the trench was overlaid by a new sound, something like wind blowing through a tunnel.

It was a sound she had never heard before—a sound she nonetheless recognized in her bones.

A hundred yards down the trench, earth exploded into the air with a thunder of impact, smoke blooming up to follow.

Instinct drove her to a crouch, her boots sinking in the mud. Lily rose from it, looking across the ten rain-drenched yards that separated her from Strangford. Horror snapped through her, a wrenching fear sparking into life. It stole her voice, leaving her breathless.

They were being shelled.

"Go, Lily." Strangford shouted, bolting toward her. "*Go!*"

TWENTY-EIGHT

$\mathscr{T}$HE FUTURE BORE DOWN on her, inexorable.

Lily was distantly aware of a cascade of impacts, a relentless booming like that of thunder she could feel through the shaking earth under her boots. It rose like a drum, low and constant inside her chest as the cold rain pounded down against her, soaking her to the skin.

Around her, men were running or curling up like pill bugs exposed to the light. Her face was flecked with mud that flew across the ground from another impact site.

The world around her slowed to the pace of a heartbeat as the fact of it pulsed again and again through her brain.

They were being shelled.

There was no time for horror, only a stabbing twist of anticipated grief as her mind buzzed with what was coming next.

The moment she had been dreading for four years. The obliterating blast that would take him from her.

An urgent electricity raced across her skin. Every cell vibrated in tune to it, every fiber of her focusing on a single ferocious instinct.

It was an act of will. A rejection.

NO.

Lily did not open herself to the onmyōdō. There was no time for that. She threw herself into it like a missile.

Doors spill out around her in the thousands, whirling into blinding fractals of possibility. Lily rages through them, grasping,

417

opening. A hundred futures fall to her in a breath, all of them revealing the inevitable outcome.

Mud and wire. Falling earth and loss.

She refuses it.

Lily forces herself deeper.

Doors blur, merge. Crumble to dust at her touch, all of them opening to the same terrible path.

You must find acceptance. Let go of desire.

Ash's words carry to her on a stench of scorched metal and the screaming of gulls . . . but there is nothing of acceptance in this. It is rage—at Strangford for being too honorable to refuse danger, at Kazi for serving as a catalyst. At the forces that shape the world into the nightmare that surrounds her, the war and its glut of the dead.

Ash never understood. Desire isn't her weakness. It is everything.

She feels it pounding through her—her want. Her need.

Glowing with the force of it, Lily does not reach for doors. She lets them fall away from her, pushing instead into the empty space that lies between.

It bows with tension, resisting her.

Lily presses harder, sharpening her will into a blade.

If she cannot find a way to save what she loves, then she will *bloody well make one.*

The fabric of time parts, and she is through it.

Bone screams. A black wind tears at her, ripping away pieces of who she is. They flicker out into the howling void—a void pierced by a thousand points of pure, glittering light.

Lily Albright hears their song in her soul, a strange and exquisite harmony, and for the briefest moment, it is clear to her.

How the doors were only an illusion.

How there has never been anything but possibility.

It spills out around her, the veins of a pulsing, living thing. There are no pivots. There is only impulse, the natural movement of vital force through an eternity that is creation, spiraling with potential.

There can be no resistance here. No grief. No hope. Only power.

It tugs at her, the pull of a shifting and irresistible sea. With each wave, more of who she was gives way, slipping into dust.

No.

The thought that disturbs the silence is a relic of something that should be lost.

She is one with the currents of the universe. She is the organ that weaves the threads of the world. There is nothing else.

No.

The small remaining thing that was Lily jolts to awareness, anchored by that word, as soft and regular as a heartbeat. It strikes a note of quick, unpleasant dissonance in the symphony that surrounds her.

No.

Lily grasps it.

The wind howls around her, demanding her release. The effort of holding on is an agony like birth. Lily screams into the glittering darkness, pulling herself together against an void that threatens to dissolve her.

No.

Clinging to a thin, tattered sense of who she was, Lily extends, claw-like, into the emptiness.

Something inside of her cracks, splintered by the strain of it. It pulls away with a rending like cloth, spinning into the void as she drags another future into life.

It beats in her hand, soft as flesh, fiery as a tiny sun, and she is thrust out.

Lily landed on her knees in the mud.

The earth trembled under her clenched fingers. Missiles violated the ground around her with the shrieking of banshees. Her arms shook with weakness. Her insides were hollow, lessened in a way that felt like pain—and yet, in the midst of it glowed a single, shining point of hope.

The form of it seeped into her, melting into her bones. Lily rose with it, pushing herself up from the floor of the trench.

A sound like the flapping of black wings swept through the back of her brain as she did the only thing in the universe—in the entirety of what was possible—that would save the man she loved.

She ran towards him.

Strangford's face fell, his eye darkening with fear. His lips formed the word—*Go*—as Lily's boots hit the ground like drumbeats.

Earth and time suspended around her, balanced delicately between her movements and the weight of steel and cordite that blasted toward them.

She struck the rough wool of his chest. The momentum drove him backward, a few stumbling steps to the north. Lily felt the rightness of it with something like joy as they hit the rough wall of the trench.

Then the world blew apart.

TWENTY-NINE

FIRST CAME A BLUR of soft gray light.

It winked in and out of existence above her. Voices sounded thick and muffled as though underwater. A face swam briefly into focus—mud-streaked tan skin, familiar dark eyes.

Sam is shouting, Lily thought vaguely.

Something arched across the soft gray sky behind his head, an intricate pattern of tapering black lines.

An archaic symbol. No—something else. Something she recognized.

A black shape flapped to a heavy landing on top of it, letting out a croak that cut through the fog in her ears.

Hands dragged at the earth that held her like a lover.

Pain came, screaming into her awareness.

The world sank into darkness.

~

She was floating, jolting and awkward. The dull sky came back into view, the horizon at the periphery of her vision titling as the angle changed. It was jagged with the forms of a large company of men, a field of dull green khaki.

The hats, she thought distantly. There was something odd about the hats.

"Oy! Clear the road, mates!"

The English of the call was strangely accented. Lily placed it as the clouds swam overhead, briefly interrupted by the appearance of a mud and blood-splattered young male face.

New Zealand. What was a New Zealander doing here?

The incongruity almost made her chuckle. The movement sent a sharp, terrible pain through her chest.

The gray faded to a point and slipped away.

~

Lily came to herself again in a darkness that hummed quietly with the murmur of low voices, a rustle of cloth, and the soft ting of glass. It was softened at the edges by the low warmth of lamplight.

Slowly she oriented herself. She could feel cloth under her back. Some kind of cot? A breeze blew on her gently. She could hear the chirp of a few crickets.

She blinked her eyes, willing them to focus. The light glowed across wooden poles and canvas that angled to a peak somewhere beyond her view.

It's a tent, she thought blurredly. A big one.

Lily attempted a slow, careful turn of her head to the side. The movement hurt. She made it far enough to see rows of beds housing an irregular terrain of ragged bodies. Some of them shifted, the odd moan or bark of dull laughter punctuating the softer landscape of sound that surrounded her.

Other forms moved lightly and quietly along the aisles, carrying water and clean linens.

She was in a hospital tent.

The bed beside her was empty, the blanket loosely thrown back as though someone had just left it. Beyond that, above her head, the side of the tent was open to a night scented with spring grass.

She took a silent, careful inventory. There was a sharp pain in her chest. Her left arm ached. Something tight was wrapped around it.

Her right leg felt thick, heavy . . . almost distant. She resisted the urge to test it, instinct urging her to caution.

Something else was off as well. She felt it like a sharpening of sensation in her skin. It was as though her nerves had heightened in counterpoint to some other absence, one she could not yet name.

Fingers brushed against her arm. Lily looked up into the brown oval of a female face. It stared down at her briefly, then flickered away.

A moment later, there was a deeper creak of movement, canvas settling over a frame against some substantial weight. A large, gentle hand lifted her right wrist, big fingers slipping over her pulse.

Lily willed her head into another turn.

"Hello, doctor," she rasped, her voice a sandpaper whisper.

"Glad to see you are once again with us," Dr. Gardner replied.

His big frame was perched on a camp stool beside her bed, dressed in the uniform of the Royal Army Medical Corps, the cross-shaped badge visible on his sleeve.

"Have you made your assessment?" Lily asked.

It felt like she was speaking through gravel. Gardner gently released her.

"Fractured left wrist," he listed. "Punctured lung. I was able to relieve the pressure with a needle, at least, so you haven't a great bloody hole in your chest. Multiple lacerations—I won't bother to list them. You'll find them for yourself soon enough. The most concerning is at the side of your calf, below the right knee. You were pierced by a splinter of the planking from the trench wall. The wound itself is minor, but there is damage to one of the nerves. I cannot say what that will mean. Your head, hard as it is, is more or less intact, for which you owe a great deal of thanks to every deity from here to Timbuktu."

He paused, looking down at her meaningfully.

"So is the rest of what you're carrying."

Emotion flooded in, burning away the remaining fog of indifference in a crashing wave of horror, fear, and relief. Lily choked on a sob, her hand clenching weakly at the fabric of her shirt as though making a feeble and belated effort to protect the life that sheltered within her.

The madness of it threatened to drown her—how much she had risked, how dearly it might have cost her—even as the truth resounded under her skin, plain and undeniable.

It was the only way.

She looked up at her friend, absorbing the small miracle that it was his hospital she had landed in, and forced out the most important question—the one she was terrified to ask.

"Anthony."

"He is alive," Gardner answered.

He took her hand again, this time simply for comfort as the relief of it washed over her, leaving her breathless.

He is alive.

"Tell me," she demanded.

"He dislocated his left shoulder. There is some damage to the ligaments, but they should heal on their own with time. Four fractured ribs. You'll be able to tell him all about how that feels while healing, won't you? A particularly nasty slice to his back that took twenty stitches or so to tie up and a mild concussion. He was asphyxiated for longer than you, but some clever bastard managed to get him onto oxygen on the way here. And, of course, he's more or less one enormous bruise . . . but he'll be fine, Lily."

She absorbed the list of damage. It was so much less than it should have been.

At the sound of that terrible word—asphyxiation—she remembered the choking sensation of the earth. The way it had closed over her, thick and cold as the grave.

"Where is he?"

"A colleague of mine is seeing to the stitches. They'll tidy him up and bring him back shortly."

Her fingers brushed against the empty bed. The blanket was still warm.

Alive.

"How?"

The word was heavy with all the terrible weight of what should have been.

"Sam saw you go down," Gardner replied. "Hauled a sergeant and two privates into digging. Still might not have managed it if he hadn't also set a handful of rats to sniffing you out. I gather the wee monsters went to it without the usual rigmarole. Must've sensed his desperation."

Lily thought of what she knew of how Sam's power worked. Yes, she thought distantly. The rats would have known. Would have understood that he was trying to save the lives of those he loved.

Gardner's kind face was drawn.

"I don't think I have to tell you how near a thing it was. A minute or two longer …"

Lily gave his hand a squeeze. She knew perhaps better than anyone just how close it had been.

"But the shell …" she protested.

"Should have torn you apart," Gardner agreed. "Would have, too, if it weren't for the tree."

"Tree?"

"Or what was left of one. The pair of you just happened to fall against the root system buried in the wall of the trench. It took the brunt of the impact, sheltering you from the worst of it. You were really only buried by a foot or so." He paused. "One of the lads who brought you in said it was an ash."

The impact of it dizzied her. For a breath, she was back in the place beyond the doors—the threads that held the world together glittering in the light of distant stars.

"I'm afraid I've men waiting on me," Gardner said, breaking the spell as he shifted to his feet, glancing at something behind her. "I'll leave you to it and check back in a little while."

Lily turned her head.

Strangford had returned. He looked like hell.

His grizzled cheek was marred by a red abrasion. A cut crossed his forehead, set off by neat black stitches.

He dropped his Navy jacket on the empty cot with his free hand. The other was strapped to his chest by white bandages that immobilized his shoulder. The blue wool of his uniform was filthy with dirt and blood. Someone must have given him a new shirt.

His eyes were darkly circled, his face pale.

Lily pushed herself up instinctively, trying to rise to meet him. The pressure of her elbow against the cot sent a sharp dart of pain through her left wrist, which was encased in plaster. It made her gasp.

A hand came to her chest, halting her with exquisite gentleness. Strangford dropped to an awkward knee beside her, wincing.

"You really ought not do that."

She felt the words echo across time and choked out a laugh as she slipped a hand across his bare fingers, clutching at them.

"Everything hurts," he admitted.

His words were touched with a natural wryness. The warm seed of relief grew inside of her.

Lily reached up to touch his face, fingers following the familiar line of his jaw under the rough texture of his stubble.

It was the most perfect thing she had ever felt.

His expression shifted, growing lean and desperate.

"You shouldn't have done it."

Lily slipped her hand into the back of his hair. Threading her fingers there, she uttered her reply.

"I could not lose you."

He let his head fall to her breast, still clutching her hand.

The night breeze danced across her skin as he pulled back, then kissed her. It tasted of everything that had very nearly gone wrong.

Pale fingers glided across her cheek.

"Remind me to show you how grateful I am . . . just as soon as I figure out how to get back up again."

Lily laughed, joy bubbling out of her.

Alive.

~

Lily wasn't certain whether she had slept. It was too noisy in the hospital tent, even at the low murmur of the night watch. Then there was the pain. A nurse had offered her morphine, but Lily refused it, uneasy with the prospect of oblivion when she had only just escaped it.

That strange feeling of absence also itched at her like a healing wound, a subtle hollowness she couldn't quite mesh with any of the list of injuries Gardner had diagnosed in her.

A shift of movement to her right drew her attention as a dark figure slipped up from the camp stool by her cot.

"Sam," she said softly.

He stilled, his shoulders drawing up under his coat.

"You weren't supposed to wake up," he complained.

His face was lined with exhaustion, his dark hair mussed. He must have washed up, but his coat was still splattered with mud and something Lily strongly suspected was blood, only hastily wiped away. He still hadn't shaved.

"What happened to your shirt?"

The words felt thick in Lily's mouth.

Sam glanced down. He wore only the black coat over his trousers, his chest bare save for the bandages that wrapped around the middle of it. They were softly tinged here and there with seeping spots of blood.

Lily thought of the injuries she had seen on him during the battle. He would have new scars to add to his collection.

"Some nurse ran off with it. Wanted me to put on one of those bloody johnnies." He scratched at the bandages. "Woman asked if I was in the canine unit. Told her I was a pilot. Should've seen the look on her."

He pulled out a near-empty pack of cigarettes. The nurse in the next row meaningfully cleared her throat, and he sadly returned them to his coat pocket.

"Heard you're alright, then," he noted, his voice clipped.

Lily looked up at him—her beautiful, dangerous friend.

"I gather we have you to thank for that."

Sam's words took on a thin edge of desperation.

"Just don't bloody do it again. Alright?"

She turned her head. Strangford lay on the next cot, his face relaxed with deep sleep. She felt a sad smile tug at the corner of her mouth.

"Anthony would tell you we have no intention of it."

"Him, I might even believe," Sam retorted.

He rose.

"There's something I need to take care of."

Lily came to an instant decision.

"I'm coming with you."

His eyes widened with alarm.

"Are you cracked?"

She managed, carefully, to maneuver herself into a sitting position with one hand. Her chest twinged, making her short of breath.

"Help me up," she ordered.

There was a brief internal war before he gave in. He took hold of her good arm, lending his strength to lever her up from the cot.

Her injured arm ached in protest. So did a dozen other places in her body. Her right ankle and foot felt strange—numb and wooden. She tried to take a step. It felt as though the limb was dragging, her foot refusing to answer her commands.

"I might need a little help," she admitted.

Wordlessly, he came to her side, slipping his arm around her waist. She set her own over his shoulder, and they hobbled together out the side of the tent.

A horse waited in the darkness under the shadow of a chestnut tree. It was a black gelding, sleek and powerful. In the shadows, one could almost overlook the fact that it had not been tied up.

"Who's that?" Lily demanded.

"It's not like he gave me a name," Sam countered crossly.

"But where did you get him?"

"What do you mean, 'get him?' Maybe he's the one who followed me."

"Sam ..."

"You coming or not?"

Lily eyed the animal warily. It was massive.

"I'm not sure I could get up there," she admitted.

"No worries about that," Sam cheerfully replied. He clicked his tongue. "Tch. Come on, you."

With surprising grace, the gelding knelt down on the grass.

"Climb behind me. Use your good wing to hang on. I'll keep you steady." Sam promised.

Lily carefully settled herself at Sam's back. She wrapped her good arm around his waist, resting her splinted wrist against her thigh. The wound in her calf twinged with mild protest, along with a host of other bruises, but it was tolerable.

Sam gave the gelding another click of the tongue, and with terrifying strength, the horse pushed up from the ground. Lily tightened her grip on Sam, but he was solid as a rock, his seat on a horse rivaling even Strangford's.

"You alright?" he asked.

"Yes," Lily replied.

"Nice and easy, then, mate," Sam instructed the horse.

They set off at a smooth, steady walk, following the rutted track of the road. Lily let herself fall against his back, comforted by the warmth of it and the steady rhythm of his movement.

Darkened fields gradually gave way to scattered fires and clustered tents as the dark hulk of Mont Noir rose before them. The gelding moved aside for a row of transport lorries that trundled past, their headlamps painting the landscape with a stark glare, illuminating a field gun rolling slowly through an intersection.

Something about the busy scene struck Lily with surprise.

"There are too many men," she exclaimed, straightening. "Where did they come from?"

"They're ANZACs," Sam replied shortly.

"Australians?" she echoed with shock.

"Mostly Kiwis, so far as I can tell," Sam corrected her.

"But what are they doing here?"

"Seems there was a bit of a mix-up with the transportation logistics. A maintenance crew shut down the railway tracks halfway between Hazebrouck and Poperinge just as a run with two New Zealand companies was headed through. Their captain marched them to the line to find a way to communicate with headquarters and get updated orders ... and it just happened they showed up as our lot was getting shelled. Boche spotters must've seen them coming and thought they were proper reinforcements. After their first wave had failed to break through, that was enough to make them call off the rest of the attack." He glanced back at her, his eyes glittering in the darkness. "Funny sort of mix-up that drops a load of fresh troops an hour's march from our position."

"George," Lily whispered, feeling the truth of it in her aching bones.

She recalled her brother's "dreadful puzzle"—the complex web of men, roads, rails and supplies that was the lifeblood of the war—and the brief, crackling words over a bad phone line in Bergues.

... *never underestimate ... schedules ...*

The warmth of it washed through her. He had made a bit of the earth move to bring her the help she needed on nothing more than her word.

Her brother.

"Bit farther to go," Sam said, tapping their horse on the shoulder.

The flank of Mont Noir was highlighted by a strange orange glow.

Beyond the familiar stink of petrol from the passing lorries, the air smelled of fresh grass, turned earth, and smoke.

Fire bloomed into view as they rounded the shadowy bulk of the hill, approaching the front line. It burned low and smoldering from a pit dug by an artillery shell. The ruddy light spilled across a barren stretch of ground near the trenches. A few figures were silhouetted there, watching the smoldering blaze.

As the gelding halted at the outskirts of it, a kilted Black Watch private and a hatless ANZAC soldier hauled something toward the pit. Between them, they tossed it in on top of the rest of what was burning.

The recognition dawned over her, carried as much by the smell as the sight.

They were bodies.

No one spoke as Sam dismounted, then helped her down with careful hands. Lily climbed awkwardly to the edge of the hole. The man next to her turned to see who had come, and she recognized the bruised, drained face of Captain Ambarsan.

He had a crutch under his arm, clearly favoring one leg. Blood still darkened the bandage around his thigh.

Lily wondered if there would be any football for him after this.

He gave her a respectful but wary nod before moving away.

She looked down at the burning corpses. Even though they looked different in death, some of the monstrosity drained out of them, Lily knew exactly what they had been.

"It's them," she said softly. "Isn't it?"

"All twenty." Sam grimly confirmed.

"You're burning them."

"It was his idea," Sam replied.

She followed the jerk of his head to another who stood at the edge of the flames.

Kazi raised his face from his contemplation of the pyre, meeting her eyes across the pit.

Sam tapped out a cigarette, lighting it with the flare of a lucifer. He glanced between the pair of them.

"I'd best make sure they didn't miss any pieces."

He set off into the night.

Lily doubted he would be executing that search alone. There were others Sam might call upon for assistance who could perhaps more easily distinguish between the mundane and the monstrous dead on the cluttered battlefield.

Gazing down at the terrible embers of the pyre, Lily was struck by the compulsion to see if it was truly over.

She could, of course. She knew that with just a simple push of her onmyōdō, she would know if this fire had irrevocably destroyed the last vestiges of the Wulfstruppen. Whether the vial Kazi had stolen and handed over to Army Intelligence would open the door to another trail of horrors.

The thought of it exhausted her in a way that went deeper than the renewed aches in her bruised body, but she felt the need for it like an obligation.

There was no one else who could do it, and so of course she must.

Lily took a breath, focusing herself, and reached for that place inside her—a place she had become more and more easily accustomed to going—and found . . .

Nothing.

Standing by the pit, Lily blinked with surprise.

The onmyōdō had always leapt up at her invitation like an eager pet hovering outside the door, just waiting for a chance to come in. Lily had spent most of her energy wrestling to keep it at bay. To ask for it and not find it was something so unexpected, it felt absurd.

With more will, she pushed for it again . . . and again. Harder. Gritting her teeth, shaping her will into an arrow and letting it fly into the space where her power had always been.

It was like throwing punches into the air.

With rising alarm, she tried for something else. Lily opened the way for her old and ordinary foresight, the power that had been with her since she was a child.

Tell me what is coming, she ordered it. *Tell me what will happen next.*

Nothing answered.

The shock of it made her stumble. She fell to a knee, her wounded leg jolting with protest . . . and felt what was not there. She had been feeling it ever since she woke up in the hospital tent. It was as though

431

all the ever-present traffic of London's streets had suddenly vanished, leaving behind a bizarre and uncanny silence where there had always been sound. Always been *something.*

Lily flailed through the memory of the last moment she had used her power. It had been in the trench with Strangford. The moment had the distance of a long-past dream, but there had been doors and then the space between them.

Beyond that, a power so great it threatened to dissolve her. A sharp and painful tearing as she had grasped what she had risked it all to find and wrenched herself away.

"What have I done?" she gasped, shocked into speaking the words aloud.

"Lady Strangford?"

She startled, surprised by the presence of someone standing beside her. She looked up to see Kazi, his brow creased with concern.

"Do you need assistance?" he asked.

"I . . . think perhaps I do," she replied.

His hand slipped under the elbow of her uninjured arm, firm but careful. With his help, Lily returned to her feet. Her limbs protested the movement. They were weak, trembling.

She took a breath, willfully anchoring herself. She set the shocking and uncomfortable questions aside, not ready yet to consider what they meant, or to share them with the man who stood beside her.

"I am . . . glad to find you unharmed," she said.

"Appearances can be deceiving," he replied thinly.

He raised a hand, breaking off her instinctual response.

"I am better off than I have any right to be," he quietly assured her.

His elegant face was drawn, the lines of it stark in the firelight as he watched the flames in silence.

"I owe you an apology."

Lily looked up at him in surprise.

"You were right," he continued, closing his eyes as the rest of it spilled out of him. "I should never have given them the serum. I should never have lied to you."

He opened them again, meeting her gaze without flinching.

"You knew, all along, what this was. You and your husband both, far better than I possibly could have. I should have listened to you. I thought I was being . . . rational."

The word sounded like a curse.

"Some things in this world aren't entirely compatible with what's rational," she said.

"No," he agreed with another sideways glance at her.

It didn't feel like a vindication. She wondered how much he had seen of her on the battlefield. Did he think her monstrous too?

Perhaps she should have joined the others roasting in the flames, those men who had volunteered themselves for violence, mistaking it for duty or the chance of glory.

The pyre crackled in front of them with the pop and hiss of irretrievable destruction.

"The matter of your status, and that of your husband, has been settled."

"What?" Lily asked, startled.

"I sent word to London," Kazi replied tightly. "That the assault on the officers in Dunkirk was the result of an unfortunate misunderstanding. Clarifying that you did not desert your duties but followed them to the front at great personal risk to yourselves. Somehow the Minister of Munitions was personally copied on the communication and made it known to the Prime Minister."

"The Minister of Munitions," Lily echoed carefully. "You wired Churchill."

She recalled the uncomfortable and compelling presence of the big man in her study.

"I did not think he would remember us so well," she remarked.

"He has a weakness for heroes."

On the other side of the fire, one of the battered Black Watch soldiers threw a pile of smashed wood into the fire under Ambarsan's watchful eye. The flames swelled up in response.

"Army Intelligence need not concern you anymore, either," Kazi said.

"Why not?"

A world burned in his golden eyes—responsibility, guilt, determination, regret.

"Because I'm going to fix it."

~

She became aware of Sam's presence sometime after Kazi trudged from her side out into the night. In the pit, the flames had begun to lower.

"It's done," he said. "We'd best get you back before his lordship notices you're missing."

She accepted his arm without protest this time. Their horse waited patiently where they had left it, munching on a few tufts of grass. It knelt obligingly once more for Lily to mount, the maneuver hurting more than it had before as her bruises protested the additional movement.

The ANZAC camp was quiet as they rode past, only a few scattered sentries keeping vigil. The great field of their tents was thick with the strange presence of a thousand sleeping men.

Exhaustion crept over her, deepening the ache in her bones.

They stopped in the darkness just beyond the soft glow of the hospital tent.

"We done with this, then?" he asked as he helped her dismount. "Because I never thought I'd say it, but I'm ready for my kip and a few dull observation runs for a while."

Sam took a step or two towards the tent before he realized she hadn't followed.

"You alright?" he asked.

"I ..."

He came closer.

"What? What is it?"

The words spilled out of her, falling like small stones from her lips.

"I ... I think I broke it."

"Broke what?" he asked with alarm, looking from her to the horse as though ready to blame the animal for a new injury.

The sight of it made her laugh in spite of it all.

"No, it's not that. I ..." She took a breath, forcing out the rest. "I mean the rest of it."

Sam stilled.

"You mean what I think you mean?" he asked.

She nodded.

"How's that even possible?"

"I don't know. I think it was in the trenches. When Strangford was going to ... when we were both ..." She looked up at him, struggling for the words. "It wasn't supposed to happen. I was forcing it to find another way, and there wasn't. There wasn't any, so I kept pushing ..."

Sam's hands tightened. Lily didn't realize the point at which he had taken hold of her shoulders—the point at which she started to shake.

"Is it ... just the fighting bit? Or—what's that Cairncross calls it?"

"Everything."

"Oh," he quietly replied.

Lily fought to hold steady against the avalanche of what she had just acknowledged.

"He was supposed to die," she said.

She thought of how terribly close it had been. The future had been certain, impenetrable as a wall ... one that she had blasted apart.

"Well. It weren't like you were ever going to stand by for that," Sam noted dryly.

Tears cooled her cheeks as she gasped out a laugh.

"What's it feel like?" he asked carefully.

"Like it's all ... burned away. And where it was, there's only this ..."

"What?" Sam prompted as she trailed off.

She probed at the feeling, searching for the right word to capture it.

"Stillness."

"Does it hurt?" he asked.

"No," she replied. Her mouth twisted into the shadow of a wry smile. "Everything else does. But not that."

"But how do you ... *feel* about it?"

Lily considered the question with surprise. The epiphany of it was so new, she hadn't yet had the chance to think about it.

"I'm not really sure." She forced herself to meet his eyes, voicing the quick, fluttering fear that had risen in her. "Would it change things? If I wasn't like you anymore."

Sam's brows drew together crossly.

"What do you think, you lubber? What—would it change things for you?" he demanded.

"No!" Lily exclaimed. "Of course not."

"Then stop asking stupid questions. *Would it change things?* I oughta knock you for that one. Shake your brains back in order. Only I suppose it wouldn't be fair now that you can't fight back."

His grin was a white flash in the darkness. Lily jabbed a finger at him.

"I can bloody well still use a stick, and you know it."

"Well. Ain't that much changed then, is there?" Sam concluded neatly.

Lily realized what he had done and how tidily he had done it— setting her straight, banishing that terrible little flash of wretched insecurity.

She burst into tears.

"Oh bugger," Sam swore.

He put his arms around her, pulling her in against his chest. Her knees had weakened, and it brought both of them down to the ground. Her shoulders shook with the force of the emotion spilling out of her.

And then it passed.

The cool of the earth seeped up through the grass into her legs. Sam's skin was warm under his bandages, her wounded wrist tucked between them like a broken wing. He smelled like wool and soap.

"I should really stop doing this to you," she noted quietly.

"Naw," he countered, stroking a hand through her hair. "It's alright." She could almost feel his mischievous grin through where she leaned against his chest. "I dry up quick enough."

Lily shoved him back with her good arm, laughing through an ache in her chest.

"Shǎguā," she said, echoing the insult she had heard Zhao Min use in the carriage on the way to Vianden.

Sam's smile brightened the darkness.

"There you are. Now you're getting it."

He stood up, extending a hand.

As she looked up at him, the black of his coat seemed to weave into the shadows, the beard he still wore sharpening his features, making them rougher. It was almost as though she could see the dark wings extending from his back, merging with the night. The thought of it sobered her.

"What about you?" she quietly demanded.

He dropped his hand, stiffening a bit.

"I'll go back. Before they decide I'm a deserter after all."

"That's not what I meant."

"You needn't worry about that," he countered stiffly. "You know I'll be alive, whatever else happens."

His tone was a whip, striking back at itself as it pushed her away.

Lily knew better.

She reached up.

Sam hesitated only a moment before clasping her hand, helping to gently lever her from the ground. Lily winced with the movement, her wounds sparking with various forms of pain. She dropped Sam's hand to clasp at a particularly sharp pang in her side, working to catch her breath.

"You really need to stop running about," Sam complained tersely.

Lily straightened awkwardly. She felt her way toward what she needed to say. Searching for the right words almost reminded her of what the onmyōdō had been like.

"Someone once asked me what my feather was," she began carefully.

"Your what?"

"The thing that decided whether I had a vision or went on happily ignorant of what was coming in the future."

Sam's eyes tightened, icing with a quick flash of pain.

"It was him. Wasn't it?"

"Yes," Lily admitted.

The unspoken name hung in the air between them, entangled in a complexity of resentment and grief. She pressed on, knowing it had to be said, even though it wouldn't be easy.

"I haven't been part of this war as long as you have, but even what little I've seen has made one thing very clear to me. There's no system to who dies and who survives in it. It's not logic. Not justice. Not skill. And if it's not any of those things, Sam—then what is it?"

He blinked, his shield dropping.

437

"I don't know," he stammered.

"Maybe it's just pure chance," Lily continued. "But chance doesn't need an army of black-winged rotters running about doing its bidding. Chance doesn't need . . . you."

He stood before her in his black coat, bloodied and ragged, staring at her with all the vulnerability of the boy he had once been.

"What are you saying?" he demanded, the words rasping in his throat.

"That maybe . . . something chooses. Something a bit more than just luck. And perhaps before you go on hating yourself for what you did in order to survive, you might just . . . try to find out what that is."

She put her hand to his beard-roughened jaw.

"But whatever it is—and whatever you decide to do about it—you will always have a place with me," she vowed fiercely. "*Always.* Do you understand that?"

A night breeze danced sweetly through the darkness around them as she waited for his answer.

"Yeah," he said at last, meeting her eyes. "I do. We're jiā."

The word felt powerful—like a presence, filling up the grass and trees and silence that surrounded them.

"That word," Lily said, remembering it from his terrible conversation with Zhao Min. "What does it mean?"

"Home," Sam replied, voice stripped raw with the feeling of it. "Family."

"Yes," Lily agreed. She slipped her hand to the back of his neck, gently pulling his forehead down to hers, her words a promise. "*We are jiā.*"

THIRTY

$\mathcal{L}$ILY WOKE AT DAWN to a clatter of empty bedpans and knew that Sam had gone.

A hobble around the hospital camp confirmed it. She found she was not surprised. He had matters of his own to attend to, and they had said their goodbyes last night.

The camp buzzed with activity. A row of ambulances arrived with the dawn, gray lorries marked by distinctive red crosses. There was a bustle as Gardner and the orderlies worked to quickly triage who was stable enough to be transported to the proper hospitals west of the front.

There was no sign of Kazi, either. She thought of what he had said the night before about "fixing" his mistake with the serum. Whatever his purpose was, he would pursue it doggedly to the end. That much she felt certain of.

She found Strangford two rows down, sitting on a camp stool. He spooned porridge into the mouth of a man who no longer had any arms, chatting away beside him.

"So the lad says, 'I'm taking the cow to the bull.' The vicar asks him, 'Couldn't I help instead?' And the boy replies, 'I'm sorry, Reverend. It really has to be the bull.'"

439

There was a roar of pained laughter. Lily winced at the punchline. As he caught sight of her, Strangford's smile turned into something warmer.

Those smiles had been rare when she first met him. The man he was now had been shut up inside, only little glimpses of him escaping into the world.

It should have been impossible. Strangford should not have been there. Lily had changed that. She didn't yet fully know what it had cost her, but at the moment, all she could feel was gratitude.

"There you are."

She started a bit at the deep timbre of Dr. Gardner's voice as he stepped up beside her.

"You shouldn't be larking about," he noted. "You'll stress your lungs. And that hole in your leg."

"I'm using this," Lily retorted, tapping the crutch she had stolen from an empty nurses station.

"When it swells up from all the jolting about, and the rest of your foot goes numb, don't say I didn't warn you."

Lily glared at him but lowered herself to sit on the empty cot behind her.

"Anyway, you've a visitor," the doctor continued.

"What—me?" Lily protested.

Gardner's response was a tip of the head toward the back of the tent. Lily turned to see a man who starkly contrasted with the wounded soldiers that surrounded him, thanks to his finely tailored civilian dress, obvious age, and the bearing of someone who regularly dined with the king.

"Who's that toff, then?" asked a wounded Black Watch private on the cot to her left, leaning up a bit on his elbows for a better look.

"My father," Lily replied with quiet shock.

~

Edward Carne, Lord Torrington, sat down beside her on a camp stool that looked too small for his tall frame. He somehow still managed to make his perch on it seem elegant.

"How are you here?" Lily demanded.

She was still shocked by the sight of his leonine profile, marked by the deeper lines the war had carved into his features.

"I had a rather alarming wire from your brother the day before last saying there had been a raid on some pithy little hill in France. That he strongly suspected you might have been in the middle of it, and would I mind terribly confirming that you hadn't turned up on any of the casualty lists. So here I am," he finished neatly. "Confirming the lists."

He gave a practiced nod of acknowledgment to one of the nurses, who bobbed a quick curtsy as she moved past. The fact that there was an earl in the tent had clearly made its way around.

Torrington was contained and courteous, as he always was. Lily wasn't fooled by it.

"You traveled all the way to the Western Front just to check up on me?"

The cool gray eyes he turned on her were identical to her own. The emotion she saw scored in them was familiar to her as well.

"How is your husband?" he asked, choosing not to voice the deeper feelings she had just glimpsed.

Then again, he didn't have to.

"Well enough to be over there telling dreadful vicar jokes," Lily replied past the lump in her throat.

There was another burst of laughter from Strangford's post. Lily noticed a few additional men seemed to have limped over to join the circle.

"I suppose it would be futile for me to inquire as to the reason you turned up here instead of running your far more modestly danger-ous courier route back in England. I'm sure it wouldn't at all be related to that curious little flurry of memos that went flying about Westminster yesterday afternoon just as I was preparing to leave— the ones marking you exempt from interrogation by MI1b following extraordinary service to the crown."

Lily opened her mouth to respond. Realizing she had no idea where to begin, she closed it again.

"Our mutual acquaintance," she said, mouth dry. "She was well, the last I saw her. If you were wondering."

Torrington absorbed that.

"She was of some service to you?"

441

Lily pictured Zhao Min in the clearing as she turned away from her chance at escape to walk back into the heart of the fray.

"Very much so."

"I am not certain whether or not to be grateful to her for that. Had she not helped you, perhaps you would not have ended up here." He motioned to the sprawl of wounded men that surrounded them, tension beginning to show more clearly through his facade. "I can only imagine what you have been through in this place, Lily, but it cannot be something any father would wish on his daughter."

She felt the horror of the fight. It had been only two days before. On the slope behind Mont Noir, they were digging a new cemetery, deep holes in the earth where most of that battered company of the Black Watch would be laid down.

No—it was not a burden she would ask for again.

"So. Have you any further life-threatening adventures you need to throw yourself into?" her father asked. "Or might I escort you and your husband safely back to England?"

Lily reached out across the distance that separated them and took his hand. She felt how he held it back and thought of all they had been through over two weeks that felt like a thousand years. Of the wounds that needed to heal, both in her body and elsewhere, injuries she still did not know the full impact of.

The Lily of four years ago would have wanted to hide in the face of it, crawl away to where she could suffer it alone. That was not the impulse that rose inside of her now. Instead, an unexpected answer presented itself with surprising and steady certainty.

"I know exactly where I would like to go."

~

Her farewell to Gardner was brief, the loading of the ambulances sparing him only for a few moments.

"I've a fair bit of leave due me. I'll make my way back to England sometime in the next few weeks to check up on you," he said. "In the meantime ..."

"Yes, I know. Stay off of the leg," Lily filled in for him.

He squeezed her shoulder.

"Why not let someone else fight a few of the battles for a while?"

he suggested warmly.

Her father had acquired a carriage. It was black and gleaming, pulled by a fine pair of horses, parked beside the hospital tent like something plucked out of the previous century and set into the middle of the war. There was even an elderly chauffeur in proper livery standing by to wait for them.

"It belongs to a friend," Torrington explained.

Lily wondered whether the friend was some ambassador who owed him a political favor or the great-grandson of a deposed French duke whose assets conveniently found their way across the channel during the revolution. Her father had connections everywhere, a threaded network she had no desire to fully understand.

A cluster of ANZAC soldiers moved out of the way as she, Strangford, and her father approached. They were eyeing the carriage like something from a film set. One of them beat the chauffeur to the task of opening the door for Lily as she hobbled over, offering her a hand.

"Here you are, then, love." He winked as he helped her up, then straightened abruptly as he realized the slight, scarred figure following her was wearing the uniform of a Navy lieutenant commander.

"Sorry, sir. Let me get that for you," the gallant neatly offered, tone switching from flirtatious to deferential in a heartbeat.

The men parted like water as the stoop-backed chauffeur snapped the reins, the carriage rolling into motion. Lily looked back to see them lingering by the tent, one of them doffing his hat while the other blew her a kiss before they broke into an easy flow of shoves and laughter.

The dark shadow of Mont Noir shifted outside the glass of the carriage window, thinly hazed with smoke under a low gray sky. The battlefield was not visible, only the unsightly sprawl of cart tracks, tents, campfires, and supply depots, but Lily could sense it—the broken ground, the torn nests of wire. They would even now be shoveling out and reinforcing the blasted sections of trench. The whole line would dig in, sprouting sturdier fortifications until it became an all but impenetrable barrier.

It was the place where she had shed so much blood, where the men she fought with had died. Where Strangford should have been buried, lost to her forever.

The place where part of her had shattered, leaving only questions behind.

Her father sat across from them in his flawlessly tailored suit. In the periphery of her vision, the stark relief in his eyes was laid bare.

Black leather brushed over the back of her hand. She opened it, letting Strangford's fingers slide between her own. She leaned in to settle her head on his uninjured shoulder.

~

They sailed from St. Malo. It was little more than a quaint fishing village located far enough west of the front to attract minimal interest from the Army and Navy. Torrington's double-masted yacht was waiting for them at the harbor, all sleek polished wood and elegant white finish. The gray skies opened into a soft rain as they boarded, painting the clustered shops and cottages of the village in muted hues.

They made the crossing under sail alone, their passage marked by nothing but the soft splash of water against the hull. Lily watched its progress through the round window of the cockpit, looking out over the churning gray water as the rain tapped against the glass. Strangford kept his arm around her waist, his chest warming her back.

He didn't speak of what she knew he must have learned from that touch, not with her father and his captain sharing the space with them—but then, he didn't have to. The burning of the Wulfstruppen, the loss of her power. Sam. Strangford wouldn't just know what had happened. He would know how Lily felt about all of it. There was no need to struggle awkwardly for the words that might start to fit.

His lips brushed her hair. Lily leaned against him, suffused with quiet gratitude. The dim hulks of Jersey and Guernsey slid past on either side of them as they left France behind.

~

It was nearing evening when the horizon darkened with the rolling line of the English shore. As they approached, it took the form of a familiar profile of crumbling red clay cliffs topped by softly waving seagrass.

Lily faced her father as his captain readied the launch.

"Are you sure you wouldn't rather we bring you round to the harbor?"

"It would take another hour. Then we'd have to call for a carriage, and who knows how long that would take? I'm just . . . ready to be done. We can manage. Slowly." she finished with a tired smile.

She put her arms around him, holding him as tightly as she could without bumping her wrist.

"Thank you. For coming for me."

"It was the very least I could do," Torrington replied, hugging her back.

His captain rowed them across the lapping waves in the yacht's launch, driving it neatly up onto the sand. Strangford planted Lily's crutch in the wet ground before gingerly helping her out of the boat. She watched it row back to the yacht, the rain now dissolved into a typically damp mist.

Her father's lean figure watched them from the deck until the boat slipped from view.

She faced the narrow, curving path up the cliffs with Strangford at her side. The mist caught against the dark threads of his hair, glittering there like stars.

"I'm afraid I can't carry you," he admitted. "But I could go ahead. Send on a few strapping lads from the village."

"Wouldn't you be jealous?"

"Oh, entirely." Strangford assured her. "I should rather like to be carried myself at the moment."

Lily laughed.

"Shall we, then?" he said, offering her his arm.

"One step at a time," Lily agreed, accepting it.

By the time they reached the top of the path, her lungs were burning, exhaustion weighing her limbs. She wondered whether the harbor might have been a better idea, even with the extra time it would have taken them, but at last they came to the end of it.

The seagrass danced around her boots in acknowledgment of their arrival. The eccentric sprawl of the manor came into view, windows already flaring to golden life against the dimming of the hour. It was unchanged, a timeless clutter of stone and ivy ending in the dull glass of a conservatory.

They set off across the spring-green field. When they reached the door, Strangford gave it a firm knock.

It swung open as though they were expected, but the tall, ginger-haired figure who greeted them revealed his surprise in a slow blink.

"Lord Strangford. My lady." James said in greeting, opening wide the door of Taddiford. "Do come in."

He motioned them inside as though there were nothing at all untoward about filthy, wounded relatives turning up on the doorstep by way of the sea.

The familiar contours of the front hall warmed her, from the gleaming wood paneling to the worn but beautiful Turkish carpet on the floor. A side table held a decorative pewter bowl filled with shells instead of a pivotal vase.

When Lily looked at it, she felt nothing but a quiet relief.

The smell of baking bread floated to her down the hall from the kitchen as her brother-in-law, Walford Eversleigh, wandered in. He wore fleece slippers, his new spectacles doing nothing to conceal the magazine-perfect proportions of his features.

"You two look terrible!" he exclaimed cheerfully. "Come to us straight from the front lines or whatnot, have you?"

A slighter, smaller figure pushed forcefully past him as Strangford's sister, Virginia, barreled into the room. Her sharper eyes flashed from Lily's crutch to Strangford's immobilized arm by way of a rapid and relentless inventory of the cuts and bruises on their visible skin.

She strode forward, pulling her brother firmly into her arms, her perfectly-coiffed brunette head fitting just under his chin.

"You have a very great deal of explaining to do," she proclaimed, her voice muffled a bit by Strangford's shoulder.

She reached out to grasp Lily's arm as well, pulling her into the embrace.

"Could we have a bit of tea first?" Strangford asked with a tired smile. "And you are hurting my broken ribs."

"Broken ribs?" Virginia exclaimed at a near shriek as the children poured in from the stairs.

THIRTY-ONE

Thursday, May 9
Two o'clock in the afternoon
Taddiford

In the field behind the manor, Lily concentrated on her tendons. She had left her crutch. Instead, she had Estelle, the taller woman bracing Lily with a sturdy elbow.

"Try it again," she urged.

Lily attempted to step forward.

Her foot refused to move the way it ought to. Instead of lifting neatly and instinctively at the ankle, it stubbornly hung down, the limb responding to only the dullest and most general of her commands. To move it forward without tripping herself, she was forced to lift not just her calf but the entire leg, raising it from the thigh and setting it carefully forward, toe first, before letting her foot fall flat against the ground.

The effort of it was both tiring and deeply frustrating. She was conscious, painfully, that certain things she had previously taken for granted might well be beyond her now—the thoughtless lope of a run, the neat plant and pivot before she swung a weapon.

She might still have had those powers had she lost Strangford.

There was not a shred of doubt in her mind about which she would choose if she had a chance to do it all over again.

There was a wind today, a regular breeze blowing in from the sea.

It smelled fresh and briny. Lily and Estelle did their exercises beside a tall brass monument, positioned nobly within view of the drive with a fine vista of the coast. The obelisk was topped by the sculpture of a squat and ungracious pug—Virginia's tribute to her beloved Horatio, who had finally passed away in 1915.

Horatio's successor currently loped around the back field, alternately chasing and being chased by the children. Titus boasted far larger proportions than the departed pug, being mostly of Great Dane extraction. Though Lysander was eight and the girls, Rosalind and Dorcas, both teenagers, the happy squeals and shouted admonitions as they wheeled about the yard didn't sound much different from those of 1914.

It all contributed to the feeling that coming to Taddiford had been the right choice. Even though London or Northumberland was home, going back to that quiet isolation would have felt too much like retreating to lick her wounds.

Life at Taddiford felt more like healing.

Lily felt oddly ready to heal.

Estelle had shown up three days before, arriving at the door with her trunk and promptly installing herself in one of the guest rooms. Lily still wasn't certain whether Virginia invited her or someone dead clued her in, but either way, she had been a very welcome addition to the household. She fit herself into the life of the Eversleighs with confident ease, discussing the charms or flaws of various marriage-eligible European nobles with Rosalind and weighing in on ghost stories with Dorcas. Miss Bard had joined her just long enough to express her very heartfelt gratitude that Lily and Strangford were safe before hurrying back to London to help with a veterans' fundraiser.

"She had a loaf of bread in the shape of a pair of conjoined twins from Kent for you," Estelle had informed her after Miss Bard had gone. "Only you were gone so long it went stale."

Out in the cropped grass by Horatio's monument, Lily attempted another step, hissing with pain and frustration when her foot caught once more against the ground.

She thought with a pang of her walking stick, the old branch of yew that had been with her for so many years. It had been abandoned back in the lab at Vianden, where she let Kazi have it to brace the handle of the door when a half-burned berserker was trying to tear through it and kill them. The irony was not lost on her that it would be rather useful to have now, not just for purposes of self-defense.

"Has there been any change, then?" Estelle asked gently.

Lily knew what she was asking. It was there in the careful sympathy of her tone. She wanted to know whether Lily had felt any indication that her khárisma had not been entirely obliterated by the events at Mont Noir.

There was little to say about it. Every once in a while, there was something like a distant hum, a low electric crackle that felt vaguely familiar, but it went nowhere, like a spark lacking fuel.

Mostly all she felt was space, a quiet absence where the tumult of her power used to live.

"I had another letter from Sam this morning," Lily said, neatly changing the subject.

"Oh?" Estelle replied, just as neatly allowing it as she carefully matched Lily's agonizingly slow pace across the lawn.

It was the second letter she had received since returning to England. Both were short, hastily scribbled on scraps of paper and tucked into battered envelopes, but they at least included actual words rather than blank postcards and magazine clippings.

Lily was also capable of reading far more into the messages than they actually said.

That he was well. That he missed them all. That the things he would never write down in a letter had not yet consumed him.

"He says the food is rotten. There are Americans everywhere. And apparently, they have managed to find him a new plane."

"Will he be glad to be in the air again, do you think?" Estelle asked.

Lily considered the question.

"Yes," she replied. "I believe he will."

There was a crunch of wheels and hooves on the gravel of the drive. Lily and Estelle slowly rounded the corner of the manor to see a hired carriage stop by the door. The man who emerged from it had to bend to get out of the door, the crown of his silver hair emerging first.

"Well, look what the cat dragged in," Estelle called out cheerfully.

"Miss Deneuve," Cairncross, now descended to the drive, returned with a bow.

Though pleased to see him, Lily could immediately see that he looked uncomfortable.

"What's the matter?" she demanded.

"Is his lordship available?" Cairncross asked. "I believe this may relate to him as well."

~

Ten minutes later, they were ensconced in the library. Walford poured Cairncross a neat finger of scotch from one of the finer bottles on his bar.

"Will this do?" he asked.

"Thank you," Cairncross replied.

Lily wondered if anyone else noticed that his hand was shaking a bit as he accepted it.

"Anyone else need a nerver?" Walford offered.

He was so robust and cheerful, it was strange to remember that Lily had once stood over him in a room just down the hall as he bled from a bullet wound to the chest in front of his wife and eldest daughter. Walford had recovered with vigorous English energy from his injury.

He would still have the scar, and there were stains in the floor-boards under the new carpeting in the study.

"I believe we can find our way to the bar should the need arise, Mr. Eversleigh," Estelle replied.

"I'll leave you to it, then," Walford said, kindly ducking from the room.

Cairncross stood by the window, looking down into his glass. Lily reclined on the couch, her aching leg propped up on one of the pillows. She felt worn out from her earlier exertions. Strangford perched on the arm of the sofa behind her, his hand on her shoulder.

Estelle occupied an armchair, her blue caftan contrasting richly with the upholstery as she tapped her fingers impatiently.

"Well?" she prompted. "Are you going to tell us what's the matter, or must we continue sitting here in dire suspense?"

Cairncross set his untasted drink aside. He pulled a small package wrapped in brown paper from his pocket and handed it to Lily.

She looked up in surprise at his drawn, weathered face, his uncharacteristic silence spelling a reverent and cautious air over the room. She pinched the package with the mobile fingers on her plaster-cast left hand, tugging the twine loose with the other. Unfolding the paper, she lifted the flap of the box within.

A slender glass vial fell into her lap, topped with a wax-sealed cork. Inside, a thick liquid slid into place, colored a dark and viscous reddish-brown.

Lily stared down at it, frozen with shock as a wild blend of horror and relief pounded through her.

"You know it, then," Cairncross stated flatly.

"Where did you get this?" Lily demanded as she gingerly picked it up. The vial felt alive in her palm—both dangerous and contained.

"It showed up in the post this morning," Cairncross replied. "And before you ask, there was no return label or any note."

"How did you know to bring it to us?" Strangford demanded calmly.

His hand had tightened on Lily's shoulder.

"Well, honestly, who else would something so bizarre possibly relate to?" Estelle offered breezily.

Lily looked up at Strangford, the weight of the vial cold against her fingers.

"I can't be absolutely certain ..."

He took off his gloves, setting them on the back of the sofa, and extended his hand.

Lily placed the vial in his palm. A shudder went through him, his mouth twisting into a grimace.

"It's the serum," he confirmed. "The same one. Not a replica. And no, it has not been opened."

"But how did it get here?" she protested.

He shook his head.

"It was placed into a container by someone who feels ... military. And that's it. There are no impressions after that."

"Well, someone obviously took it out," Lily retorted shortly.

"But why was it sent to James?" Estelle demanded.

Cairncross was pale as he gazed out across the quiet green fields behind Taddiford.

"I knew it," he said bitterly. "I knew that it was to do with that summons to the beach at Gravesend."

"But no one knew that was you," Lily pointed out.

Strangford looked thoughtful.

"Give me the package," he said.

Lily handed over the slender box, taking the vial back from him. Strangford ran his pale fingers over the paper, frowning—and then stopped.

"Well," he exclaimed with a soft note of surprise.

"Well what?" Lily pressed. "What do you feel in there?"

"Kazi," Strangford replied.

The world slowed for a breath. She was conscious of Cairncross's careful attention at the window, Estelle's thoughtful frown from her chair.

"Kazi," she echoed.

"Yes, Lily." Strangford returned meaningfully.

"But he sent it to Cairncross."

"Indeed," Strangford agreed. "It would seem that he did."

Her mind spun. She glanced up at Cairncross—the old soldier with the terrible secret running through his veins.

Kazi had always been tenacious about chasing down loose ends and obnoxiously good at putting things together.

She remembered his face in the light of that gruesome fire on Mont Noir.

I'm going to fix it.

The vial was smooth in her hands. It seemed so innocuous.

She held it out to Cairncross.

"It was given to you," she said. "What would you like to do with it?"

~

They were an awkward procession to the cliffs at Taddiford. Lily made use of both her crutch and Estelle, Strangford following behind them as Cairncross, straight-backed and grim, led the way along the beaten earth of the path. The tide below them was high, waves brushing against the base of the cliffs under a soft gray sky. The grass danced around them in a delicate breeze that tasted of the sea.

They came to a stop at the edge, lined up to face the water.

Cairncross looked down at the vial in his hand.

"Will this be the end of it, then?" he asked, his voice edged with years of guilt and regret—of the most bitter of secrets.

Lily's instinct was to put that question to her power—to whip along the threads of her onmyōdō until the true answer presented itself to her. She was thrown by the recollection that her power to do that was gone. She could no longer tell them what the future held.

With a softly dawning realization, she discovered she did not have to. An answer to his question was there, based not in foresight but in something else—something more like faith.

"Yes," she replied.

Cairncross's shoulders shuddered with relief. With a neat twist of his hand, he broke the wax seal on the vial. Pulling the stopper, he extended his arm, emptying the contents out over the edge of the cliff.

Shoving the cork back into place, he pulled back his arm and launched it out into the void. The spinning glass caught a glint of the soft morning light before it slipped from view, lost to the sea.

THIRTY-TWO

Wednesday, May 29, 1918
Morning
Lancaster Gate, London

$\mathcal{L}$ONDON EXPLODED WITH vibrant green as spring leaned into summer. The trees in the park were in full leaf, flowers dotting the pathways where groups of women collected donations for wounded soldiers.

In the house at Lancaster Gate, Lily stretched against an uncomfortable cramp in her hip. Her body had been aching lately in a way that had nothing to do with her injuries and everything to do with the life growing inside her. It had made her intolerant of her general wardrobe, her corsets and gowns all feeling constrictive and uncomfortable even though there was only the slightest swell to her abdomen.

Today she had eschewed them for her motorcycling trousers and a loose shirt. She had no need to leave the house. Her days with the WRNS were done. The organization would have immediately dismissed her as soon as they learned she was pregnant. When Lily had floated the idea of seeing how long she could get away with it before she was discovered, Strangford had wisely pointed out that she couldn't drive a motorcycle with a broken wrist. By the time the cast came off, her situation would be undeniable.

She had still practiced sitting on her Triumph on its kickstand in the yard, feeling her way through the once-familiar motions of piloting it. She had to use different muscles to work the controls involving her foot but was feeling confident she could manage it. In a way, her disability was far less apparent when she rode than when she walked.

Lily limped into the kitchen, where Mrs. Jutson stirred something at the stove.

"Is lunch ready yet?" she asked.

"Bless you, it's barely ten-thirty." Mrs. Jutson exclaimed. "That babe of yours must be growing. Let me fix you a wee bite of something."

Lily sat down at the kitchen worktable. She had been dreadfully hungry lately.

Her eyes fell on that morning's newspaper. She turned it around to face her as Mrs. Jutson set a bit of brown bread and jam down in front of her.

"The Prince of Wales has been spending an awful lot of time with that Freda Dudley Ward," Mrs. Jutson announced, noting Lily's interest. "Oh, and the Americans have retaken Cantigny."

Mrs. Jutson's order of priority for the updates was not surprising. Lily felt a warm relief at the news of Cantigny. The transports of American troops had been arriving in France thick and fast now, with estimates that there would be as many as a million of them at the front by mid-July. Though the Germans continued to throw their battered divisions at the line, here and there succeeding in driving the Allies back a few miles, it already felt like the momentum of the war had swung around. Germany was starved, exhausted, and increasingly demoralized. It could not possibly hope to press on against a million fresh-faced Yankee troops.

In the warm cheer of the kitchen, Lily quietly acknowledged her part in that. What she, Strangford, and the others had done may very well have made the difference between victory and defeat—or perhaps even something worse.

It had only been four weeks since she had returned to England, but it already felt like a memory from a distant world.

Mrs. Jutson tugged loose the ties of her apron.

"I'm off to pick up the rations, but I'll be back in time for lunch. There's a package for you out in the hall. Looks foreign."

Mrs. Jutson said the word as though it were both fascinating and slightly dreadful.

Curious, Lily rose, popping the last bit of bread and jam into her mouth as the housekeeper pulled on her coat. She went to the hall table where Mrs. Jutson routinely deposited the mail, finding the usual assortment of letters—a handful of society invitations they routinely declined. The usual packet of papers from their steward up at Allerhope, their estate in Northumberland. A fat missive from Virginia—she sent at least two a week and would undoubtedly descend upon them in person with her brood before long.

There was also a package. It was odd in shape—long and narrow—and cluttered with an array of foreign postage.

Lily studied it, curious, noting that it was addressed to her and not her husband. A better look at the stamps revealed that it had originated in Cairo.

Surprised, she took the letter opener from the holder and cut the string open, working a bit awkwardly around her left wrist, still encased in its cast.

A slender wooden box slid out of the thick brown paper. A white envelope was neatly tied to it with a piece of twine, labeled *Aunt Lily*.

Understanding clicked. Lily had only one connection in Egypt, after all—her eldest niece, serving there with Queen Alexandra's Nursing Service. Lily had received letters from Portia before. They were informative and sharply observant, with an affection that did not spill across the page but had to be read more carefully between the lines.

This is the first time Portia had sent a package.

Both the box and the letter showed signs of having been opened, but then, something this unusual from so far afield would have caught the notice of the censors. Whatever Portia sent must not be too alarming, as it had been allowed to come through.

Lily pulled out the letter.

Dear Lily,

Cairo is home to woodworkers of unusual skill, but an unfortunate dearth of yew. Hence I had to furnish this to you in acacia. The tree was once sacred to the ancient Egyptians, so perhaps it will help you make yourself a new sort of luck.

With love,

Portia

Lily blinked in surprise. Setting aside the letter, she opened up the box.

Inside was her walking stick.

She blinked, clearing her mind. Of course it was not her stick, lost in Vianden. The grain of the wood was different, the lines of it more pronounced, showing deeper contrast of light to dark. The brass at the top was longer and oddly tapered. There was a band of ornamentation a hands-breadth down from the knob.

Lily held it, running her palms along the beautifully polished length of it. The height was perfect, and there was a solid, almost delicious weight to it . . . one that she realized seemed ever so slightly off.

Following a rogue instinct, Lily gave the brass a twist with her good hand.

The top of the stick, from the band of ornamentation up, popped loose. Lily tugged it free to reveal a long, gleaming flow of silver—the narrow and dangerously sharp blade of a rather wicked short sword.

Her mouth curved into a smile, the sight both surprising and delighting her.

"Cheeky, clever girl . . ." she murmured softly.

She took a closer peek at the band decorating the hilt of the sword. It was a ring of brass embossed with a circle of delicate stars.

The sight of it set something ringing quietly inside of her. Lily's posture was more solemn as she slipped the blade back into its casing.

~

Strangford was outside. Lily followed the sound of his voice through the garden, behind the yew hedges to the back wall.

"Honestly, I don't believe I'm asking all that much of you," she heard him say as she rounded the corner.

She found him in eyepatch and shirtsleeves, staring at a sad assortment of warped and jagged boards that hung awkwardly from a pair of rusting hinges.

"Asking much of whom?" Lily inquired.

"The door," Strangford replied. "Shouldn't it be willing to come back together rather than find itself in the dustbin?"

Lily took a closer look at the door in question.

"Anthony—this garden gate was rotted when I met you," she pointed out, looking at the sad, sagging boards.

"Exactly." he agreed. "And it would be terribly ungrateful of me to give up on it when it is responsible for bringing you into my life."

She leaned her new walking stick against the garden wall and slipped her arms around his waist. It was wonderfully accessible to her in the absence of his coat. She slid the tip of her nose along the clean-shaven skin of his cheek.

"I have a key now, you know," she noted.

"Nor do I think a proper door would stop you were you determined to get through it," Strangford replied, his own hand beginning a slow exploration of the curve of her back. "I know I simply ought to take it down and build a new one, but between the ribs and the shoulder, it's a bit past my capabilities at the moment."

"Have Roddie help you," Lily replied distractedly, lifting a hand to the top button of his shirt.

Strangford's glance turned curious.

"Roddie's in France."

Lily started, catching herself. Of course Roddie was in France. Their awkward young footman had been drafted a year ago. Mrs. Jutson had received another letter from her nephew just a few days earlier.

"Sorry." she said, shaking her head, which felt momentarily foggy. "I must've forgotten myself for a moment there."

She let her finger glide around the curve of the button. He had, of course, forgone any sort of neckcloth when he had gone out to tend to the door.

"You know—you never did tell me whether you knew how to handle a sword."

He leaned back for a better look at her, mouth quirked into a smile.

"What on earth prompted that line of thought?" he asked.

"Portia sent me one." With a flick of her finger, Lily freed the button from its hole. "It's in my new walking stick."

"Is it?" Strangford echoed a little hoarsely.

She moved to another button. He swallowed. She could see the motion of his Adam's apple.

"Might I remind you that there is not much left to this poor garden gate. Should we attempt to make use of it," he added thickly.

"Then perhaps we should go inside," Lily mused, moving on to the third button.

She leaned in as her hands moved lower, brushing her lips over his ear.

"Mrs. Jutson has gone to fetch the rations."

"Bless the woman."

Strangford grasped her hand and tugged her, laughing, back up the path to the house.

~

An hour later, they sprawled on the bed in a sated tangle. Lily was tracing lazy circles along the sculpted form of Strangford's bare back when she heard the door open downstairs.

"Mrs. Jutson is back."

"Maybe she forgot something at the shops." Strangford's voice was muffled by the pillow. "She should head right back out for it."

"At least she didn't come in ten minutes ago," Lily commented, thinking of how that timing might have stretched their housekeeper's notions of propriety past the breaking point.

"If there is one thing to be said for injuring ourselves, it does promote a certain degree of creativity." Strangford agreed warmly.

"I am not going to be responsible for breaking your ribs again," Lily protested staunchly, pausing her circles.

"My ribs thank you for it. As do my hands, my hips, my—oof." he protested at a sudden jarring of the mattress.

The enormous orange form of Cat had landed on Strangford's calf. He turned a bit to glance back at the animal.

"Has it been here the whole time?" he asked.

"I am fairly certain Cat can pass through walls," Lily replied.

She ran a finger down the newest feature of his skin, the long scar where he was cut during the shell blast at Mont Noir. The stitches were taken out weeks ago, but the mark was still there, a dark reminder against his pale skin.

"One more for the collection," Strangford commented.

Lily's hand stopped. She moved her fingers to his chin, turning his face to look at her.

"I love all of you. Every shape. Every scar."

His mouth pulled into a wry smile.

"You are quite welcome to demonstrate that to me anytime you like."

Lily made a playful sound of disgust. She moved to rise from the bed. He reached out a lazy arm, pulling her gently closer as he rolled onto his side until she was tucked against him.

"The latest assessments at NID are that the war will be over by Christmas, based on an arcane calculation of German losses and American reinforcements."

"Such romantic pillow talk," Lily commented wryly.

She could feel him smile behind her and knew when his expression had shifted to something more serious.

"Will you mind it terribly, do you think?" he asked.

"Mind what?"

"Living … quietly."

Lily considered it. No more war. No terrible prophecies. After all they had been through—all the terrible responsibility, the loss, the struggle—to find only life. With Strangford. With all those that she loved and had gathered around her.

"No," she admitted, feeling the truth of it. "I don't believe I shall mind that at all. Not that I expect it to be quiet for very long."

Strangford's hand traced its way to her abdomen, slipping across the gentle curve of it lovingly, possessively.

"Can you feel her yet?"

"Him," Lily corrected automatically.

She caught herself, shaking her head. "I'm sorry—I have no idea why I said that."

"Well, I suspect one of us is right, at any rate," Strangford countered warmly.

Lily laughed, but it ended oddly, breaking on a strange and unexpected notion.

Strangford's bare fingers paused on the skin of her abdomen. "You're thinking something."

"I ... yes," Lily admitted, the feeling still strange and uncertain.

Strangford gently turned her towards him.

"What is it?"

She looked at the face of the man she loved, the one who knew her like her own soul, beautiful and weathered by the life they had already shared together. She studied the strange bubbling impulse that had risen up inside of her and realized there was something familiar about it. Different—lighter, more tentative, more delicate—but familiar.

"It feels like both," she admitted, almost scared to say it.

Strangford raised an eyebrow, his mouth quirking up on the scarred side of his face.

"Both?" he echoed.

Lily blushed ruefully.

"Never mind it—it was nothing. Just a passing fancy."

A sound from downstairs broke the lazy quiet of the late morning as the front door opened once more.

Strangford raised his head with a wicked smile.

"What do you know? She really did forget something at the shops."

He moved in on Lily once more, and was almost immediately interrupted by a great cry from below, an exclamation of some wild and unexpected emotion.

Strangford was out of bed in a moment, pivoting with leonine grace and tugging on his trousers. He paused with his hands on the buttons as Mrs. Jutson's voice echoed up the stairwell.

"My lord! You must come down! It's Roddie! Roddie has come home!"

He turned back to Lily, who had only half risen, still tangled in the sheets. His eye warmed as he dropped slowly to his knees in front of her. He reached out an ungloved finger, drawing it slowly over the subtle curve of her stomach.

"Both," he declared, looking up again to meet her eyes as Lily felt her own surprise well through her—along with a gentle, quiet certainty.

A whisper breathed through the space where something else had once lived, warm with promise.

"Oh blast," she exclaimed as her mind caught up to it, taking hold of his hand and laughing with the shared wonder of what was coming next.

NOTES FROM THE AUTHOR

Thank you for joining me on Lily and Strangford's adventures in *The London Charismatics* series.

Not quite ready to say goodbye yet? There is a special bonus story for the series you can get for free by subscribing to my newsletter at JacquelynBenson.com/LCEpilogue.

By subscribing, you'll also be the first to know about any new book releases. (I haven't completely ruled out playing with some of these characters in the future.)

And to make staying in touch even more tempting, you'll also get a free download of *The Stolen Apocalypse*, an exclusive novella featuring a young Lord Strangford.

~

Please take a moment to rate or review *What the Ravens Sing*—or, if you haven't yet, pop a review up for *The Fire in the Glass* to let folks know what you thought of the series as a whole. It's a simple thing that makes a profound difference for independent authors like myself.

ACKNOWLEDGMENTS

The book you hold in your hands owes much to many. Cathie Plante, Kaitlyn Huwe, Kori North, Dr. Laura George, Matthew Dow, and Chris Mornick provided invaluable early feedback.

Jennie Siegal and Nicholas Atwater graciously helped me with my French. John Carroll tuned up the German.

Sahrish Hadia lent her insight into making Kazi as authentic and respectful as possible. Zhui Ning Chang did the same for Sam and Zhao Min, while also cleaning up my atrocious Mandarin. Any remaining errors are entirely my own. Casey Fenich repaired my wonky grammar and worked tirelessly to cure me of my disdain for Oxford commas.

The backers of the *What the Ravens Sing* audiobook Kickstarter campaign—each and every one of you—made it possible for me to bring this work to life in audio, and I could not be more grateful. Special thanks goes to Melissa Acquaviva, Gail Johnson, Nazima Rashid Khan, Virginia Northington, Martha Prybylo, and—with a bit of extra love—Donna Benson.

But of course, this story is more than just the book you hold. It is the conclusion of a very long journey. Lily began taking shape in my mind nearly a decade ago, and coming to the end of her story carries a feeling much like grief.

For the entirety of *The London Charismatics*, there are more thanks to be given:

To Alex Picard for her breathtaking work bringing my characters to life in the audiobooks, and Alise Ashby for composing their lovely theme music.

To the authors of The Lamplighter's Guild—Olivia & Nicholas Atwater, Suzannah Rowntree, Intisar Khanani, Rosalie Oaks, and

Charlotte English—for invaluable advice and inspiration.

To Dan, for his gracious and wholehearted support through all the long hours, mood swings, historical rants, and minor hysteria. And for simply, completely believing in me and in the worlds that I am building. Your faith is contagious, babe.

And finally, to my readers, for opening your hearts to Lily, Strangford, Sam, Zhao Min, Estelle, Cairncross, Gardner ... George. Mrs. Liu. Even bloody Roderick. Every one of them is as real to me as the people who live across the road. Carrying the burden of some-one else's existence on one's own is rather onerous. Knowing that so many of you are willing to share it with me makes the load quite a bit lighter.

ABOUT THE AUTHOR

Jacquelyn Benson writes smart historical thrillers where strong women wrangle with bold men and confront the stranger things that occupy the borders of our world. She once lived in a museum, wrote a master's thesis on the cultural anthropology of paranormal investigation, and received a gold medal for being clever. She owes a great deal to her elementary school librarian for sagely choosing to acquire the entire Time-Life *Mysteries of the Unknown* series.

When not writing, she enjoys the company of a tall, dark and handsome English teacher and practices unintentional magic.

If you'd like to be friends:

- **Join the email list on her website:** JacquelynBenson.com.
  You'll also get a free download of an exclusive novella,
  The Stolen Apocalypse.

- **Follow on Bookbub:** BookBub.com/Authors/Jacquelyn-Benson
  and stay informed about deals and discounts

- **Follow on Goodreads:** Goodreads.com/JacquelynBenson

- **Find her on social media:**
  Instagram: @jbensonink
  Twitter: Twitter.com/JBensonInk
  Tiktok: Tiktok.com/@JBensonInk
  Facebook: Facebook.com/JBensonInk
  Pinterest: Pinterest.com/JBensonInk

CPSIA information can be obtained
at www.ICGtesting.com
Printed in the USA
LVHW041746010423
743158LV00002BA/315

9 781959 050063